I0712860

CALL IT HOPE

AMBER LEE

Copyright © 2024 by Amber Lee

All rights reserved.

No part of this publication may be reproduced, distributed, or transmitted in any form or by any means, including photocopying, recording, or other electronic or mechanical methods, without the prior written permission of the publisher, except as permitted by U.S. copyright law. For permission requests, contact Amber Lee.

The story, all names, characters, and incidents portrayed in this production are fictitious. No identification with actual persons (living or deceased), places, buildings, and products is intended or should be inferred.

Book Cover by Books and Moods

Editing by Indie Editorial LLC

To all the women who hope to experience the type of love she reads about in books.

Especially with a hot, morally grey billionaire.

This one's for you.

CONTENT WARNING

This book contains topics that may be sensitive to some readers, including explicit sexual content, profanity, and a death of a loved one.

PLAYLIST

1. *Wildest Dreams— Taylor Swift*

2. *Lavender Haze— Taylor Swift*

3. *On My Mind— Ellie Goulding*

4. *Close— Nick Jonas (feat. Tove Lo)*

5. *Birds of a Feather— Billie Eilish*

6. *Earned It— The Weekend*

7. *Hands to Myself— Selena Gomez*

8. *Lust for Love— Genrey*

PROLOGUE

Every summer, my mother took my brother and me to the beach house. She said it was a way to recharge our energy, to get in touch with our spiritual side. My mother married my father because of love. She was easily the only person my father truly cared about on this earth. I never could have imagined the struggle we'd all have to go through the moment we lost her.

At times, I still remember the way her hair flowed in the wind and how bright her smile was, only because she felt sand in between her toes and the salty water on her skin. That day felt free and... happy. I wished the day would last forever—until that night.

"No! Please, my boys are upstairs! No!" I jumped from my bed, hearing my mother's screams from the kitchen. I turned to my younger brother Aaron, who was still fast asleep. "Please." As I heard my mother's sob pray out of her mouth, I could feel my bones becoming weaker. I shook with fear and covered my ears.

It only took my mother's screams turning into cries to lead me to run from my room, all the way down the stairs, and into the kitchen. I stood against the wall, inches away from the stove, and peeked at what was happening. When I did, my fears rapidly turned to anger as I saw how they were taking advantage of my mom. There were two masked men, holding her down, constantly beating her while having their way.

My mother saw me in the corner of her eye and began to scream louder. "Go! Run, Adam! Run!" My heart was beating wildly against my chest. I felt as if it might explode at any moment. I tried to run away, but the only direction I could run was toward these massive men hurting my mom. I should have known it was a guaranteed loss with how young I was.

I began to hit them as hard as I could, with all my strength. It was never enough; I couldn't protect her the way I wanted. My mother only cried and cried as she witnessed my failed attempts. One of the men slashed my collarbone with a knife, blood soaking the white shirt I had on.

The blood ran down my chest, distracting me, and it only took one hit for me to fall to the ground. Once I regained consciousness, I saw my mother lying on the floor, completely motionless. I crawled to her, wincing at my bruises. As I got to her, I noticed her breathing was slower than usual; I could barely see her chest rise and fall.

"Mama?" I carefully shook her. She never answered. I began to cry with everything I had at the thought of losing my mom, the only person who took care of me, who loved me with everything she had.

My eyes were closed when I felt my mother's hand against my cheek. "It's okay, shh." Her soft voice calmed me down.

"I'm sorry," I sobbed against her touch, a mix of my blood and hers.

"It's not your fault. I love you, Adam." She coughed as she tried to form her last words. "Promise me you'll look after your brother." I nodded as she formed a slight smile. "Good. And promise me that you'll always have *hope*, trust in love, and act in kindness. It will always take you far. I will always be with you, no matter how this night ends." Tears fell from my eyes as I heard her speak to me as if it would be the last time I heard her voice. "My baby boy, everything will be okay."

Her voice became hushed, and her skin pale. I held her head in my lap and caressed her hair as I waited for someone to come. I slowly saw the light dim in her eyes as she stared up at the ceiling. Any hope I held on to, just like her, was gone.

My father came not long after and rushed her to a hospital. I already knew she was gone, but they officially pronounced us motherless. I'd always thought I'd lost my hope and ability to care for another forever.

That was, until *her*.

CHAPTER 1
KATHERINE

"KATHERINE! HURRY UP, WE NEED TO HEAD OUT NOW IF WE want to make it on time to our shift!" Elaina screamed while running out the door. It was Wednesday morning, and I was running later than usual. I had always been the type of person who's on time for everything. But today felt different than other days. I grabbed my bag with my keys, left the apartment, and headed toward the café I worked at part-time on 11th street.

I had been working at this café for about four months now, and I have to say, it wasn't as bad as I thought it was going to be. Certainly not with one of my good friends working there with me—Elaina. She and I were walking out of our favorite romance bookstore a few doors down from the café. We saw the 'help wanted' sign and decided that it wouldn't be a bad idea to apply for a job in the same area where our favorite bookstore is.

It made sense. We spend money on books every weekend and gain money every paycheck a few doors down. On top of that, we needed to pay rent, but splitting it with Elaina made it easier to both save and spend some extra money. Still, New York wasn't the cheapest place to live in, especially not when you're a struggling author trying to make it. Much less an unpublished author whose goal was to get at least one romance novel published. Plus, I was only twenty-two, so it was normal to feel out of place...

Right? Wrong. Fast-forward two years to the present, and I still feel the same.

I moved to New York from California for college five years ago. I was an English major. It was a big step for me to be so far away from my mother; it had always been just me and her. But I wanted something different. I wanted to take my writing seriously. College was one of the best decisions I had ever made. It was where I met my girls. The four of us—me, Elaina, Celeste, and Valery—met at a fundraiser our college had thrown, and ever since, we'd been inseparable.

Things back home in California just weren't working out for me, including certain people. So, the decision was easy to make when I found out I had the choice to start a life here. New York had its flaws, but it continued to throw me surprises that I ended up loving. I was still hoping New York would do something special for me within this year, preferably with my writing.

"Got the keys?" Elaina asked, as I caught up to her. Café Luna was a fifteen minute walk from our apartment, and we weren't about to spend money on a taxi that would get us there in the same amount of time. Morning in New York meant the streets were crowded.

"Yeah, I got them. Why?" I answered Elaina, holding up the keys as proof.

"Okay, good, because I forgot them." Elaina gave me a charming smile as I shook my head while we continued walking. Elaina was a forgetful person, so it didn't come as a surprise to me. It wouldn't be Elaina if she'd remembered. As we arrived at the café, we settled in and started preparing everything for opening. Café Luna was mostly empty around this time of day, but we'd get busier when lunch came around.

I looked out the window and became distracted with how

beautiful it looked outside. It was the beginning of August, and the colors screamed Autumn. It was my favorite time to write; it felt cozy to me. With that, I had some ideas to write about in the current book I was working on.

"Hey, can you take care of the customer coming in? I need to use the bathroom," Elaina said, dragging me out of my thoughts. Elaina was the type of person who looked for any excuse to not work early at this time of day. "Yeah, okay," I replied while putting on my work apron with the word's Café Luna on it, with a white coffee mug and a yellow half-moon dangling over it. I then walked over to the cash register.

"Welcome to Café Luna. How can I serve you today?" I said with a simple, thin smile on my lips before looking up. I took my attention from the register to the green pair of eyes already set on me. I suddenly forgot my next words from simply returning this man's eye contact.

"A double espresso to go," he replied in a dark tone and looked back down at his phone. If my legs weren't already weak before his reply, they were shaking now from the sound of his voice. It was demanding, yet comfortable, in a way that I'd obey. *Maybe it was the fact that I worked there that made me feel like I'd have to obey.*

Christ Kat, get with it.

"Of course, anything else?" I questioned, before turning away to prepare his double espresso. His facial expression remained still while typing on his phone, completely ignoring my question.

It was obvious that he was a man of money because of the way he presented himself. He had a dark gray suit on and a dark —almost black—tie with it. It hugged his muscles so perfectly it had to be tailored. He was tall, at least six-foot-two, give or take. Which didn't help because I had a thing for tall guys.

I couldn't help being curious about why a guy like him would be in a café like this one. Not that Café Luna wasn't good, just that it wasn't luxurious. While I thought of who this man was and why he was here, I didn't realize that a line of customers had formed in the midst of my thoughts.

"Kat, we've got customers," a strict voice stated behind me. I turned to see Auther, our café manager.

"Sorry, Auther, I'll get right to it," I replied quickly while running to complete this man's order. I was surprised that he hadn't hurried me or left the café, but he stayed in the same position, still typing away on his phone, this time aggressively.

I turned to pour his double espresso in a cup, placed a lid on, turned again to where the man was standing, only to find him gone. I'd turned away for a matter of what seemed to be seconds, and he'd completely disappeared. A strange feeling of disappointment crept up on me.

"Kat, where is Elaina? We need her out here. Go get her for me, please." Auther tried to ask me kindly, but I could hear the irritation in the back of his voice for basically having to attend these customers without much help. I nodded, collecting my current thoughts.

Auther was in his late fifties. He seemed like a pretty understanding and patient person with us, which was one of the reasons we loved working here, or at least I did.

"Got it, Auther. I'll be right back," I responded, already halfway toward the bathroom. I walked in to find Elaina sitting on the floor, editing some of her videos she'd post for the next week. Elaina was a social media influencer with her fashion blog, and she was known to have a European style when it came to clothes.

She was amazing and my go-to when I needed help to pick out my outfits. I must admit, my closet had improved drastically since I moved in with her two years ago.

"Elaina, you can't be here. Auther asked me to come get you. It's crazy busy outside." I kneeled beside her, patting her thigh. "Did you really think he wouldn't find you in here?"

"No, but the fact that he's a man and he can't come into the women's bathroom to get me out tells me yes," she explained, her eyes still fixed on her phone, determined to finish. *Touché.*

"You need to hurry up and get your fashionable butt out there. Or you're going to get us both fired," I replied, slightly chuckling as I stood to my feet, lending out my hand for her to hold on to while I dragged her up.

"Okay, fine. I'll just have to edit it later tonight after my interview," she said, before sighing. "What time do you think you'll be home tonight?"

"It's Wednesday, so I think I'll be home around one, two at the latest." I replied as we walked back out to our current job. After my morning shifts at Café Luna, I worked a night shift as a bottle girl at Avenue Nightclub. It was quite popular and known to attract celebrities and big names. It also paid well. I took the next customer in line, and without me realizing it, my mind drifted to a familiar pair of green eyes. I wondered if I'd see him again and if my body would react in the same way it had earlier this morning.

"Let me ask you something, *asshole*. Do I *look* like a stripper to you, for you to be throwing a bunch of ones in my face?!" I heard Celeste shout from behind the bar at some drunk man.

"I—" The man tried to fight his case, but Celeste cut him off by spraying him down with beer. Security grabbed the man and led him out of the club. Celeste was known for having a fire to her, a mean temper that could be easily reached. When she gets pissed off, nobody stands in her way.

"What happened with him?" I asked while I swung the bar flap door open and entered behind the bar.

"You know how it goes, assholes being rude and drunk assholes being pervs," she said while cleaning up the mess of beer she had made. I replied with a simple nod and tugged the sides of my denim shorts up. Celeste's eyes scanned me from top to bottom.

"Woah, mira la mamacita. I like the fit," she complimented in a playful tone. Celeste and I were the only Latinas in our friend group. She's Colombian, and I'm Venezuelan.

"Gracias, amor," I replied in a playful tone. As bottle girls, we had to wear tight black clothes. Tonight, I chose to wear my favorite high-waisted black shorts that fit me like a pair of leggings. They were decent in length, from my waist down to my mid-thigh, paired with a black tank top that fit perfectly around my chest. The women in my family were known to have curvy bodies, so I didn't need to put on scandalous clothes for the figure of my body to pop.

"Tú también," I said to Celeste. Though, I didn't need to compliment her. She truly was gorgeous, and she knew it. You wouldn't need to ask what nationality she was. She's the image of a "Latina mami" with her jet-black curly hair and curvy body.

"Oh, please, stop it," she teased as she mixed drinks. Celeste started working here long before me. Avenue was a hard job to land, simply because of its reputation. The only reason I even got a job here was because of Celeste and her good words to the manager.

"We have a party group at the booth," one of the other bottle girls informed me before grabbing the light up 'happy birthday' sign and a light stick. I spared Celeste a *'here we go'* look before I grabbed a champagne bottle and joined the group, heading toward the table.

I held the bottle in the air with both my hands and fell in line behind the rest of the girls. *I could be writing my novel right this second,* the author voice in my mind said. *But you need to pay the rent somehow,* my reasonable voice argued. *Great. Now I'm arguing with voices in my head.*

"Okay, girls, show time!" the group leader called out in front of us. We all started dancing to the beat while surrounding the booth with our hands in the air, swinging light sticks. I kept falling behind as I was preparing to pull the cork from the champagne.

Once I finally got around the table, I came to face a familiar pair of green eyes. *Ay, Dios mío.* It was him. My mystery guy from this morning.

He was seated in a relaxed position at the end of the couch with his legs spread apart and a smug look on his face. He was wearing a white button-down shirt with the sleeves rolled up and a pair of black pants. His outfit was a lot more casual than what he had on this morning.

He hadn't seen me yet. *Not that I wanted him to see me...*

I took advantage of him not noticing me to study his face, to really take in every one of his features. He had these luscious lips and the bone structure of a literal god. His hair was a dirty, almost golden shade of blonde that was fixed in a brushed back hairstyle.

Suddenly, the top came off the bottle and sprayed the champagne directly at him. I gasped, realizing what I had just done. I had gotten so lost in looking at him that I had forgotten that I needed to shake the bottle in the air and not keep it positioned right at his face.

Everyone surrounding the table fell into a state of shock, and I did what any embarrassed girl would do. I grabbed some napkins from the table and kneeled right in front of his legs, trying to wipe dry the liquid his pants were drenched in. I felt his muscles tighten at my touch and looked up to his face to see his sight stalled on me, his pupils dilated. He clenched his jaw the moment my hand moved a little higher.

Oh, dear god.

A warm, heavy feeling rolled through my body, a tingling tension between my thighs. "I-I'm so s-sorry," I said, at a loss for words. The intense stare he was giving me made me feel like he saw right through me. I felt so vulnerable to his sight, I might as well be naked in public because it felt no less than that.

"Oh, shit," one of the guys said, laughing with the rest of the group that was witnessing the most embarrassing moment in my entire life.

"It's fine, get up," he replied with irritation bleeding through his voice. I got up and stood next to my group leader.

"I am so sorry, Mr. Pearson. Our Kat is still learning how to open bottles. Your entire tab tonight is covered," she said in a sincere voice, and *WAIT. Did she just say Pearson?? As in Pearson Book Group?!*

There's no way it's that Pearson. Dread washed over me at the memory of me spraying a bottle at possibly one of the biggest book publishers in the world. Life had a fascinating way of torturing me, and this, I've got to say, was gold.

"Great, keep them coming, then," the guy sitting at the center said with a smile while *Mr. Pearson* shook his head in annoyance.

The walk back to the bar was a dreadful one, with my group leader insisting on letting this one incident slide. I forced myself to continue working and finish this shift. The whole night, I purposely avoided the booth they were at.

I'd messed up my chance before I knew I even had one. I couldn't walk up to him now with a manuscript; he'd see the attempt as a joke. I wouldn't blame him.

This is going to be a long night.

CHAPTER 2

ADAM

The last time I attended a funeral was when I was twelve years old. It was my mother's funeral, and it felt like my entire world had shattered. I didn't think I could ever feel a pain greater than that. My father was a wreck. He had wanted nothing to do with the responsibility of raising two boys. He threw himself into work and never stopped.

He paid the company more attention than he did his own two sons, leaving me to take care of my younger brother, who, at the time, was only nine years old. In his choice of picking the company over his family, he turned the Pearson Book Group into the successful publishing company it was today. The passing of my father hit me harder than I expected. Not in an emotional way, but in a 'my whole life became hectic' kind of way. It had been six months since the funeral, and everything at the company was transitioning.

My father was the CEO of the Pearson Book Group, and our uncle was the current CFO. I was preparing for the transition of me becoming CEO before discovering my father had left bearing gifts...

After speaking with our family lawyer, we found out that, in his will, he predicted me becoming CEO under one condition. I'd have to earn it. I, however, had not a single clue about the stipulation. My brother and I were supposed to take over the company, with him being the new CFO. Only to find out there had to be an election between two candidates, me and...my uncle.

This mishap had made me way behind on my schedule, and I was a man who liked order. Now I had to think of a way to convince the company board and shareholders that I deserved to be CEO, not only because I was a Pearson, but because I knew what I was doing. My uncle didn't deserve it; he didn't even deserve the current position he held. I'd see fit of him being gone and have my brother Aaron take over.

I knew that if my uncle were to gain that power, he'd use it to get rid of us. And that wasn't a possibility.

It was morning, and I had just gotten back from my morning run. I got out of my workout clothes, soaked with sweat, and hopped into the shower. Then I changed into a casual suit for work. I was leaving my penthouse, walking through the lobby, when I felt a vibration in the pocket of my pants. When I saw who was calling, I answered with irritation rushing through my body.

"What?" I spoke.

"Go-Good morning, Mr. Pearson. I'm sorry to be calling you this early," a nervous voice responded over the phone. It was the new intern working as my assistant. The company thought it would be a good idea to bring young, inexperienced people in. "The coffee shop is under construction right now, and everywhere else is packed, and uh... I won't be able to get you, your, uh... your coff—"

"You're fired," I interrupted and hung up before he had a chance to explain further. What type of idiot did you have to be to call your boss this early in the morning to say you couldn't get them coffee? A decently smart human would look elsewhere for it. *Completely useless. What a good idea that was...*

But then the realization kicked in that I had no one to get me a coffee, and Lord knew I would be needing it today, with the lawyer stopping by to discuss more details of my father's will. I walked through the lobby doors to exit the building and outside to where I usually meet my chauffeur, Henry. Only to find absolutely no one parked outside. *What the hell.* Henry had never been late, much less missed a day without my permission.

I emailed Henry to see where the hell he was, and he responded at once. *'Good morning Mr. Pearson. I was informed that you would not be needing my services today by Mr. Edward. I send my regards.'* Edward. My uncle. Why the *fuck* did he speak to my chauffeur? Something was up, and it was just a matter of time before I found out what that was.

The only option I had was to call a cab. Without much choice, I walked back inside the lobby to the front desk, where a young lady stood.

"Call in a cab for Adam Pearson," I told the woman typing on the computer. She instantly paused when she heard my name and looked up at me with flushed cheeks.

"Mr. Pearson, yes, of course. Good morning, I hope your day is going well," she stuttered between words as she wrung her hands together. She stared at me, standing incredibly still.

"Thank you, I need that cab now..." I paused to look at her name tag. "Miss Adre," I finished. She smiled as she reached for the phone with shaky hands and dialed for a cab. I took a seat while I waited for my delayed ride to arrive, answering some emails in the meantime.

Once my cab arrived, I gave him my destination, sat back, and stared out the window. With the stunt my uncle had just pulled, I sat uneasily in my current position. A million suspicions ran through my mind. I had a habit of doing the most thinking when riding in cars. Outside the window, we passed by some small gift shops, a flower shop, a pinkish bookstore, and... *Café Luna.*

"Pull over," I ordered as I kept my eyes on the property.

"Listen, man, I got other rides to do, and I ca—" I interrupted him by pulling two hundred-dollar bills out of my wallet and handing them to him.

"Wait here," I said as I got out of the cab and walked into the café that had plants and flower vines wrapped around the entrance. It happened to be empty, and it also happened to be incredibly small. Inside, the walls were the color of green sage that matched well with the white tables arranged with plants on them.

All types of pastries were placed in a glass compartment next to the register. The wall behind the counter had mini shelves drilled into them, holding cookbooks. Across the register was a woman putting on an apron before walking over to acknowledge my presence. I took advantage of her distraction and took a good look at her as she tied her apron. She had her hair in a loose, low bun with strands falling out the front.

She had beautiful, clear golden skin that seemed to be soft, giving me the temptation to caress her cheek with my hand to see if my impression had been correct. A bizarre wave of warmth washed over my body as she met my eyes. Weird… "Welcome to Café Luna. How can I serve you today?" she asked in an inno-cent voice. Her voice seemed as soft and delicate as she did. Never had I heard such a sweet sound come out of someone's mouth.

"A double espresso to go." My response came out in a huskier tone than I expected.

She had these big bold eyes in the color of a rich gold, almost pure honey. Holding eye contact with her made my body feel out of my control, and I didn't like it. I took my attention from the woman standing in front of me to the small device I held in my hand. I had a total of four missed calls and five emails from my younger brother, Aaron. Panic filled my body as I opened the first email.

A line had formed since I'd stepped back to read. *'Edward is here early. He said that the lawyer will be here in twenty minutes.'* What? Why would... *Shit.* That was the reason behind his stunt with my chauffeur. That bastard was trying to leave me out of the meeting. I've got to give it to him; if it weren't for my brother, he would have succeeded in pushing the meeting two hours earlier.

My coffee had not been made yet, and the woman looked so busy now. The man taking over the register had her rushing around the entire place, and I couldn't find it in me to hurry her. If she had been anyone else, I would not have shown any type of mercy. I was a lot of things, but merciful was not one of them.

So, why show it to her?

I ignored the thought and rushed out of the café. Getting into the cab and driving there felt like the longest trip of my life. Once we arrived at Pearson Book Group's offices, I rushed into the elevator and got off with much anticipation of what I would walk into.

I made my way straight to the head office where the meeting was being held. I barged in, finding the two men about to start. My uncle's face transformed from a welcoming smile to an aggravated expression. *Good.* Knowing I'm the reason behind *that look* gave me much pleasure.

"Adam! You made it just in time," Richard, the family lawyer, greeted me.

"Yes, I had a mishap earlier this morning, but it was nothing I couldn't handle," I admitted with a smile, looking directly at my uncle. A flash of hatred crossed his eyes. I took a seat on the chair beside him. "Shall we begin?" I said in a delightful tone.

"Yes, let's start," Richard replied as he put his glasses on and opened his briefcase, drawing out the file with a stack of papers. He pulled out a document and cleared his throat before speaking.

'*To my dear son and brother, If you are reading this, you both must already be aware of the election. What you are not aware of is the job you will both be doing. You both must find an author yourself and bring them up to be on the New York bestsellers' list...* Okay, that's not so bad. All I had to do was find someone and leave it to the Pearson team to do the deed. '*...Without the use of Pearson Book Group advantages.*' Shit. Looking over at Edward confirmed I wasn't the only one feeling tense.

Richard continues reading. '*You'll have six months to complete this task, and if you fail, you will be eliminated from the election. This should not be an impossible task to fulfill. Adam, you are my son and have my knowledge and my determination that will help you. And, as for Edward, we both brought this company from the bottom up. Let's see if you have remembered how to do the job without help. Good luck, and may the best man win.*'

Richard placed the document back in the file and looked at us. I had no words. How was I supposed to respond to that? I mean, come on, *six months*. Where was I going to find an author with actual talent and manage to have them placed on the best-sellers' list in a matter of six months? It was absurd. Richard recognized our stunned expressions and decided to cut things short.

"Well, gentlemen, now that we have gone over the details, I'll see myself out. I'm sure you both have some work to do," Richard said as he was packing his briefcase. "Please feel free to contact me if you have any questions."

"Yes, it's been a pleasure, Richard," my uncle responded as he rose from his seat and leaned down toward my ear. "You don't have a chance," he said in a low voice that only I could hear. "May the best man win, Adam."

"That won't be necessary. We both know who that is," I responded in a polite manner, hiding my anger toward his attempt to belittle me. He was sure to give me a threatening stare before walking out the door. The door shut behind him and I turned my attention to Richard, who had just finished packing his briefcase.

"Adam, it's been a pleasure," he said before walking toward the door.

"Richard," I called out, needing to clarify some things. "Richard, what exactly was my father talking about when he said *without the help of Pearson Book Group advantages*?" I was determined to find some loophole.

"Well, just that you would be the one to come up with ideas instead of the creative department and edit the novel instead of the editorial department and so on."

"What about working here at headquarters? Are we allowed to use our office for our client meetings and the head office to present the work we have so far to the other employees?" I suggested. He paused for a moment before responding.

"He didn't mention not being allowed to use the property for those types of purposes. I suppose it's alright if you don't use the advantages of the departments." I could work with that. With some presentations, I could basically take care of the publicity in the interest of my employees and events.

"Good to know. Have a great rest of your day," I replied before shaking his hand and heading toward my office.

Opening my office door, I was greeted by the sight of my brother Aaron sitting in my chair. "Get out of my goddamn chair," I said, causing him to jump in fright at my sudden response.

"Christ, Adam, why can't you be a normal person and make your presence known?" He got up from my chair and moved to the couch I had across from my desk.

My office at Pearson Corps was decently spacious. It was also quite private, which I liked. I wouldn't have appreciated it if everyone knew about my business from outside my office. Not that I had anything to hide, just that I liked to have my own space where no one could bother me.

"How was the meeting?" Aaron asked, pulling my attention toward him. I took a seat before explaining everything that had just happened a few doors down from my office. "Six months?" he said with a concerned look on his face.

"Yes, and I plan on finding someone within the week. I have a few candidates," I lied. I didn't have any candidates whatsoever, but I tried to sound as confident and convincing as I could. Still, I couldn't help having this doubt at the back of my mind.

"As long as you have a plan..." Aaron's shoulders loosened with my response, and he got up and walked toward the door. "Hey, are we still on for tonight?" he asked, looking back at me.

"Tonight?" my brows scrunched together in confusion.

"Yeah, Micheal's birthday. You said you'd get him an entrance at Avenue." *Shit, that's right.* It had completely slipped my mind with all the chaos I'd been dealing with.

"Yes, it's already been handled," I assured him. Aaron responded with a simple nod and saw himself out.

The moment the door shut behind him, I was already getting on the phone to make the call. Micheal is someone I consider to be a close friend of mine. We were good friends in college. I hadn't seen him since my father's funeral, since I had been so busy with everything that I barely had the time to have a drink with him.

I had promised Micheal that I would get him a table to celebrate a few months ago. Avenue was a high-end nightclub that had many celebrities and big names on their list. When I called to reserve the booth for tonight, with the use of my name, they more than welcomed our group. Having the name Pearson had its perks in New York City, and anywhere else, if I'm being blunt.

Once I finished with work at the office, I'd head back to the penthouse, change, and make my way to Avenue.

CHAPTER 3

ADAM

The moment we arrived at Avenue, the host immediately showed us to our booth. "I can't believe you actually got us a table for tonight," Micheal said as he placed his arm around my shoulders, completely amazed with the spot.

"I'm a man of my word," I responded simply as we reached our booth.

The place was packed. The whole room was filled with purple neon lights, crowds of people squished together on the dance floor. I would hate to be at this club without a reserved spot; I hated busy crowds altogether. Micheal had chosen to bring two other guys aside from Aaron, who I hadn't met until tonight.

We all took a seat around the booth that faced straight out toward the partying crowd. I had requested a full Avenue experience for Micheal that included unlimited drinks and the party group.

"How's everything, man?" Micheal asked as he took a seat beside me.

"Everything's been alright." Micheal glanced at me with a skeptical look.

"Everything's alright? The transition and the company?"

"Never better." My jaw locked at the reminder of what was at stake. "Enough with the ridiculous questions and enjoy the night." I indicated toward the bottle girls making their entrance. Micheal smiled in return and placed his full attention on the women, swaying to the beat with bottles in their hands, surrounding our booth.

Micheal's expressions were priceless as he realized the bottles they were holding cost more than two months of his rent altogether. I grinned at the sight. Just as I turned to face the group, I was drenched in champagne. *Great. Just great.*

Everyone paused and became quiet as they saw what had just happened. I looked down at the mess some girl made in anger. Whoever it was who had done this was in for a ride. More specifically, she was getting fired tonight. The girl kneeled in front of me with a decent number of napkins in her hand and began to pat dry my thighs.

My muscles tightened at her touch. She brought her head up to meet my eyes, and I realized... *It was her.* The woman who took my order this morning at Café Luna. Those amber eyes looked almost black with the lighting in the room. My jaw clenched to the point I felt like I was going to pop it right out of place.

"I-I'm so sorry," the woman said, almost breathless.

"Oh, shit," Micheal said, laughing with the rest of the guys witnessing this moment. I glanced at him with an intimidating stare that shut him and everyone else up.

"It's fine, get up," I said in a demanding voice. She got up and stood beside one of the women in black.

"I am so sorry, Mr. Pearson. Our Kat is still learning how to open bottles. Your entire tab tonight is covered," she said, afraid I would make a scene. I didn't care about anything she was saying except the mention of the girl's name. *Kat.*

"Great! Keep them coming!" Micheal said while I shook my

head in disapproval. Micheal always took advantage whenever certain incidents happened to me. Mostly because whenever something did happen to me, every single soul did something to make up for it in fear of me threatening them.

The girls left the bottles on the table and walked back toward the bar. I stood up to make my way to the men's room. "You're leaving?" Aaron asked while Micheal and his friends busied themself with the free champagne.

"No, going to the restroom to try to dry most of this off." Aaron nodded and continued talking as I made my way there.

Once the bathroom door shut behind me, I turned on the faucet to a cold temperature and splashed it on my face. What the hell was going on with me? The place was cold and yet I felt like my body temperature was a hundred degrees.

My heartbeat was fast, as if I had run a marathon. My hands were sweating at the reminder of the girl in all black. *Kat.* She had worn her hair down tonight, silky brown hair that reached to her hips. Her dark uniform hugged the most amazing curves of her body. She had to be one of the most attractive women I'd ever seen.

I'd seen plenty of beautiful women, but not one who came in contact with me made my body react this way. *Get yourself together, Adam.* Feeling out of control made me feel uneasy. I knew the moment I left this bathroom, I would be doing every-thing and anything in my power to avoid Kat. I *finally* got myself together and opened the door.

"Hey, you're Adam Pearson." A woman with dark curly hair approached me when she caught me coming out of the restroom.

"Yes," I responded, bored with the conversation already.

"Pearson, as in Pearson Book Group?" she asked in an amused tone. I didn't have time for this. I didn't have interest in conversing with people who had stupid questions, so I walked around her as if I had never heard her in the first place.

"Wait! I know of someone who is an incredible author!

Perhaps you'll be interested in publishing them," she shouted with desperation to get my attention. Normally, I would continue walking, especially with the number of people who have tried to stop me and talk about the latest book they were writing, which turned out to be awful.

Pearson Book Group wasn't a publishing company open to just anyone; publishing was only granted to those who had high respect in the literature world. Whether it was a known author, or an author recommended by a high-end agent. We only took and published the best of the best. However, with the current task needing to be done, I did the most unusual thing. I reached into my pocket and handed her a card.

"Here's my card with my personal email. Send me the manuscript of what this author is currently working on. If I see that it has potential, we'll set up a meeting." I would have never in a million years willingly done that without an alternative motive. But I was desperate, having time as my enemy.

"Thank you! You won't regret it!" The woman smiled with all her teeth and headed back toward the bar. Won't regret it? *I probably will.* What was the worst that could happen? The worst thing would be receiving a horrible manuscript that wasted my time.

As I made my way back to the booth, I realized that it would be smart to make a game plan ahead of time. I didn't necessarily need to wait to find an author to make a schedule of the times we would be laying everything out. With that thought, I reached the booth and excused myself for the rest of the night.

"Oh, come on, bro. It's early, stay a little longer and relax. You're twenty-eight, live a little," Micheal suggested, a blonde girl sitting on his lap constantly distracting him from my gaze.

"It's quite late for me. I have matters that need my attention," I briefly explained, before turning to leave.

"Are you sure everything's alright?" Aaron asked, concerned.

"Yes, no need to worry. Go on and enjoy the rest of your night." With that, I left the club and called a cab to take me back to my penthouse.

I entered my penthouse, exhausted, taking my shoes off at the entrance. The place smelled freshly cleaned, a sign that Petra, my housekeeper, did a deep cleaning today. My place never really had a signature scent. It always just smelled like luxury furniture. Although, that's when Petra doesn't cook.

When she did, she left the entire penthouse smelling like freshly cooked food. I preferred it when it smelled like fresh food to just clean furniture; it had a more 'home' scent to it. Although, no place had ever felt like home to me. The growling of my stomach interrupted my thoughts. I hadn't had a proper meal throughout the whole day.

I made my way to the kitchen and opened the fridge to find some meals Petra had prepared in glass containers. I pulled a random container out of the fridge and popped it into the microwave. Five minutes passed, and I retrieved the container.

I turned to the island in the middle of my kitchen and took a seat on the bar stool on the right edge. I ate in silence, allowing my thoughts to take capture of me again. *Should I make a big announcement that I'm looking for fresh, new authors? Should I contact one of the authors at Pearson to ask if they know of anyone? Should I just run the streets of New York with a big sign that says, 'Authors Wanted.'?*

I shook my head at the fact that I was really considering the 'authors wanted' sign. Desperation wasn't a good look for me. *Pathetic.* I had six months, starting at the end of this week. It was Wednesday, so I still had four days to find someone who was worthy and talented to make this work.

"Have a little faith, have hope." My mother's words popped into my mind.

I wasn't a hopeful person. I believed everything came with work and determination. Hope was something that made one weak and lazy, living up to this thought of things working out just cause. Hope was to ease one's mind instead of accepting the reality of their lives. As for love, it was the weakest emotion one could have. We could not lose if we did not love. And I never lost.

Tomorrow, first thing in the morning, I'd start making calls and sending out emails. Hopefully, receive some as well. Until then, I needed to release the tension I felt throughout my entire body. I stood and dropped the dirty container and utensils in the sink, then made my way to my bathroom.

I turned the shower on to its hottest temperature, took my clothes off, and stepped in. The shower head was placed on the ceiling, allowing the water to fall directly on my head like a waterfall. I dipped my head back, allowing the steamy hot water to fall onto my chest.

With my eyes closed, I took a few breaths. I unconsciously ended up picturing a certain woman with amber eyes and a pretty shade of pink plastered on her cheeks looking up at me, causing my arousal. My hands hardened at my sides in frustration.

What the hell was happening to me lately? This woman who I hadn't had a real conversation with had the power to constantly take over my thoughts, and I loathed it. I loathed myself for being the smallest bit curious.

I refused to have my thoughts consumed by her. I turned the nozzle to cold to gain control over my mind. After a while, I got out of the shower and headed to bed. I had a busy day tomorrow, and it would need one-hundred percent of my attention.

With that, I allowed my mind to drift off through all the chaos.

CHAPTER 4

KATHERINE

L AST NIGHT HAD TO BE ONE OF MY MOST EMBARRASSING NIGHTS ever. It most definitely made top three on my list, possibly over-taking number one. People talk about how they felt in those moments when something happened, but no one talks about the moment after. When they end up replaying the scenario in their mind repeatedly for what seemed to be forever.

I woke up with that embarrassment as the first thought in my mind, and I despised it. I finally got the courage to get out of bed and start my day, even though it was thirty minutes before noon. Café Luna was closed for the next three days, due to Auther's mini vacation to Saratoga Springs, which meant a mini three-day vacation for me.

I walked out of my room to find Elaina and Celeste sitting at the coffee table with Valery on FaceTime. "Good morning, sleeping beauty!" Elaina said, thrilled to see me.

"What's going on?" I asked, while walking to the kitchen to get a glass of OJ. Celeste had a humongous smile on her face that concerned me.

"CC did the impossible for you!" Valery gushed over FaceTime.

Valery was attending culinary school abroad in Barcelona. The time difference had made it difficult to communicate with her every day, but we never left out any important details. Which indicated that whatever Celeste had done was big. I took a seat at the coffee table, anxious to know what Celeste did.

"Okay..." I encouraged one of them to start talking with a swift movement of my hand.

"Yesterday, CC happened to meet someone who is HUGE in the literature world." Elaina's knees jumped with excitement as Celeste started talking.

"And I happened to tell them I knew an author who was worthy of their attention. And well, they gave me... THEIR CARD!" Celeste screamed the last phrase while pulling out a card from her jean pockets.

"You-you what?" I was speechless, slow to comprehend what had just happened.

I took the card out of Celeste's hands with shaking arms. "He said to email him a manuscript of what you're currently working on, and if he likes it, he'll set a meeting!" Celeste finished with wide arms as if she just cured world hunger.

"This is a huge opportunity, and if anyone deserves it, it's you, Kat," Elaina said, while holding my hand.

"You're going to become a published author!" Valery yelled over the phone.

"We don't know that yet," I replied while I looked at this card like it was a golden ticket to my dream life.

"Of course we do," Celeste added. I turned the card to look at the personal information on the back.

'adampearson@pearsonpublishing.com'
Adam Pearson.

AKA Mr. Pearson from last night.
"No way." I spoke without thinking.

"What? Why?" Elaina asked with narrowed brows.

"Celeste, you remember when I said I sprayed a man with a bottle?" I spoke.

"Yes..."

"Well, it was him. I sprayed him with the bottle. I doubt he'll give me a chance the moment he recognizes me." I shrugged before drinking the last drop of OJ.

"Okay... Well, he can't recognize your face through email. He'll read your manuscript and judge it strictly on how good it is." Elaina was right, he wouldn't recognize me through email.

"Yeah, Kat, take a chance," Valery added.

I took a moment to myself before giving the girls an answer. I shut my eyes and shook my head. "Okay. Fine, I'll send the manuscript tonight," I said, already slightly doubting it.

"Yes!" all of them screamed in unison at my response.

"But I'm going to need wine and you guys beside me when I send it." I pointed at both Elaina and Celeste.

"Consider it done," Celeste replied with her hand in the air as if she were taking an oath.

"Aw, I'm jealous!" Valery admitted in a whining tone.

"You were the one who decided to go to culinary school in fricking Barcelona instead of here in New York," Celeste said with crossed arms.

"Yeah, yeah, whatever." Valery rolled her eyes before saying her goodbyes. Valery hangs up, leaving the three of us. I get up and go to my bedroom to change, grabbing my bag and laptop. I walked out of the room to Elaina and Celeste, still sitting at the coffee table.

"As much as I love you both, I'm going to head down to the bookstore to write." This bookstore wasn't just any plain old bookstore. It was a bookstore that sold only one genre, which was romance. It was the one place where I felt most comfortable and creative.

"Okay, we'll see you tonight," Elaine said while Celeste

waved goodbye. I left the apartment building and walked to the bookstore. I personally loved walking to the store. It was peaceful and gave me time to be alone with my thoughts and to also enjoy the beautiful views. New York was beautiful, and I couldn't get enough of it.

Fifteen minutes later, I arrived at the bookstore with the name 'Happily Ever After' in pink plastered on the top. The whole shop was pink on the outside, with pink and white roses surrounding the entrance. It was beautiful, but the inside was the best part. As soon as you walked in, there were pages of all different types of romance books plastered on the walls and open books attached to the ceiling. It had beautiful white shelves and a white sliding ladder that allowed you to reach the books at the very top.

The whole shop smelled like books and roses. It was small compared to other bookstores, but it was literally filled with love. This was one of my favorite spots in the entire world, and I hoped it would never close.

"Hey, Kat!" Judy, the bookstore owner, greeted me. Judy knew who I was, due to how constantly I visited, just to soak up the energy that surrounded me.

"Hey, Judy, it's good to see you."

"Anything new in your book?" I always read Judy everything I had written in my book. I felt like I owed it to her for allowing me to be here without needing to pay for a book. Judy was sweet to everyone who entered her store. She was a representation of the place—love.

"Hopefully, I will in the next two hours..." I responded, taking a seat and pulling my laptop out onto the small coffee table that faced the window. "I feel a bit of pressure if I'm being honest. Whatever I come up with now is what I'll be sending to a publisher later tonight."

"A publisher? Well, that's great!" Judy smiled as she walked over to me. "You shouldn't be worried. Whatever you write will be amazing. I would know." Judy placed a reassuring hand on my shoulder before walking away to attend to a customer that had walked in.

While I looked at my laptop, I couldn't help but feel doubt. I doubted that what I had wasn't good enough, causing it to be rejected. I was afraid because I knew if I were to be rejected, it would hurt me more than anything.

Wanting to be an author and having the dream of becoming a well-known author was easy and great, but taking the next step to actually doing it was terrifying. It was terrifying putting a piece of yourself out in the world and waiting for it to be accepted. But the dream would just remain a dream if I didn't do anything about it.

'Don't leave any untold stories inside of you. You were born to tell stories.' That's what my mother used to say whenever I found myself stuck, convinced I should just give up. I wasn't about to do that now. I was going to do this for myself. For my dreams.

I looked out the window and saw a couple walking down the street. The woman was eating ice cream while talking and the man watched her like she was his favorite thing in the world. I smiled at the sight; they were happy. Seeing them gave me an idea for my book.

I turned toward my laptop and started writing. Words and words fell from my mind to my fingers, typing on the keyboard. I found a flow that had me writing for the next three hours. Within that time, I had written four chapters, twenty-two pages, and more than five-thousand words.

"Hey, hun, I hate to stop your flow, but I'm closing a bit early today," Judy said, interrupting my thoughts. I was only supposed to write for two hours, but as a writer, when you catch that flow, it's impossible to stop on your own.

"Oh, it's okay, I understand. Thanks for letting me write here, Judy." I thanked Judy before packing my bag and standing up.

"Don't be silly, hun. I love to witness the magic." Judy smiled and walked me out. I waved goodbye to Judy as I headed back to my apartment.

"Just send it already!" Celeste yelled in irritation. The girls and I sat on the floor in the living room with two bottles of wine, the second one opened already. My laptop sat right at the center of us, and I looked at it like I was afraid of the damn thing. I picked up my glass of wine and drank it. This was my third glass already, and let's just say I had poured each above the average serving.

"CC, stop pressuring the girl," Elaina argued.

"Peer pressure always works." Celeste grinned as she lifted her glass up in the air before taking yet another sip of wine.

I wouldn't say we were drunk; I'd say more like tipsy. Okay, we were drunk. So what? I needed to release the stress that was basically suffocating me. I waited my whole life to be given this opportunity. I *had* to take it. I closed my eyes and took a deep breath. I reached for my laptop and placed it on my lap.

"Card," I ordered with my hand out while keeping my eyes strictly on the screen. Celeste and Elaina gave each other a cautious look before placing the card in my hand. The weight of the card was light, but it felt like a brick, making me want to put it down.

I logged into my email and started typing out the information on the card. Celeste and Elaina hovered over at my sides, watching my every movement.

"I'm so proud of you," Elaina whispered.

"Shut up, you're distracting her," Celeste argued back in a whisper.

"Both of you, shh!" I replied, also in a whisper.

I wasn't sure why we were whispering, but it was one of

those moments when the energy felt so intense, making it feel like something greater than myself. I slammed the laptop shut, terrified of how this made me feel.

"What are you doing? Send it!" I didn't respond, causing Celeste to grab my laptop off my lap and pull onto hers.

"I can't do it," I said in a soft voice with my head lowered, trying so hard to not tear up.

"Yes, you can," Elaina replied in a soft voice, wrapping her arm around me.

"Katherine, you are such an amazing and talented author. The world deserves to read your books. You deserve to have your books known." Celeste brushed my hair out of my face and grabbed my hand. "Elaina and I, we're here for you. You're not doing this alone."

I looked at both and gave them a simple nod. "Thank you, you're right."

"Of course, I'm right." Celeste grinned while placing the laptop back on my lap. "This is your chance. You need to be the one who sends it." Celeste was the crazy one in the group, but she took on the role of a mother and a therapist when one of us really needed it.

Once again, I opened my laptop and logged into my email. I retyped the information on the card and opened my files. There were two identical blue files, leaving me to question which one was the one I was currently working on.

"What is it?" Elaina asked, seeing my confused expression.

"Nothing. I must have saved the draft twice." I didn't think twice as I clicked on the first file. A notification popped up, letting me know it was going to take twenty minutes for the file to upload and attach to the email. The timer on my screen caused me to feel more anxious by the minute.

"So close!" Elaina clapped her hands in a beat.

I started nibbling on my right thumb nail as I watched the time pass. I had a bad habit of biting my nails when I felt extremely anxious. It started when I took my first big exam in the third grade. It was for English; most kids didn't feel worried because English happened to be their first language. Whereas, I was struggling because I was bilingual. At that time, I only spoke Spanish in my household, causing me to suffer when it came to school. Now, I took that habit into adulthood.

Looking back at it, it's funny how I started off struggling in English to wanting to be an author who writes in English. I worked so hard on my English for years just so I could feel confident in it. I should feel confident in it right now.

"It uploaded. It's time to send it," Elaina said to me as she handed me my glass of wine. I took a sip from my glass, took another deep breath, and sent the email with one click.

"Oh my god. I-I really sent it," I said to myself, hardly believing it.

"Hell, yeah, you did!" Celeste exclaimed.

"I fricking did it!" I jumped up, screaming my lungs out. I broke out into my famous victory dance, a dance that was more jumping than dancing.

They both jumped up and joined me. We were jumping and screaming like a bunch of teenage girls would after associating with an innocent crush. In the middle of my dancing, I felt a wet stream running down my cheeks. I took a moment to wipe it off with the back of my hand—tears of joy.

I might have only just sent a publisher my manuscript and there was a possibility I wouldn't hear back from them. But that didn't matter. I had won. I felt free, like a bird finally escaping a cage it trapped itself in. I had overcome something greater than me, and dammit, I was proud.

The rest of the night, the girls and I celebrated.

CHAPTER 5

ADAM

I HAD RECEIVED OVER TWENTY DIFFERENT MANUSCRIPTS OVER the past two days after putting out that I was looking for a new author. I read all of them and only one caught my attention, an author that went by the name Katherine Trujillo. She had sent in a fifteen-chapter romance-fantasy. Normally, I didn't read that genre, but something about it intrigued me.

It had everything a book needed to hold a reader's undivided attention. It was engaging, exciting, and thrilling. I had set up a meeting for an hour from now. I would sit down with them to explain my plan to fully get their book out on the market and on to New York's best-sellers' list.

Some would say it was impossible to accomplish that in a matter of six months, but nothing was impossible until I declared it to be impossible. Until then, I was going to give it my all. Reading Katherine's manuscript gave me an extra boost with all of this. I knew if I found the right publicity method, it would sell all on its own.

A knock at my door interrupted my train of thought. "Come in," I announced, with annoyance seeping its way through my voice.

"Sorry to interrupt, Mr. Pearson. Someone is here to see you," my assistant, Jackson, said.

I checked the clock on my computer. *2:30 p.m.* I had lost track of time while thinking of all the things that would be discussed during this meeting.

"Bring them in." I got up from my chair and buttoned my suit jacket. I made my way toward the door, only for my brother to barge in.

"Adam," my brother greeted me with a smile.

"Aaron," I replied, not returning the smile. "Is there a specific reason you're here in my office?"

Aaron nodded at my question before answering. "Yes, I had my suspicions about our new author." That was crap. Aaron liked to come by my office and annoy me, thinking that it would entertain him until he found something to occupy himself with. Which was ironic because he owned three other businesses. The moment he became CFO, he'd have loads of work to do. Which meant lowering the 'annoy your brother' hours during the day.

"*My* new author," I interfered, already sick of his presence. He took a seat across from my desk, obviously trying to piss me off. I didn't have time for this crap.

"Something wrong?" Aaron said sarcastically. Just before I jumped out of my chair to strangle my brother, a knock interrupted, saving him.

"Mr. Pearson, a Ms.Trujillo is here to see you."

Aaron and I glanced at each other before getting up. Jackson moved out of the way and showed the woman through the door. She had her head turned toward Jackson, thanking him, before turning it toward me.

Golden, amber eyes, long, silky brown hair, curves that were created to torture me. It was her again. Kat was short for Katherine. *Fuck my life...*

"Hello." Her voice came out soft and delicate. *God, that voice.* If I didn't watch out, it'd be the death of me.

"Hello, it's a pleasure to finally meet you, Ms. Trujillo." Aaron stepped up, offering his hand out to the woman. He brought her hand up to his mouth and landed a soft kiss on top. Red flushed through my eyes. The hell was he doing putting his hands on my client?

I rearranged the cuffs on my wrists as a way to compose myself before holding my hand out to her.

"Hello, Katherine." My voice was deep, the grip in my hand strong. A low, quiet gasp escaped from her mouth. I was the only one able to hear it with the advantage of being close. A smirk crossed my lips. That sound shouldn't have given me as much pleasure as it had.

I held on to her hand for a beat longer, craving the heat that radiated off her body to mine. Within the next second, I dropped my hand, as if it could catch on fire at any given moment.

"You must excuse my brother, Aaron. He won't be joining us today. He has someplace to be at the moment." I looked at Aaron with an intense stare that said *go along, or else.* Aaron spared me a knowing look and played along.

"Ah, yes, apologies. It must have completely slipped my mind. Enjoy your evening, Ms. Trujillo." He gave Katherine a charming smile before looking back at me. *Dick. I'll deal with him later.* He finally turned around and walked out the door, leaving Katherine and me to get down to business. Because that was all it was, strictly business.

I walked back to my desk and took a seat. "Sit." I pointed toward the chair in front of me. It came out more as an order rather than a suggestion.

"Oh, okay." Her response was nervous. For a brief moment, I had forgotten the whole point of this meeting before I quickly returned to my senses. I placed a copy of her manuscript I had printed prior to this meeting on the desk.

"I noticed you only sent me fifteen chapters of your novel. Is that all you have written at the moment, or there's more?"

She looked at me like I just spoke an entirely different language.

"I'm sorry, fifteen chapters of what?" she asked, as if she was dreading the answer.

"Night Span. The romance-fantasy novel...?" Okay. Now I was confused. Why was she asking me about *her* book? Her face had turned about five different shades of red. She dipped her head down to look at her shoes. If I hadn't known any better, I would've thought she was about to lose it. But to my surprise, she lifted her gaze from her shoes to my face with a soft smile before speaking.

"Yes, of course. Fifteen chapters... That's all I have so far..." I looked down at her hands and noticed her knuckles turning white with how hard she was gripping the seat.

"I see, how unfortunate..." I explained, causing her to cut me off.

"In what time period would you like me to finish it?" she asks, not afraid of the answer I would give her. She surprised me when she took charge, not allowing me to have the chance to turn her down. Not that I was going to do that.

"How fast do you think you could finish it?" I asked, intrigued by how she would answer. If she was a fast writer, it would be better for me.

"Just give me the deadline." *Interesting.* She really didn't beat around the bush. I liked that. I could respect that.

"Five months." My expression was serious, not showing any type of emotion. Her eyes grew wider, her skin turning paler at my sudden response. I didn't blame her. I would think it was absolutely ridiculous. It *was* ridiculous.

"Five months?" she questioned, waiting for me to correct her. I nodded, causing a cautious look to spread across her face. She crossed her legs, making her skirt hike up an inch. She wore a red off the shoulder sweater with a black skirt and black pantyhose under. But her bold red lip was what had my gaze returning to her.

"Is there a problem? I leaned forward, resting my arms on the desk in an attempt to get a closer look at her. Katherine was the type of woman I could stare at for hours, never wanting to look away. Simply looking at her made one want to bow down shamelessly and praise the heavens for such beauty.

Focus.

"No... just such a tight schedule." Katherine shakes her head.

"Yes, well, there's no need to worry about that. I've prepared a timeline for us." I sat back and reached toward the right cabinet in the desk, pulling out a file with all the information and handing it to her.

"Read this and let me know if you have any questions regarding the schedule." Katherine nods as she scans through the documents while I watch her closely. She bites her lower lip as she gives the documents her undivided attention. Her brows draw together as she reads.

"You want my book on the New York bestsellers' list in six months?" She sounded uneasy about the idea.

"Ever heard of manifesting?" I joked, trying to lighten the mood. I was taken aback by my decision to make a joke, only to make her feel more comfortable. She laughed, the sound vibrating throughout my body.

Her smile died down as she continued to read. I couldn't help but feel disappointed at the loss of her smile. Seeing her smile for the first time was like experiencing a beautiful sunrise after years of it being midnight. I couldn't grasp what it was about her that intrigued me so much. It bugged me.

"I have to travel?" she asked, pulling me from my thoughts. It took me a second to respond, earning a skeptical look from her.

"Yes, for publicity purposes." I had set up book signings and a book launch for when we would release it. I had picked locations in New York and around the U.S. None had been confirmed, but it was just a matter of time until I got each venue to comply with my plans.

"I'm not sure if I can leave. I have two jobs."

"I'm aware." I knew this because of our past encounters. My sudden reply triggered Katherine's cheeks to redden. I bit my tongue in an attempt to stop my smile from escaping.

"I—"

"The moment you sign with me, you'll drop everything and anything when you are called to," I said, pausing before finishing, "That is your job. That and writing." Katherine kept quiet, not answering me.

I wanted nothing more but to know what she was currently thinking about. What did she think of this whole arrangement? Would she follow through, or would she back out? Suspense filled me as I waited for her to give me an answer. Then, she put me out of my misery with her response.

"I understand. I'm willing to fully dedicate myself."

My lips formed a slight smile.

"Perfect. I'm going to need you to sign these." I handed her a thick pile of papers and a black pen.

"I should probably go over these with my lawyer," she insisted as she looked down at the first page.

Bullshit. We both knew she didn't have a personal lawyer waiting around on call. But I respected her attempt at trying to make it seem as if she did. I decided to make it easy on both of us and get this over with as quickly as possible.

"No need. All the details you need to agree to and understand are in the first three pages." I flipped through the first three pages and shortly summarized it. Each time earning an approving nod from Katherine.

"Now that we've gone through that and you understood it, sign here." I pointed to the bottom of the page where her signature was needed. She gave me a suspicious look, squinting her eyes.

"If I was trying to trick you, you would know," I suggested, eager for this woman to finally sign the damn thing. She looked me in the eye for a long beat before returning her gaze to the box that required her signature. She hesitated before picking up her pen and placing it on the paper.

"I'm not worried about that," she finally spoke up, surprising me. "I just—This whole thing is important to me, and I want a good outcome from all of this," she explained as she looked into my eyes, giving me the impression that this was her first time attempting to put a book out.

I understood where she was coming from. I had worked with multiple authors while my father was still CEO, and the amount of time and thought that goes into writing a novel, it's intense. I wanted Kat to know that her book is going to be in good hands. My career counted on it, *literally.*

"I understand. You won't have to worry about any of that. I will personally work through everything." I wasn't lying. I had no choice but to do so. Her eyes lit up with joy.

"Really? Wow." She came down from her bliss and raised her right brow. "But why? I would've thought that someone else would be in charge of it."

"Your novel has great potential. It would be an honor to work on it personally." I couldn't let her know about the election, nor the task that had everything to do with her. I couldn't have anyone know, for that matter. Everyone thought I was in transition to becoming CEO, which I had no intention of changing.

I was telling the truth when I said her novel had potential—it did—which was the main reason I picked her novel in the first place. Though, doing all the work without a proper team did come across as a burden for me, but I was determined to make it work. *It's only for six months.*

Working one on one with Katherine for six months worried

me. I'd just have to make sure I stayed focused. Yet, with her in front of me, it seemed like an almost impossible task.

"Thank you. I look forward to working with you," she said as a soft shade of pink rose on the surface of her cheekbones, her smile small and soft. She was a mess of gorgeous chaos; I could see it in those golden eyes. Everything inside me told me I should run the other way before I became consumed by her. But I chose to ignore it.

"Monday, 9 a.m., we'll brainstorm for your cover. In the meantime, write me five to ten chapters." I was giving her the weekend to brainstorm and come back with fresh ideas. I stood from my seat and walked Katherine toward the door. She turned to face me.

"Thank you for... your time today." She smiled, and I knew I was in trouble. She turned and walked out, leaving me even more intrigued than the moment she first walked in. I shook my head and closed my door.

Walking back to my desk, I heard a knock at my door. Whoever it was didn't have fucking manners because they just walked in. I turned to face him—*my uncle.* God, I hated how my stomach twisted every time I laid eyes on him.

"What do you want?" I asked impatiently, waiting for this encounter to end. My uncle had an expression that was only used for one emotion—desperation. Now, I was interested.

"I see you've found an author." His response was simple, trying to hide the obvious. He had seen Katherine walk out of my office. He hadn't found an author. No one would willingly work with him. My uncle was weak, and he lacked creativity; two things you did not want in a publisher. Another reason I'd be the only rightful choice for the CEO position.

"Yes. Now that you have fed your suspicions, you can leave. Your existence is giving me a headache." I thought I would find this conversation amusing, but really, it's just a waste of time.

He laughed, his eyes filled with hatred as he looked at me. If looks could kill, I would be six feet under the ground next to my father. I was a step ahead of him, and it drove him *crazy*.

"I'd keep my eyes open if I were you. Others might offer her a better deal." His smile was wicked. He was trying to mess with me, trying to get me to be paranoid throughout the process. Whatever it was, it wasn't going to work. I knew I had to keep an eye on my uncle; he was more than capable of cheating.

I felt relieved that I had Katherine sign the contracts today, because if she did try to leave... Let's just say it was going to be a difficult, very unpleasant process.

"Edward, please. No need to worry. I see and hear everything." I meant it as a warning. A warning to *fuck off*. I was more than positive he got my message, giving me a black look. He walked out of my office, slamming my door. I held on to the sweet thought of finally defeating him once and for all. For nothing would get in my way of achieving it.

I would make sure of it.

CHAPTER 6
KATHERINE

I messed up.

To my surprise, a day after sending in my manuscript, I had the Pearson Book Group contact me for a meeting. I was in complete and utter shock. Except, it was because of an entirely different manuscript; one I was never planning to send. The day I had sent the email, there were two identical files in the folder on my laptop.

One of them was a novel I had started at the age of nineteen and gave up on. While the other was the one I was currently working on. Both files were blue, and I had been drinking a lot of wine with the girls, so I couldn't tell the files apart. I was never able to finish the novel Night Span. It was stressful for me, causing me to throw it aside, not giving it a glance for the past *six years*.

I had tried to pull myself together the moment I had realized which manuscript he was talking about, and I had no choice but to go along with it. It's now been two days since my meeting with Adam Pearson and it was not what I was expecting. He liked it so much, he was willing to work on it with me, *personally*.

He told me he saw great potential in my writing—in this story. I couldn't make out the right words to tell him the truth. His confidence in me as a writer made me want to try to finish it. That unfinished novel was a heavy burden for me, constantly reminding me that it was there.

"Write me five to ten chapters." His voice popped into my head. It was easier said than done. Trying to figure out how to continue the book was hard. Though, he didn't know that, and I wasn't planning for him to know, either. To him, I knew what I was doing, and I constantly had new ideas.

Except, after two days of sitting in front of my laptop, trying to brainstorm for the next chapter, I had nothing. This was a fantasy-romance, featuring a princess and a guard. Their love was forbidden, a love so passionate they were willing to fight an entire kingdom to be together. The story plot was easy to follow; it was the characters that were difficult.

I couldn't find the right way to present my characters in the story. Nothing truly served them justice, and I refused to write something that was the complete opposite of passion. The truth is, at the age of nineteen, I went through a breakup that almost broke me. I had given three years to the relationship, only for him to end all of it for his own benefit.

That was in the past now and I'd moved on, but it was the reason I had given up on it, because I gave up on love. I hadn't been with anyone since. The only love I experienced was in the books I read and wrote. Sad, right?

My mother had been by my side and helped me get back on track. She had reminded me why I loved to write, and it took some time to figure out how to write romance without it hurting me, but I got it. Now, I just had to overcome another obstacle and finish this book. I desperately needed inspiration to stimulate some new ideas, so I decided to take a little trip to my favorite place on earth—the bookstore.

As I made my way toward the store, I passed Café Luna.

Auther had just returned from his mini vacation and expected me to be there tomorrow for an early shift, but I had a meeting with Adam.

"The moment you sign with me, you'll drop everything and anything when you are called to. That is your job. That and writing." Adam's voice resonated in my mind twenty-four seven; it never seemed to back down. I made a commitment that I would have to follow through, no room for excuses. I didn't want to leave Café Luna. I enjoyed working there, but I had no other option.

I took it upon myself to walk into Café Luna and tell Auther I could no longer work for him. He deserved to hear it from me in person. As I opened the door, the bell rang. Auther was cleaning up behind the counter and looked up at me the moment he heard the bell.

"Kat, what a lovely surprise. I was expecting to see you tomorrow." I was fond of Auther. He was like a father figure, which was why it truly hurt me to tell him.

"Hey, Auther, about that... I have some news," I said in a pained voice. I took a second to think of how I was going to break it to him. There was no easy way, there was only the truth...

"Sure, what is it?" He stopped what he was doing and walked around the counter. He pulled the hand towel off his shoulder to clean his hands as he patiently waited for what I had to say.

"I... I signed with a publishing company that requires a lot of my time..." I paused to find the right words. "And I won't be able to work morning shifts anymore. I hope you understand. This is one of the best jobs I've ever had." Auther looked at me for a second, then his whole expression changed to... happiness?

"A publisher? Oh, Kat, that's amazing. I'm so proud of you for finally doing it." I looked at him, confused, yet relieved to hear him say that.

"You're not mad that I'm quitting?" I asked. He smiled and shook his head before he answered.

"Of course not. You didn't think I was expecting you to work here forever, did you?" I shook my head in response, so relieved. "You deserve a shot at making this happen, and I support it." I was pleased that Auther understood, more that he supported me. Having my friends cheer me on gave me the motivation to make the most of this.

"Thanks, Auther. Really, you have no idea how much that means to me," I said.

"Anytime." He winks, then his eyes travel down to my bag and back up to my eyes. "Are you staying, or is this a quick stop?"

"Quick stop. I wanted to speak to you in person. I was actually heading to the bookstore," I admitted.

"Well, I appreciate you coming to me. You can go on to your bookstore now. I have to wipe these tables clean for tomorrow." He gave me a soft push toward the door. I gave him a smile and left, making my way to the bookstore.

I entered the bookstore and noticed there were fewer books up on the shelves today, and curiosity ran through me. Judy was probably in the back restocking books, so I took a seat at my regular spot and started writing. For the first time in a long time, I wrote one chapter for Night Span.

It wasn't much, but it was something. Tomorrow, when I met with Adam, we'd discuss the cover. I knew he wouldn't like the fact that I only wrote one chapter, but maybe if I lied and told him I was brainstorming more, then it would pass. I'd find out what he thought about it tomorrow.

Later that night, my phone rang in my room, stopping Elaina and me from cooking. I made my way toward my room and unplugged my phone from the cable. My mom's name flashed across the screen, and I swiped to answer the call.

"Hola, Mami," I said, not expecting this call. I hadn't spoken to my mother in a week. That was the longest I'd gone without speaking to her. I normally would call every Friday, but with all the changes that have been going on in my life, it simply slipped my mind.

"Hola back, Mija, you're alive!" my mother said sarcastically, yet very dramatically. I could picture my mom making her irritated face through the phone. "What happened to you on Friday? I was worried sick. I called you, but you didn't answer." Her voice instantly switched from sarcastic to angry in a matter of seconds.

"I'm sorry, Mami. I've had so much on my plate lately. I didn't even realize you called," I explained, hearing her huff through the phone. My mother and I were close; she knew everything except what my life had been like for the past week.

"I actually have something that I've been meaning to tell you..." I said, ready to finally spill the beans. "I met Adam Pearson, and I had a meeting with him two days ago." I expected my mom to know who Adam Pearson was, but I guess not...

"Ay, Mija! Tienes novio?" My mother's voice switched from anger to happiness. I aggressively shook my head no, as if she could see me through the phone.

"No, Ma! I don't have a boyfriend! Adam Pearson is *not* my boyfriend." I tried to make it as clear as I could. I caught a glance of myself in my mirror hanging over my vanity. My face had turned as red as a tomato. God, I hadn't blushed this much since my junior year of high school. The thought of Adam Pearson being more than just my publisher was… something.

"Adam Pearson is a publisher; he owns the Pearson Book Group. One of the biggest publishing companies worldwide," I exclaimed, trying to say the words fast before she could suggest anything else. I heard silence for a second, then checked to see if the call got cut off. Nope, she was still on the phone... but why was she so—

"WHAT!" she screamed through the phone without warning, leaving my ear with a loud ringing. I moved the phone away from my ear. "Katherine! How could you not tell me this sooner?" My mother pronounced my name with a Spanish accent.

"I know, I wanted to make sure it went well before I told you anything..." It was true. I never wanted to tell my mother about things I wasn't sure would have a good outcome. I always wanted to make her proud.

"It went pretty well. He said my work had great potential," I said while I heard typing from the other side of the line. "Ma, what are you doing?" I asked, confused about why she was typing so aggressively with me on the phone.

"I'm looking up Adam Pearson." Of course she was; my mother was always checking people out the moment I mentioned them. She was successful with most, and she'd *definitely* be successful with this one. Adam Pearson was well known, and the internet loved him, not only for his name but for his face. The camera loved him. "Wow, he's gorgeous," my mother continued.

"Yes, he is an attractive man, but that isn't the point," I pointed out, trying to make it clear to my mother that it was not going to happen. *Or are you trying to convince yourself?* an annoying voice pitched in.

Yes, looking into those green eyes made it difficult to focus, and yes, he was too gorgeous for his own good. But again, not the point.

"Mhm. Okay, well, you never know," my mother continued, trying to torture me. I pinched the bridge of my nose and took a deep breath before cutting the call short.

"Yes, Mami, sure. I have to go now; Elaina and I are making dinner, and I can't afford to leave her out there alone for so long," I explained, getting up from my bed.

"Okay, sweetie, love you. Talk to you next week?" she asked, waiting for my answer.

"Si, Mami, love you. Bye." I hung up the phone and placed it on my nightstand. I swear I was planning to leave my room to help Elaina out, but she could handle another minute alone. I unlocked my phone and opened Google, and typed in 'Adam Pearson'. As soon as it popped up, I saw news of his father passing away and him taking over the CEO position.

I hadn't known his father had only passed a few months ago by the way he and his brother carried themselves so well. I guessed they were used to it, dealing with so much work and having to put their feelings aside. It was sad, but I had a feeling there was way more to Adam than just the obsessive CEO. Within the next six months, time would only tell if I was right.

I clicked on images and looked at recent photos taken of Adam. God, he was gorgeous, but I noticed he didn't smile in any. Without noticing, I got lost in time, simply just looking at him. One could get lost in his eyes, and I guess I did...

"He's hot." I jumped and threw my phone across the room in shock. I snapped my head toward Elaina while trying to calm my heart rate.

"Oh my god, Elaina!" I exclaimed, as Elaina gave me a confused look.

"We live together, Katherine. Who else would it have been?" She shook her head as she walked toward my phone. She bent down and picked it up.

"I got it!" I said as I quickly ran, trying to take the phone from her hands. Elaina happened to be way taller than me, which was a curse. Elaina dwarfed my five-foot-two at five-foot nine. She could have a career as a runway model if she wanted to, yet she chose to be the one behind the curtains, preparing all the clothes.

"Who is *this*?" she asked, pronouncing the last word with a long duration. She ran out of my room with my phone still in her hands. Panic set in and I ran after her, feeling like I was chasing a dog with a bone in his mouth—almost impossible.

"This is Adam Pearson??" She stopped running, causing me to crash into her, and we both fell flat on the ground. "Oh, this is good... You've got a thing for your publisher!" she smiled. Dread filled me as she figured it all out, so I did what anyone would do... deny.

"No, I don't! I was just researching. I have the right to be curious about who I'm working with." I tried my best to sound convincing, though I knew she saw through my lie. Elaina knew me so well; she knew when I told a little lie. To be honest, it wasn't really a lie, when I was just curious.

"Katherine, researching would be reading things about the man. You were straight up staring at his photos." I covered my face with both of my hands and shook my head. Elaina let out a chuckle as she stood up from the floor.

"I happened to cross by a few of his photos online while researching him. It's normal. You just walked in on me at the wrong time," I said, getting up from the floor as well. Elaina spared me a skeptical glance before handing me back my phone. I'd admit that I was looking at his photos, but not that I was interested.

"Okay, Kat. I would be careful, though. At the end of the day, he *is* your publisher." I knew that, of course I did. I wouldn't willingly do anything stupid. Plus, I hadn't been with anyone in years, so why suddenly give *him* any attention?

"I know, El. I wouldn't do anything to mess up this opportunity." I gave her an honest look, and I meant every word. Elaina gave me a curt nod before speaking again.

"Good... He is *gorgeous,* though," she said as she entered the living room. I rolled my eyes at her response. Why was everyone saying that? I walked toward the living room, where Elaina had placed the dinner plates. Elaina and I never used our dining table; we always sat on the couch to eat while watching TV or to just talk. I reached to grab my plate of pasta and noticed two black balls on top of it.

"Elaina... what is this?" I asked, pointing at the black balls with my fork. She spared me a shy smile before explaining.

"It's a meatball! You were the one who left me in the kitchen alone for so long, and I'm not Valery," she said, right as she took a bite of the burned meatball. Not a second later, Elaina spat it out. "Yeah, definitely not Valery," she clarified as she coughed. I laughed so hard that my stomach started to hurt.

The rest of the night was filled with laughter and dumb conversations, making me forget any ounce of stress I had. And I was grateful for it, not taking moments like these for granted.

CHAPTER 7

ADAM

It was Monday, 9 a.m., and I kept looking at my Abbot Wood Pendulum clock hanging on the wall of my office. The clock changed from 9:00 to 9:01. She was late. I thought I had made it clear to her that our meeting would start at exactly 9. Where could she possibly be if not here? I am not a patient person; for someone to keep me waiting pissed me off.

Time is money, and a minute is worth thousands of dollars to me. I was prepared to discuss the ideas I had for the cover, and I was eager to hear about the progress she had made throughout the time I'd given her. I waited about ten minutes before deciding to dial my assistant to see where she was. As I motioned my hand toward the phone, it rang. I picked up to hear my assistant's voice on the line.

"Ms. Trujillo is here for her nine o'clock meeting." I glanced at my clock: 9:14.

"Send her in," I said as I retained my anger, just for it to vanish the moment she walked through the door. How could one glance at her make all my anger fly out the window? She was soft, but in a dangerous way, her little black dress, with a brown coat on top, hugging her curves.

I looked down at her hands that held two cups of coffee from Café Luna. She spared me a shy smile as she walked toward my desk to hand me my coffee. My heart beat harder with each step she took as she came closer. I took the coffee from her, our hands touched, and electricity and tension filled the room.

One touch made me feel like I'd been hit by lightning.

Suddenly, my hands turned sweaty, and a suffocating feeling started underneath my zipper, my erection bulging against my pants. I placed a hand over my length and tried to cover the reaction she had caused with a single touch. I was furious that I had lost control over my own body.

Katherine took a seat across from me without saying a word, completely oblivious to my reaction to her light touch. She patiently waited for me to say something. She was nervous; I could tell by the way she couldn't figure out where to rest her hands. I then realized I wasn't the only one who was affected by our interaction, and a part of me liked that.

"What's this?" I said as I lifted the coffee she handed me, curious why she would get me a coffee. She responded with a small, nervous smile and shrug.

"I owed you a coffee from Café Luna." She remembered our first encounter; the morning I ran out of the café before receiving my coffee. I stared at her, which caused her to break eye contact by speaking again.

"You left before you could get your coffee, so it's basically already paid," she joked while I tried to hide the smile I felt emerging. I never smiled. No one made me *want* to smile. Yet, all it took for her was a simple coffee.

Are you sure it's the coffee? I pushed the thought to the back of my brain.

"Yes, I remember. Thank you for the coffee, but I'd prefer it if you were on time." I indicated toward the clock behind her. She looked back at the clock, then back at me.

"Right, sorry. I must've lost track of time," she shyly apologized as she wrapped both her hands around the coffee cup. The image of her red nails wrapped around a round object tortured me. My mind drifted to her red nails wrapped around something else. *What. The. Fuck?* I shook my head before realizing I had her waiting for a response for about ten seconds. I cleared my throat before speaking.

"Don't apologize, just show up on time," I said, my voice husky, rougher than usual. But that was what she did to me, simply tortured me with her existence. Katherine nodded at my sudden reply. I hadn't meant to come off so aggressively; it was something I couldn't control. I quickly changed the subject by asking about her progress with the book.

"Let's see the chapters you've written over the weekend." I leaned forward as I watched Katherine pull out an incredibly thin folder to hold five to ten chapters. Her hands slightly shook as she placed the folder on my desk.

"It's not much. It's one chapter," she finally spoke, meeting my gaze. *One chapter?* Over the past two days, she'd written only *one* chapter? I took a deep breath before replying.

"One chapter? How come?" There had to be a logical reason for her only writing one chapter. That or she was slow. If she was a slow writer, then I was fucked. I opened the folder to find six or seven pages.

"I spent most of the weekend brainstorming and writing ideas before writing the actual chapters. I wrote this one last night. I'll have more on your desk by next week." She kept eye contact, not breaking it once, making me want to believe her. She sounded convincing. Part of me thought she had writer's block. It was quite common with authors, though we did not have time for that.

"Alright, I expect ten chapters on my desk by next week." I let it go, wanting to trust her. The reality was, if this was going to work, I had to trust she would finish by her deadline. It was only the beginning, so I supposed brainstorming was okay. *This is the second time you let her off the hook,* a voice in my mind crept in.

Something about Katherine did not allow me to be hard on her. I wanted her to feel comfortable, while, with anyone else, I'd make sure they felt my wrath. Still, it was a mystery why I was being so lenient.

"Yes, of course, Mr. Pearson." A smirk crossed my lips. The way she so willingly went along with anything I said pleased me. It shouldn't, but *Christ*, it did. I pulled out the multiple cover design ideas I had in a file in my cabinet. I spread them out on my desk. Katherine broke into a huge smile as she got up from her seat and walked around my desk.

"Oh my god. These are amazing," she emphasized as she picked up a sample. She then bent over next to me to pick up the next, remaining still as she analyzed the rest that were laid out. I took advantage of her being distracted and smelled her hair. *Lavender.* A rich scent of vanilla and lavender.

Her scent was so sweet, so rich, so *intoxicating.* Her scent was like a drug to me. I was sure that if I had a taste of it, I'd become addicted. I looked at her face, and genuine joy filled her smile. I didn't realize it until she turned to face me that I was smiling. A small yet noticeable smile for someone who never does.

Her smile slowly disappeared as her eyes grew wide. Heat spread throughout my entire body, causing the tension in the room to become thicker. We stared into each other's eyes for what seemed to be forever, making it feel as though time had stopped just for us. I looked down at her slightly parted red lips.

Fuck. What was I doing? What were we doing?

"Which cover do you prefer?" I asked, quickly killing the mood that was clearly about to eat us alive. She took a step back as she tucked a strand of hair behind her ear. She walked back to her seat before answering me.

"I like this one the most, but I still feel like it's missing something," she breathed, crossing her legs. She pointed to the cover featuring a crown settled next to a sword covered in blood. I examined the cover she picked and couldn't think of anything that could make it better.

"Any suggestions?" I asked as I pulled out a stack of sticky notes and picked up my black pen. As she started to make a few suggestions, I jotted them down, wanting to make sure I got every detail. One of the most important things about publishing was the book cover because it was the first thing readers would see.

Like a first impression when meeting someone important, the cover needed to intrigue readers, leaving them wanting more. Readers would pick up the book if the cover called to them, and with this cover, I was going to make them want it.

"Perfect, I'll look into it." I placed the sticky note on top of my Apple laptop and got up from my desk, needing to investigate my other cabinet. I kneeled in front of the cabinet and looked through the files, finally finding the one I was looking for. Pulling it out, I got up and adjusted my tie, meeting Katherine's gaze from across the room.

"Do you have a question?" My sudden question caused her to blink back to reality. *She was checking me out.* A smug smirk pulled at the sides of my lips.

"Um, yes... Could I see your creative department, please?" she quickly requested as she got up from her seat. I was not allowed to receive any type of help from any of the departments, so I wasn't sure if I could show her. Yet I didn't want her to become suspicious about the nature of her contract with Pearson. I took a moment to myself before deciding whether it was smart to comply with her request.

"What for?" I decided to ask, wanting her to back down. But she surprised me the moment she opened her mouth.

"Because I want to." Because she *wanted* to. I didn't get

angry or irritated, I became interested. In that moment, I made the decision to give her what she wanted.

"Alright. Since you asked so nicely." Her face turned a shade of red, similar to the one she was wearing on her lips. I walked toward the office door, holding it open as she claimed her bag. She didn't spare me one glance as she walked through the door. I kept my eyes on her, as if my life depended on it.

I closed the door behind me and walked in front of her, leading her toward the creative department.

It was on the tenth floor, and we were currently on the eighteenth. We arrived at the elevator, and I pressed the button and waited. The elevator took longer than expected, causing both of us to stand awkwardly in silence. Finally, the elevator doors opened. I placed my hand on the small of her back and gently pushed her in.

She entered and immediately stood in a corner, so I took the corner across from hers. I pressed the button to the tenth floor and stood back.

The elevator walls were glass, showing us a perfect view of New York City between floors. If my office felt small with Katherine in it, then the elevator felt like nothing. I clenched my hands, forcing myself to stay still.

"The view is beautiful," she finally said as we descended four floors. *Four more to go.*

"Yes, it is," I said, keeping my eyes on the floor numbers as they changed. *Fourteen, thirteen, twelve, eleven, ten.* Finally, after what felt like an eternity in hell, the doors opened. I quickly walked out, leaving Katherine behind.

Get a hold of yourself, a voice in my mind said.

I needed to keep my distance. Katherine was now a signed author here at Pearson Book Group, which meant that me being associated with her in any way other than professionally was not a good look for me. Not with the elections coming up. I wanted nothing to do with Katherine either way.

Keep telling yourself that. Maybe you'll start to believe it.

"Shut up," I quietly said to myself, like the psycho I was clearly becoming. I didn't know how I was going to do this, but distance was a start. I waited for Katherine in front of the creative department.

Breathe. I was going to survive whatever this was. I had to. I had no choice.

CHAPTER 8
KATHERINE

I HAD ASKED ADAM TO SHOW ME THE CREATIVE DEPARTMENT because it was the only thing that I could think of. After the past interactions I had with Adam, my mind was a bit hazy. The moment he kneeled in front of the cabinet, my mind went blank. He was so tall, seeing him kneel did things to my mind. I was basically drooling over this man and didn't even realize it.

'Alright, since you asked so nicely.' Adam's voice became my brain's favorite subject, constantly replaying his words. It was impossible to stop. And the way he made me feel excited over a damn department was ridiculous.

I had followed him to the elevator and waited for the doors to open. When they did, we had both walked in. I took it upon myself to stand in the corner far, far away from him.

The tension between us in that elevator was eating its way inside me, causing me to press my thighs together. I looked out the window in need of some type of distraction, and it worked for a few seconds. The view was breathtaking. I could see all of Central Park and the buildings surrounding it. I was convinced that this elevator was the spot photographers used to take those amazing pictures of New York city.

"The view is beautiful," I said, trying to lighten the mood.

"Yes, it is." A simple reply, and yet he didn't even bother to look out, his gaze focused on the number of floors we were passing.

The moment those doors opened, Adam had rushed out of the elevator in the blink of an eye. I was left behind, shocked at his sudden disappearance. For some reason, I felt like he didn't like me that much, like he couldn't tolerate me. I finally walked out of the elevator before it closed again.

"Katherine." I snapped my head toward him. He was standing outside these big wooden double doors with a sign that read 'Pearson Creative Department' in bold, black lettering. I walked toward Adam, anxious to see what was behind these doors.

"Can we go in?" I asked, running out of patience. Adam gave me the smallest smirk I had ever seen, almost missing it altogether.

"So impatient." His response was dark and rough. I felt my cheeks heat to a burning temperature, and I knew I looked as red as a tomato. *How embarrassing.*

Adam opened the door, and I tried to walk in without showing how weak my legs had turned due to his little comment. They felt like two strings of cooked spaghetti.

I walked in and was left speechless with the place. Shelves and shelves filled with books that were probably all designed in this very room. Vibrant colors painted on the walls and couches that looked so comfortable, I'd willingly choose them over my own bed. As I walked further in, I noticed multiple conference rooms with long wooden tables and rolling desk chairs that surrounded them.

Instead of regular lights, the spaces had modern glass pendant lights hanging in each room. No wonder all their covers were amazing; the place they worked in basically provided unlimited inspiration.

Adam placed his hand on my lower back as he showed me around. The small gesture messed up my breathing patterns and made me feel like I belonged to him, like he owned me. *You're reading way into this.*

"I'll introduce you to some of our main creators." He suddenly spoke as he directed me to an occupied room. I walked in to find a group of people brainstorming and designing with music playing out of speakers at full blast. Adam cleared his throat loud enough for everyone to hear and stop what they were doing.

The whole room paused with his presence. Adam was the type of man with so much power that anyone who came across him bowed at his feet, and I was witnessing it. After all, he owned the place.

"Adam, what a lovely surprise," a woman said as she got up from her chair, making her way toward us. She looked like she was around the same age as Adam. She had beautiful curly blonde hair and eyes that were so blue. They made me feel like I would suddenly freeze if I stared into them for too long.

"Victoria," he greeted her before continuing. "This is Katherine, our newly signed author." She looked at me without saying a word.

"Hi, nice to meet you," I said, trying to avoid this conversation becoming awkward. I was normally a shy person when it came to meeting new people, so the fact that I initiated the conversation said a lot.

Victoria looked at me from bottom to top, clearly giving me the vibe that she did not like me. Discomfort sat at the pit of my stomach, and I looked at Adam, whose gaze was already on Victoria. I couldn't figure out what he was thinking about. Just as I thought things couldn't get more uncomfortable, he finally spoke again.

"Victoria, it's impolite to not introduce yourself, especially to ignore someone." His voice was demanding, causing Victoria to snap out of whatever trance she was in. She quickly met Adam's gaze, then mine.

"Right, I apologize. I have quite a few things in my mind. Hectic day," she said as I looked around the room that seemed to be running smoothly. I decided not to read into it much and kept it moving.

"If you don't mind, I'd love to see some designs you guys are working on," I asked, walking further into the room. I didn't know what possessed me to just walk in without getting an answer. I was extremely curious about what was being created. Maybe I could get some ideas for my cover.

My cover. This moment felt surreal.

As I walked around, a certain cover caught my attention— beautiful gold armor with a woman's hand resting on the right shoulder. With that, an idea crossed my mind for Night Span. My cover could be a gold crown being placed on a woman's head by a man whose hands are covered in blood. It would signify the guard crowning the princess as Queen of the kingdom, already hinting at their affair. It was perfect.

I smiled, waving the rest of the creator's goodbye as I found myself out. I had passed by Victoria and gave her a simple nod. I felt Adam's presence behind me as I walked out the door, and I turned to face him, eager to tell him about my idea.

"What did you think?" he asked before giving me a chance to say anything.

"It was incredible; the entire room screamed inspiration," I exclaimed as I kept walking toward the elevator. I felt his gaze burning a hole in my back as I faced forward, waiting on the elevator. The doors opened, and I walked in.

"I have an idea for the cover," I spat out, unable to keep it to myself any longer.

"Do you now?" he responded as he walked into the elevator behind me. He looked at me like he wanted to pick at my brain, like he wanted to know everything that went through my mind.

He intimidated me, and I felt like I needed to guard my mind with all my will, scared to even reveal half of it.

He patiently waited for me to continue after pressing the button to the eighteenth floor, my gaze following his hands as he dropped them to his sides. His hands were veiny, and they seemed far from soft, too rough for my own good. I stared for a good minute; he looked at me, then followed to where my gaze rested.

I quickly switched my gaze from his hands to the black boots I wore on my feet, feeling embarrassed he had caught me staring twice today. I nervously bit my lip, refusing to look at him again.

"Katherine." His voice was dark. Our eyes met and suddenly, I forgot to breathe. Those green eyes, they had the shine and sparkle of an emerald. They conveyed warmth and intensity; I wanted nothing more than to look away. But it seemed almost impossible.

"Hm?" was all I could make out with the hold his eyes had on me.

"The cover idea," he said with a smug expression. *He knows, he definitely knows.* I hesitated before explaining the idea I had, almost forgetting it altogether. Once I remembered, I had told him all the details about it.

"Not bad. I'll see it through," he simply responded as the elevator doors opened. We made our way back to Adam's office in silence until an older man approached us, stopping us halfway.

"Adam, it has come across my attention that you were in the creative department," he said, keeping his eyes solely on Adam.

"Yes, I was being welcoming by showing Katherine around," he replied as the air surrounding us tightened.

"I see." the man smiled as he faced me. "Katherine, please feel free to call me if you have any questions regarding Pearson Book Group." He took my hand and gave it a gentle shake.

"Oh, okay. Thank yo—"

"If she has any questions, she'll call me," Adam interrupted me, not taking his eyes off the man. "Edward, it's always a pleasure," he said as he gently gripped my arm and steered me around Edward.

"Who was that?" I asked, confused by the vibe I felt. They definitely hated each other.

"My uncle. He's not important." His *uncle*. Who interacts like that with their family? They acted so cold toward each other. I would never in a million years treat any one of my family members like that. To be fair, I am Hispanic, so we are anything but cold near each other.

"I would have never guessed," I admitted, without giving it a second thought. We arrived at his office door, and he turned to face me before opening it.

"Not everyone is good, Katherine." His reply was short and to the point. Of course, I knew that not everyone was a nice person, but I still believed that everyone had *some* good in them. It would be humanly impossible to not have one ounce of good in you.

He swung the door open, waiting for me to enter. I looked down at my phone: 12:46 p.m. The time had flown by. With Adam, it hadn't even felt like an hour had passed. I put my phone back in my bag and looked at Adam to find him already looking at me. He didn't look away, didn't even blink, not ashamed of staring.

"I, um, I have to go. I work a late shift tonight, and I want to get some writing done before then," I breathed. I couldn't even speak correctly, knowing that he was looking at me like *that*. He tilted his head higher while keeping his eyes on me. *Is it hot in here?* Because suddenly I was burning up. I felt like my body was on fire, like a horrible fever was building.

"I understand. Wednesday, we will meet again to go over the progress you've made. Same time." He hadn't turned his gaze from mine, causing my heart to beat rapidly.

"Okay. Thank you, Mr. Pearson." I was used to calling him

Mr. Pearson. It was more professional. Calling him Adam seemed a bit intimate, and I knew he wouldn't necessarily like that.

"Adam." I'm taken aback, surprised by his sudden request. Or maybe I had heard him wrong. Maybe he meant something else.

"What?" I needed him to clarify before I made a fool of myself and said something I'd soon regret.

"You can call me Adam. We'll be working one on one with each other." My lips slightly parted with his response. "It's only fair since I call you by your first," he then added, clearly realizing the way it stunned me.

"Okay. Thanks, A-Adam," I stuttered, unable to comprehend what had just happened. I gripped my bag on my shoulder and quickly walked away. The moment I passed the corner, I ran. Okay, I didn't really run, more like speed walked. Once I made it out of the building, I let out the breath I wasn't aware that I had been holding in the first place.

He asked me to call him *Adam,* and it was only our second meeting. It left me wondering what our third meeting would be like. It was something I dreaded and something that excited me. Hidden butterflies in my stomach emerged when a certain pair of green eyes came to mind.

I hadn't had those in years, and it terrified me that they were finally back. *Because of him.*

CHAPTER 9

ADAM

WHAT WAS I THINKING? I HAD ASKED KATHERINE TO CALL ME BY my first name. I wanted this to be strictly professional, but I had insisted on her calling me Adam. I didn't know what the fuck had gotten into me, but the way she said my name… I could practically taste how sweet it sounded. Hearing her say my name was my new favorite melody, music to my ears.

I watched her leave in a hurry. The stolen moments I had with Katherine were interesting, different. I had to force myself to focus and remember that I had to do work. Before I could make it past my door, Aaron stopped me.

"Aaron, what are you doing here?" Aaron wasn't needed here at Pearson Book Group, not yet anyway. He wasn't CFO. He didn't have any important work that needed to be done, which caused my mind to jump to the worst assumptions.

"Edward is signing an author later this week," he said, proving my suspicions correct. He found someone. Who could it be? Whoever it was, they were our competition, and I had every intention of beating them.

"Who?" I asked. The Pearson Book Group was a big building, but news traveled like lightning around here. Someone had to know who it was, or at least have an idea of who it could be.

"It's someone who works at Pearson Book Group." That could be anyone. Many people worked here just to have an opportunity to get their work published by us. Of course, the moment my uncle threw them a bone, they'd desperately jump on it.

"I heard you went down to the creative department. Is that true?" Aaron asked. I looked around us and pushed Aaron into my office. Once the door shut behind me, I spoke.

"Technically, yes, but it wasn't to receive help from the department," I explained. Aaron gave me a 'bullshit' look before allowing me to continue. "Don't look at me like that. Katherine asked, and I was polite enough to show her around." Aaron looked at me like he had missed something.

"You showed her around because she asked?" What, like I was incapable of doing something nice? I just told him why I showed her around.

"Is that so rare for me?" Seriously, I knew I was an asshole, but I wasn't that big of an asshole. I was nice when I wanted to be, and I happened to want to for Katherine, a client.

"Yes," he said with a contemptuous expression on his face. *Dick.* Moments like these make me question why I even allowed Aaron to set foot in my office.

"Get out." I clenched my teeth, already done with this conversation. Aaron's smile slightly grows as he leaves my office. One of these days, I was destined to kill my brother. But today, I was too occupied to do so.

I took a seat and opened my laptop to begin going through some of the manuscripts that were sent to me, trying to find a lead on who it could be. No one would willingly go straight to my uncle without getting rejected by me. As I scrolled, I came across five candidates who worked in the building. I wrote the names down and told myself I'd come back to investigate them further.

Now, I had to make some calls and set up book events starting in two months. They wouldn't be for Katherine's book specifically; the events would be for a community of romance readers. We didn't need the book to be finished for that, as they would be more of a teaser, meant to reel in readers earlier than the release date. She would read the first five chapters at each book event to prompt excitement.

It would work like a charm. The first location we'd visit would be Los Angeles. The event would last for three whole days, the entire weekend. I picked up my phone and dialed my assistant. "Jackson, book two hotel rooms at the Hotel Bel Air for October thirteenth to the fifteenth in Los Angeles," I ordered.

"Will do, Mr. Pearson." I hung up and continued my work.

I had sent emails to other publishers seeking a collaboration and had gotten two of them to agree. It was settled. I'd inform Katherine of the current plans the next time I met with her. I then went over the chapter Katherine had turned in, only to be interrupted by my phone ringing. Micheal was calling me; I quickly answered the call.

"Adam, what's up?" Micheal greeted me with much enthusiasm. I pinched the bridge of my nose, irritated as I realized that he interrupted my work for a stupid call and not an emergency.

"What do you want?"

"Jesus, I can't even get a proper greeting from you these days," he joked, wasting more of my time.

"Talk or I'm hanging up." If Micheal needed to tell me something important, now was the time. But knowing him this long, it was far from important.

"The guys and I are going to Avenue tonight. Come with us." I was confused about how he had found an entrance to Avenue, but chose not to give it much thought. I was about to turn down the offer, as usual, until a certain woman popped into my mind.

'I, um, I have to go. I work a late shift tonight.' Katherine worked the late shift at Avenue, which meant if I were to go, I'd be sure to see her there. Not that my decision had anything to do with Katherine.

"I'll be there," I said before I could change my mind.

"Really? Wow, I didn't even have to push." I rolled my eyes at his stupid response. "See you there at eleven." He hung up, leaving me to regret my decision.

Later that night, I found myself waiting behind a crowded line of people trying to enter Avenue. The sight made me physically ill, instantly making me regret my choice of answering Micheal's call in the first place.

Fuck this. I pushed through the crowd to the front doors.

"Adam Pearson," I said to the bodyguard standing outside the door. He looked down at his tablet to check for my name, obviously brainless to not recognize it. Five minutes passed, every passing second further pissing me off.

Then a man appeared behind him, patted his shoulder, and whispered something in his ear that immediately triggered him to move aside to let me in.

"Adam Pearson, a second visit. What a pleasure." The man stuck his hand out for me to shake. I looked down at his hand, not making any movement to grab it. He chuckled as he brought his hand back to his side.

"Diego Ford," he clarified. Right, the owner of Avenue. I'd heard of him before; he had a reputation for doing dirty business. I personally would never go into business with this man, even if my life depended on it. Still, my expression remained unchanged, making it clear that this conversation was completely irrelevant to me.

He shook his head, giving me a slight smile as he stepped aside. I spared him a brief look before withdrawing myself from the conversation. Whatever he wanted from me, I would not be interested.

I walked deeper into the club, looking for a specific brunette with amber eyes. After scanning the entire room, my eyes landed on a woman in all black clothing, the curve of her ass engraved in my mind, difficult to forget.

She was standing in front of the bar, conversing with the bartender, who looked extremely familiar to me. I made my way toward her and instantly felt an arm rest across my shoulders. I turned to find Micheal standing beside me.

"Hey, man, I didn't see you walk in. We're over here." He pulled me in the opposite direction from where Katherine stood. There were two other men sitting at the booth, the same two men that had come the first time I had brought Micheal for his birthday.

"How did you manage to get the same booth as last time?" I asked Micheal as we promptly made our way through the crowd.

"Dylan Cruz. I've been working with him and Nicolas, and they've been showing me the right way to work in finance. I'm making more money than what I'm used to."

"I see." Out of curiosity, I walked up to them and introduced myself. Micheal excused himself before moving toward the bar to get some drinks.

"Adam Pearson. I believe I've seen you before, but never properly introduced myself." The man with glasses stood and offered me his hand.

"Dylan Cruz. It's a pleasure to meet you." The name Cruz was ringing a bell in my mind, but I couldn't fully put my finger on it. He looked like he could be a pro basketball player, except for the glasses. The man next to him was quick to stand and offered me a swift nod.

"Nicolas Geneva," he announced before returning his attention to his phone call. Nicolas Geneva was the prince of Ludornia. He was first in line for the throne. He was known for having a reckless reputation, constantly traveling the United States to party before having to settle down and become responsible over a whole country.

My guess was that he was trying to stay as far away as possible from Europe. Until recently, when I had read an article about the royal family in the New York Times, I wasn't aware that Ludornia was even a country. Apparently, people here were very fond of the prince, excited to see someone with such responsibility roaming around the busiest city in the world.

Micheal had gotten into finances once he graduated from college. He took business administration, which was the class I had met him in. It didn't take a rocket scientist to know that Dylan and Nicolas had an upper hand in the business. I would look further into Dylan when I found time, but for now, my attention was solely on the woman who was laughing at the bar. I watched from a distance, not able to take my eyes off her. Micheal returned with a few glasses of tequila—the most expensive brand they offered.

"You paid for this?" I asked him. Micheal wasn't the type of person who could afford a couple hundred dollars on a few drinks. It made me cautious about what type of business Dylan and the prince had gotten Micheal into.

"Yeah, I did. Problem?" he replied, displeased with my question. What the fuck was his problem?

"Right. Certainly, no problem. Much less my problem." Micheal's sudden remark made me chuckle that he thought he could speak to me any other way. Especially amongst others. I rose from my seat, leaving the booth.

"Where are you going?" Micheal asked as he took a drink from a glass, shooting it into his system. He was getting even more wasted—my cue to leave.

"The bar to put the drinks on my tab," I said, knowing it would make him feel small in front of his company. I'd deal with him once he was sober; I wasn't going to get any answers out of him like this.

Once I had turned to face the bar, I noticed a man approaching Katherine.

He rested his hand on her lower back, and I instantly saw red. He then lowered his head to speak in her ear. Suddenly, jealousy filled me. I was envious of the man she allowed to touch her. I could explode here, right in the middle of the club. But I shouldn't be jealous; she wasn't even mine to begin with. But that didn't stop me from approaching them.

As I got closer to the man, it took everything in me to keep calm. I placed a hand on his shoulder, forcing him to look me in my eyes.

"Get the man whatever he wants, and put it on my tap." I smiled at the bartender, throwing her a random card from my wallet. He looked happy at my request. My grip on his shoulder tightened as I pulled him closer to me, making sure what I was about to say was only in his earshot.

"Look at her again, and I'll make it my life's mission to make sure you regret it. You so much as lay a hand on her again, I'll kill you myself." His smile disappeared, his face turning pale. He was smart enough to walk away without looking back, leaving Katherine shocked by my appearance. "Not going to take the free drink?" I yelled from the bar as I saw him disappear.

"What are you doing here?" she asks, confused by the stunt I had just pulled.

"Friends." I took a step closer to Katherine, causing her back to hit the bar.

"Friends?" She seemed surprised by my response.

"Yes. Why? Is that so hard to believe?" I looked deep into those golden eyes. It had only been a few hours since I'd seen her, and I craved this.

"No..." she breathed. Something about the energy surrounding us compelled me to ask her the next thing.

"Dance with me." It was more of a demand than a question.

"I'm on my night shift right now..." She looked back at the curly haired woman behind the bar, who was gesturing for her to go out onto the dance floor with me.

"I think they can survive three minutes without you, Katherine." I placed my hands on her waist, slowly pulling her closer to me. I could feel her shake underneath my touch, and I smirked at how responsive her body was to my touch.

"I'll cover you," the woman said, winking at Katherine.

"Celeste!" Katherine spared her an obvious 'I'm going to kill you' look before following me out to the dance floor. I gave her friend an approving nod as I directed Katherine away.

"Have you danced before?" she asked as I pulled her into the crowd.

"Yes, of course I've danced."

"But not with me." Her bold remark took me by surprise. The Katherine I knew didn't do bold, other than the red lipstick she wore all the time. But then again, I didn't really know her that well.

The energy on the dance floor felt hot and heavy. The music tempo switched to a more alluring sound, captivating both of us. Katherine slowly started swaying her hips to the beat. I hadn't ever seen Katherine release herself the way she did with music. The air in the room suddenly felt tight, making it hard to breathe properly.

My heart rate was rapidly increasing, our bodies colliding with each other. Goosebumps rose on my arms and the back of my neck. Katherine turned around, her ass brushing against my crotch, causing my cock to pulse. The way she moved drove me insane, and my grip tightened on her hips, encouraging her. A groan escaped from my mouth as she pressed up against me.

"Christ, Kat." I lowered my mouth to her ear, earning a soft moan from her. I twisted her around to face me. Our eyes locked, and everyone surrounding us disappeared; it was just us and the music playing. Our lips were only inches apart. I looked at Katherine, then down at her lips.

I wondered if she tasted like vanilla or sweeter. I wondered if her lips felt as soft as they looked, and I was close to finding out. I'd never been one to crave someone, but I craved everything that had to do with Katherine. My lips lightly brushed against hers, compelling me to give in until someone bumped into me, causing Katherine to fall backward. I caught her in my arms just in time before she could hit the ground.

Suddenly, it hit me. Where I was, who I was with, and what I was about to do. Everything was completely out of my control. Fuck. *Fuck, fuck, fuck.*

I let go of Katherine and stepped back, giving us some much needed space. I ran a hand through my hair. *What were you thinking?*

Apparently, I wasn't the only one who thought this. Katherine refused to look me in the eye. I was about to cross a line I couldn't come back from. I would have to find a new author and start from zero. That was not an option for me.

"I should go."

"I have to go."

We spoke at the same time, unable to bear the awkward vibe between us. I instantly turned the opposite way and left. I called Henry, my driver, to come pick me up and take me back to my penthouse and waited outside.

This is your fault. I was the one who thought dancing would be a good idea. *No,* I knew it wasn't a good idea, yet I wanted some type of excuse to be closer to Katherine, to touch her, to feel her.

She was like a magnet, and I was the stupid metal that clung to her whenever I was in the same room as her. How was I going to approach her at our next meeting? I already knew it was going to be awkward.

Fifteen minutes later, Henry arrived. I slid into the car and stared out the window. The night was dark, with an atmosphere of mystery and uncertainty. For a night in New York City, it felt awfully quiet, allowing me to drown in my thoughts.

"Everything alright, Mr. Pearson?" Henry asked as he looked at me through the rear-view mirror. I avoided looking directly at him, unable to speak about tonight.

"Yes, tonight was... unexpected." The rest of the ride, we rode in silence, relieved Henry didn't try to push any answers out of me. The moment we arrived at my building, Henry got out of the car and circled around to my door and opened it. As I stepped out of the car, he stopped me to say one last thing to me.

"You know, Mr. Pearson, sometimes the best things come unexpectedly." Oh, *if he only knew.* Henry had been my driver for years now, and I had no doubt that he was a wise man. But I was positive he was wrong about this; he wouldn't have mentioned it if he knew. I dismissed him and made my way to the top floor.

When I got to my door, I took out my keys and placed them in the lock. I then noticed the door was left open. *Someone broke in.* I gave the door a gentle push, causing it to squeak open. I placed one foot through the door, looking around for any other signs of a break in. It was impossible for someone to break into my building, let alone my penthouse. The building was ensured of high-level security, which was the main reason I even chose this place. *Liars.*

I'd deal with them later. First, I needed to deal with the idiot who thought he could break into *my* penthouse and get away with it. I slowly walked toward the main living room, taking each step at a slow pace, careful not to make a noise. I made my way toward the small wooden drawer that held the pocket pistol that I had purchased as soon as it was legal for me to have it. I'd already experienced a traumatic break in when I was just a kid. That was enough reason for me to get it.

I tucked the pistol into my waistband and headed toward the kitchen. The lights were off everywhere, making it difficult to make out an intruder. I walked along the kitchen island and heard footsteps coming from the hallway, so I quickly ducked behind the island.

The footsteps became clearer as they entered the kitchen. A cabinet opened, and I heard a plastic bag rustling as it was filled with items. I moved toward the edge of the island, placing my right hand over the pistol. I took a deep breath before standing and heard a familiar voice.

"Esta lata está dañada." *This can is damaged.* Relief filled me as I realized it was Petra, my housekeeper. She must have left the door open by mistake. She doesn't stay late unless she's doing one of her deep cleanings; I guess one was due for the week. I got up from the ground and flicked the light switch on.

"Ay, dios mío!" *Oh my god!* Petra dropped the trash bag on the floor and placed a hand over her chest.

"It's me, Petra. What are you still doing here?" I picked up the trash bag from the floor, handing it back to her. She placed a hand over her forehead and looked at her watch.

"I'm so sorry, Mr. Pearson. Me olvidé la hora." '*I forgot the time,*' she says in a heavy accent. Petra didn't speak much English. She mostly spoke and understood Spanish. What she knew of English was pretty basic.

"Esta bien, vete a casa." '*It's okay, go home,*' I said in Spanish. I wasn't fluent, but I had taken some classes in high school that helped. I only used it to speak to Petra. Other than that, no one else knew I spoke any Spanish.

"Si, Mr. Pearson. Buenas noches." She quickly grabbed her bag and left, shutting the door behind her. The place fell silent, and I was left alone with my thoughts yet again. It wasn't that I didn't enjoy my alone time; I was just tired of always being alone.

Tomorrow, I'd meet with Katherine again, but I had a feeling she wouldn't show. Why would she? I wouldn't if I were her. I blocked out the rest of my thoughts and called it a night. *Maybe she'll show.*

That next morning, I woke up to a 'sick and can't make it' email from Katherine with ten chapters attached.

CHAPTER 10

KATHERINE

Two weeks ago, I almost kissed Adam Pearson, and I couldn't find it in myself to face him the day after. So, I took the easy way out by sending an email explaining how I was 'sick' and unfortunately had to reschedule for this afternoon. Over the past two weeks, I'd been sending him chapters and keeping up with my deadlines. I had been able to write a fair number of chapters since that night with Adam.

I could still remember the effect his touch had on my body. The feel of his fingers on my bare skin, how his grip tightened on my hips and left tingles running down my spine. I had been completely consumed by him on the dance floor. I was never someone who craved attention. I was a romance author for God's sake, and yet, I craved his.

"Kat," Celeste calls out, dragging me out of my daydream. I'd been daydreaming about that moment often, and I didn't know how to stop. Celeste gave me a knowing glance as I returned to planet Earth.

"Sorry, what did you say?" Celeste and I had decided to go shopping for Halloween costumes since it was already October.

Avenue was throwing a party, and we were going as the devil and angel. A duo costume, since Elaina had plans of leaving for Miami and with Valery still gone.

"I *said* this white dress would be perfect for you." She lifted the hanger that held a white, mini satin slip dress. It was a bit too small for my taste, but it did look incredibly soft.

"Hmm, I don't know. It's a bit short..." I explained as I held the dress in my hands, getting a better feel of the material. Celeste gave me a critical look and pointed toward the fitting rooms.

"Just try it on. I'll look for shoes." She pushed me forward and disappeared into the store. I huffed as I walked to the fitting room and entered a stall. I pulled the dress up over my legs and looked in the mirror. The white material cupped my breasts perfectly and outlined the curve of my body. It felt a little revealing to me, even though it covered the essential parts of me. I wasn't used to dressing like this; it was more of Celeste's style than mine.

"Katherine!" Celeste yelled from the hall.

"In here!" I replied. Celeste pulled the curtain open, her eyes widening the moment she saw me.

"This is the one! Try on the shoes!" she exclaimed, handing me beautiful white stilettos with diamonds placed on the laces. I sat on the bench and put them on. Once I had them on, I stood up. The heels gave me an additional four inches, sealing the look together.

"You look so hot!" I shyly smiled at Celeste's compliment. I *felt* hot. This dress made me feel ten times more confident than I was. But I would only wear this on Halloween. It was the one time of year that I allowed myself to dress completely out of my comfort zone, whether it was dorky or slutty.

"What did you pick out?" I asked as I changed out of the dress. Celeste picked up a black corset and a tight black skirt with a smirk on her face. *Of course.*

After Celeste tried on her outfit, we got in line to pay. I had ordered the devil horns and an angel halo online, so our costumes were ready for the Halloween party. I checked the time on my phone and realized I would be late to my three o'clock with Adam if I didn't leave right away.

"Shoot!" I blurted, causing Celeste and everyone else standing in line to turn and look at me.

"What's wrong?" she asked as I bit my bottom lip.

"I'm going to be late for my meeting if I don't leave now." Celeste turned to face me and pulled the clothing out of my arms.

"I'll pay for it."

"You're a lifesaver. I'll pay you back!" I smiled at her as she shook her head.

"Oh, I know. Don't worry, I got it." I gave Celeste a goodbye hug and ran out of the store. I had twenty minutes to get to Pearson Corps, and it was too far away for me to walk. The streets were packed with cars, the drivers honking at each other like that would help. I would never make it in this traffic.

I chose Plan B and ran down to the subway. I hopped on train A, which would take a total of ten minutes to get there. I took a seat next to a woman who was holding a book in her right hand and a coffee in her left. I didn't think much of it until the train pulled out of the station in a harsh movement, causing the woman to spill her coffee all over me.

Awesome.

"I'm so sorry!" the woman said as I stood up, attempting to wipe most of it off. It wasn't her fault that I chose to sit next to someone who had a beverage on the train. *I should have known better.* I was about to show up at the Pearson Book Group drenched in coffee.

"It's okay," I reassured the woman as she sat back down. It was nowhere near okay, but what was I going to do? Whether or not I got mad, it wasn't going to change the fact that I had a huge coffee stain on my shirt.

Once the train pulled into the station, I got off and sprinted toward Pearson Book Group. I would have to deal with a few dirty looks from others, but at least I'd be on time.

I finally arrived at the building with shortness of breath. I was already receiving judgmental glances from the people walking in and out of the building. I minded my business, lowering my head while walking to the elevator.

I hopped on to the first elevator that came and pressed the button to the eighteenth floor. The doors closed, and I leaned by the glass, looking out toward Manhattan. The doors opened on the tenth floor, and Victoria walked in. She was wearing a tailored black jumpsuit that looked amazing on her. I spared her a small smile that she ignored. She took a moment to look at what I'm wearing, specifically staring at the coffee stain on my white shirt.

Her glance was critical, but I could tell it pleased her to see me like this. *What did I ever do to her?* She didn't press any buttons, so she must have been going to the same floor as me. The rest of the elevator ride was silent, but I could feel her stare burning a hole in my skin. When the doors finally opened, Victoria stepped out before me and walked in the opposite direction I was headed.

I decided not to think much about it and made my way toward Adam's office. This was the first time I'd see him since that night at the club. Each step had my heart beating a bit faster than the last. *Relax, Katherine.* It was just another meeting. What could possibly go wrong?

Being here was a choice for my book and my career. That was it. I gently knocked on the door, stepped back, and waited for a response.

"Come in," I heard in a deep voice. I opened the door and walked in to him sitting at his desk, reading some documents.

He looked up from the papers to meet my eyes. "You're late again."

"I'm on time," I said as I crossed my arms. He raised a brow at my response.

"You're positive about that?" he pointed toward the clock behind me. I turned to read the time—3:04, four minutes late. *Is he serious right now?*

"You're kidding." I chuckled; I was certain that he was joking. There was no way this man was *this* uptight. He shook his head as he told me to sit down in the chair in front of him.

"I don't joke." *Okay... maybe a little too uptight.* I stayed silent. He paused and looked down at my shirt, not moving his sight. I looked down and noticed that the coffee stain had caused my shirt to become see-through, allowing him to see my red bra underneath.

I knew one shouldn't wear any bold colored bras under a white shirt, but it was the only clean one I had available.

"Is coffee always the reason you're late?" he said as he stood from his seat. He walked across the room toward me. My legs weakened as his scent became stronger, the same intoxicating scent that had me shamelessly giving in to him that night.

He looked into my eyes, then down at my shirt again. I felt my cheeks heat, and I covered the sight with my arms. He turned toward the cabinet on his right and opened it, pulling out a white button-up shirt before handing it to me.

"Here, change into this." Without saying anything else, he walked out and closed the door, giving me the privacy to change.

I looked at the shirt in my hands and brought it to my nose. I inhaled a deep sniff, unable to contain myself. I couldn't describe what his scent smelled like, just rich, clean, and expensive. I took off my current shirt and put his on. Once I had changed, I opened the door. Adam was standing right outside, staring at his phone. His green eyes looked down at me and darkened as he took me in.

"Thank you. For the shirt..." I said as I opened the door wider for him to come in. He simply nodded as he walked in, closing the door behind him. He cleared his throat as he went back to his desk.

"I'm glad to see you're feeling better," he said as he slightly reclined in his chair.

"Excuse me?" I was confused about what he meant. *Does he mean about that night?* He seemed amused by my confusion and quickly clarified.

"Well, were you not sick? That was the reason you couldn't meet last time. Or am I mistaken?" And it all hit me—*the email.* I had forgotten the excuse I used to avoid him the moment I walked through the door.

Go with it, the voice in my head said.

"No, you're correct. I, um, I'm glad I'm feeling better, too." I tried to sound as convincing as I could, but with the look in his eyes, I could tell he knew it was bull. Why was he so hard to persuade?

"I see." He slowly nodded as he opened his laptop. "We must discuss the events I have scheduled for this month." I crossed my legs as I fixed the top button on my shirt. Well, his shirt.

"Okay." I waited for him to explain the plans. He turned the laptop around, facing it toward me. I looked at the website pulled up... 'Bookery Con: Romance Convention.'

"We'll be attending this event this month, from the fourteenth to fifteenth," he explained. The event was a romance-only book convention. I had always wanted to go to one, but never had the time. I looked at the location—Los Angeles, California.

"It's in California?" I asked as I turned the laptop back toward him.

"Is there a problem?" he asked, and I shook my head 'no' as I bit my lip. "You'll be reading a few chapters at this event as well," he added effortlessly, as if it wasn't a big deal.

"My book?!" I exclaimed. Bookery Con was one of the

biggest book conventions ever. It had book signings, book sales, classes and panels, and a vendor floor. It was every reader's and writer's dream, and *I* would be reading *my* book there.

"Yes, it'll be perfect marketing." Of course, it would be perfect marketing; it was like Coachella, but for book lovers. The only thing that bothered me was that it was located in California. California is beautiful, but it was a place I had left years ago for a reason. Returning now seemed a little frightening...

"Great! So, when do we leave?" I asked. Adam was studying my expression, seeming as though he wanted to know what was going on in my head. I was never the finest at hiding my emotions or the battles that went on in my mind. It was something that bothered me ever since I was a child, and I hoped Adam didn't see through me.

"The thirteenth. We'll return on the fifteenth," he said, resting both of his hands on the desk. The position he was in made him look like a literal model. It would be the type of shot you'd see on the cover of People Magazine's 'Sexist Man Alive' edition. It was captivating.

"Let me guess: we're flying economy?" I asked, as a joke.

"Don't be ridiculous, angel, we'll be taking my private jet," he said, his tone normal. I was taken aback by both the name and the response. *Private jet? Angel??* It took him a second to realize what he had said, and he seemed just as shocked as I was. He pulled at his tie and adjusted his cufflinks. I chose to ignore the name to avoid the situation becoming more... *complicated.*

"We'll be taking your private jet," I repeated. He continued speaking as if he didn't just call me angel. Why would he even call me that?

"Don't tell me you thought we were flying commercial," he said with a grimace.

"Well, yeah... I would think first class, maybe, but private jet?" I knew Adam would never fly economy. He was rich, and I understood why we would fly first class, but a private jet? I mean, who owns that? Only an *insanely* rich person.

"Hope that's not a problem," he said sarcastically. I was at a loss for words. I had never flown private, much less seen a private jet in person. "Also, pack presentable clothes." *Pack presentable clothes?* What was that supposed to mean? I dressed very well, thank you very much.

"Of course, I have a very presentable wardrobe." I smiled at him. When I said 'I', I meant Elaina, but he didn't need to know that. He smirked at my remark and leaned closer across the desk.

"I don't doubt it, just making sure we're both on the same page." What was I, a teenager that made horrible fashion choices? I admit I did wear *comfortable* clothing when I wrote, which was every day... But, obviously, I was more than capable of picking out a decent outfit.

"We are," I assured him with a smile. "So, where exactly are we staying?"

"Are you always this curious?" Adam raised a brow.

"Most of the time, yeah." He huffed as he typed on his laptop.

"We'll be staying at the Hotel Bel Air." Of course we were. We would be flying privately and staying at one of the best five-star hotels. I looked at the images on his laptop, and God, the rooms were gorgeous. The rooms seemed more spacious than the apartment I shared with Elaina. The longer I glared at the photos, the more the reminder of having to go back home resonated in my mind. Adam seemed to catch on to my thoughts as he spoke again.

"Is there an issue I should know about?" His voice was gentle; it could have been mistaken for a whisper if it weren't for his strong tone. He patiently waited for me to answer, which encouraged me to tell him the truth. I was going to be on this trip with him, so I might as well be honest, right?

"I just—it's been a while since I've been home."

"Home?"

"Yeah, I grew up in California and left for college a few years ago," I admitted. I could never hate California, but it never seemed like the right time to go back. After what had happened with Martin, I knew I didn't want to go back for a while. I moved on a long time ago. I really did, but I never wanted to remind myself of my heartbreak.

"Just leave!" That was all Martin had said the night before. We had gotten into an argument in his college dorm about how he wanted more time from me now that I was busy finishing the novel I had started—Night Span. I gave him attention, but I guess he wanted and expected more and more from me. The argument between us quickly escalated, so I had decided to walk back home to give us both time to cool off.

Immediately when I got home, I sat in my bed and cried. I felt like I was a horrible girlfriend, I only wanted us to be okay. Overnight, I decided that I should apologize because I hated to be in fights and that was all we'd been doing for the past five months. The next day, early in the morning, I walked back to Martin's college dorm with a box of donuts that spelled the word 'sorry' in strawberry frosting, which was his favorite. I gently walked in, not wanting to wake him up early.

I set the box of donuts down on the counter and walked toward his bed. He was shirtless, with the comforter covering the lower part of his body. Next to him seemed to be a large pillow that was buried beneath the covers.

"Martin," I whispered, giving his shoulder a gentle squeeze. He tossed around, resulting in the comforter lowering a bit. Brunette hair peeked out from under the comforter, causing my heart to instantly drop to my feet. I took a few steps back, having trouble processing what I had just seen.

He cheated on me. Martin cheated on me.

Martin opened his right eye, still asleep. He must have seen me in the corner of his eye because he rapidly jumped out of bed, covering his exposed parts with the pillow he was lying on. "Katherine," was all he could think to say. My eyes filled with tears, making my vision extremely blurry.

Don't cry, don't cry, *I kept repeating to myself in my head.*

The girl lying in bed slowly rose to stretch her arms, unaware of what was currently happening. She turned her face toward us and.... It was Ali. My best friend Ali. The tears I fought so hard to keep inside had burst out at the sight of her, of them together. The pain of betrayal was almost too much to bear.

"How could you?" I spoke. I looked at Ali, then at Martin, and ran out of the room.

"Katherine, wait!" Martin ran after me, leaving Ali in the room alone. "Katherine!" He grabbed hold of my arm and pulled me back toward him. At that point, I was drowning in my own tears, unable to catch my breath.

"Let go of me! I never want to see you again!" I screamed into his face, hating him for breaking my heart in the worst way.

"You don't mean that. Please let me explain," he argued while his grip on my arm tightened. I looked into his blue eyes, and deep down, I could see regret. But nothing could make this better, he could never make it better. I stomped on his foot with as much strength as I could to escape from his grip.

It worked, his grip slightly loosening. I took the chance and bolted out of the building. My heart felt like it was about to explode at any given second. My entire body shook as if it was below freezing, but it was as warm as California could get.

I ran and ran until my own legs gave out on me. I stumbled to the ground, scraping my knees and bawling my eyes out.

I wasn't aware a human could cry this much. My legs felt exhausted, my mind felt exhausted, and my heart felt exhausted. I had been with Martin for three years, since we were seventeen years old. He was my first everything—first kiss, first time, first real boyfriend. As for Ali, she had been my best friend since freshman year of high school.

My heart had been shattered, smashed, and destroyed by the two people I least expected it from. That same night, I chose to attend college in New York and never looked back. I never spoke to Martin or Ali again.

"Hm, bad memories?" Adam's voice brought me back to reality. It was almost as if he knew I was reminiscing on a complete nightmare. He waited for my answer, genuinely interested in what I had to say, in what I *felt*.

"You could say that." I hid my sadness with a smile, not wanting to get so deep during this conversation. I'd never told anyone what I really went through with my heartbreak. I was... *I am* embarrassed. I quickly switched the subject, unable to continue the conversation. It was what I did. I shut down, and I wrote. "Either way, it'll be great!" I added.

Adam nodded. He didn't push me for an answer, which I deeply appreciated. He was my publisher, though, at times, I forgot. I wanted to tell him things, but it was difficult and it wasn't professional. The room fell silent, giving me the urge to cut this short. I found it weird to be in such silence for a long period of time.

"I think I'm going to go and get some writing done. Is this all you had planned for today?" God, please let it be all that he had planned for today... Adam had a puzzled look on his face.

"You're more than welcome to write here." Wait—did he want me to stay longer? *On purpose?* I didn't really think I would be able to accomplish as much writing as I'd like to with Adam present.

"Thanks, but I have a spot I usually like to go to." I tried my best to decline the offer as kindly as I could.

"Do you have a ride?" he asked as I got up from my seat.

"Uh... no, I usually walk."

"Don't bother, Henry will drive us." I'm sorry, *us?* The number of times this man had surprised me... It was like watching a telenovela, constantly getting hit with unexpected news. Maybe he needed to go somewhere, anyway, and was being polite by offering me a ride. "If you don't mind, I'd like to see where this 'spot' is." There was no way I had heard that right. I couldn't decline this offer; he made it hard to do so.

"Okay." I hoped that taking his offer wasn't going to turn out to be a mistake. But again, I never knew what to expect from Adam.

CHAPTER 11

KATHERINE

ADAM ESCORTED ME DOWN TO THE PARKING GARAGE AND WAITED for his driver to arrive. This day only kept getting weirder and weirder. First, I was currently wearing his shirt, and second, I was about to get in his car. All the things I could have said no to, but simply couldn't find it in myself to do so.

He stood next to me, with his eyes glued to his phone, not saying a single word. I prayed that the car would arrive faster, given how horrible I was with silence. Not a few seconds go by, and I gave in.

"So..."

"So," Adam repeated, steering his eyes in my direction. I found it hard for the words to roll out of my mouth when he looked at me. His eye contact always did things to me. It felt so... intense. Intimidating.

I didn't think anyone looked at me the way Adam did, as if he'd miss something if he blinked. I cleared my throat before speaking.

"Why offer me the ride?" I knew it was risky to ask questions like these, but I honestly wanted to know more about the way Adam's mind was wired. I wanted to know his motives, his goals, and the reasoning behind every decision he made that had to do with me.

Adam opened his mouth, only for it to close again when an all-black Rolls Royce rolled up against the mini curve. My mouth fell open at the sight of his car. The window rolled down, revealing Adam's driver. He was an older man with a black driver's cap on his head and an all-black uniform. He must *really* like the color black.

"Good afternoon, Mr. Pearson and Miss..." He waited for me to tell him my last name.

"Katherine. Katherine Trujillo." The man nodded and got out of the driver's seat to walk around the car and open the door.

"Miss Trujillo," he greeted, holding the door open. I slid into the back seat, with Adam following behind me. The door closed, leaving the both of us alone in the back seat. The car had an all-black leather interior. It was absolutely breathtaking.

The backseat was a mini privacy suite with a wall meant to keep sound and sight out of the driver's compartment. I scooted toward the window on my side, not wanting to make physical contact with Adam.

Once we were settled in, a tiny light flashed between Adam and me, and he pushed down on the button for about three seconds. The wall blocking us from the front of the car slid open, allowing Adam to speak to his driver. Never in my twenty-four years of living had I experienced that. It just demonstrated the many things Adam Pearson owned.

"Where to, sir?" his driver asked while making eye contact through the rear-view mirror. Adam looked at me, scooting a bit closer, making my cheeks flush with him being only inches away from me.

"Where to, angel?" His voice sounded confident, huskier than usual. Heat settled in the pit of my stomach. I gripped the sides of my thighs, attempting to control myself.

"I—Café Luna," I breathed. *Was my voice shaky? God, I hope not.*

"Café Luna is your *spot*?" He sounded unimpressed, not trusting the process whatsoever.

"No, but you'll see." I managed to put a playful smile on my lips. Adam gave me a puzzled look, but didn't think twice about following my lead.

"Henry, take us to Café Luna."

Henry nodded as he shifted the gear and drove out of the parking garage. The wall slid closed again and silence filled the space. He must have hit a curve, because my thighs slammed against Adam's. The touch was sudden, like lightning hitting a branch, a crash you never expected. The space we had between us was suddenly gone. Adam placed a hand on my thigh for balance; it made little tingles crawl down my spine. His eyes met mine, and they flickered with desire.

Every time I found myself getting lost in those green eyes, I felt compelled to do anything this man could ask of me. I wanted nothing more than to give in to him. There was also this powerful need to know everything that he was thinking about. And if the cause of desire in his eyes was for me.

Adam must've caught on because he swiftly removed his hand and scooted further away from me, taking the heat of his body with him. He avoided looking at me and pulled out his phone. My eyes remained on him as he answered emails.

Does this man ever take a break? The only time I'd seen him relax was that night we spent at Avenue. He was a completely different person, free from his mind. I sat there in silence for a few minutes, but after a while, I couldn't bear it any longer.

"Do you ever take a break?" I asked, seeking some type of reaction from him.

"Hm?" He didn't look up from his phone, making me more aggravated. I decided to take a more playful approach, curious if I could get a reaction taking this route.

"You just seem so... uptight. It's bad for your condition."

"Condition?" He finally looked up from his phone that he placed between us. *Okay... I'm getting somewhere.*

"Yea, you know... the Stickuptheassitis." Adam's lips twitched. If I hadn't been paying attention, I would have missed it. If I didn't know any better, I would say he was actually about to smile. Wait—he was *definitely* pressing his lips together to avoid smiling.

"Huh, and what's the cure, Dr. Knowitall." My eyes widened at his attempt to do a follow up with my joke. Adam Pearson had a playful side to him, and I brought it out. Maybe he wasn't so uptight after all. I planted a single finger on my lip, pretending to think of a response.

"Mm... little vacations here and there. Give yourself time to enjoy life," I said, placing my hands on my thighs. Adam rested his head back on the seat's headrest as he maintained eye contact. Adam had a gift of doing the simplest things and turning them into the most alluring, charming acts.

"Will you?" His voice was soft, almost as if he didn't want to scare me off.

"Will I, what?"

"Help me 'enjoy' my time." And just like that, my lower body was shivering.

A strand of hair fell out of my bun, and Adam delicately brushed the strand from my face. He leaned closer, and heat spread across my entire body, my skin on fire. He lifted a hand to the hem of my shirt and played with the collar. I slowly leaned into his touch, seeking more.

"I—" *God, Katherine, you're pathetic.* Adam lifted a brow.

"You, what?" he asked, challenging me. Just as I was about to speak, the car stopped, ruining the moment.

"We've arrived, Mr. Pearson," Henry said over the speaker. Adam snapped out of whatever trance he had been in and clicked the car door open. He held the door for me as I quickly gathered myself together and slid out.

"Thanks, Henry, I'll be in touch." And with that, Henry then drove off, leaving us in an awkward silence that Adam soon broke. "The spot is..." Adam probed, taking a look around the area. I knew this corner like I knew myself; it was part of home. I gave Adam a small smile as I walked down the street.

My back was turned to him, and he quickly followed. I could tell by how strong his presence was. I kept walking down the street until I arrived at the small, all-pink bookstore. I stopped right in front of the entrance, taking it all in. Adam stood beside me, checking out the building.

"It looks like the color pink threw up all over it," he said in disgust. I couldn't comprehend how his first impression was that pink threw up on it. Okay, so maybe it did look like it, a little. But once we walked inside, his whole interpretation of the place would change.

"It does not. This happens to be the best place on earth," I argued.

"Sure it is," he said sarcastically. I rolled my eyes and grabbed hold of his arm, dragging him inside the store. The doorbell rang as we walked in.

"Katherine!" Judy welcomed me with open arms. "And who might this be?" She indicated toward Adam; he gave her a simple nod before responding for me.

"Adam Pearson. Pleasure." He offered his hand and gave Judy a gentle handshake.

"Oh, wow, very glad to meet you. Katherine has never brought company before." I looked at her with cautious eyes. *This is not happening right now.*

"*Of course* I bring company, Judy. I brought Elaina last time," I argued, as I avoided making eye contact with Adam. I knew that the bastard was somewhat enjoying this. I could tell by the smug look he had plastered on his face.

"Exactly, not male," Judy finished as she grabbed a pile of books off the counter. I bit my tongue, attempting to contain my composure. *TMI, Judy.* As if this moment couldn't get any more awkward, I made my way toward my usual table, leaving Adam behind.

I took a seat and pulled my laptop from my bag. I knew it was unsafe to be carrying my laptop around the city, but I couldn't risk losing ideas that popped up at spontaneous times.

Adam walked around the store, looking at all the books that were spread out on the bookshelves. The sight of him scanning the bookshelves was a God-given gift. But again, anything he did was appealing. He met my eyes, and I quickly looked away like some high school girl getting caught staring at a crush.

Focus, Katherine. You're here to write. Adam took a seat across from me, resting his arms on the table.

"What do you have written so far?"

"About five chapters. It's coming along pretty well, I think." I opened my laptop and began typing. I pressed random letters on the keyboard, pressured to come up with something. Adam locked his gaze on me, making me even more nervous.

"Why do you write?" His question caught me off guard. I'd never been asked that question. Others just assumed it was a hobby, nothing worth asking more about.

"Huh, no one's really asked me that."

"Well, I just did." He reclined on the chair, giving my thoughts some space.

Why did I write? Because I loved it, but what was the reason I started? I sat back as I dug deep in my brain to seek an answer. It all began when I picked up my first romance novel. I had never given it a second thought. After getting rejected by my first crush, I wanted to fall down a sad hole, like listening to love songs. Except reading completely changed my perspective on love, my entire view on who was supposed to be "the one."

I loved the way it made me feel like I was experiencing it

myself. It made me forget I felt alone in the first place. I was transported into a different world, and I kept seeking more of it each time. That was, until I started to write.

It gave me a similar feeling, except it made me feel more in control, more creative. I knew that I had found my true calling, and I never pictured myself doing anything other than writing.

"Because of the way it makes me feel, how it might make others feel as well," I confessed. Adam's lips tugged at their sides.

"And what do you feel now?" This time, he leaned closer, wanting to hear every word that would come out of my mouth.

"Like I have a purpose." Adam and I gazed into each other's eyes. I felt vulnerable with him, like I was giving him permission to look into my soul. "I know it's a bit cliché, but my favorite novel happens to be *Pride and Prejudice*." I played with the strings of my ripped jeans before speaking again. "And my favorite author at the moment is Julia Lark."

"Of course it is," he said, as if he had me all figured out; like I was a completely open book to him. And I knew nothing about him. "You were right about one thing," he added unexpectedly.

"About?" I asked as I raised my brows in question.

"This being one of the best spots on earth." This time my body wasn't the one warming up, it was my heart. I didn't need his validation on this, but it pleased me to know I wasn't the only one who thought this.

Then, out of the blue, his phone rang. He checked the name before answering, and his face transformed from this state of tranquility to an irritated expression.

"Speak," he said without removing his gaze from mine. After a few seconds, he spoke again, ending the call. "I'll be there." Suddenly, disappointment descended on me, but I was unsure why I even felt that way in the first place.

You don't want him to leave. No, that couldn't be it.

"I have a matter that needs urgent attention," he said as he stood from his seat. "We will meet next week for the event." *Right, California.*

"Okay, great," I replied. That was all I could say, incapable of coming up with anything else. As if Adam felt the vibe, he said one last thing before heading out the door.

"You can call me if you have any questions, Katherine. You know that." That was his way of saying goodbye. I watched him as he exited the store.

How did I go from not wanting him to come along to not wanting him to leave? I had a bad feeling that if I wasn't careful, this feeling would end up doing some damage. Damage that would take me so long to piece back together, but would never be fully repaired.

I packed my bag and left the store, unable to write anymore. While walking back to the apartment, I decided I would begin packing for Los Angeles. The moment I arrived at the apartment, I had planned on taking advantage of Elaina still being here before she left for her trip to Miami. Her opinion of my clothes was much needed.

'Also, pack presentable clothes.' Please. I could pack presentable clothes.

"These are not presentable clothes whatsoever," Elaina said while Celeste sat and ate a sandwich on my bedroom floor. She didn't even bother defending me.

"What do you mean?! It's not that bad," I argued as I pointed at the clothes spread out on my mattress. No one was home when I arrived, so I picked out some outfits before Elaina got back with Celeste. Apparently, I should never make fashion choices without Elaina's approval.

"Celeste, what do you think?" Elaina asked, looking back at Celeste. Celeste took another chomp out of her sandwich, hinting at the obvious... She didn't want to interfere. "See," Elaina added.

"Help me, then!" I exclaimed, becoming antsy. I knew I still had two weeks before the trip, but those two weeks would pass in the blink of an eye. Plus, I happened to like being extra prepared, just in case of pre-disasters. The type that could leave things upside down like a tornado had passed over. If anything were to happen, it wouldn't be the first time.

Elaina scanned through my closet, pulled out a few items, dumped them on my bed, and walked out of my room. Celeste and I glanced at each other in confusion. Elaina returned with her arms loaded with clothes from her closet.

"This is what you'll take," she declared as she dumped them onto the pile. Elaina had clothes that were to die for; clothes from past runways and past model shoots.

"Oh yeah, wayyy better," Celeste added as she scanned the clothes laid out. I gave her an annoyed expression. Now she decided to share her opinion. "What? It's true." I shook my head before taking the first outfit and trying it on.

The rest of the evening, I packed the rest of the clothes in a small suitcase. I placed the suitcase right by my bedroom door, ready to take. A wave of relief washed over me at the sight of my preparations being completed.

CHAPTER 12

ADAM

My assistant had called, informing me of the meeting my uncle had set for five-thirty this evening, but I had gotten caught up with Katherine. Once again. I was a man who valued his time, yet for some reason, I was more than willing to spare some for Katherine. More than some... A lot, actually. So much so that it agitated me. The second I exited the bookstore, I called Henry to drive me back to the office.

The drive allowed my thoughts to take me captive. I cursed the fact that silence consumed me, and I cursed the fact that my thoughts constantly drifted to Katherine. I craved more of her when she was gone. More time, more words, more glances. It was not common for me to allow another to utterly consume me. Distract me. Trick me. And yet, I desperately needed her.

Once I arrived at the office, my thoughts switched tracks, focusing on the bigger picture I was about to deal with. I had a feeling this meeting had to do with the elections coming up. I walked into the head office, prepared for what might be coming.

To my surprise, the room was filled with Pearson Book Group's investors and the company board that would be voting in the elections. Edward stood at the center of the room.

"Adam, glad you could make it." He wore a shiny new Zegna suit with an even shiner Rolex. He only wore that when he wanted to impress. His greeting toward me might have seemed genuine, but I could read between the lines.

Why are you here, and who told you about this meeting?

"I am glad I could as well." I gave him a cordial smile and glanced at my watch. 5:32. I took a seat at the table. He continued his presentation on the board, and as I looked around, I noticed our family lawyer, Richard. *Why was he here?*

"For the upcoming election, I feel it is beneficial to introduce our authors to the media at the following event in Los Angeles." *This asshole better not be talking about my idea.* "The Bookery Con Romance Convention, biggest book event of the year," he finished as he kept his eyes on me. *Dick.* He was so useless he had to steal my idea.

"I think that is a brilliant idea," one of the investors spoke up. Of course, it was a brilliant idea. It was *mine*.

Edward had a smug smile plastered on his face as he took a seat in the center chair of the table. This was a bunch of bullshit. I hadn't been planning to tell the company board my ideas. I was planning for the outcome to voice how successful it was. Now, I had to share the event with Edward and his mystery author. *Fuck this guy.*

"The idea is approved. It does not cross with the following rules," one of the people on the board spoke, after conversing with the rest. 'Does not cross with the following rules', meaning it didn't go against my father's stupid will. "Adam, do you have anything you'd like to share with us?" I bit my tongue, cursing my uncle under my breath.

It was a tough act to follow, especially when I had nothing now. I accepted my defeat and stood down. "Unfortunately, I don't."

"Well, I guess that concludes today's meeting. Thank you,

gentlemen." And with that, everyone left the room, leaving my uncle and me alone.

"Taking my idea? I knew you were useless, but I didn't take you for a coward," I said as I stood from my seat. He chuckled in response.

"Call me whatever you want, but this job, I *am* keeping," he said. I looked down at my watch, annoyed at how much time this pathetic talk was taking.

"This *job* was never yours to be 'kept'," I simply replied, walking out the door and closing it on my way out. I made my way toward my office, seeking some peace and quiet. It was a matter of time before I exploded and burned down this entire building along with me.

"Hey, man." I turned to find Micheal waiting by my door. *So much for peace and quiet.* I didn't greet him in return. Instead, I walked straight into my office, still pissed off with this remark from Avenue. "Listen, I wanted to talk to you. Apologize for that night." Suddenly, I was all ears for whatever he had to say.

I considered Micheal a close friend. Knowing him for quite some time now, I could tell what's like Micheal and what's not. And as for that night, it was nothing like Micheal. "I've just been dealing with a lot of shit," he explained as he walked in behind me.

"Care to elaborate?" I suggested, taking a seat. He shook his head as he rubbed the back of his neck.

"At the moment, I can't. But all I can say is I'm dealing with it." *Hm.* I wasn't sure I liked where this was headed. If Micheal ever needed my assistance, I would more than gladly give it to him. But with what I was thinking, my resources wouldn't come in handy with what he needed. "But the point is, I'm sorry I jumped on you the way I did."

It came easy for Micheal to apologize, and he meant it when he did. I gave Micheal a simple nod, accepting his apology. As for me, I never apologized. It was a sign of weakness on my part. I never felt the need to, anyway.

A knock stole both of our attention, and Aaron was standing by the door. "Am I interrupting?" he asked as he strolled in.

"Aren't you always?" I said as Micheal chuckled, giving Aaron a pat on the back.

"How was the meeting?" Aaron asked, adjusting his tie. This time, I stood and walked toward my secret cabinet. It opened, revealing my stash of whiskey. I pulled out three cups and poured each of us a drink, then I walked back, handing a glass to each of them. I kept a stash for certain emergencies, only using it when I felt most anxious.

This situation called for a drink.

"Damn, that bad?" Micheal said, looking down at his cup like it was poison. I shot back my drink, the liquid burning its way down my throat. Aaron and Micheal glanced at one another, then shot back their drinks as well.

"Give me the news," Aaron said, closing the cabinet for me.

"It seems that our dear uncle decided to take *my* ideas to the board." I gripped the glass in my hand like my life depended on it, near shattering it. "And now, both of our authors will be attending the same event, head-to-head."

"Do you know who the other author is?" Aaron asked. I shook my head in response.

"I might be able to find that out for you," Micheal interjected. Aaron and I spared a look before asking Micheal how he could possibly get that information. "I have contacts that have a connection with Diego Ford." Diego Ford was a wealthy man who hacked into his enemy's histories and dug for dirt to blackmail them into doing anything he wanted. He was not one to be trusted. I wondered why Micheal would have those certain contacts. It's dirty business.

"No," I demanded.

"Contact whoever you need to," Aaron spoke over me,

completely overriding my suggestion. "We need to be prepared for anything. Adam, as future CEO, you should know that." Aaron was right. I did need to always be prepared, but getting help from Diego felt way below my style.

I gave much thought to what was riding on this entire election. I looked at Aaron, then at Micheal, and finally spoke.

"Fine. Contact who you must."

I had a bad feeling about this, but I'd rather know what I was up against. I knew getting information from Diego Ford was going to come with a price, and I'd eventually pay it, but I could only pay it when I had power as CEO.

CHAPTER 13
KATHERINE

"Take the next exit!" Celeste screamed at our taxi driver. He had his personal GPS on, but Celeste never trusted it if she couldn't directly see which route it was taking us. She had suggested coming along to drop me off at the private jet terminal. Adam had offered to give me a ride, and it was probably the most reasonable thing to do, but I wasn't fully comfortable spending additional time with him. I was already going to be trapped with him on the plane for a total of six hours. And about to spend the next three days with him, only God knew how that would go...

"Excited?" Celeste asked as she noticed my timidity. I was beyond nervous. This would be the first time I read my book to strangers, and the first time I'd be back home after being away for what seemed to be an eternity.

"Super!" I replied, biting back the emotions that were threatening to emerge. I needed to remain cool, calm, and collected throughout this entire trip, even if I didn't feel like that at all. *Fake it till you make it, right?*

Our taxi driver pulled up near the terminal. Looking out the window, I could see the breathtaking black jet parked, with

Adam's black Rolls Royce next to it. The sight caused Celeste and I to drop our jaws in awe. Nothing screamed filthy rich like having a matching jet and car.

I got out of the car and walked toward the back to retrieve my luggage. I lifted the trunk and grabbed the luggage by the handle to pull it out, but a firm hand came to rest on my hip. I turned to find Adam behind me. My arms became weak, dropping my luggage. Adam caught it before it had a chance to hit the ground.

"You shouldn't be carrying your own luggage," he said as he looked toward the front of the car. The driver was resting his eyes, waiting for his money. "Wait here," he added before making his way to the front.

"He is even better looking with proper lighting," Celeste said, standing next to me. I was confused about what she meant until I realized this was her third time seeing him. Adam returned, closing the trunk. The car immediately drove off. Celeste and I glanced at each other.

"I didn't pay him," I argued as I picked up my luggage from the ground. "And that was Celeste's ride." Celeste stayed quiet behind me, not wanting to interfere.

"His service wasn't worth paying for if he didn't help you with the luggage. As for your friend, Henry will drive her back." My face reddened at his sudden response as Celeste choked on a cough behind me.

"You didn't pay him?" I asked, becoming aggravated with how he chose to handle the situation.

"I paid him what he deserved," he said, his expression bored.

"Which was?"

"Half. For half the service. Any more questions?" I stayed quiet, not wanting to get deeper into this conversation. I could tell Celeste felt uncomfortable as she moved closer to me.

"Great, I think I'll take that ride now." Celeste gave me a small hug before getting into Adam's car. Adam then grabbed my luggage and handed it to the baggage handler. I followed behind Adam as the jet door opened, revealing the flight attendant and the pilot. They both greeted him before returning to their jobs. We walked up the stairs, and I paused right at the entrance, completely stunned by the beauty inside.

The interior was much lighter than I expected. It was carpeted and decorated in beige and creams. It made the darker oak woodwork of the tables and storage furniture stand out. All the furniture seemed hand-crafted in leather, crystal, and the finest woods. It left me speechless. I took a seat in one of the high-quality leather seats.

The moment I encountered the seat, I felt like I was floating on a cloud. I fully reclined in the chair, seeking more comfort, and heard a chuckle behind me. It was low and deep, causing my entire body to flush with warmth. I faced Adam as he took a seat across from me.

"Comfortable?" he asked, obviously seeing how much it felt like heaven to me. I nodded as I fixed my posture. A few seconds passed, and I pulled out my laptop from my bag. The flight attendant walked out with two glasses of champagne.

She handed me a glass before handing Adam his. She smiled at Adam as he settled his glass on the table between us.

"Anything else you'd like from me, Mr. Pearson?" she gushed with ogling eyes. I rolled my eyes at how obvious she was drooling over him. I was sure Adam received a ton of attention from women; I'd just never been around to witness it.

I didn't like the way it made me feel. I felt... *jealous*. Jealous over him. I couldn't recall the last time I'd gotten jealous over someone else. Adam dismissed her with a flick of his finger. I focused on the plain document in front of me, waiting to be typed on and... nothing. I was completely blocked. Nothing came to mind but the interaction with the flight attendant.

What was wrong with me? I had no right to be bothered by a small interaction. She was just being friendly. Yeah... *A little too friendly.* As if Adam could read my thoughts, he interjected.

"Everything alright?" I fixed my eyes on him.

"Yes, everything's great." He didn't seem to believe it, but he jumped to the next question.

"How's the writing coming?" Just *great* because of your wonderful employee. God, jealousy was not a good look for me. I hated how obvious my emotions were.

"It's coming along just fine," I spit out. His brows narrowed, baffled by my response.

"Read it to me." Damn, this man could not catch a hint. I looked at him, my attitude quick to make an appearance. "I said, *read it* to me, Katherine." His voice became dark and demanding. Why did that do things to my stomach? It had just flipped and rolled over a total of ten times in a matter of seconds. My hand tightened around the chair handle. Maybe it was the champagne.

"Excuse me for a second." I instantly got up, retrieving my carry-on bag, and made my way toward the bathroom. My body begged for some type of release. I entered, closing and locking the door behind me.

The restroom had a vast amount of space. I could practically do some gymnastics without hitting anything. I looked in the mirror and realized how red my face had gotten.

Tingles resonated at the spot between my thighs, reminding me of the effect Adam's voice had on me. I placed my bag on the sink and searched for a specific item. Suddenly, the need for a release became vigorous. It had been years since I'd had the real deal. I wasn't one to sleep around; I only gave myself to someone I *wanted,* and I hadn't wanted someone in such a *long* time.

After much thought, I lifted my skirt, my underwear soaked with my arousal. I slipped a hand under my panties and applied pressure on my clit with a finger. A moan escaped from my lips.

I bit my lips together, not wanting anyone to hear what I was really doing in this bathroom. I closed my eyes and pictured Adam's face and his voice.

I pictured him telling me what to do, giving me orders on how to please myself. I imagined his hand replacing mine, that it was his finger inside of me instead of my own. I pumped a finger in and out, not taking my mind from Adam. *'I said read it to me.'* His voice taped in my mind, I replayed it over and over. I imagined his body hovering over mine, then his lips replacing his fingers. I slid down the wall onto the floor as I lost strength in my legs.

It all felt a bit too real as I reached my climax. My vision blurred as I saw stars, and my breath intensified. Once I gained stability, I got up and fixed my clothes. I checked myself in the mirror as I washed my hands, trying to calm my breathing.

My cheeks were pigmented with my release. I splashed cold water on my face, hoping it would wear off. After a few seconds, I unlocked the door to exit, feeling ashamed of what I had just done.

As soon as I opened the door, I found Adam standing right outside. Suddenly, the color of my cheeks returned, stunned by his presence. I wanted to hide under a rock at the thought of him hearing what I was doing behind the closed door.

"I was about to check on you. You were in there for a while," he said. I walked out of the bathroom, closing the door behind me, scared that I could've missed any evidence while I was cleaning. I stood there with my legs shaking, praying that he wouldn't give it much thought.

He stared at me, and I peeked at the small, smug smile growing on his face. *God, please no.* He straightened his posture as he took a few steps closer to me. He stopped exactly an inch away from me, causing my back to hit the door.

"Are you? Alright, that is." His stare was intense, his pupils growing by the second.

"I-I'm fine," I stuttered, hating how I couldn't make out a simple sentence.

"Right..." He leaned down, his lips only a breath away from my ear. "Are you lying to me, angel?" If it weren't for him holding me up, I would've melted right there. "Because if you are... you'll find out I'm not one to be lied to." My breath became unsteady as he moved back, looking deep into my eyes. I swallowed a gulp of saliva stuck in my throat.

I tried to step back, only to be reminded of my back being plastered against the door. He lifted his right hand and used it to caress my left cheek, studying the color spread on my skin.

"Such a pretty color," he whispered, his body tensing as I wrapped a hand around his wrist. I closed my eyes, not wanting to do this. This was wrong. All of this was so wrong, yet it felt so right. This lust was a burden that we both shared.

I opened my eyes again, finding Adam still staring into my soul. He slowly leaned in... wanting to give in. I wanted him to give in. Suddenly, his phone rang, interrupting the moment. *Just in time.* We both moved away, giving us room to catch our breath. My heart was racing, my hands sweating. Adam looked down at his phone, switching back to business mode.

"I must take this." He turned and walked out of the area, leaving me alone with my thoughts. What was happening? I was stunned by my own actions, stunned by my interaction with Adam. I wanted to be living under a rock right now, jealous of Patrick for being able to hide out in his spacious rock in Bikini Bottom. *Lucky pink star.*

I decided to move from my current seat and lay on the couch across from me. I turned my entire body toward the window, wanting to hide away from the world. *Four more hours to go.* As I looked at the beautiful view outside, my mind drifted off to a deep dark sleep, forgetting my surroundings all together.

CHAPTER 14

ADAM

"Adam Pearson, I didn't believe it when I heard you needed my services," Diego voiced over the phone. I had asked Micheal to contact him for information on my uncle, but I didn't think he would call me directly, and yet, so quickly.

"Cut the bullshit, Ford. Do you have what I want or not?" I asked, my mind still mildly hazy from my moment with Katherine. God, I couldn't help myself. At first, I had gone to check on her, worried that I'd scare her off with how demanding my voice had come off.

But then, seeing her come out of the bathroom with flushed cheeks had my mind going to places it shouldn't. I had a good idea of what she was doing in there. She looked guilty about it. Sweet, innocent Katherine taking such a risk just to please herself; the idea made my dick harden.

"Straight to the point, I see," Diego said, dragging me from my thoughts. "Yes, I have the information. But you do owe me something in return; a favor in the future." Of course, I didn't doubt him doing this without a price. I took a second before deciding to make a deal with the devil.

"Done. Now tell me what you know." Diego then proceeded

to speak, and I quickly became impatient. I glanced back at the sitting area, unable to see Katherine in her chair.

"He has an election coming up against surprise, surprise... you." My jaw ticked at the fact that he was so deep in my personal business. But that was expected of Diego; he'd dig into anyone he was working with. It was his way of assuring his 'payment' was set in stone.

"Tell me something I don't know," I said, aggravated by his unnecessary announcement. He knew that I was aware of the election; he only wanted to get under my skin. A reminder that he now knew things about me. To use against me.

"I was able to discover your *mystery* rival." He meant the author my uncle had signed. It had been driving me insane not knowing who it was. I had an idea of who it could be, and now I would be prepared with the news. "And it happens to be someone who works in your company." I would be lying if I said I was shocked. I had a list of candidates who worked for Pearson Book Group.

"Go on." Diego had taken a dramatic pause, knowing it would toy with my mind. I despised the need to have Diego find this out for me, and I despised that I now owed him something in return. I owed absolutely no one, and I was more than certain he knew that. He was one lucky bastard to be doing this over the phone.

"Victoria Mora. Director of your Creative Department." I blinked in shock. I was heedless of the remaining manuscripts in my mailbox, but I must have skipped hers. Or probably skimmed through it, hated it just as much as the others, but never acknowl-edged her name.

Then it all clicked—why she had scorned Katherine that day I showed her around and why she was randomly on my floor for long periods of time. "I happen to have more information on your uncle, though I'm certain that was all you needed."

He was right. It was all I needed to get the advantage of

being ahead. Eventually, following up with the elections, I would need more information, but with this, I was good. "Yes. We'll be in contact soon." With that, I ended the call.

How foolish, how *brainless,* of her to go against me. *With* my uncle. The moment I became CEO, she would be fired from Pearson Book Group. Along with a dreadful, detailed email description of what a horrendous employee she was sent to other publishing companies she dared to walk into. Loyalty had no price, and for someone to give it up this easily was pitiful.

As I fixed my suit, I walked back toward the area Katherine and I shared. Katherine had moved to the couch, asleep. Her hair draped over her face, robbing my chance to acknowledge her beauty. Katherine was beautiful when she was awake, but asleep... she looked like an angel.

An angel because she was the most beautiful, pure, and kind creature to walk the planet. The sweetest thing on my side of hell, making me want to seek redemption in her name. If you were to ask me to give you my description of an angel, I would show you this exact moment, with Katherine at full peace.

I marched closer toward her, unable to contain myself. With a hand, I gently caressed her hair, the touch tender to my skin. She smelled the same as always, lavender and vanilla. Quickly, those scents had become my favorites, completely devouring each whiff I was able to steal.

Katherine twitched beneath my touch, and I swiftly removed my hand, careful to not wake her. I forced myself off the seat and back to my own. There was a short amount of time left on this plane, so I sat there with a drink in my hand and my attention directly on Katherine.

As her current publisher, I was never given the chance to look at her, and I mean *really* look at her. Yes, I stole some glances here and there, but never to study her like she was my life's work. To count each time her chest rose to inhale and exhale, to admire the tiny birthmarks she had on her shoulder, to acknowledge the small slit on her right eyebrow. I'd looked at her, but never *saw* her, until now. And she was breathtaking.

Two hours later, we arrived in Los Angeles at exactly nine. Katherine slept the entire flight. She walked off the jet behind me, her hair ruffled with the constant turns she had made in her sleep. The car I had ordered for the entire weekend was parked outside, with our luggage loaded into the trunk. Katherine and I slid into the car and rode toward the hotel in mute.

The rumbling of her stomach broke the silence. "Hungry?" I asked, already looking up the room service menu the hotel offered. She could order something once she had her room. That way, she could eat without worrying about what restaurant was still open.

"Just a little," she said, looking out the window. Her stomach grumbled again, demanding to be fed. She met my eyes, her cheeks flushed with embarrassment. I handed her my phone with the menu pulled up, and she grabbed it and looked. "Thanks." I nodded in return before turning my head in the opposite direction.

A few minutes passed, and we arrived at Hotel Bel-Air. I opened the door and got out of the car. "Stay here," I ordered Katherine, shutting the door before she had a chance to get out of the car behind me. I made my way toward the lobby to check-in, where a woman stood behind the front desk.

"Adam Pearson, I have two suites booked for this weekend." She gave me a flat smile before fixating her eyes on the computer in front of her. She typed aggressively on the keyboard for a brief moment before looking up with a pained expression.

"Hey, we all checked in?" Katherine emerged through the lobby doors. Could she not follow simple directions? All she had to do was wait, and it pissed me off. I gave her a bitter look, which made her step back, crossing her arms. I faced the woman again, whose expression remained the same.

"Yes, Mr. Pearson. It seems we have a small mix up. You

only booked *one* suite for the next three days, not two." What the fuck was she talking about? I was sure to ask Jackson to reserve two suites. There had to be a mistake. That or my assistant was completely dull.

"Check again." She continued to type on her computer, shaking her head. After a long pause, she spoke again.

"Nope, only one room. Still." My body tensed at the thought of having to share a bedroom with Katherine, even if it was for one night. I reached for my wallet and gave her my black Amex card.

"Then book another." She looked at my card like it held a disease. That was a first.

"Can't do that. We're all booked." *Shit. Now what?* "And to save you the trip, everywhere else is booked. It's a busy weekend —we have a concert, a lakers game, and... Oh, a book convention," she exclaimed happily. *Excellent.*

I rubbed my temple, frustrated. I hadn't slept the entire trip due to focusing on Katherine and the news with Victoria. I couldn't think of a solution because of how exhausted I felt, so I decided to take the room for tonight and figure out sleeping arrangements tomorrow, early in the morning.

"I'll take it," I said through gritted teeth. She smiled, handing me two room keys. I forcefully took them and turned to Katherine, who stood behind me the entire time.

I handed her one of the keycards, her body stiff with having to share this room with me. I guess I wasn't the only one feeling uneasy with this arrangement. I walked toward the elevator; Katherine speed-walked behind me to catch up.

"What about our bags?" she said, out of breath. I looked down at her, pressing the button to our floor.

"They'll be bringing them up later."

"Oh, okay." The rest of the elevator ride was silent, something about being trapped with Katherine in such a small space driving me insane. It took everything inside me to remain still, and I regretted getting in without a single soul stepping in as well.

If it felt like this in an elevator, how would it feel in a bedroom? I was, without a doubt, fucked if I didn't figure something out. The doors opened, and this time, it was Katherine who ran out first. *Does she feel it, too?* Interesting...

Katherine looked down at the key while walking down the hall, looking at each door number. She stopped in front of room 112.

"This is it." She inserted the keycard, and the lock lit up in green. The room had a grand deluxe king bed, with a patio and a fireplace. Across from the bed was the sitting area that contained chairs and a couch. One would say the room was sufficiently wide, but I'd strongly disagree. It was nowhere near wide enough for both me and Katherine.

"So... you'll be taking the couch?" Katherine interfered with my thoughts. I slid out of my jacket, folding it on the chair beside me. I rolled up my shelves and faced Katherine.

"No. I'll take the right side of the bed." She crossed her arms, looked at the bed, then back at me. I was not about to sleep on a crappy couch when, logically, there was more than enough room on the bed. One night, only sleep. It was manageable.

"And where do you suggest that I sleep?"

"On the left side." Her eyes widened at my response. "It's a grand king bed; it'll fit the both of us." Katherine spared me a glance. "Relax, angel. I'm not interested in touching your precious side." *Liar.* No, it was true. This was just one night. Tomorrow, I'd fix the problem.

Katherine stared at me at a loss for words. *Shit. Did I really just call her that? Again.* I needed to get a hold of myself.

A knock came from the door, most likely room service with the meal I had ordered for Katherine. I took the interruption as a miracle. I strode toward the door and opened it. They had brought up our luggage with the meal and dropped the bags inside the room while I retrieved the food from the mini cart.

"What's that?" Katherine asked, staring at the takeout box, practically drooling at the sight.

"For you." I handed her the box. She opened the lid and inhaled a deep whiff. I'd ordered her a medium-rare cheeseburger with lettuce, onions, and tomatoes. Ketchup on the side, in case she didn't like her sauce on the bread. I didn't know if she'd like anything else on the menu, so I made the safe choice of a cheeseburger.

"For me?" she repeated, not taking her gaze off the burger.

"Yes, earlier you said you were hungry. Do you not like cheeseburgers?" Anticipation instantly struck in my gut, contemplating whether my 'safe' choice was actually safe. So what if she didn't like the burger? It wasn't like I cared that much, it was just food.

"No, I like them. Thank you." Relief washed over me. Katherine and I made eye contact for a brief second. *Get out of the room.* I listened to the voice in the back of my mind and left the room. Stepping out into the hallway, I collected myself. I reached for my phone and called Aaron.

"Hello, brother. Miss me already?" he answered the phone. I had called him to check in on the office, as he was my eyes and ears while I was gone. Plus, I was in much need of a distraction.

"Cut the shit. What's new?" Even I could hear the irritation in my voice, and Aaron enjoyed prolonging scenarios unnecessarily just to piss me off.

"Edward landed in Los Angeles an hour before you. The corporation is running smoothly at the moment, and I intend to keep it that way." Aaron was a pain in my ass, but I felt at ease with him in charge of my position. "Everything going accordingly?" he asked, noticing how mute I was over the phone.

"I've settled in my room... with *Katherine.*" I emphasized her name. Aaron laughed, the sound causing a sharp earache. I clenched my jaw, regretting telling him the current situation I was dealing with.

"I won't ask," he then added, as if he could feel my urge to wrap my hands around his neck from across the line. I heard one more chuckle before he ended the call.

I stood right outside the door, my shoulders tense at the thought of walking back in. *Here we go...* one night. Control yourself, you're not an animal, for fuck's sake. With one swipe of my card, the door unlocked. I pushed it open, steadily walking in.

CHAPTER 15

KATHERINE

The door shut behind Adam as he left the room, leaving me alone with my thoughts. I looked down at the burger he had handed me not long before he stepped out. I took two bites of burger and quickly lost my appetite. I closed the lid of the box and stared at the bed I'd lay in with Adam. Sharing a room with him was never part of the plan, much less a *bed*. I was expecting him to take the couch, but obviously, he had no intentions to do so.

The thought seemed extreme to me, and I began to feel jittery. *Stay cool, Katherine.* I decided to take a hot shower to release some tension. I turned on the shower to the hottest temperature; I had a problem with liking the water being so hot that it practically burned my skin.

I stared at the wall of royal beige tiles and contemplated whether or not I should sleep at my mother's. *No,* this was one night. I was sure Adam would fix this. *Or do you like the idea of being in the same room as him?* No. There was no way that was the reasoning for my decision to stick around.

He is my publisher, for God's sake; this was strictly a professional relationship. About the time the water started running cold, I hopped out of the shower. As I wrapped my towel around myself, I checked the floor and realized I had left my bag outside.

Crap.

I opened the door, letting the steam from my hot shower out. As I took a step out to quickly retrieve my bag, Adam came into view. He was standing only inches away from me, his eyes fixed on the towel wrapped around my body, looking at the water drops on my chest and shoulders. I hadn't even bothered drying off. I wasn't supposed to run into him.

"Adam," I breathed. His pupils were dilated at the sight of me.

"Katherine," he said in a breath.

"My bag..." I pointed at the floor where my bag was settled. He looked back and reached for it.

"This bag?" he asked, wanting to tease me. I was afraid to play along with the look he had on his face. It was pure hunger.

"Adam... please," I begged, wanting him to just give me the bag already. I couldn't stand to be in front of him, drenched and in a towel. I couldn't control myself for much longer. He saw the desperation on my face and handed me the bag. "Thank you," I whispered, leaning closer to him, taking in the way his lips parted.

"You're welcome," he whispered back. I stepped back and tried to gently close the door, but Adam placed his foot in the way, stopping me. "Wait." He said as he opened the door again and walked toward me. My heart beat wildly against my chest.

"What?" I had to control my heart rate. He stopped and shook his head.

"Nothing. I—" He looked into my eyes with longing. He suddenly left without saying anything else, shutting the door behind him. I stood there, shocked by what happened. I locked the door behind him and splashed cold water on my face before I could do anything else.

Afterward, I went through my bag and thanked the big man upstairs for Elaina and her idea of packing comfortable, *appropriate* pajamas—a pink sweatshirt with heart-printed pants.

Heading out of the bathroom, I climbed straight into bed, claiming my side. The pillows on the couch caught my eye, giving me an idea. I quickly ran across the room to retrieve them and hopped back into bed.

With the pillows, I created a wall. Adam glanced at the wall I assembled, chuckling as he reached for his luggage.

"A bit paranoid, are we?" he said without looking up.

"It shouldn't be a problem."

"I didn't say it was." He looked up this time, focusing on what I had on. After a beat, he strolled into the bathroom without another word out of his mouth.

I watched him make his way toward the bathroom, more specifically, admiring his ass. I swear, this man had to be dedicated to going to the gym because his body was something to be praised. *Snap out of it, Katherine.*

I shook my head and pulled out my laptop, incapable of going to sleep at this time. I glanced at the pages I'd written for Night Span, shocked at the amount I had been able to complete.

Whenever I wrote, it always seemed like I did so little until I skimmed through everything. If you always stared at one part of an art piece and never stepped back to acknowledge the full painting, you'd miss the beauty of it altogether. And that's how I'd found writing to be.

Without realizing it, I had gotten caught up in writing. Adam came out of the bathroom in gray sweatpants and a black t-shirt. Something so simple, yet it was my favorite thing I'd seen on him so far. The gray sweatpants outlined his bulge, being the reason for my throat drying out.

"How's the writing?" he asked as he slid into bed, careful not to mess up the pillows I had placed between us.

"I'd like to think it's going okay." I cleared my throat, clearly needing some water. Adam's expression remained the same as he leaned in to look at my screen.

"Let me see." He grabbed the laptop from my hands and set it on his lap. He read through it, and my stomach suddenly felt sick. I always felt so nervous when he read the things I wrote. Yes, I knew many people would read my book, but it was *him* that made me nervous. Which was ironic, with him being my editor and publisher.

"I like the tension you're building with the characters and the conflicts that come along with it." What he didn't know was he happened to be my muse for that part. "I do think you should go more into detail with the upcoming coronation. You want the war to start there, right?" I nodded as a response. "Okay, then I'd focus on that during the next two chapters. Really go in depth with it."

One thing about Adam was he always knew what he was talking about. He knew his stuff. And he was amazing at litera-ture. It felt like a breath of fresh air whenever I received his feed-back. I stared at him while he typed on my computer, fixing errors.

The sight leaves me speechless. Lying next to him in bed while he wore *that* and helped with my writing made my heart thump harder than it ever had. I focused on a lock of golden hair that dropped at his forehead.

I'd never seen his hair messy before; he'd always styled it back with hair gel. The black t-shirt he wore hugged the muscles in his arms perfectly, distracting me from any other thoughts I had.

"Katherine," he called out, and I blinked. Shoot, did I just zone out like a complete freak?

"Yes?"

"I asked if you have any ideas on what to write toward the end of the book." The answer was no, but I didn't want him to think I was out of ideas. Either way, I was sure I'd figure something out.

"Yes, I have some ideas. But I'll figure that out when I'm at that point." He looked at me as if he was dubious about my response.

"Might I remind you that your deadline is in March?"

"I'm aware." Did he not think I'd be able to finish on time? I mean, I wasn't sure if I'd be able to, but at least one of us should. And it should be him.

"Good," he simply said. "There is a lot riding on this, Katherine." I spared him a puzzled look.

"My career?" I asked, unsure of what he meant.

"Yes." He hesitated, then cleared his throat before speaking again. "You have a very long day tomorrow that requires you to be at your best. I suggest you get some rest." He handed me back my computer.

Our fingers slightly touched, causing both of us to glance into each other's eyes.

"Right," I said, as Adam moved his hand. I've noticed he always tried to get as far away from me as possible whenever he made physical contact with me. A part of me wished he'd stay, curious to see why it felt so... *different.*

He flicked the lights off and turned to face the opposite side from me.

"Goodnight," I spoke, unsure of what else to say.

"Goodnight, Katherine," he merely said.

I couldn't see him clearly through the pillow barrier I built between us. It was dark and silent. I stared up at the ceiling, trying to fall asleep. I even made an attempt to count sheep, but that was a complete failure. I kept getting distracted by Adam's breathing. It was the only thing in this room that I could hear.

A constant reminder that I wasn't alone. I tossed around to find a comfortable position to sleep in because nothing else was working.

"Are you going to keep doing that?" Adam said in a drowsy voice. I immediately stopped moving, scared to wake him up more. Though I had a feeling he was already awake.

"Sorry," I whispered, while slowly switching into one last position, hoping that I wouldn't have the need to move again. I faced the pillows that separated us, looking through to Adam's side.

"Try to get some rest, Katherine," he softly said.

Adam tossed around, facing the pillows. He still had his eyes closed, his hair ruffled by the pillow, and yet he looked so perfect. The moonlight shined through the window, casting a light on his face. I took the advantage of staring at him like he was my favorite painting, admiring the details that made him different from others.

I noticed he had a faded scar on his collarbone that must have happened a long time ago. But that didn't stop me from wondering what the story behind it was.

None of your business, Katherine.

I shook my head and continued staring. Watching his chest rise and fall in a rhythm allowed me to fall into a deep sleep, drowning all the things that surrounded me.

CHAPTER 16

KATHERINE

THE FOLLOWING MORNING, I WOKE UP TO ADAM'S SIDE OF THE bed empty. He must have been up early because everything on his side of the room was left organized. His clothes were fixed into the drawers, his nightstand spotless, and his luggage placed under the desk, empty. Meanwhile, my bag was still on the floor, opened, with clothes spilling out.

Across the room was a silver and glass room service cart that held toast, fruits, and a glass of orange juice. I noticed there was a note placed next to the fruit. I checked the time on my phone—eight-thirty. The room temperature was freezing, so I checked out the thermostat, and it was set to seventy-two degrees. I rolled out of bed with the comforter wrapped around me like a burrito, otherwise I wouldn't be capable of leaving the bed.

I grabbed the note and read it. *'Be back soon, angel. Eat.'* I snickered at the message. Did he always have to be this demanding? Though my heart pinged at his nickname for me, I still didn't understand the meaning of it. I wiped the small smile that had formed on my lips and reached for a piece of toast, taking a bite as I walked toward my bag on the floor.

I kneeled in front of it and searched through the clothes

Elaina had packed for me. I spotted the mint and pink floral dress I had planned on wearing today and laid it out on the mattress.

Looking at the dress made me feel anxious about today's event; I had no idea what to expect. Would anyone be interested in my book? What if they hated it? What if I messed up while reading the first chapter? What if my accent popped out while I was speaking?

I shut my eyes and pushed all my thoughts to the back of my brain, no longer acknowledging them.

I quickly changed into my dress and fixed myself up, then looked at my reflection in the mirror. The dress was flowy at the bottom and tight at the top, with long sleeves and a small bow placed on the back. I had decided to wear my hair down, not touching it much. I also went with my signature red lip today, hoping it would give me some luck.

The lock on the door clicked, distracting me from applying my lipstick. The door creaked when Adam pushed it open. He wore a heathered navy blue suit with silver cufflinks. He'd styled his hair back with gel, making me crave his ruffled hair instead. I looked down at his hands, that held a cup of coffee.

"Good, you're awake," he said as he strutted across the room toward me. If he wanted, he could get cast as a runway model; his walk held so much confidence. Power. "Coffee. I figured you'd like to start the morning with some," he added, handing me the cup.

"Thank you." I took a sip of coffee, and my eyes widened at the taste of it. Chai Tea latte with a pump of white mocha and vanilla—my favorite. How did he know? "This is—"

"Your usual," he cut me off.

"How did you know?" I asked, as I gave him a puzzled look.

"It was listed on your cup the time you brought coffee to my office." I was surprised he would remember something like that, shocked that he paid attention to that detail about me. I took another sip, unable to grasp that it was perfectly recreated, not one mistake.

"Why's it freezing in here?" he commented while looking at the thermostat. He then changed it to seventy-nine degrees.

"I thought you changed it."

"I didn't. I hate the cold," he stated. "I take it you don't like it, either." He pointed at the comforter on the floor that I had ripped off the bed.

"I actually like the cold." I shrugged as he gave me a disbelieving glance. "I also happen to love snuggling in warm blankets." He huffed at my remark.

I turned to face the mirror and lined my lips with red liner, then filled them in with red lipstick. Adam stared at my reflection in the mirror.

"What?" I asked, meeting his gaze in the mirror. He walked up behind me and caressed my shoulder, spreading tingles down my arm.

"You should know better than to do that in front of me." I shivered at his remark, unable to move. His words held me like an anchor. No matter how strong the waves were, I still wouldn't budge.

"Do what...?" He looked away from my gaze and focused on the lining of my dress.

"Put on red lipstick." I lowered my hand that gripped my lipstick. It felt like he had me trapped there for years, but I compiled without a complaint. He then cleared his throat, as if he had snapped out of his thoughts. "We must be heading out now. Arriving early will allow us the advantage to prepare." He walked out of the room, the door shutting behind him.

Disappointment crawled through me. I yearned for his touch, needing more. It was ridiculous. I didn't act like this, like a highschooler. *Forget it.* I reached for my purse on the couch and left the room.

We arrived at the book convention; it was empty due to us being early by two hours. Usually, the convention was held at a convention center, but this year, it was being held at an exhibition hall. The area was so spacious, you could easily get lost in the place. But Adam walked into the building like he owned it, making his way through random rooms like he knew his way around.

I followed Adam to an empty, dark room. I gripped his arm, unable to see where he was taking me. He then settled me in what I thought was the center of the room. "Don't move," he said as I heard his footsteps fading. I stayed locked in my current position, curious about where he'd brought me.

With one flick of the switch, the entire room filled with light. The sight left me in awe. He had taken me to an auditorium that I wasn't aware they even had. I gasped at the Romanesque-style architecture—massive stone walls with incredible details and dramatic semicircular arches—with warm white lights shining on everything. The building alone wasn't big, but it gave the illusion that it was.

"Read me your chapters," Adam said, bringing my attention back to him.

"What?" He wanted me to read? Now? Here?

"You can practice reading here. I know this is your first time doing a reading for your book, and it can be nerve-wracking." He adjusted his hands in his pockets as he walked on stage with me. "This will help. You'll feel prepared." He reached into his suit pocket, pulled out a folded copy of my first chapter, and handed it to me.

He wanted me to feel prepared. The thought alone was sweet, like he cared about me. *He's your publisher, it's his job to prepare you.*

"O-okay." God, I needed to get a hold of this stuttering

problem I had *only* when I was around him. Adam spared me a small smirk as he walked off the stage and sat in the audience, front and center. His presence felt overpowering, like it was a full crowd instead of it only being him. I was nervous.

I began to read the first chapter out loud and messed up. "Try again," Adam suggested. I tried again and repeatedly made reading errors. I started to become anxious.

I looked at my phone and noticed I only had one hour to get this right. Panic set in at the realization that if I couldn't read in front of one person, how could I read to hundreds? I buried my face in my hands, wanting to hide from the world.

Adam noticed my minor breakdown and made his way toward me. He stood beside me, leaving some space in between us, careful not to touch me.

"Hey," he whispered, his voice soft and faint. "You can do this. Don't doubt yourself, I don't," he added.

It had always been difficult for me to read in front of others due to my fear of messing up. As a little girl who knew nothing but Spanish, many made fun of me for not being able to pronounce certain words correctly. It had always been an insecurity of mine. I'd worked hard to become confident in my writing, but reading… I'd always had that fear, that doubt.

"I-I don't know if I can do this," I whispered in half a sob. Something in Adam changed, causing him to completely close the gap. His eyes softened as he reached out to grab my face. His hands were warm, quickly reassuring me without saying a word. Adam was surprisingly patient with me, careful not to hurt me. I felt safe in his touch.

"Let's try one more time. This time, I'll help you." He grabbed the crumpled copy from my hands, standing at the very center of the stage.

He began to read the first chapter, carrying off what I was clearly struggling with. He spoke with confidence, dominating the room, the audience, if there was one. He handed me the next page to read, and with a little hesitation, I followed along. This time, I made progress, only mispronouncing one word. Finishing the last word on the page, I jumped with excitement.

"I did it!" I smiled, cheerful. I busted out in my famous happy dance, then jumped on Adam to give him a hug. My arms wrapped around his neck, with my entire body lifted off the ground. I heard a deep chuckle in my ear, and my entire body melted at the sound.

My feet then touched the ground, instantly missing the feeling of them being off it. I glanced at Adam's face, and for once, I saw him smile. Not a small smile, a genuine, all white, teeth showing smile. He has deep cut dimples that felt like a sharp stab to my heart when I wasn't prepared for it. And I wasn't.

Adam's smile was easily qualified as the one and only thing I knew could ruin me. I admired it for as long as he wore it. His smile slowly disappeared as he looked into my eyes; I couldn't decide whether I was disappointed at the loss. But as I held his gaze, I recognized the sensational feeling I got at just the sight of the emerald green.

He cleared his throat before speaking. "Feel prepared?" he asked, not taking his gaze off me.

"Now I do." A strand of hair fell to the front of my face. He took the strand and tucked it behind my ear, sending shivers down my neck.

"Good," he said in a husky voice. "Let's introduce them to the best book ever written." Did he really mean that? My cheeks flushed with warmth at his admiration for my writing. I wasn't sure if it was meant to ease my nerves, but either way, it worked.

"Let's do it!" I exclaimed, hiding the nerves crawling through me. I felt like I was agreeing to jump off a cliff without a parachute to assure me of a safe landing. But maybe this time, with Adam, I'd fly regardless.

CHAPTER 17

KATHERINE

IF YOU TOLD ME I'D BE READING A CHAPTER FROM MY BOOK AT the biggest book convention in California two months ago, I would not have believed you. Within the hour, the entire hall was filled with readers and authors set up in their stations. Adam and I made our way toward the reading area, where the name 'Night Span' was spread everywhere.

Adam had set up the area with Night Span posters and a 'Book Reading' poster with my picture on it. The entire setup was a dream. I'd always pictured it to be just like this in my mind. My eyes clouded with tears at the sight of others interested in my book.

"You're on in five," Adam said, directing me to the front. "You're more than prepared for this. You'll be fine."

He gave me a soft push up to the stage. Walking up sent an adrenaline rush through my body; each step felt heavier than the last. Suddenly, the coffee I drank this morning was making its way back up my throat. I *really* shouldn't have finished that drink.

Adam caught my attention from the front of the crowd, and seeing him eased my mind. I shut my eyes closed and breathed, then opened my eyes and gripped the microphone positioned at the center of the stage. My hands shook. I hated that I couldn't control my own body. Oh, man.

Then, Adam's voice made an appearance in my mind. *'You can do this. Don't doubt yourself, I don't.'* Okay.

I read the first sentence without making an error, *not too bad.* The second sentence I mispronounced my character's name, but I shook it off, hoping no one noticed. I looked at Adam, who gave me an encouraging nod to keep going. I read the entire chapter without making another mistake.

As I finished the last sentence, I was showered with applause. I heard a familiar voice screaming my name in the crowd—my mother. She had her phone held high in the air, recording the entire event; hard to miss. I had told my mother about my event today, but I wasn't sure she would show, with how busy her work schedule was.

My mother had started working in television as an assistant director for a telenovela on Telemundo. It was one of the biggest Latin television networks, and I was incredibly proud of her. But given such a big role, it consumed most of her time.

Someone in the crowd raised their hand, and I was confused about whether I should call on her. Was I supposed to be answering questions? I figured it was okay and called on her, anyway.

"Yes? You have a question for me?" I asked as I pointed directly at the woman.

"When will your book be released?" she asked with a friendly smile. I felt excited that someone would want to get their hands on my book as soon as possible.

"Well, it's planned to be released within the next five months," I answered. Several hands rose to the sky after answering the first question. This time, I called on a teenage girl.

"Hi, I'm Ameila. This is my first book event," she stated shyly. "I'm very intrigued by your novel, and I'm very excited to read it! What helped you get out of your comfort zone and take that step to publish it?" Jeez, that was a great question. But my answer was clear as I made eye contact with Adam in the crowd.

"Great question, Ameila. I'd say it was my friends and family who believed in me." I took a beat before adding, "And having an amazing publisher who cares also helps *a lot*." I prolonged the last two words without looking away from Adam's gaze. He gave me a small smirk and looked away. Did I make him feel nervous?

Ameila gave me a small nod, and I called on the next person. After I answered most of the questions, I walked off the stage.

"You were incredible," Adam stated as I moved closer toward him, and I blushed at his compliment.

"I wouldn't have been if it weren't for you." I meant every word. Because of Adam, I had gained the confidence to give it a try.

"That's not possible. You're always incredible at everything you do," he admitted in a deep voice. "That had nothing to do with me." He looked at me with much intensity, holding his gaze felt like my soul was ascending with his. It was so easy to fall for Adam. He always said the right things at the right time.

"Katherine!" We both spun our heads toward my mother.

"Mami," I said, unhappy she ruined the moment. For once, I wanted to see how much longer Adam could influence me. It was like I was experiencing a new high from an exotic drug, and I craved more of the effect.

"Ay, mija, estuviste increíble." *Oh, darling, you were incredible.* She grabs my arms and pulls me in for a hug.

"Gracias, Mami. I wasn't sure you would make it."

"Don't be ridiculous, Katherine. *Of course,* I would make it," she exclaimed with a very heavy accent. She looked at Adam, who stood beside me, observing the entire encounter. "Y este guapo quien es?" *And who is this handsome guy?* My cheeks turned red with embarrassment. I only prayed he didn't understand a single word coming out of my mother's mouth.

"Mami! Por favor! Él es mi editor." *Mom, please! He is my publisher,* I explained, desperate for my mother to catch the hint. She had a certain glint in her eyes, the type she got when she felt like a matchmaker. "Mami..."

"Katherine, por que no estás saliendo con él?" *Why are you not dating him?* Oh God, please save me. We already had this conversation over the phone. "Hola, I'm Katherine's mother, Gloria." She introduced herself to Adam as I stood there, clueless about what to do with myself.

"Gloria, such a pleasure to meet you. Adam Pearson." He gave her hand a gentle shake.

My mother looked at me and whispered, "Que hombre tan atractivo." *What an attractive man.* I awkwardly smiled, wanting this moment to end. Adam spared me a smug look, as if he could understand what she was saying. It wasn't rocket science to get the point my mother was making, but he didn't know the exact words. Thank God.

"Invítalo a cenar a la casa esta noche." *Invite him over to dinner at our house.* There was no way in—*excuse my language*—hell I would do that.

It seemed way too personal. I shook my head 'no' and she spared me a glare. The type of glare parents give their child when they do something they qualified as disrespectful. Adam was enjoying all this a little too much, as he did not try to walk away.

"Please, join us for dinner tonight," my mother said to Adam. I prayed and begged the lord he would decline, because a night with my mother and Adam would not be pleasurable.

"I would be delighted to," he responded, looking directly at me. *'Delighted to.'* Ugh! I was in no shape or form ready to deal with this. Training for war wouldn't prepare someone enough for this.

"Perfecto. See you tonight." She gave Adam a pat on his shoulder before facing me. I gave her an irritated look as she kissed my check goodbye. "Tranquila, es una cortesía invitarlo. Él te esta ayudando con mucho." *Relax, it's a courtesy to invite him. He's helping you a lot.*

She was right. He was helping me with more than I could imagine. But I didn't think this was the *best* way to thank him.

"Lo se, Mami." *I know, Mom.* She gave my arm a gentle squeeze before leaving.

"So, taking me home so soon, angel?" I'm sorry, did he mean to make a joke about what just happened? I was astonished by the attempt. It came out so effortlessly, charming even. And his nickname for me made an appearance once again. A smile creeped on my lips; I fought extremely hard to thin it out.

"I—" I got cut off by two familiar people.

"Fancy seeing you here," Edward, his uncle, said.

"Fancy, no. Unfortunate, yes." His composure was elegant, but his expression screamed with rage.

A woman came into view—Victoria. What was she doing here? The moment she appeared, Adam's demeanor changed. I couldn't quite describe it; all I knew was it didn't change for the better.

"What a great choice, signing with my uncle," Adam said to Victoria.

Signed with his uncle? The only reason she would be signed to his uncle would be—no. She was the other author. I knew Adam and Edward Pearson were looking for new authors, but I didn't know that it would be some type of competition. At least that was what it felt like whenever I had an encounter with Victoria. She always made it feel like we were competing for the title of New York Best-Selling Author.

Not only that, I knew she hated me. She saw me as a threat because Adam chose me and not her. It had been right beneath my nose this entire time, and I chose to never give it much thought. I sensed Adam's shoulders tense beside me. I wanted nothing more than to comfort him.

"Oh, I know. It would have never worked out with you, anyway." Her smile seemed true, yet it was anything but real. Adam stood tall. No one would know he was filled with fury. Edward seemed like he wanted Adam to make a scene, but he knew deep down that it was impossible for Adam to act out. "Now. Please be a dear and get out of my way," she said to me as she moved toward me.

"Victoria, I know you're incapable of holding good manners, but I suggest *you* walk away." Adam looked at her like he was throwing daggers at her head. He was so defensive of me. I was not expecting it.

Victoria seemed very miffed by his response and walked the other way. His uncle, however, stayed put. He looked at Adam like he had just found gold.

"What?" Adam spit out.

"Nothing, I just find it interesting," he replied, carefully seeking to trigger Adam.

"What would that be?" Adam asked. He seemed uninterested in where this was going.

"I'd be careful. It's not... appropriate to be anything but colleagues." I looked at Adam, who gave him a mild smile.

"I wouldn't worry about that. I take *my* CEO position very seriously," he emphasized the word 'my', as if he was making the message clear to his uncle. There was something more behind it, but I had no idea what it was. It could be anything, with the way they despised each other.

"Edward," Adam said, dismissing the conversation. Edward's face turned red; what Adam had said hit him harder than he thought it would. He looked like he wanted to kill the man. Adam placed a hand on the small of my back and directed me away from the conversation.

"We're leaving," he said. I was aware that now wasn't a good time to receive tingles up my spine, but I couldn't control it with Adam. He moved his hand and rested it on the side of my hip and gripped it tight. We walked toward an empty hallway.

"What time is dinner tonight?" Adam asked, surprising me. Was he considering showing?

"You're actually coming?" I didn't think he would waste his time at a family dinner.

"Yes... Were you not?" I stayed quiet, and his eyes widened at my hesitation to answer. "I don't believe it. You're too much of a good girl for that." For some reason, the term 'good girl' didn't seem like a good thing coming from him.

"I *am not* a good girl," I argued. He gave me a disbelieving glance.

"Right," he said bluntly. "You're a girl who can do no wrong and spends her time writing romance novels." Ouch. Way to say my life is anything but exciting.

"You seem like a good guy," I said softly, scared it would offend him. But it didn't. Instead, with the hand he had on my hip, he spun me until I faced him. A gasp escaped from my mouth as he tilted my chin up, studying my facial structure.

"Let's make one thing clear." He caressed my chin, warmth pooling between my thighs. "I'm not a *good* guy, Katherine," he growled, not taking his eyes off me. "Sooner or later, you'll realize I'm not the gentleman you think I am." He meant it more as a promise than a warning.

"Enlighten me." It was bold of me to put Adam on the spot. I wanted to get a taste of the forbidden, the wrong. He yanked me toward him. He tucked a strand of hair behind my ear, then gripped my hair in his hand and tugged on it. My head fell back, my lips parting an entrance for him.

"Don't provoke me. I must warn you, it's not what you want," he said in a dark voice. His eyes darkened as he glanced down at my lips. My eyes watered at how hard he was tugging on my hair.

"What if it is what I want?" I admitted, desperately wanting him. It was a need. I needed him. Our bodies crashed together, his thick erection pressed up against me.

"It's not," he spoke. Our lips were inches away, only for Adam to let go of me. "Fuck," he whispered to himself. "What are we doing?"

"I—"

"We need to leave. I have a few calls to make," he said through his teeth, as he ran his hand through his perfectly styled hair. He looked at me once more before walking out the double doors. I felt embarrassed after basically throwing myself at him. If there was one situation that could leave a girl feeling unwanted, it was opening ourselves up and getting rejected.

CHAPTER 18
ADAM

I HAD ALMOST GIVEN IN TO THE TEMPTATION OF KISSING Katherine. Last night was hell for me, knowing I had Katherine right there beside me and I couldn't have her. Today, our moment in the hallway, the way her lips parted, giving me a welcoming entrance. I wanted to dominate her mouth, hear her whimpers as I explored her body. Seeking and discovering the things that threw her over the edge.

At last, all of that flew out the door when I heard footsteps roaming the halls. I didn't want to risk someone catching us at that moment, and I had a strong feeling someone was watching. But whether someone was watching or not, we should not have gotten as far as we had. Katherine's bold remark made it absurdly difficult to decline.

It was like hanging a piece of raw steak in front of a starved wolf and expecting it not to demolish it. No good would come out of that; the entire situation would remain a complete mess. Though, I noticed I wasn't the only one with hunger that filled their eyes.

Katherine sat beside me in the car on our way to her mother's house. I found it way too entertaining to decline the offer earlier.

Neither of them was aware I knew Spanish. Which would only make things more interesting tonight.

I looked down at Katherine's thigh, which bounced with anticipation. She was nervous. Should I comfort her? After all, it was because of me that we were doing this. "Are you alright?" I asked, glancing over at her. She abruptly turned to me.

"Why do you always ask me that?" She seemed upset and irritated with me, and had every right to be.

"It's just a question, angel," I simply said, in a cool tone. She flinches at my nickname for her.

"Don't call me that," she snarled. I blinked, shocked at her response. She had a kick, a fire to her, and I was insanely intrigued.

"What would you rather I call you?" I asked, fascinated with what her answer might be.

"I don't know, not *that*." This time, she couldn't look me in the eye, a sign of her shyness emerging. Just like that, the fire dimmed. I became slightly disappointed.

"Mhm." I hummed under my breath. I caught her by the side of my eye, staring.

"Why did you say yes?" she blurted out, almost as if she was fighting to hold it in, but hopelessly lost at the attempt.

"I need you to be more specific Katherine, I could have said 'yes' to anything." My tone came across more sarcastic than serious, which seemed to push a button.

"Adam," she says, looking at me. There was no escaping from her gaze, and I wasn't about to look away first. I was the intimidator, not the one who got intimidated. So, what was going on with me?

"Katherine," I softly said her name, matching her tone. She flicked her gaze to my lips for a quick second before returning it to my eyes.

"Why?" she pleaded.

Shit. Why was it hard to deny her? How could I tell her the

reason I agreed was that I desperately wanted to know more about her? Her childhood, where she grew up, what she thought of me. Even when I couldn't give two shits what others thought of me. That I wanted an excuse to spend more time with her, not in a room where she mentally blocked me out.

Katherine stared at me, waiting for an answer that wasn't coming. Her big brown, amber doe eyes stared into mine, her brunette hair falling in her face, the air conditioning blowing it out of her way momentarily.

Her plump, red lips rubbed against each other. I wanted to brush my fingertips against her bottom lip, to get a feel of how soft they were.

The car came to a stop, saving my ass from confrontation. I opened the door, urgent to get out. I held it open for Katherine to slide out, only for her to use the other door instead. My jaw clenched at her attempt to ignore me.

It shouldn't have bothered me as much as it did.

I stood in front of a one-story white cottage home with a black roof. It had a small porch with an orange swing attached to it and gray brick tiles cladding the exterior of the house. It looked warm, cozy—it looked like a *home.* Something I never had.

I followed Katherine to the porch and stood right outside the door. She gave the door a soft knock and stood back.

As we waited, I observed the items they stored on the porch. There were books and magazines under a coffee table that had a glass compartment and plants placed on each opposite side of the swing.

The door swung open, revealing Katherine's mother, Gloria. She had a warm smile placed on her face as she expanded the door open for us to come in. I noticed Katherine's body stiffen as I placed my hand on the small of her back, motioning her in.

"Bienvenido a mi casa! Welcome!" Gloria greeted me.

"Thank you." I flashed her a charming smile that had her

winking at Katherine. I shouldn't be pleased with how she praised me in front of her daughter, but I was. I heard and understood every comment she made to Katherine, and the reactions Katherine had to them earlier today.

"Please, make yourself comfortable. I just need to finish something in the kitchen." She asked Katherine to come with her. Katherine looked at me with wary eyes, not wanting me to snoop. I spared her a quick nod before she completely turned her back to me and followed her mother.

"Ustedes dos se ven bien juntos." *You two look good together,* Gloria whispered to Katherine.

"Mami! Shh!" Katherine shout-whispered back to her mother. The smirk that was growing on my lips was inevitable to stop.

Once I saw her turn the corner, I took the chance to look at the pictures laid out on the table. It was the first thing that caught my eye when I had first walked in, but I didn't want to seem like I was intrigued. I picked up a white wooden frame of Katherine as a child in a graduation cap and gown. In the picture, she smiled, her two front teeth missing. Her hair was up in two individual ponytails, with pink bows attached to each side. It was the cutest thing I'd ever seen; I suppressed a smile just looking at it.

Placing the picture down, I scanned the others. All of them were of her and her mother, but none of them held a father figure. It made me curious about what the story behind that was.

"That's fine, Ma." I heard Katherine's voice returning from the kitchen. I quickly stood. "Come on, table's ready," she said as she gave me a quick look and turned back around.

I chuckled at the attitude she was clearly giving me. I caught up behind her and pulled her in by the waist.

"Control that attitude, or I will," I managed to whisper in her ear before entering the dining room. I felt her tremble beneath my hand, my grip tightening before letting go. I passed by her and took a seat at the table.

Shocked by my comment, she remained still in the position I had left her in. Katherine promptly shook her head, coming back to reality. I pulled out the chair next to mine and watched her approach the table. She smiled at me and her mother, then complied and sat down.

Good.

"Oh! How rude of me. Did you want some ice in your drink?" Gloria asked, pointing at my cup.

"Please, if you can," I responded, handing her my cup. She then made her way out of the dining room, leaving me and Katherine alone.

I took the napkin laid on the plate and placed it on my lap. Katherine huffed at my action, and I spared her a glance that had her looking away from me.

"You do remember your manners, yes?" I asked her in a quiet voice, one only she could hear.

She rolled her eyes, which irritated the fuck out of me. I purposely dropped my napkin on the floor to reach down and retrieve it. As I grabbed the napkin, I placed my hand on her ankle. She shivered under my touch.

She wore a red dress tonight, with long sleeves. The clothes she wore made it easy for me to access her skin, her legs.

I ran my hand up her slim leg as I settled back in my seat. When I made it to her knee, I delicately spread her legs open, giving me access to her inner thigh. I made contact with a warmer area and rested my hand there, squeezing her inner thigh and watching her cheeks flush with red.

"What did I say about that attitude of yours?" I reminded her, my voice huskier than before. I removed my hand from Katherine's thigh as I heard footsteps coming back from the kitchen. I placed the napkin on her lap before turning my attention to her mother.

"Aquí tienes." *Here you go,* she said, handing me the drink with ice. Truth was, I'd rather have my drink without it. But I saw an opportunity to have Katherine alone, and I took it.

"Thank you, Gloria. This dinner looks amazing." Gloria smiled in return. The table was filled with food. She had cooked chicken with rice, a salad, bread, and black beans. She took a seat and began to say grace.

"Katherine, por favor, ora por la comida." *Please, pray for the food.* Katherine bowed her head and shut her eyes. Gloria grabbed my hand and told Katherine to grab the other. Katherine cleared her throat as she held my hand.

"Gracias dios, por la comida, um, bless the hands who made it," she stuttered before saying the rest, "and those who eat it. Amen." We all released each other's hands and began to eat. Gloria speared a knowing look at Katherine as she reached for her drink.

"So, tell me. How did you come across Katherine's writing?" she said, reaching for the bread.

"I was on a hunt for new authors, and I came across Katherine's manuscript in my mailbox," I explained as Katherine listened.

"I had sent him a manuscript of Night Span," she clarified, and her mother's eyes widened.

"Night Span," she said flatly, unable to grasp the fact she had sent in her novel. Katherine nodded, tucking a strand of hair behind her ear.

"It was very well written. It was the only book that caught my attention." I wasn't lying; no other manuscript had been entertaining to me. Katherine had a way with words that grabbed a hold of you, leaving you in *real* suspense. It had been a while since I'd seen that in a book.

Gloria smiled at Katherine, who had her attention on the food she was playing with on her plate. "I have always told Katherine she had talent," she admitted.

"She does. I haven't worked with an author as talented as

her." It slipped out of my mouth without much thought. Katherine blushed next to me, warmth radiating off her.

"Que lindo." *How cute,* Gloria said to Katherine.

"A veces." *Sometimes,* Katherine responded to her. Sometimes? I formed my hand into a hard fist, annoyed by her comment. *Sometimes.* I should *always* be to her. I supposed I'd let that one slide. Just this once.

"What do you plan for the book?" Gloria asked the both of us. We briefly looked at one another before answering.

"I have big plans. I plan on getting your daughter on the New York Best Sellers List." Her eyes gleam with excitement and then confusion.

"Amazing. When would that—" Katherine cut her mother off by giving her an answer.

"Seis meses. Pues, cinco ahora." *Six months. Well, five now.* They shared a look before Gloria spoke again.

"Wow, that's... El es..." *He is...* Gloria tried to find the right word.

"Cabeza dura?" *Hard-headed?* Katherine finished for her. Huh, it was funny how she felt safe making this bold comment, thinking I didn't understand. This, however, I would not let slide.

"Creo que la palabra correcta es inteligente." *I think the right word is intelligent,* I voiced. Katherine dropped her fork on the plate, and it rattled on for a brief second. "Or high achiever. Whichever you like best." Silence filled the room, both women sitting at the table in complete shock.

"You… speak Spanish...?" Katherine asked, cautiously. All the color suddenly drained from her face at the realization that I had understood everything that had been said in front of me. Out of the blue, Gloria broke into hysterical laughter.

She slammed her palm against the table, unable to catch her breath. Her eyes filled with tears that fell down her cheek. Katherine, on the other hand, was still unable to process it. Stone-still in her seat, only her chest rising and falling rapidly.

"Ay, que risa!" *Oh, how funny,* Gloria cried out. "This whole time, you knew?" I gave her a quick nod, chuckling with her. It wasn't because of Gloria, but because of Katherine's expression. I could tell how embarrassed she was. She was practically trying to hide from me.

"How do you know Spanish?" Katherine asked, struggling to form the words.

"I learned in high school. I've been practicing it with Petra." Gloria raised a brow, seeming impressed at my response.

"Petra?" Katherine quickly asked.

"My housekeeper."

"Eso es espectacular." *That is spectacular,* Gloria said. Katherine stayed quiet as she listened.

"Definitely has its perk. Don't you think?" I said to Katherine. She speared me with a glare, her jaw slightly locking. Katherine looked even more attractive when she was upset. It turned me on.

"I suppose it does," she agreed.

Gloria rose from her seat, becoming slightly uncomfortable with the tension between us. "How about dessert?" she exclaimed, looking at Katherine.

"Sounds wonderful, Gloria," I said to her. She cleared her throat and instantly left the room. I turned my head to Katherine, who had her sight focused on her lap.

"You speak Spanish with your housekeeper?" She spoke softly, still not meeting my gaze.

"She doesn't know enough English to speak it," I explained. "She's a single mother, and she couldn't find anyone in New York who would hire her." She then met my gaze. "So, I did." Her eyes softened, the anger slowly dissolving from her face.

"That's... very kind of you," she admitted, placing a hand on my thigh. My muscles tightened at her touch, and I felt heat flush my body. The most innocent gesture sparked the most electricity between us, and I wondered what else she could make me feel.

"Yeah?" I asked, looking deep into her eyes. A shred of vulnerability showed in my voice, and I quickly pushed it down. I was not an open person. I didn't ever feel the need to explain myself. I never cared enough. And no one had ever thought of me as kind, much less called me kind. That was a first, and it meant everything to hear those words come out of her mouth.

"Yeah," she repeated with stars in her eyes.

"It was so nice having you over, Adam. Thank you for coming." An hour had passed and Gloria showed us out the door.

Surprisingly, the entire night went by smoothly. Gloria spent the majority of the time telling stories about when Katherine was a little girl. When she lost her first tooth, when she first picked up a romance novel, when she began to write.

The conversation never took a dark turn; it always stayed in a positive light. I couldn't recall the last time I had good company over dinner or the last time I felt sad that something had come to an end. And that was how I felt about tonight.

"Please, thank you. I had a good time," I said to Gloria.

I stepped out the door and waited for Katherine to follow behind. "Estas segura que no te quieres quedare?" *Are you sure you don't want to stay?* My chest clenched as I waited for Katherine to voice what she wanted. I wanted her to come back with me.

I was aware that I had said I'd fix the sleep arrangements today, but it had been hectic. *Lair.*

I could tell myself whatever I wanted, but the truth was, I wanted Katherine in the same room as me. It was torturous, but I liked not feeling *alone.* Even if she ignored me, I knew she was there. Her presence was there.

I stood outside the door, waiting for her to say if she wanted to come back with me. Katherine pulled at her sleeves, deciding whether or not she'd stay.

"I think I'll stay for tonight," she said gently. Such a soft, smooth voice, yet it caused my chest to tighten. I hated that I reacted this way over the choice she made.

"Of course. I'll send a car tomorrow morning." Since she wouldn't be riding with me, she'd still need a ride to the convention tomorrow, which would be the last day. The following morning, we'd fly back to New York.

"No need. My mom will give me a ride." My expression remained the same, but inside, I felt like I'd been punched in my gut multiple times. It was a mystery why I felt this way. It was new, different… unsafe. "But thanks for the offer," she added with a small smile.

"You're welcome," I replied. I tucked my hands in the pocket of my pants, glancing down at my shoes like a nervous teenager. God, what was wrong with me? "Goodnight, Katherine," I added before turning and walking away with the small amount of dignity I had left.

As I made my way to the car, I fought hard not to look back at her. Because if I did, I knew I'd find her already looking at me, and it would be incredibly hard for me to leave.

CHAPTER 19

ADAM

"What do you mean, there's a 'little' problem?" I said to Aaron. He had texted me saying that there was a 'tiny' problem, and I immediately called him. Panic rushed through my mind, on edge with just how 'little' this problem could really be.

"Hello to you, too, brother," he replied. I waited for him to elaborate, but nothing. He wouldn't speak until I greeted him back, like the pain in my ass he was.

"Aaron. For once, make my life easier and just answer the question. I'm working," I said in an irritated tone. It was half true. I had just arrived at the Bookery Romance Convention at that exact moment as I waited for Katherine to arrive.

Last night, I had left Katherine at her mother's house. The entire ride back to the hotel felt lonely and quiet. The room hadn't felt the same as the night before; there was no tension pulling at me while I slept. I should have been glad, but I wasn't. I still woke up with the same thought I had when I fell asleep. Which was red lips, slim legs, tan tone shoulders, and long glossy brown hair that covered the small amount of back she was showing.

Aaron sighed before speaking. "The company board sent a

very elaborate email on the 'no dating policy' that the Pearson Book Group has. They said it has been brought to their attention that you and Katherine seemed a tad too... friendly." I rolled my eyes, already knowing who it was that had 'brought it to their attention.'

My uncle always had a knack for finding the smallest things to use against me, especially to the company with the upcoming elections.

To be fair, I had always thought the no dating policy was necessary with other employees, but it bothered me that it still applied to me.

I wasn't CEO yet, which meant I had no say in this situation. *This should be an easy rule to follow.* Right, most things stopped being 'easy' the moment I met Katherine.

"Shit." I could hear Aaron huff in frustration when I didn't say more. "What else?" I said, knowing that his huff had some type of meaning attached to it.

"Diego Ford called the office this morning. He said he might be needing that favor from you. What does he mean?" I could hear the tiny bit of concern in Aaron's voice.

"Fuck," I cursed at the mention of his name. "Diego said I'd need to grant him a favor for the digging he did on Edward," I explained, my hand gripping the phone a little too hard. As if it could run away if I didn't keep a firm grip.

"You have no idea what this favor is?" Aaron asked. He sounded troubled about the arrangement. He was my little brother, and we had gone through some tough shit when we were kids. We saw things that we shouldn't have at our age, and that led to us having physical and mental scars.

"Aaron, I have it covered. Call me if you hear anything else," I reassured him. Even though we were both adults now, I always felt the need to take care of everything. To take on the worries myself. To fix them myself.

"Okay. Take care of yourself, Adam." The word 'care' bled through with heavy meaning.

"I will." That was all I said before I ended the call. The need to win the position became grander than it already had been. The need to defeat these assholes and prove that I wasn't one to fuck with was bigger than I anticipated it to be.

I paced the concrete floor, trying anything and everything to not think back to that night. The night that I got the scar on my collarbone. It was healed and faded, but every time I thought back to it, it was like it got cut open again. I shut my eyes and fought to think of something else, someone else.

Without much of a fight, red lips and amber golden eyes came to mind. I released a breath I wasn't aware I held in the first place. But that was how Katherine made me feel—relieved. A breath of fresh air after being underwater for what felt to be an eternity.

"Adam?" My eyes snapped open at the soft, delicate voice calling my name. I turned to find Katherine stepping out of a white Lexus. Hearing her voice and seeing her face shone a bit of light on my darkness that threatened to take over.

"Katherine, just on time." I greeted her as I looked down at my watch. 8:45 a.m., the exact time I told her to come.

"Just for you," she said with a soft smile. *Just for me.* I realized the tension in my shoulders loosened at the sight of her smile. Even if it was small and quick, it was all I needed for the day to go by decently.

She noticed the way I looked at her. She cleared her throat, which brought me back to reality.

"Let's head in," I suggested. Katherine followed behind me, her heels clicking against the floor. I kept my gaze straight forward, trying to refrain from looking back.

Today was our last day at the convention, and I had set up a Q&A booth for her book. I noticed yesterday that many potential readers were interested in asking her more questions, hence the idea. She was amazing up on that stage, commanding everyone's attention. Including mine.

As I got closer to our booth, another blue table was set up beside it. A blonde woman sat at the center of the table, holding her book—'Into The Blue'. The entire set up proved my uncle didn't have any type of imagination or vision for this business. I bet he didn't even bother reading Victoria's book like I had for Katherine.

Though, I didn't blame him. I couldn't even get past chapter one when I received her manuscript. Which was quite pathetic if you asked me.

Her blue eyes strained on Katherine. I could feel her becoming uncomfortable as we stood at our booth.

"Pay her no mind, you're here for your book," I reassured her, handing her a packet of fan art I had created for her book. I had also made bookmarks that were in the shape of swords and crowns.

"What's this?" she asks, looking at everything I had arranged on the table.

"Merch, for your book." She picked up the poster of both characters gazing into each other's eyes.

"You interpreted them beautifully. It's perfect." She admired the artwork in her hands, scanning her finger across each detail. "Thank you, Adam." Her approval of the poster I created was like winning an award. I felt appreciated and valued.

"You're wel—"

"Katherine?" a deep voice interrupted us. I turn to see a man in a pair of blue ripped jeans with a black shirt. He had a gold chain around his neck. The least appealing outfit I'd seen.

"Martin?" Katherine sounded surprised, like someone had suddenly held her at gunpoint. How did she know this guy? Most importantly, what the fuck did he want?

"I knew it was you. It's good to see you, Kat," he said,

scratching the back of his neck like an idiot. I looked at Katherine, who wouldn't meet my gaze.

"What are you doing here, Martin?" I could hear the discomfort bleeding through her words. Whoever he was, he had hurt her. And that made me hate him more.

"To see you." He wouldn't take his eyes off Katherine. A green-eyed monster emerged within me. I was quickly filled with jealousy, yet I stepped down to let Katherine take charge.

"How did you even know I would be here?" she said to him.

"I still follow your mom on Facebook..." Of course he did. I fantasized my knuckles slamming against his face, breaking his already fucked up nose. "And I saw that you were back home, now publishing your book. Congratulations, by the way," he added.

"Thank you," Katherine said in a wary tone.

"And I just..." *Great. There's more.* "I wanted to see you. It's been six years, Katherine. When I saw that you were here, I had to come see for myself." I clenched my fists.

"What is it that you want?" Katherine asked.

"I thought we could talk over some coffee. Maybe even rekindle things." Yeah, fuck that. I was taking charge. "I'm afraid that's not possible. We leave first thing tomorrow," I interjected, gaining both of their attention.

"And you are?" he said to me, straightening his posture. I chuckled to myself at his 'I'm the alpha' gesture. I was still a couple of inches taller than him.

"This is Adam. My publisher," Katherine interfered, resting her hand on my bicep, spreading goosebumps down my arm.

"Adam." He scanned me from the bottom up. My neck felt warmer, and I slowly became angrier.

"Like he said, Martin, I leave tomorrow." A smirk pulled at my lips.

"How about tonight?" he asked, returning his gaze to Katherine.

"Don't think that's possible either," I answered his question for her. Katherine gave me a confused look and instantly looked at Martin.

"Who are you to speak? She can answer for herself," he rebuked.

"I'm aware. But the answer is no," I said to him, trying to restrain myself from doing something foolish.

"The hell it is!" he yelled at me. Katherine stepped in front of me to face him.

"I think it's best if you leave, Martin." He ripped his gaze from me to Katherine, grabbing hold of her arm, and Katherine gasped at his harsh grip.

"Just give me one chance to explain myself. I've tried to move on, but I just can't," he said hastily. This man was so desperate, it was almost too miserable to watch. I would feel sorry for him, but instead, I felt like ripping his head off.

"No, Martin," she said, her voice becoming smaller.

"You will hear me out. You think you're so perfect. Listen here, bit—"

"Leave. Now," I said in a dark voice, as I gave him a threatening look. He let go of Katherine and marched over to me.

"Fuck you, man!" he yelled. I smiled, rubbing my chin.

"That's not a smart answer, *man*. I can easily *ruin* your life, your career, and everything you've ever worked hard for—faster than you can say the word 'sorry'. When I say leave. You. Leave." I towered over him, not once looking away from him. He harshly swallowed, looking down at his phone. "This is your *final* warning."

He looked like he wanted to hurt me, and I wished he would, only so I could have my turn. He looked around before he stepped back, turned, and left.

"What was that, Adam?" Katherine asked in shock, looking flustered at the scene *her Martin* created. I wished I had ripped out his tongue when I had the chance. I instantly regretted making him leave so quickly.

"I rectified the situation." Even if I didn't want to.

"No, Adam. I meant… I can handle myself," she argued. Her nostrils flared, confirming that she's fuming. "I can handle an ex." I figured.

"Yes, I know you can, but I could not stand the way he spoke to you. With me here, I wasn't about to allow it," I argued.

"I don't care if you're here. It was *my* problem to deal with." She was right. I had no business interfering in their conversation. I had no right to be jealous when she wasn't even mine. Yet, I still did it. And to be frank, I'd do it again.

"Well, I'll make sure to step back the next run-in you have with your *little* ex. I must say, you have impeccable taste," I said sarcastically.

"God! What is with you? I don't get it!" she exclaimed with her hands in the air. "You know what? I need a moment. I'll be behind the booth," she said, crossing her arms.

Having Katherine mad at me was doable, but having some bastard's hands on her wasn't. It was an instinct to protect her, to destroy whoever came close to her. I loathed that I felt so strongly toward her.

I watched her stand behind the booth, talking to potential readers. How was I supposed to approach what I was feeling? I was clueless about how to make it stop. I had so much at stake, and because of Katherine, I could lose it all.

She was my weakness. And she alone could ruin me.

CHAPTER 20
KATHERINE

The drive back to the hotel was quiet; I hadn't spoken a word to Adam since that scene with Martin. I didn't understand why he acted so defensive of me, possessive even. He had no right. I'd been single and alone for a while now, and I could handle a small run-in with the one person who broke me.

Though, Martin showing up was a total surprise, and not the good kind. Out of all the scenarios I had thought of, that was not even close to what I was expecting. I always thought Martin would travel from California to New York just to come see me, to get me back.

I waited for years for him, but he never came. I had been devastated, more upset with myself for even wanting him to reach out. Who wanted their ex who had cheated on them to talk to them? I guess a person who wanted an explanation that might take the pain away.

Of course, I never wanted him back. But I wanted him to want *me* back. Martin was never the aggressive type. His confrontation today was nothing like him. He looked lost, desperate, off-track with his life. It hurt me to see him like that.

Even for a split second, I felt allayed by Adam's presence. I was overwhelmed with everything. I wanted to be angry with Adam, to ignore him. But there was something pushing me toward him. God, even when I hated the man, I still wanted him.

"Katherine," he called out, attracting my attention. "I know you're still upset with me, but we should really be getting out of the car now." I then noticed that I'd been daydreaming while the car was parked right outside of our hotel. I had no idea how long I'd been sitting here, not moving.

"Right," I said, placing my hand on the door handle. Adam covered my hand with his, spreading heat to my chest.

"Stop opening the goddamn door, Katherine." He spoke in a rough tone, making me feel on edge, the hair on my arms standing on end. He sighed, looking down for a brief moment. "Just. Stay put, angel."

He got out of the car and walked around to my door. He opened it wide, offering me his hand. I looked at it like it was some type of trickery.

"Get out of the car, angel." With shaky arms, I placed my hand in his. My feet touched the ground, all my worries gone momentarily with my fingers tangled in his. My hand felt incredibly small against his, his grip strong and firm. His touch was rough, and yet delicate with me.

We walked to the elevator with my hand still in his, as if it belonged there. We got on and waited till it reached our floor. I kept my gaze on my shoes, as there was nothing else to look at other than Adam, and I refused to look at him.

The elevator dinged open on our floor, and Adam removed his hand from mine and withdrew himself from the space. My hand suddenly felt cold, empty. I followed behind him, as I always did.

He placed his keycard on the door and opened it for me. He stood in front, waiting for me to walk in first. "Thanks," I said, unsure of what else to say. He spared me a solid nod before entering.

The door slammed shut behind him, the room instantly feeling thick with tension. Last night, I slept at my mother's because I didn't trust myself around Adam. I didn't know what it was, but something had changed between us. The energy was heavier and too strong to deny.

"Why did you react the way you did today? With Martin," I snapped. Adam walked toward the living area, shrugged out of his jacket, and folded it on the chair. "Answer me, Adam." He glanced at me from the side of his eye, removing his cuff links in the process. He dropped them in the tray on the coffee table.

"I already clarified that. I didn't like the way he chose to treat you." He paused, looking down at his shoes. "No women deserve to be spoken to that way," he added.

"I understand, but it wasn't your place to jump in when you did," I explained. His answer was not what I was looking for. There was more to it. There had to be. He sighed, rubbing his temple. "I want the real reason, Adam," I added. It was probably smarter if I remained ignorant about this, but the need to know was greater.

He clenched his jaw, barely able to contain whatever information he was keeping from me.

"Please," I asked, losing the last bit of patience I had.

"You want the *real* reason?" I hesitated before nodding. "I wanted to beat the guy bloody for speaking to you that way, for even looking at you," he admitted, the muscles in my legs suddenly feeling weak. "I saw the way you looked at him, Katherine. He hurt you. I hated the fact that he had you. He doesn't deserve you, Katherine." His voice turned dark. "Just the thought of you with him *irked* me. I don't give a shit if it's just coffee." My heart pounded against my ribs.

"W-why?" I faltered. He strode toward me with determination written all over his face.

"I don't know, Katherine. You think I want to feel this way? To feel jealous over any man you allow the privilege to speak to you? To look at you? To... *touch* you?" He pronounced the last two words with disgust.

"I-I didn't know." What was I supposed to say to all of that? How wasI supposed to deal with what he was telling me?

He shook his head, running a hand over his perfectly styled hair. "Tell me, Katherine. Because I don't understand how any man could look at another woman after looking at you. I don't get how they could ever think about anyone else after thinking about you. I have no idea how they do it. I have no idea how to *stop* it." He was only inches from me, slowly pushing me toward the dresser.

"I haven't been able to function properly after meeting you. Much less when I'm around you." As I tried to move backward, my back hit the furniture. His look was intense, and it felt too intimate, this moment between us.

"I don't know what to say," I admitted sadly, as I tried to fight the tears from falling.

"You don't need to say anything," he murmured, caressing my cheek with his hand, brushing a stray tear that fell. His eyes bore into mine. "You know how many times I think about what crosses your mind when you look at me?" His voice was soft, and I slowly shook my head. "Far too many."

He brought his thumb to my bottom lip and played with it. "How many times I've thought about these lips?" I gasped as he pulled my lip down. He grinned at the noise.

The heat of his touch burned a mark onto my skin. I bit down on my lip and closed my eyes, trying to figure out if this was really happening.

"Fuck it," was all the warning I got from Adam as he slammed his lips onto mine. My heart started to race, tingles spreading from my lips all the way down to the area between my thighs. He kissed me like he wanted to consume me.

And he did.

I ran my fingers through his hair, slightly tugging at the

strands, eager to have more of him. He pulled me onto the dresser, lifting a leg up to his side. His grip on my thigh tightened, earning a moan from me.

He licked the seam of my lips, seeking entrance. I granted it and allowed his tongue to slip into my mouth. He explored as his hand reached up to cup my breast and drew circles around my right nipple. Another moan slipped out of me. His erection strained against his pants and pressed up against my core. I could feel how big he was underneath the fabric.

I shamelessly ground against him, seeking and begging for any type of friction. He groaned into my mouth, gripping my hair in his hands. He tugged at the strands, making my eyes water. I was addicted to his touch.

My hand slipped between us and rubbed the center of his pants. My fingers were slightly brushing against his hardness. I began to unbuckle his belt, and he suddenly pulled away from me, leaving me panting on the dresser.

"Did I do something wrong?" I asked, confused by how rapidly he pulled away.

"No. This is—" For the first time, Adam Pearson was at a loss for words. As if he couldn't believe he'd lost control. "Fuck," he cursed, catching his breath. He rushed out of the room, slamming the door on his way out.

The impact of the sound made me shake in shock, my chest heaving in the most outrageous way. I'd been kissed before, but never how Adam kissed me. Like he was obsessed with the way I tasted, like I was his first meal in days.

The electricity still lingered on my lips. I kept reaching for where he left his mark. His name was branded on them. I felt unhinged from the way he departed, like he had instantly regretted kissing me in the first place.

We'd leave tomorrow morning, leaving everything that had happened behind us.

Adam had been gone for the past two hours. Within that time span, I'd showered, changed, and gotten into bed. I'd be lying if I said I didn't care that he disappeared, or that it didn't hurt me that he'd been gone for so long.

Was it me? Was I the problem? Because why else would he just leave like that, without an explanation? I glared up at the ceiling, feeling exhausted.

I felt tired, worn out by everything that had been thrown at me today, a series of unsettling emotions washing over me. And yet, sleep didn't seem like it was going to solve any of my problems.

The door clicked, promptly opening to reveal Adam. He stood at the entrance, looking in. I rolled over and stayed still, hoping he'd think I was asleep. He didn't turn on the lights, instead he walked in so quietly I thought he was still standing.

Adam took off his shoes and slid into bed. This time, I hadn't built a wall of pillows to keep us apart, clearly giving him the benefit of looking straight at me. My eyes were shut, but I could feel his heavy gaze on me.

"You awake, angel?" he whispered, as he slowly moved closer to me. I didn't respond to him; I didn't feel like speaking to him. He sighed heavily, my body warming at the simple sound.

"This is what's best, what's smart." He spoke softly. I never knew his voice was capable of being so faint, so delicate. It was not what I would have expected from someone as hard as Adam. He was powerful, ambitious, serious, and very intimidating.

"Understand that I'm trying to protect you," he said with a hint of sadness in his voice. "To save you…" he added. *Save me? From what?*

"…From me."

I could tell Adam held some dark secrets within him. I could also tell he was slowly getting tired of holding on to this 'act.' I wanted to dig and find the real him, unsure he would even dare to reveal himself to me.

But still, it wasn't his place to decide if I needed saving. Because he couldn't save me if I didn't want to be saved.

And I didn't.

"You what?!" Celeste screamed at the top of her lungs. I had gotten back from my trip to Los Angeles and was having a late brunch with the girls. Celeste and Elaina joined me. Elaina had returned from Miami, while Valery was still in Barcelona.

"I know, it just happened." I had spilled the beans about my kiss with Adam, and Elaina choked on her mimosa, a grin growing on Celeste's lips.

"Did ya bang him?" she asked. Both Elaina and I turned red at her bold question. But that was Celeste, bold as always.

"Jesus, Celeste!" Elaina whisper-shouted. Elaina wasn't comfortable with these types of conversations in public, and I couldn't say I blamed her.

"What?" Celeste looked genuinely confused. "I was just curious. How do you share a kiss like that and not bang?"

She was right, and the Lord knew I was practically begging for it. But it never got to that point due to Adam's vanishing. The girls saw the disappointment written all over my face.

"Did he..." Celeste paused to search for the right word suitable for this question, "bail?" Bingo. Bail, he had. But I wouldn't sound like a foolish girl who was affected by it; I refused to be. "Hey, no worries, girl. The best way to get over a man is to get under a new man." She shrugged.

"I don't even like Adam that much." I did, I really liked him. But why would I admit it, especially after what had happened? It was a recipe for disaster. Also, it just made me seem wretched, and who wanted to be that?

Celeste and Elaina both raised a brow, giving me the *'yeah, okay, you can lie to yourself but not us'* look. "Katherine, talking seriously... This is the first guy you've liked in years. Don't you think you'd feel something for him after a kiss like that?" Yes, of course I did. Honestly, this conversation made me want to crawl into my skin and hide.

The mood began to switch to a depressing one, so Celeste jumped on an opportunity to lighten it. "That doesn't matter. How about we focus on the Halloween party coming up," she said cheerfully. I'd totally forgotten about the party and that we needed to plan it.

We wouldn't be working that night as bottle girls or a bartender. We'd be guests, kind of. Doing all the planning and decorations, we'd basically be going to keep an eye on everything, make sure things were running smoothly. But Celeste found any party as a profit.

"Yeah, we do need to start planning," I responded, taking the last sip of my mimosa. The girls had ordered a huge pitcher of it, and we'd drunk every last drop.

"I'm not talking about the planning. I'm talking about the guys..." she huffed, picking up the empty jar. Our waiter walked by, and Celeste fluttered her lashes at him. "Can we get more?" He looked at Celeste with a shy smile and grabbed the pitcher.

As he walked away, Elaina barked out a laugh. "The poor guy almost forgot what he was here for," she said as Celeste smiled proudly. I wished I could have the confidence Celeste had with men. After years of being single, I forgot how to flirt. And even doubted I was good at it when the moment came.

"Now, about the party. I know of a few candidates who you might like..." Celeste said with her iconic scheming look.

CHAPTER 21

ADAM

Monday morning came around, and I had some meetings to attend to. One of them being the reason for my uncle's *fantastic* observation between Katherine's and my relationship. God, it was the first day back, and I already felt ready to strangle these asswipes.

"Wonderful morning, isn't it?" Edward said as he passed me in the hallway. I spared him a deadly glare, prepared to remind him who he was messing with. I made my way toward the conference room that held this meeting. As I got closer, I could hear all the voices in the room.

I stood beside my uncle and gave a firm knock on the door, and suddenly the room fell silent. Within the next few seconds, the meeting director opened the door. "Edward, Adam. Please, come in and take a seat. We were about to begin," he said. I took a step in, only to be cut off by Edward.

How childish was this man? Seriously, he was older than death. I'd pay good money for his time to be cut short. But that'd be the cowardly way out, and when I gained this position, which I would, I wanted to be proud of it because I knew I earned it.

I took a seat at the round table. The board was set up with a

PowerPoint presentation of the company guidelines, as if I wasn't raised in this company. I knew these rules like I knew the back of my hand. This was going to be a long, wasteful meeting.

I tried to give the presentation my full attention, but my phone vibrated in my pocket, distracting me. I took a look to find Aaron and Micheal texting in a new group chat they added me to. I never willingly wanted that, obviously. The group chat was named 'The Broskis.' I instantly knew Micheal had named it.

> Micheal: I'm in your office, snooping around your shit.

> Aaron: I tried to stop him.

> Micheal: He didn't. He basically opened the door for me.

> Micheal: Important question. Halloween party next week? I need myself a playboy bunny or a hot vampire.

> Aaron: Not feeling it.

> Micheal: Don't give me that crap, you're supposed to be the fun brother.

> Aaron: ....

> Micheal: Convince your antisocial brother.

I rolled my eyes at the messages. I could always count on them to annoy me on my shittiest days. And what was Micheal on?

"Adam, is there something you'd like to share with us?" Rod, the board chairman, asked, pausing his presentation. Everyone surrounding the table turned my way.

"Perhaps some good news with the authors?" he added. He

completely caught me off guard with his question. Even with my phone being silent, they could still hear the vibrations of the incoming messages. I had put my phone on 'do not disturb', but that didn't help with the men in the group chat. More specifically, *a* man.

I should put a special restraint on Micheal's contact. He was always the one who jammed his finger on the 'notify anyway' button, blowing off the entire concept of being on 'DND' in the first place. Knowing he was only a few doors down from me, waiting in my office, made me want to excuse myself to unalive him with my bare hands.

I readjusted my tie before rising from my seat. "Yes, I do, actually." I paused and tried to form an idea that would be worth sharing. I looked over my shoulder to find my uncle, whose grin is wider than Mars. "It looks like our deadline will be cut a month short. Due to how quickly my author is writing." His grin dropped faster than when he formed it.

The first thought that came to mind was how Katherine was going to take this. Cutting a month off her deadline, knowing she needed an extra added. Not good, I imagined.

"You don't say? That's very good news," he replied with a smile. "Looks like you have some work to do, Mr. Edward," he added. My uncle's face turned red.

"I suppose you're right," Edward said with a half choke. "I wonder if perhaps we could cut this meeting short. I assure you we know these rules, and you can understand where my urgency is coming from." Typical coming from him, when he was the reason we were in this meeting.

"Perhaps, we could... Only with the acknowledgment of you both understanding the presentation. The main points, if you will," Rod said, taking his seat at the table. "Mr. Pearson, what do you say?" This must have been the first time that I agreed with Edward.

"I have to say that I agree with Mr. Edward. We all understand the main concept and will follow through with each one," I said, avoiding eye contact with the man seated beside me. Rod gave me a swift nod as he redirected his attention to the rest of his colleagues.

"It's settled, then. Meeting adjourned," he said as he looked toward the clock hung on the wall. I rose from my chair and exited the room, not wanting to waste more time. I was relieved to be out, and I made my way to my office in long strides, itching to kick Micheal out of my building.

I forced my office door open, not caring enough to knock; it was my office to begin with. I found Micheal sitting in my chair, slugged off, while Aaron was in the chair across from him. Both swung their heads in my direction at the stentorian sound of the door slamming against the wall.

"Knock on the door, will you? I thought you were the polite brother," Micheal breathed, his hand positioned dramatically over his heart.

"It's my office," I announced, noticing my shirts that I kept folded in my drawer, spread out around the mini couch. "Why are you here without advising me?" I looked over to Aaron, who sat still, looking down at his phone like it was the most interesting thing he'd ever seen.

"Oh, I 'advised' you. In the group chat," Micheal said as he took out his phone to show me the chat that I'd already seen. "See?" he added while scrolling, with the proudest look on his face.

"I had nothing to do with it," Aaron added, and Micheal rolled his eyes as he put his phone away. "The Broskis? No one would willingly name a group chat that, unless they were you."

"It's a good fucking name. Catchy even," Micheal argued. "You both lack taste, but I'm willing to put that aside if you come to the Halloween party Avenue is throwing." His eyes glinted with exhilaration.

"No," I said, without giving it a single thought. I hated big crowds and parties; they were a waste of time. Drinking and having girls throw themselves at me became boring at the age of twenty-seven. But for Micheal, it seemed it'd take much longer for that itch to settle.

"You're on the list. The Pearsons must make an appearance," Micheal said to Aaron and me. Aaron wasn't the type to party. One thing I had in common with him. Though I wasn't aware that he and I were expected at this party. I looked over at Aaron, thinking he might have had something to do with him.

As if he knew what I was thinking, he said, "Again, I have nothing to do with it. Do I look like I have time to spare for a Halloween party?" I looked over to Micheal, who had a grin on his face.

"What did you do?" I asked in a cautious tone.

"Nothing. I was informed that you two were placed on the list by Diego Ford," he said as he sniffed his nose. "I'm Dylan's plus one that night, and apparently you're Diego's," he joked. Aaron looked at me, confused, as if he was trying to say, *'what the fuck is he talking about?'*

Honestly, I didn't know what he meant. Did Diego want to speak in person about this personal favor I owed him?

"I see. I suppose Aaron and I will make an appearance after all," I said as Aaron raised his brow, but didn't argue.

"Perhaps I can make time to see you with your *date*," Aaron pestered. Micheal straightened his poster in my chair.

"Plus one, goddammit!" Micheal corrected. I had to admit, seeing Micheal bothered was the best thing that happened the entire day.

"How was the meeting?" Aaron asked, changing the subject.

"As you'd expect," I answered. That meeting was, by all means, unnecessary. I was left with the burden of telling Katherine about the changes made to her deadline and not a good change. Knowing her for this long, she might freak. But she'd also work her ass off to get it done in time. Which I admired about her.

"Right," he said, looking down at his watch.

"Am I the only one who's excited to see playboy bunnies? I mean really?" Micheal exclaimed. I chuckled to myself, the type of chuckle when you're trying to keep yourself from losing it.

"Get out of my goddamn seat, Micheal," I managed to say.

"And for a second there, I thought you were actually laughing," he said as he rose from my chair.

"Pick up my damn clothes," I demanded, pointing at the shirts thrown over the couch. Aaron chuckled as he watched Micheal pick up my shirts and fold them with a scowl on his face.

"Katherine, I have news," I said to myself, practicing before picking up the phone and dialing her number. "Katherine, unfortunately, I have some news you might not like." Hm, no, that'd make her think it was the worst news. "Katherine, I—"

"Katherine, I'm obsessed with you," Aaron said, strolling into my office without knocking. He was just at my office yesterday with Micheal. I didn't know why he kept coming around.

"I am not. She's my colleague, and we're business partners at the moment, if you will." Business partner—nothing sounded so disturbing coming out of my mouth. We were anything but that —we were more. That kiss with Katherine proved it. There was no way it could have been one-sided.

However, I wasn't going to let Aaron know of this kiss. It wasn't that I didn't trust him—I did, more than anyone—but I couldn't let him know how I felt about Katherine when he walked into my office acting like a child. It didn't matter how old Aaron was; if he saw the opportunity to sing 'kissing in a tree' to piss me off, he'd do it.

"Yeah, okay," he simply said as he took a seat. It was like my office was slowly turning into a hangout spot for these guys. How the hell did I make it stop?

"Can I help you?" I asked in an irritated tone.

"No, but maybe I can help you," he said with much confidence. I knew that look he was giving me. He was up to something.

"Okay..." I said as I waited for his explanation.

"I know you moved Katherine's deadline a month earlier." *Yeah, no shit.* "That seemed to piss off our *dear* uncle, which pushed him to cut his deadline short as well." I didn't like where this was headed. "Word in the office is he's planning to set up a book launch and book signing event at the Barnes and Noble located at 105 Fifth Avenue."

"And you want me to secure that spot before he does," I summarized as Aaron nodded in approval.

"Excellent idea brother." He smiled. I wouldn't have jumped on the opportunity Aaron had just granted me if it weren't for Edward trying to steal my Los Angeles event. Now, it was payback and two could play at this game. Only one could win, and with Aaron on my side, I knew it would be me.

"I'll send an email to schedule the date," which would be four months from now, "right after I make this call," I said. Aaron spared me a knowing look as he left the room. I could only set the date if I knew my author was on board with the new deadline. I couldn't release it unfinished.

I stared at the phone, contemplating how I should break the news to her. After a few seconds, I got irritated with myself for acting like a nervous teenager calling the most popular girl in school to ask her on a date. I was her boss. She was obligated to do anything I said.

I shook my head and picked up the phone. I dialed her

number on the keypad with a vigorous grip on the phone. The line rang for a few beats before a woman answered. "Hello?"

The woman's voice was light and airy, but not as soft and delicate as Katherine's. I instantly knew it wasn't her.

"Hello, I'm trying to reach Katherine. Is she around?" I asked, waiting for her to pass me over to Katherine.

"Yeah... she's a bit busy with balloons right now. I can take a message," she said, sounding distracted. She's busy with balloons...? What could she be doing that involved balloons? I was about to demand she pass the phone to Katherine, instead I cleared my throat before answering.

"Yes, tell her that her publisher has some news regarding her current deadline. I'll be waiting for her call," I clarified, anxiously tapping my finger on my desk.

"Her publisher... yeah, I'll be sure to tell her," she said, sounding amused by my call. Like she knew something I didn't or something she wasn't supposed to know. My guess was if she was close with Katherine, she knew about the kiss. I wondered if Katherine thought I didn't enjoy the kiss after how I left things.

Of course, I liked it. I more than liked it. I was extremely close to ripping the clothes off her body, spreading her legs, and taking her right there on the dresser. I truly had no clue how I was able to leave, but I pulled away with every ounce of strength I had in my body.

I wanted nothing more than to have my hands roaming all over her as she shivered under my touch, begging for more. But the sound of my belt getting unbuckled sprung the tiniest amount of common sense I had. I realized that she would most likely regret that night with how upset she was with me. I didn't want her to feel taken advantage of.

Also, the fact that I happened to be her publisher and boss. Though, slowly, without me realizing it, that didn't seem like a big enough reason to stay away from her.

"Thank you," I said before hearing the line disconnect.

CHAPTER 22
KATHERINE

Celeste and I had spent the last two hours getting ready for the Halloween party tonight. We finished the preparations for it yesterday. I'd never tied as many balloons as I had yesterday, and I had calluses on my fingers to prove it.

"Can you tie the lacing on my corset?" Celeste asked me while holding it to her chest. "And tie it tight. I mean it. I don't want to breathe with this on." She stood in front of a mirror, handing me the laces.

"You sure?" I asked, knowing that she'd ask me to loosen it later. She met my gaze in the mirror and pulled her hair up.

"Yes. Now pull like your life depends on it."

"Okay..." I began to lace her corset downwards, alternating the sides until I reached her waistline. "Alright, this is where you're going to want to breathe in," I warned, gathering every bit of my strength to pull. Celeste took a deep breath, as if she was going to be underwater for longer than five minutes.

With a few harsh pulls, I managed to make her waist appear like an unrealistic hourglass. I doubted she'd go the whole night like this. "Perfecto," she said, satisfied, as she checked herself in the mirror. I still had to put on my costume, though I pushed it to be the very last step.

"Need me to help you with yours?" Celeste asked, grabbing my white dress from the bed. We only had about half an hour left to get ready, and if we wanted to get there early, I'd have to be ready now. I gave her a quick nod, fitting into my dress.

I turned to face the mirror, pulling my hair out of the way for her to zip me up. "There. Perfect." She emphasized 'perfect', wanting to give me confidence. I looked at my reflection, stunned by the final product of everything together. Hair, makeup, dress, shoes. I looked like a brand-new person.

A person who was confident in herself, who was worthy.

My hair had been styled in loose curls that fell to my waist, and I had worn a shimmery nude eyeshadow for a natural, radiant look. I added the tiniest bit of glitter to my eyelids and cheekbones for a more 'angelic' look. I paired it with a bright pink lipstick, a color I tended to shy away from. Only because I never thought it paired well with my complexion, but Celeste thought otherwise.

"We are so ready for tonight! I cannot wait for you to meet your bachelors!" Celeste exclaimed, placing both her hands on my shoulders. "I'll be your wing woman." I felt nauseous. I hadn't flirted or been 'in the game' for such a long time. I was afraid I'd lost my touch, if I ever even had it...

I was young. This should have been exciting for me, but instead, it was completely terrifying. I smiled at Celeste as she walked out of the room. "I'll be waiting outside," she told me. I turned to face the girl in the mirror one last time before leaving. To remind myself that this Katherine was completely different from the Katherine I was used to.

I joined Celeste outside, my heart pounding at the realization that I was really doing this. Finally putting myself out there. To fend for myself...

We started walking toward Avenue, as it was only half a mile away from where Celeste lived. Which was why it was so easy for her to work every night till late. No one in their right minds would take her job, working as late as she did, if they lived far.

It was New York City. If you had a car, parking was a pain. If you didn't have a car, the subway was a pain. Walking when you lived close by was an advantage; it saved you from having to pick one of those options.

"You seem quiet. What's on your mind?" Celeste asked, bringing me back to earth.

"Just thinking. I don't really know what to expect from tonight," I admitted, looking at the building lights instead of Celeste.

"Well, expect some fun. Maybe even a fling. You know, live a little on the wild side." Celeste had *lived* her life more than anyone else I knew. She knew everything about living on the wild side; making every time a good time. It was one of the things I admired most about her. Her bravery, her confidence to grab life by the ear and direct it to where she wanted it to go.

"Yeah, you're right. It's all new to me." I gave her a timid smile as she put her arm through mine, directing me to the right.

"I am always right," she said with a smirk on her face.

"Eh, I wouldn't say *always*, but I'll give you this one."

We made a turn at the corner and were greeted by bright red neon lights spelling the word 'Avenue' in all capital letters. They had set up a gigantic 'Halloween Party' poster with a green hand gripping a glass of martini. Security was set up beside it, only letting people in who were on the list.

Avenue was always so popular for their parties and events. Which explained why they always had endless lines of people wanting to get in, like the one Celeste and I stood behind. "Come on, we're skipping," she said, grabbing my hand and steering me through a crowd of angry people.

"Celeste Castaño and Katherine Trujillo. We're on the list," she told the security guard, who seemed to be in a bad mood. He scrolled through the list on the tablet, and Celeste tried to take a peek at it. He noticed, moving the tablet out of Celeste's eyeshot. "Oh, come on, Lev. I can find those names faster than you can."

He looked up at Celeste, rolling his eyes. "Just go," he said, unhooking the red velvet rope to let us pass.

"Thanks, Lev, you're the best. Even though our names were on the list," she cooed at him, making him blush. Celeste always had a knack for making the grumpiest men nervous.

"You truly are something," I said to her as we walked into the club. She turned back to smile at me for a brief second. The music got louder with every step we took, getting deeper in. The entire venue was decorated in a spooky theme—dark purple and green lights, skulls placed at every table, and spiderwebs spread over the bar.

I felt pleased with the outcome. The hours spent setting everything up were worth it. "Do you want a drink?" Celeste yelled over the loud music.

"What?" I yelled back, unable to hear her. She lifted a finger as a gesture for me to stay put. She walked away, leaving me alone on the dance floor. I was not a person who willingly got on the dance floor on her own, yet I didn't make the effort to get off.

Suddenly, all the hairs on my neck stood on end. It was as if my body knew something I didn't. A hand settled on my right hip so effortlessly, like it always belonged there. "I see you've taken my nickname to heart, angel." A rough voice spoke in my ear.

I would know that voice anywhere. It was the only voice that made me feel on edge. The one that made me feel all hot and flustered. I turned to find Adam dressed in all black, with fake blood stained on the left side of his bottom lip. His eyes filled with desire.

His eyes shifted from my dress to the halo placed on my head. "This costume suits you," he said, reaching to fix a strand of my hair. A small gesture that could leave one panting on their knees. "Though I'm convinced this isn't *just* a costume."

He ran his hands up to my ribcage, wanting to get a feel of the material of the dress, of me. The memory of his lips on mine became clearer than water. But not as clear as the memory of him leaving, not saying a single word until he returned. Thinking I was asleep.

It was easy to guess his costume, and it happened to be an incredibly hot one. A vampire. Ironic with mine being an angel. A perfect representation of us, and our relationship... Or situationship.

An angel getting tricked and dragged into temptation by the devil himself. A devil with the face of an angel.

"I didn't wear this because of your 'nickname' for me. I'm here with a friend. It's a duo costume," I claimed, wanting to prove him wrong.

"Is that so? What a shame. I was *very* satisfied with the thought," he said, making me nervous. But tonight, this Katherine didn't feel timid, she felt confident.

"Yes, it is a shame. Now, if you could excuse me, I have my friend waiting at the bar," I lied, but I was desperate to leave before I made a fool out of myself. Before my body could betray my mind.

Adam didn't skip a beat to move out of the way. I quickly walked past him to reach Celeste. I could feel his gaze burning a hole in my back as I left. "What's taking so long? You left me there waiting for forever," I said to her, still unhinged by my encounter with Adam.

"Girl, I wasn't gone for longer than five minutes." I looked down at my phone and realized she left me four minutes ago. Talking with Adam felt longer than four minutes. It felt like a lifetime with his hands on my bare skin.

"Right, sorry." Celeste looked confused.

"Anyway, you remember how I told you I have a list of candidates?" she said, looking back at the dance floor.

"How could I forget?" I replied sarcastically, feeling unsettled by this arrangement.

"Candidate one and two are on the dance floor as we speak. I think you should go and introduce yourself. Or wait for them to strike up a conversation. They will, after seeing you." She sounded sure of it. But the thought seemed so unusual to me. "Cowboy and Top Gun guy," she clarified, pointing them out for me.

"How do you know them?" I asked, trying to distract her from pushing me toward them.

"I don't, but they come here often," she said, giving me a look. She slowly seems to be catching on to me. "Served them a drink or two."

"You know what? I think I'm going to—" Celeste cut me off.

"Oh, no you don't. Take this, drink this, and go," she ordered, handing me a lime and a shot of tequila. She grabbed the other shot glass from the bar. "Pa' arriba, pa' abajo, pa' centro, pa' dentro," she toasted, shooting the drink down her throat. I stared, unable to take it like her.

"Dale, drink!" *Go on, drink!* she exclaimed. I quickly shot the glass back, the liquid burning its way down my throat. An itching sensation, making my throat completely dry, leaving me in need of some water. I started to cough aggressively, a clear sign that I hadn't drunk straight tequila in forever. Not since my twenty-first birthday, which was planned by Celeste.

I was not someone who liked to drink. I'd rather have coffee or hot chocolate. I was also not one to party. I would rather be in a coffee shop or a bookstore, writing. I loved to travel, but not to places that were dangerous. I lived life comfortably, not wildly. And that was the problem. It was not actually *living*.

I slammed the empty glass on the counter and made my way to 'Top Gun' guy. I felt committed to introducing myself and doing it the right way. Preferably before my senses kicked back in. I stopped only inches away from the man on the dance floor and poked his left shoulder.

"Hey, I'm Katherine," I said to him as he turned to face me. Getting a good look at him, I saw how charming he was, how handsome. His brunette hair and the brown eyes hidden behind his glasses seemed anything but ordinary.

"Dylan Cruz," he said, putting out his hand for me to shake. I grabbed it and was quickly disappointed that it didn't make me feel anything. Not one spark, not a flicker, nothing. Not even close to what I felt when my body sensed Adam's presence.

"That's a first," he said, pulling me from my thoughts.

"What?" I spoke. He had caught me off guard.

"That a woman looks at me and seems disappointed. It's a first," he explained. I felt terrible. I hadn't been focused on my expressions. I opened my mouth to try to explain, but he cut me off. "It's okay. I haven't felt excited over anyone since..." He paused, like he didn't want to share much. "Since a while."

I simply nodded, not wanting to get deep into this 'I'm lonely' conversation. Which, by the look of him, I doubt would ever happen. He didn't seem like the 'talk about our feelings' kind of guy, like Adam.

There I went again. Comparing a perfectly attractive man, that I was supposed to get to know, with the only man that seemed to be living rent free in my mind. I couldn't seem to shake him off, and that was all I wanted for tonight. To let loose.

And yet, I was all tied up in his ropes.

The music was pounding in my ears, and I thought Dylan and I were using it as an excuse to not speak to each other. I looked over at Celeste, who seemed to be observing all of this from a distance. I gave her a swift head shake to tell her, 'It's not going well.'

"I don't expect anything from you, but perhaps we can make the most of this and enjoy the night," Dylan suggested in a surprisingly gentle voice. And I guessed he was right. It was the least we could do. Dancing to some music wouldn't hurt anyone, and it was better than slouching off to some dark corner in the club alone.

"I'd like that," I said. Dylan seemed like a sweet guy under the 'hard' exterior he put up. I moved to the light music playing in the background and caught a glimpse of Celeste's smile.

Before I knew it, Celeste was joining us on the dance floor. Having her next to me allowed me to loosen up to the beat. She grabbed my arms and twirled me around; I did the same until she bumped into a guy wearing a 'Joker' costume.

"Watch it," she growled at him, which only made him chuckle. He didn't seem bothered that she whipped out her claws at him, instead he seemed amused.

"You're the one who bumped into me," he said with a charming smile, but Celeste didn't back down.

"Didn't your parents teach you to stay away from the devil?" she replied. She seemed incredibly annoyed with this man. Dylan and I stood back to watch the entire thing unfold.

"Yeah, but I've always been a sinful child. Maybe you can help me with that?" he teased, moving closer to her.

"Go to hell," she snarled at him.

"Only if you're there. Then I'll go happily." He winked at her. She looked fed up with him at this point before turning to look me in the eye and signaling her 'I'm going to the bathroom' look. She walked away without looking back.

"Who was that?" he asked us, with a huge smile plastered on his face. Dylan shook his head.

"That's my friend, Celeste," I clarified.

"Easy, Micheal. I don't think that's a smart choice," Dylan said to his friend.

"Yeah, but I fucking love the game," he replied, not taking his eyes off Celeste. When she made it out of his eyeshot, he looked around until his gaze settled on someone else. "Dude! You made it."

"You didn't give me much of a choice, did you?" A warm, familiar voice spoke. "Cruz, was it?" Adam said, with a bit of venom in his words. Dylan spared him a firm nod before trailing his eyes to where Adam's sight rested.

Dylan had been gently holding my wrist, from when he helped me catch my balance after twirling so much with Celeste. Looking at Adam's face, I could tell it bothered him.

"Your hands. Off," he demanded without much context. Dylan didn't wait for him to say anything else. He grinned, yet carefully let go and stepped back with his hands up in the air, playfully surrendering. Micheal just laughed at Adam's reaction.

"What are you doing?" I whisper-shouted, confused and displeased with him. He moved and took Dylan's place, only stepping a bit closer to me than he was. His hands fell to my waist and slowly lured me into him.

"Come with me," he spoke softly in my ear, his breath hot. I despised how it sent shivers down my spine, but I mostly despised how I couldn't say no to him.

"I came with a friend. I can't just leave her," I said as a defense. It was the only thing tying me to this spot, to this dance floor. He dropped his head to my shoulder and took a whiff. I could feel his nose trailing down my neck. God, if I had a few butterflies before, I had a swarm of them now.

"Then send her a quick text. Tell her you're not feeling well," he said, gently brushing his lips over my collarbone. I tried to reject him, but how could I when my body was pushing me to him? I couldn't. So, I said something that might get him and me in a load of trouble.

"Okay." The next second, he was pulling me off the dance floor and to a nearby hallway where the bathrooms were.

I wasn't sure if it was the fact I was sneaking off with him, or the feeling of *needing* him, that was causing adrenaline to pump through my veins. His grip on my hand was solid, the music getting lower, muffled, as we walked deeper into this hallway.

He swung the bathroom door open and pulled me in. He slammed me against the wall and shut the door, locking it. "I don't know what stunt you're trying to pull, but it's pissing me off," he said through his teeth.

I was displayed against the wall, panting, begging for his hands to be on me. "But Dylan Cruz? He can't give you what you want. What you need," he said, closing the space between us. His face was only inches from mine.

"And you know what I want?" I said to him, wanting to get some type of reaction from him. He seemed challenged by it as he placed a hand on the wall, caging me in.

"I know what you need," he said. I swallowed hard, unsure if I should challenge him further.

"Right." I rolled my eyes, calling his bluff.

"Right," he repeated before crashing his lips onto mine. The same tingling feeling I had the first time was back, but with a vengeance. He wrapped his hand around my neck as he bit my lip. I shamelessly moaned into his mouth, desperate for more.

He slipped a hand between us and gripped my right thigh. I leaned into his touch, consuming the warmth of his body. I gripped his shirt in my palm, pulling him closer. He chuckled against my lips. He dragged his hand to my inner thigh and gently spread them apart.

"If I check, will I find you soaked for me?" he asked, knowing the effect he had on me. I stayed quiet, unable to answer his question, but the answer was obvious. So damn obvious.

He pulled my panties to the side and swiped his fingers along my wet folds, proving his point. He grinned as he looked deep into my eyes. "Just what I thought. A hot, wet mess, just for me," he said, his voice hoarse.

He rubbed his thumb in a circular motion against my clit, applying the right amount of pressure. I squirmed underneath his touch, bucking my hips toward him. "Such a needy cunt." His rough words drew a moan from my mouth.

He moved his thumb and slipped a finger inside me, curving it at a perfect angle. I'd been pleasuring myself for the past few years, but it never felt as good, as full, as when Adam touched me. "Not enough?" he teased before adding another finger.

"God," I moaned, unable to take the torture. He looked entertained by this, like he was getting off on teasing me. He leaned closer to me, dipping his head to my ear.

"I don't know what you need, right?" he whispered, pulling his fingers out. I was left feeling empty, eager for more.

"Please," I begged, needing to ride my orgasm out.

"Please, what?" he rasped, driving me crazy. "Use your words, angel," he added, flicking the halo over my head.

"Please, make me come," I groaned, suddenly not caring about how desperate I sounded. I wanted more, needed more. I could feel him smile beside my ear before shoving three fingers inside me, completely filling me. "Yes, God, yes," I screamed as he worked me in a rhythm. I rode his hand, chasing my release.

I shut my eyes, almost at my breaking point. "Open your eyes," he ordered aggressively. "I want you to see who's making you come. Whose hand you're riding. Whose hand you're dripping all over." I opened my eyelids, stuck in a hazy mist.

"Tell me, whose hand is it that your cunt is clenching around?" I bit my lip, unable to answer. "Whose, Katherine?" His voice was dark, filled with need.

"Y-yours, Adam," I half moaned. I was so close; I could rip apart right here.

"That's right. Now come on my hand," he said, and that was all it took for me to tear apart. For a minute, everything around me disappeared. It was just him and me. It took me a while to come down from my high, my sight clearing up. His green eyes were glued to my face, reading and studying every movement I made.

Adam stepped back with a smug look, bringing me back to my senses. "You were saying?" he asked, clearly tormenting me. I rolled my eyes as I lowered my dress to cover what he had already touched, seen, claimed.

With shaky legs, I tried to open the door to leave. He covered my hand with his, slightly turning me back to him. "What do you think you're doing?" he asked. My breath hiked at the sudden interaction.

"Leaving," I scowled, embarrassed that he had me pressed up against a wall, a whimpering, shaking mess for him.

"With me. I'll drive you home," he added, as if I had no other choice but to accept.

"I'm fine, I'll walk," I said, avoiding his gaze. I couldn't look him in the eye much longer.

"The hell you will. Don't make me carry you to the car, Katherine. You know I will." I could tell he was serious. And I also knew it would be stupid to call his bluff once again. I pressed my lips together, accepting my fate.

"Fine," I spoke. He opened the door for me to walk out and followed behind me.

CHAPTER 23

ADAM

I escorted Katherine out of Avenue, feeling satisfied with myself after the interaction I had with her in the bathroom. Satisfied that, for once, I had her speechless, without another smart word coming out of her mouth. Watching her come apart for me while riding my hand tortured me. The bulge in my pants begged for attention, but that was about Katherine; about making her feel good, giving her what she needed.

Even though she might not have wanted to admit it, what she needed was *me*. I watched her hips sway as she walked in front of me, and a smile touched my lips at the memory of my hand slipping under that dress.

I respected her request when she wanted to walk away from me, but I wasn't going to stand back and watch Cruz hit on her. Her body language was different with him than it was with me. It was why I had felt bold enough to march over there and claim her away.

Regardless, I would have, anyway.

She wouldn't even look at me. She was quiet and closed off, stuck in her own head. I wondered if she felt embarrassed or ashamed. A woman like Katherine shouldn't feel ashamed to get an orgasm from a man; it was a need. I could tell this wasn't her sort of thing.

I watched her shiver as we both stood outside, waiting for Henry to arrive.

"Are you cold?" I asked, unsure of how I'd warm her up if she said yes. I didn't have a jacket on me; this party was supposed to be a quick stop. But after seeing Katherine in her costume, I refused to leave without her. I notified Henry that I was going to stay until later.

"No," she responded, continuing to avoid eye contact.

"But you're shivering," I said, taking a few steps closer to her. She hummed in response. I got the impression that Katherine didn't want me around right now, but I wasn't going to leave her behind. No matter how much she'd hate me for it.

I figured she'd get over it after a few minutes. I'd step back and give her some space. I texted Henry to hurry the fuck up so she could get in the car and warm up. After pressing send, the car pulled in.

I motioned toward the door and opened it for her. She carefully slid in, steering clear of making physical contact, as if I didn't just have my fingers shoved deep inside her. What would be the difference if her shoulder grazed mine? But I didn't call her out on it. I knew it would only make things worse.

I slammed the door shut behind me and watched Katherine squish herself against the opposite door from mine. "If you push any further, you'll fall out of the car," I joked, trying to cheer up the mood. She crossed her arms, completely ignoring me.

This would be a fun ride.

Silence filled the space. I knew I should feel some type of remorse or regret over what I had just done, but I didn't. I kept waiting for it to kick in, but nothing. As I continued to fight for my position as CEO, this should throw me off. It should mess with my head, but the only thing that messed with me was the thought of Katherine feeling any type of regret.

As long as no one knew about this, it should be fine. I was aware that tomorrow morning, or the next meeting I had with Katherine, would be... interesting, to say the least.

"I know you don't want to speak to me, and it's understandable," I spoke, my voice roaming around the quiet vehicle. "But we need to speak about your deadline, preferably tomorrow. If you can," I carefully suggested. Katherine was like a butterfly, beautiful but easily scared off. If I was not careful, I might not be able to catch her.

"Okay," she softly said. The smallest bit of relief hit me as she spoke that one word to me. She slowly turned her head to look at me. She looked tired, like she was too deep in her head. Overthinking was killing her with exhaustion.

"Get your rest tonight," I said as we parked in front of her building. I climbed out of the car to open the door for her. "And angel," I called out. She looked up at me with those big, whiskey golden eyes. "Don't think too much about tonight."

She gave me a small smile as she got out of the car and walked past me. I watched as she made her way through the double doors, savoring the way she looked in that white dress. I was aware she wore that costume for her friend, but a part of me wanted to believe that it was for me.

The next morning, I sat in my office waiting for Katherine to come in. Today was the day I'd break the news to her. I wasn't sure how she'd take it, but I expected she'd take it as a challenge to overcome. She was determined when it came to her writing, so I wasn't worried.

A knock on the door caught me by surprise, and I yearned for it to be Katherine. "Come in." I spoke as I straightened my posture before she came in.

"How was the party?" Aaron greeted with a knowing grin.

He bailed on me last night, leaving me to show up for the both of us. I should have known that I'd need to drag him in myself. But, because of Katherine, he didn't cross my mind once. He was lucky.

"Fine," I barked out, as the memory of Katherine passed through my mind. I spent the entire night replaying the memory in my head. I also had a very long date with my right-hand last night while chanting Katherine's name under my breath. It wasn't close to the warm wet walls that clenched my fingers so perfectly.

Not close to the sweet sounds that fell from her lips, her plush full lips. If she felt that good wrapped around my fingers, I could only imagine how addicting it would feel to have her wrapped around my—

"Hey, you must admit… one Pearson is just as good as two. Especially if that Pearson is you," Aaron interrupted my thoughts. He wasn't wrong. Having me show up was enough for the both of us. I was running for CEO, and he'd be CFO. He was the younger, more reckless Pearson, just as I was the older, more responsible, 'stick up the ass' Pearson, as my brother liked to call it.

"I don't care if it's 'just' as good. I was expecting you to come with me." That wasn't exactly a lie. I was expecting him for the first five minutes. Then I wasn't.

"Hmm. Can't expect me to hold your hand, can you?" He shrugged me off, not taking my words seriously. "Did you finalize the event at the Barnes and Noble?" he asked as he adjusted his jacket.

"I have. It's set for the month of January." I hadn't picked an exact date. My writer wasn't exactly aware of the change. Again, a conversation that must happen today.

"You secured the entire month to pick out any date?" Aaron quirked a brow at me, as if he was impressed with my choice of locking the location down. I did it for Katherine, but I also loved the fact that it would greatly affect my uncle. It was his problem to find a better place and time now.

"Of course. I have the money and power to do so. Why wouldn't I?" I answered, standing from my chair and looking out at the view that lay behind my desk. He sighed, knowing me better than I knew myself.

A soft knock grabbed our attention, and I turned quicker than I thought I could. Aaron looked entertained by how rapid my reactions were to the one woman who seemed to drive me crazy. The one woman who I hadn't been able to forget. The one woman I saw every time I ripped apart. The one woman who was my client, and a client who I had important information for.

"I'll get it. I was about to leave regardless," he said as he strode toward the door. "Ms. Trujillo, pleasure to see you, as always," he cooed as he swung the wooden door wider. My jaw unhinged at how he purposely flirted with my client. He spun his head over to me and winked.

Did I mention I wanted to kill my younger brother?

"Hi, Aaron, good to see you, too." She gracefully stepped into the room. I swear, gravity pulled in her favor. "Hi," she quickly said, shy to face me. She wore a simple pair of jeans that hugged her thighs and her round, tight ass. Those jeans had the power to make a man jealous.

"Katherine, how was your night?" I greeted, ready to get into it. The conversation, that is. My mind was messing with me this morning.

"It was fine. Thank you for asking." Her head tipped down to her black boots. "Let's talk about the deadline." Right there and then, I decided that this conversation wasn't going to work in my office. We needed air, somewhere to walk, a view to look at. That way, she wouldn't need to keep looking down at the floor.

"Yes, but I was thinking, perhaps, we could take a walk and talk down Central Park. It's right across the street, if you're up for it." She released some tension from her shoulders.

"That sounds nice," she said, finally making proper eye contact with me. We were getting somewhere. I normally didn't give a fuck whether a client was uncomfortable in my office. I cared about the work getting done. But Katherine, she wasn't just a client anymore. Not to me.

We made our way down to the lobby and walked out the double doors. I was pleased with my choice as the fresh air hit my lungs. Walking along the sidewalk, I pulled her to the inside, away from the street. "Do you regularly take walks?" She finally broke the silence.

"It's New York, Katherine. Everyone walks." I knew what she meant, but I wanted to mess with her first. Steer away from being so damn serious all the time.

"You know what I mean. Like... to seek peace, or to relax? Catch a breath?" she explained, terribly missing the part where I was playing around with her.

"I know what you mean, angel. That's why we're doing this." I placed a hand on her waist and directed her toward the park across the street. October was coming to an end, leaving November to come next. The cold was setting in, but it was manageable to take a stroll. "And yes, I do take walks regularly."

"I love walking. I do it even when I don't need to." I could tell with her thighs being perfectly toned, and that wasn't a feature one casually had. "I think this has to be my favorite time to walk Central Park, other than winter." I agreed with her—except for winter. I hated the fucking cold. But now, the trees had red, orange, and green leaves falling and flowing everywhere. The air was crisp and sweet, breathing it in was refreshing.

"Listen, Katherine, about your deadline..." God, I dreaded telling her I had changed it because my uncle got the best of me. I wanted to see him lose and suffer without it affecting Katherine and her flow. "I had a meeting with the board, and with the deadline coming closer, I moved it a month earlier. Instead of it being February, it's now January. We could move it to the end of the month if you'd like. I figured a month wouldn't be much of a difference."

Katherine stayed quiet longer than I'd like her to be. I allowed her to process it. "I know it's sudden—"

"Yes, it is," she snapped.

Crap, she was not happy with this. I knew she wouldn't be. It wasn't like I was waiting for her to jump on me with happiness. Katherine shook her head, unsettled by the news. Right as I expected for her to burst out in complaint, we passed by the best hotdog cart in all of Manhattan.

I didn't think twice before heading toward the cart with the blue and yellow umbrella covering it. Why was it that all the carts with the best treats in New York had umbrellas in those two colors? It was like a national flag of 'best food in the city'. Katherine eyed me as if she couldn't believe I'd stop for this.

"Would you like one?" I tipped my head toward the large menu, with only three types of hotdogs.

"Wha—Are you seriously asking me if I want a hot dog right now?!" she exclaimed, her anger finally rising from the ashes. About time; I was missing this side of Katherine. Her spunk, her fire. What could I say? I was a sucker who liked to get burned. Mostly because I usually did the burning.

"Suit yourself," was all I said as I handed the man behind the cart five bucks. "Keep the change," I added, standing back to watch this mouthwatering treat be made. I caught Katherine from the side of my eye, gushing over the food. She might've not wanted it at first, but once the smell hit her nose, once she watched how they assembled it... I could tell that it changed her mind.

"You're positive you don't want one?" The man handed me my hotdog, and Katherine just stared at it. Ignoring my question. She wasn't fighting me anymore; she was focused on what I had in my hand. "You want a taste?"

"I... I suppose one bite wouldn't be bad..." she convinced

herself. I lifted the hotdog to her lips, and she opened her mouth, allowing me to feed it to her. Her mouth wrapped around the end of the hotdog, and it brought dirty thoughts to my mind. She took a bite and pulled back.

Her eyes were closed as she savored the taste, a small moan of satisfaction humming in her throat. Which didn't help the boner I already had. She opened her eyes to find me staring at her. When she shyly looked away from me, I cleared my throat.

"Good?" She nodded. I noticed the bit of ketchup she had on her chin and unconsciously reached to wipe it off. Electricity hit my fingertips as I accidentally touched her bottom lip. "You had a little something—" I focused on cleaning her up, "there."

Her cheeks flushed with a pretty pink. "Thanks," she stuttered, looking into my eyes. Her amber eyes matched the scenery, the colors plastered all over the concrete and grass. I didn't make the effort to move away from her; I stayed. I craved this—her.

I'd never been a fan of the color gold. I never liked how sweet honey tasted on my tongue. But her eyes; those beautiful, otherworldly creations made me think otherwise. They were sunlight and honey. They were raw and lovely; they could never tell a lie. They were the sunshine heating the dark, twisted world. They were everything.

"You know what? I think I will take a hotdog. I deserve it after the shitty news you gave me. Gotta give a writer something to look forward to, no?" I snapped out of my trance, recovering from the way her eyes held capture of me.

"That is the first time I've heard you curse," I called out, signaling the hotdog man to whip me up another one. Katherine giggled under her breath.

"Yeah, well, there was a lot more where that came from."

"Please, don't stop on my account." Katherine playfully rolled her eyes, already switching to a better mood. There was a striking difference in how my energy flipped from exhaustion to completely feeling recharged while being with Katherine. There was something about her that powered me up for the troubles to come. It was absurdly crucial. It was like she was my battery supply.

I shook the thought off once Katherine received her hotdog. We continued strolling through Central Park while stuffing our mouths in silence. She might not be saying a word to me right now, but I knew she felt more at ease. More open to what I had to suggest.

"What do you say? Can you take on the new time frame?" Reading what Katherine had so far showed her perseverance. It showed that if a writer could take on this sudden change, it would be her. Though, I wasn't one to push if the other wasn't willing to push back.

She took a moment to herself before answering me, looking out at the views. "I can try." She sighed, and that was all I needed to hear. Many would shy away from this or completely drop the entire contract, which would cost them. But not Katherine. No, she stuck around because it was what she wanted. She was hungry for her dream, and I could cook her a five-star meal that would satisfy that hunger.

"And you'll succeed."

CHAPTER 24

KATHERINE

I stared at the blank white screen, impotent to write. All because my deadline happened to be cut a month short. I repeatedly read the chapters I'd written, hoping they would spark some type of idea that could complete the story.

Just as I expected, nothing came to mind. No one talked about how difficult it was to write once you got to the middle of the story. There was the beginning, that always seems to be the easiest for me, the middle, and then the end. Which ran much smoother once the middle was complete. But, for me, I was still here. Stuck.

I hadn't written since last week. I convinced myself that it was for 'planning'. Now, I couldn't use that as an excuse. It was the first of November, which left me about two months, and it was taking everything in me to not freak out. The best way to go on with this was to be calm, but it was tough.

As my professor in college used to say, 'You must stay drunk on writing to stop reality from interfering. If you stop writing for one day, you will know. If you stop writing for two days, your critics will know. And if you stop writing for three days, your audience will know. Therefore, if you do not write every day, you might feel like you want to die, or go crazy, or both.' It was the one thing that had really stuck with me. Everyone says you take one thing from college with you, and for me, that was it.

Knowing I hadn't touched my keyboard this long bothered me. I couldn't help but feel like I was slowly letting my dream slip from my fingers. I reached for my keyboard and began to type without really knowing where it was headed.

"Okay, Katherine, focus," I said to myself as I placed the palm of my hand across my face. God, I needed to have something written by now—anything. I was dangerously close to throwing my computer out the window until I heard a key being jammed in the lock.

I stood from my chair and made my way toward the door to look through the peephole. As I rose on my tiptoes, I found Elaina quickly losing her patience, with someone behind her who looked an awful lot like Valery. I unlocked the door and Elaina pushed it open.

"Finally! I thought it would never open," Elaina shouted in frustration, as if she were the one who got it open. She stepped into our apartment with a beautiful Asian girl, with shiny straight black hair, holding a suitcase. Her features were flawless and poise—the one and only Valery.

"Valery!" I shouted, throwing my hands up to give her a massive hug. "You're back! From Barcelona... how did you even manage to come so soon?" I asked her as I suffocated her with my bear hug.

"I know. It's quite funny if you think about it. I was about to spend Thanksgiving break over there, but my parents gifted me a ticket to New York. They could no longer deal with my calls about how much I missed my girls," she explained in her elegant British accent.

Her accent didn't do her justice over the phone like it did in person. It was like being caressed by the softest feather. We hadn't seen Valery in months, since she left to go to culinary school. Of course, we were all proud of her, but we missed her like crazy. Every hangout felt like something was missing.

"You didn't tell me she was coming!" I swung toward Elaina, who watched us from a distance with a smile planted on her face.

"Well, I wanted to surprise you girls. And I had to choose the one person who could keep a secret," Valery explained as she put her suitcase down.

"I had sworn to secrecy. Plus, I knew it would be a great surprise. I called Celeste to come over for drinks tonight." Elaina reached for cups in our kitchen cabinet.

"How long ago did you call her?" I asked, taking a seat at one of our bar stools. Valery took a seat beside me. "And what time did she say she was coming?" We watched Elaina fill the glasses with water before handing them to us. Right as she opened her mouth, a knock on the door stopped her.

"Right about now." She smirked as she headed to the door to let Celeste in. The door swung open to reveal Celeste with her curly hair tied up in a messy bun. She wore her 'work' overalls, which were covered in paint, proving she was coming from the studio.

It took her a moment before she realized who was sitting on the bar stool beside me. Her eyes looked over her, then to me, then quickly back to Valery. "Shut the fuck up!" she yelled as she ran to us. "Oh my god! Valery!" She jumped on Valery, throwing her on the floor along with her.

They both laughed as Elaina and I looked at them. After a few seconds, they both got up from the floor. "What are you doing here? I mean, we love it that you're here, but how?" she asked.

"I couldn't leave my girls to cook for themselves for Thanksgiving, could I?" Valery answered, leaving all of us beyond grateful for her presence. We seriously did not have a clue how we were going to deal with Thanksgiving without our chef this year. Probably some takeout that wouldn't come as close to Valery's cooking.

"Oh, thank God! I'm going to eat like a pig again this year!" Celeste exclaimed. We all looked at her with a disbelieving glance. "Okay, fine. I would have still eaten like a pig. But at least I'll be a happy pig." She shrugged as she lifted herself onto our kitchen counter.

"So, since I'm here. I'd love for you guys to fill me in." Valery positioned herself in an elegant stance. Valery came from money; she was the image of grace in everything she did.

"I would love to go first, but my life is pretty much as plain as it gets," Celeste said.

"Nothing is plain with you. I mean, look at you." Elaina motioned toward her clothes.

"You know what I mean. You start."

"Well, I've been trying to make EStyle work. My trip to Miami didn't go as planned, but I'm sure something will pop up. It has to." EStyle was the company Elaina was trying to open. She created it to dress celebrities and important people for grand events. Kind of like those stylists that people turn to when they go to the Golden Globes.

"Oh, Elaina. I'm sorry, maybe it wasn't meant to be. Maybe it's because you have something greater waiting for you," she prompted her with a small smile.

"What about you?" Valery looked at me. I could already feel Celeste grinning from across the kitchen.

"Yeah, Katherine, what about you?" Celeste kicked her legs.

"Well, I'm finishing my book and publishing it." I summarized what was going on without going into details about having the 'hots' for my publisher. The two women who knew only about a kiss stared at me. I hadn't told Valery about it yet, but as I saw it, I didn't have much of a choice.

"And I kissed my publisher. It was unintentional. It just

happened. We were caught up in the moment, and the Halloween party. That was a mis—"

"The Halloween party?!" Celeste exclaimed as she jumped off the counter.

"No, I meant—"

"Hold on, you kissed your publisher? I mean, is he hot?" Valery looked like she missed something, and she had. Big time.

"Is he hot? That man is beyond hot," Elaina confirmed. She was already on her phone, searching for a picture to show Valery. When she found the right one, she lifted the phone to her face.

"Oh, wow. Yeah, he is." She patted me on the shoulder, like she understood where things had gone wrong.

"Okay, yes, he is good looking. But—"

"What happened at the party? Please tell me you banged him," Celeste cut me off, not letting go of what slipped out of my mouth.

"I—"

"Does it interfere with your work relationship? That can't be easy to deal with," Valery added as she took a sip of her water.

"Of course, it's not easy to deal with. It's her publisher. I told her that her book and her career should be her first priority," Elaina argued, putting both her hands on the counter.

They all stayed quiet as they waited for me to respond. A million things went through my mind about Adam. How difficult everything could become, how wrong it all could go. I still had to finish my book before my deadline.

"It's okay if you don't want to talk about it. You know you can always come to us for anything. It's perfectly fine if you're not ready to share. Just know we'll still be here when you are." Valery rubbed my shoulder.

"Thanks." Valery was always the comforting one.

"So, since you're here. Perhaps you could whip up your

special spaghetti and meatballs." Celeste mimicked Valery's accent. Valery smiled as she shook her head.

"Who has been feeding you this entire time?" she asked, getting up from her seat.

"The frozen aisle at the supermarket. Elaina tried to cook me your dish that she claims she's 'mastered' but all I got was two burned black balls." We all laughed as Celeste hugged Elaina.

"You got the burned meatballs, too?" I asked, trying to contain my laughter.

"Hey! I know I'm not her, but that is the last time I cook for you two. I don't care if you're starving." Elaina walked out of the kitchen to her room. Once our laughter died down, Valery grabbed her suitcase from the floor.

"I'm going to put this in the room and change. I'll be out to cook in a second," Valery said.

"You just got off a long flight. You should rest, cook tomorrow," I suggested, noticing the dark bags she had under her eyes.

"Don't be ridiculous. I can't leave poor Celeste hungry. Plus, it's like therapy to me." She turned to walk out, leaving Celeste and me alone. Celeste leaned closer to me, like she had some dirty secret to tell me. Or worse, she was trying to get something out of me.

"What really happened at that party, Katherine?" she asked, looking at me intensely.

"Something that shouldn't have happened," I admitted. It was the truth; I should have never followed Adam to the bathroom. My body had taken over and made all the choices that night. But what worried me was, I didn't only want him for just pleasure—I wanted all of him.

I wanted his full attention.

I wanted to know more about him. To learn about his life and the reasons for the man he was today. However, I couldn't expect that from a man who was in charge of my career. I couldn't mistake his focus for his work, for me, because the reality was, I was his work.

"Are you sure?" Celeste fixed her bun that kept falling. "Maybe it should have. You never know."

"Okay... now. Are you going to help me or watch how it's done?" Valery spoke as she walked back into the kitchen with her apron on and her hair tied back in a tight bun. Valery's high cheekbones were the most attractive feature on her face. Other than the fact that she was already painfully beautiful.

"Please, show us how a professional chef studying in Barcelona does it," Celeste said, changing the subject. She turned to look at me over her shoulder and flashed me a quick wink.

Thanksgiving was right around the corner, and I accompanied Valery to the grocery store to shop for the feast and, I've got to say, I'd never seen Valery so feisty over a turkey. But I guess after being in culinary school for about a year now, she'd know which turkey was the best.

I'd also helped Celeste with the preparations. We'd looked for table decor and the "perfect" cornucopia to place right at the center. She even went as far as painting our tablecloth with tradi-tional Thanksgiving images.

Meanwhile, Valery refused to let Elaina out and took it upon herself to teach Elaina how to cook. She had her bound to chains in the kitchen. This Thanksgiving was the same as last year's—meaningful and eventful. We took holidays very seriously with our friend group, and I adored it.

It had always been just the four of us, but this year, Elaina brought a friend. She met him on her trip to Miami, a coworker who she said had been helping her with Estyle. It made me think about what Adam had planned for Thanksgiving.

Maybe I should invite him. He might not have plans at all, and Thanksgiving is a holiday to spend with friends and family. Everyone was busy doing their own thing in the living room and kitchen, so I went to my room.

Walking in, I locked the door behind me and sat at the edge of the mattress. I looked down at my phone and scrolled to his contact. Should I call him? Text him? Send him an email? An email sounded more professional, right?

But with everything that had happened between us, a call or a text might suit the situation better. Plus, when I contacted someone, I never used email.

I sat in silence for a moment before figuring out how I was going to contact Adam. It wouldn't be awkward if he came; Elaina didn't find it awkward to bring her coworker. This could be a way to show my appreciation toward him for all the work he'd done for my book.

It felt like the right thing to do. A *nice* thing to do.

Okay, I was going to call him. I pressed on his contact and waited for the phone to ring. The first ring came through, and it immediately made me feel nauseous. The second ring came through, and I was more than ready to hang up before he answered. The third ring came, and as I motioned my finger to hang up, he picked up.

"Katherine?" he voiced over the phone. Shoot. I didn't even practice how I was going to ask him. What I was going to say. Shoot me now...

"Hey, hi! Um. How are you?" *Hey, hi? What was I saying?*

"I'm alright, are you okay?" He slightly chuckled, warmth spread through my body. Was I okay? No, thank you so much for asking! Just embarrassing myself was all.

"Yes, yeah, I'm good. I was calling to, uh, ask you something." It was so obvious that I was a nervous wreck. If he knew, he didn't show it. He patiently waited for me to finish.

"Okay... What's on your mind?"

"Well... Do you have plans for Thanksgiving?" I asked, biting my lip so hard I could draw blood. Adam stayed quiet for a second before answering. I was sure he was thinking, "What the hell does this girl want?"

"No, I don't," he answered, his voice sounding rougher over the phone. Completely throwing me off track.

"Oh." I cleared my throat before throwing the offer out there. "Okay, well, my friends and I are having dinner tomorrow night. I thought maybe it'd be nice for you to join us? You know, nothing weird, just a way to say thank you for everything you've done for my book."

Adam tried to speak, but I cut him off. "It's Thanksgiving, a holiday to spend with your friends and family. I figured it wouldn't hurt to spend it with loved ones. Not that I'm a loved one... I just... You know what I mean. And—"

"Katherine." He stopped me.

"Yes?" Did my voice sound shaky? God, I hoped it didn't.

"I'd love to come," he said. Relief hit me like a bolt of lightning. I could finally breathe.

"Okay, great. Oh! I almost forgot. You can bring Aaron as well. We'd love to have him. The more the merrier."

"I'll be sure to ask him."

"Great! That's, er, it. That was my question," I awkwardly tried to end the call. Even over the phone, he had the power to make me feel intimidated.

"I realized." He chuckled again. Was the way I'm talking funny? Probably. *I* would laugh if I could hear myself.

"Okay, bye..."

"Katherine." He stopped me again. "Thank you for the invitation. Really." If I wasn't wrong, it sounded like he was a bit shy... his voice with a hint of rawness to it.

"You're welcome. I'll text you the information," I added

before I hung up the phone. My heart was pounding out of my chest.

Adam Pearson was coming over for Thanksgiving dinner, and *I* invited him.

CHAPTER 25

ADAM

Katherine invited me over for Thanksgiving. Honestly, I was not expecting her call. For the past few years, Thanksgiving hadn't been a holiday I truly celebrated. I usually had a beer with Aaron at a bar, and Micheal joined us most times. And frankly, it always seemed easier that way.

My mother used to love Thanksgiving. She would wake up first thing in the morning to cook in the kitchen with music blasting through the house. I remembered waking up to the smell of her famous cornbread; it was my favorite dish she made. To this day, I hadn't tasted cornbread as good as hers.

Thanksgiving reminded me of my mother more than any other day. Which was why we decided to wash it over with alcohol. My first thought was to say no to Katherine, but then I heard her get nervous over the phone. I couldn't turn her down.

Perhaps this year would be different. I texted Aaron to meet me at my office, only for him to turn me down, saying he was 'busy.' It was hilarious how he bursted into my office every god given day that I didn't need him and disappeared when I did. Classic Aaron.

The best way to get ahold of Aaron when he was, and I quote, "busy" was to email him. He could never ignore an email, as a good businessman should. He later responded, agreeing to meet me at Scarlette Lounge in an hour, where we usually spent our Thanksgiving.

The time passed by quickly, then I was entering the bar and sitting at our regular spot. The lounge's interior was filled with gold and black, lights placed at the edge of the bar with all the most expensive liquor bottles stocked on glass shelves. The lights were dimmed, allowing the lights from behind the bar to shine upon the space. The bar stools were gold, with soft velvet cushions.

This lounge happened to be exclusive, allowing only the wealthy to dine and drink there. The woman bartending stared at me, waiting for me to call her over. When she realized I wouldn't, she came walking toward me. "You need a drink?" she asked with a glint in her eyes.

I was used to women hitting on me when I was out of the office, and I have to say, the attention wasn't as satisfying as it had been before. It was kind of... expected. Boring. Women threw themselves at me, and I'd never paid mind to them, not like I did Katherine.

Right as I planned to send her away, Aaron sat on the stool next to mine. "I'll have a drink, sweetheart," he said, winking at the bartender. She blushed as she walked away to prepare the drink Aaron usually ordered—scotch on the rocks.

Turning to look at Aaron, I realized just how much he looked like our mother. I never realized it until the holidays came around, when it reminded me most of her. He had dark hair, unlike mine, that's dirty blonde. His eyes are sky blue, as my mother's used to be. He was a copy of her, and I was a copy of my father.

One thing we did have in common, in facial features, was our dimples. They only became visible when we smiled, and Aaron's appeared all the goddamn time. Unlike mine...

"So, what is it that had you busy?" I asked, curious to see what he had on the side. If he was working on a project I was unaware of. He looked straight at the liquids placed on the wall, avoiding looking me in the eye. He was definitely working on something, and he didn't want to tell me. Which only made me more curious.

"A side business. I know I have our family company, but I'm working to build another empire." He wasn't telling me the entire plan, but the way he spoke showed that he somewhat cared about having it under his own name. I was the eldest, so I was the one who would carry on Pearson Book Group. "When I have more information regarding the business, I'll share it with you. As of right now, I need to figure it out. By myself."

I gave him a firm nod, understanding where he was coming from. If he did happen to start a successful business, it would only do good to our name. So, regardless of me not knowing the full details, I was on board. It would be his fourth business, but the guy couldn't help it. He needed more.

"Listen, I didn't call you over to talk shit," I spoke, swiftly changing the subject to the main reason why I brought him here. To talk about Thanksgiving. "Katherine has invited us over for Thanksgiving dinner. At first, I was hesitant to accept, but I thought perhaps it wouldn't be a bad idea." Unsure of what Aaron would say, I tried to sound as convincing as I could.

"Really? Can I ask why?" he said, amused by the invitation. He grinned like he knew something I didn't.

"She said it's to thank us for all the help we've given her. It would be rude to decline the offer," I responded in a normal tone. Aaron's grin only grew.

"To thank *you*. But I suppose attending the event is okay." The bartender returned with his drink and set it in front of him.

He winked, making her red in the process. He grabbed the cup, the condensation dripping down the side of the glass. "It's been a while since we've done a dinner," he stated, before taking a sip of his drink.

"I know," I answered. "We'll see how it goes." I stared at his cup as he set it down. The ice cubes clashed tighter, creating a sound that consumed my ears.

"I suppose we will." He played with the rim of the glass as we allowed the low music to fill the silence. I had a feeling in my chest that Aaron saw right through me; he knew I only wanted to go for Katherine. If I was going to get through this dinner tonight with Aaron, I was going to need a drink. One would say it was too early for a drink, but for me, happy hour was whenever I said it was.

I did a swift movement with my hand, gaining the bartender's attention. "Dry martini. Shaken, not stirred." Aaron snickered beside me, further proving my choice of ordering a drink was the right one.

Katherine: 11 Hanover Sq, New York, 10006.
Apartment 223, At 7:30 p.m. See you then :)

Aaron and I arrived at Katherine's building at the exact time she had said in the text she sent. We brought three bottles of wine, knowing that Katherine's friends were joining as well. "Apartment 223," I told Aaron as he punched the numbers on the apartment buzzer.

It rang for about four seconds before a raspy feminine voice answered. "Yes?" she asked. Aaron looked at me as if he had just heard a voice of an angel, only it wasn't *my* angel speaking.

"Adam and Aaron Pearson. Katherine invited us," I

responded, already becoming annoyed with the system. She took a long pause, surely checking in with Katherine. After a while of standing and waiting, she finally buzzed us in.

The building was decent, but far too small for my taste. I tried to search for an elevator on the ground floor, only for the lobby attendant to tell me they didn't have one. Great. We had to walk up two flights of stairs. It wouldn't exhaust us, but the thought still irritated me.

What if she had a foot injury? Or was feeling too weak or tired for her own good to be walking up two flights of stairs? It was ridiculous. There should be more reliability when it comes to her.

Once we arrived at her door, we gave it a firm knock. Within seconds, the door swung open, revealing a tall blonde in a brown outfit. "Adam, Aaron, come on in," she greeted as she pushed the door wider for Aaron and me to walk in.

The apartment was smaller than I thought it'd be. The kitchen was stashed in a small corner, and the dining table was next to the couch. I saw two doors on the opposite side of each other, which were probably hers and Katherine's rooms. "Please, make yourself at home," she suggested, while closing the door behind her.

Aaron handed the wine bottles to her, while giving her his signature 'want' look. "You have a beautiful home, Ms..." He waited for the woman to introduce herself.

"Oh, thanks. It's small, but Katherine and I make it work. I'm Elaina. Thanks for the bottles, we'll for sure empty them tonight," she answered him, stabilizing the bottles on the small counter.

"You're welcome," he said, flashing her a smile that purposely showed off his dimples. The main move that locked a woman in for him, but surprisingly, she didn't seem to be giving it much attention. I liked her already.

"Where's everyone?" I asked, clearly asking only for Katherine.

"In the room. They should be out in a second."

Not a few moments passed before the room door opened, revealing Katherine in a stunning dress in the color auburn. It hugged her curves perfectly, making me jealous that the material got to touch her bare skin. Her hair was pin straight, her lips bold red, as always. I'd never get tired of that color.

I planned to have lipstick stains all over my body. I planned to have her on her knees with nothing but red lipstick on. She didn't even need to touch me for me to gain a hard-on. Looking at her already did the job.

"Hi. I'm glad you could make it." She walked toward me, looking like perfection, lighting up the entire room. Rolling in like a breath of fresh air. Air that I desperately needed. I allowed my eyes to roam her curves, then locked them onto her golden eyes. I didn't think I'd be relieved to see her, but I was.

"Me too," I simply said, unable to form more words. I could feel my heart skip a beat as her hand slid down my arm, passing me to get to the kitchen. I didn't notice the other two girls walking out of the room with Katherine. I only saw her.

Aaron and Elaina had been talking during the time I was waiting. The girls set the food and beverages on the table, then everyone surrounded the table, grabbing seats. As we began to settle down, a knock disturbed us. Celeste opened the door for a man to walk in.

"Hey, Celeste, how's it going?" He smiled at her as he stepped in. Elaina turned and noticed him while he came up behind her, hugging her.

"Hey, I'm Spencer," he said to Aaron, who didn't seem impressed with his entrance.

"Aaron Pearson," he introduced himself, irritation filling his voice. I knew he was bothered that someone interrupted his conversation. Elaina only smiled awkwardly.

"Okay, let's take a seat." The British woman spoke, everyone following her command. I watched Katherine about to take the seat two chairs down from me, and I hurried to her side and took the chair next to hers. She seemed to notice as her cheeks flushed red.

I pulled out the chair for her, and she took a seat. "Mind if I sit here?" I asked, not wanting her to feel uncomfortable. I wanted to be as close to her as possible.

She nodded as I pushed her chair in. Taking a seat next to her, I could see Aaron's annoyed scowl from across the table. He was seated next to this Spencer guy; my brother wasn't the aggressive type unless he didn't like you.

"Everything looks amazing, Valery," Katherine commented, getting a beaming smile from the British Asian. She dressed very presentably. I could tell her wardrobe was worth a good amount of money. I hadn't gotten her last name yet.

"Thank you. Please dig in," she said, as she took her seat next to Elaina. The turkey was placed at the center of the table, already cut into flawless slices. This chick was a perfectionist with all her dishes, from the turkey to the gravy, that was carefully placed in a glass bowl.

"Oh, shoot! I forgot a dish," Katherine said as she pushed out her chair and headed toward the kitchen. She then returned with a plate covered in foil and placed it in front of us. The moment she removed the foil, I was left shocked.

Yellow golden crust, soft fluffy center. Bread. Not just any bread—cornbread. It looked exactly like the one my mother used to make for us. I hesitated to reach for a piece, but my curiosity got the best of me. I wanted to see if it tasted as similar as it looked.

Taking a bite, I was completely astonished. It felt soft and moist on my tongue; it had a sweet taste to it as much as salty. It had a hint of sourness, and I could taste the buttermilk added. This wasn't store-bought. It was freshly baked. It tasted just like my mother's. For a brief second, I felt as if she were serving the bread at the dinner table when I was just seven years old.

"Who made this?" I asked. It wasn't a question; it was a demand. I needed to know who it was that made this dish.

"Oh, no, did it come out bad?" Katherine reached for a piece to try for herself.

"Who made it?" I said again, eager to get a response.

"I-I did," she finally answered. My chest felt tight at her words. She made it. She managed to get the same outcome my mother used to.

"You made it," I repeated. I couldn't believe the similarity in taste, in shape, in color.

"Yeah... what's wrong with it?" She seemed wary, with a hint of disappointment in her eyes. She thought I hated it, but it was the complete opposite.

"Nothing. Absolutely nothing," I admitted, grabbing another and placing it on my plate. "It's amazing, Katherine." She smiled as she looked down to her lap. I followed her eyes to the hands resting on her thighs. I reached for them instantly. Like a reflex.

As my hand captured hers, warmth spread throughout my arm, filling the coldest spots with heat. I rubbed my thumb in circular motions on the side of her hand, as a way to thank her for giving me a gift I didn't think I'd ever have again.

I was not a man who believed in "signs", but I felt like it was a message from my mother through Katherine. And that alone had a heap of meaning to it.

"Adam, Katherine's told us a lot about you. But we'd like to know more through you. How's the book coming?" Valery asked, filling the silence in the room. Everyone was too busy shoving food into their mouths. All the dishes were very savory; she knew how to cook.

"You've heard a lot about me?" I was more hung up on the part about Katherine speaking of me with these ladies. It could possibly mean she liked me.

"Uh, about the book. She means the work that comes with the book," Katherine clarified, and I was quickly disappointed it wasn't in the way I thought.

"I see. Well, yes. The work has been diligent, keeping us actively occupied," I responded to Valery's question.

"I heard it's only been you two doing the work. More you than her," Elaina added to the conversation.

"You heard right." Looking at the faces around the table, they found it very hard to believe. I'd understand, from their point of view, publishing a book with only two people was possible, but difficult. For me, it was possible and doable. Not exactly difficult.

"Must be hard," she added.

"Perhaps. But I'll manage."

The conversation stirred in a whole different direction as everyone began to bring up multiple subjects. We talked about Katherine's book, Elaina's small company—which Spencer was helping with—Celeste's paintings, and Valery's almost finishing culinary school. Which backed up her ability to cook like a professional chef.

Before long, the entire table was wiped clean of all dishes, leaving only empty plates with crumbs. I faced Aaron, who looked overly satisfied with our decision to attend tonight's dinner. For the first dinner in a while, I could say it was a great one. But, from what I could see, every night with Katherine by my side turned out to be a good one.

And I wasn't ready for it to end just yet. Valery got up from her seat and started grabbing the plates. Katherine stopped her and grabbed the plates from her hands, telling her she and Elaina cooked, Celeste decorated, and she'd clean up. Valery gave in and allowed her to retrieve the plates to the kitchen.

I watched Katherine disappear to the kitchen, and rose from my seat, grabbing a pile of plates, and followed her. Stepping into the kitchen, I saw her turning the faucet on, about to rinse off the first plate. I set the plates next to her and placed a hand on her rib.

"Let me," I said, carefully moving her aside. "I'll rinse, you put them in the dishwasher." Her smile was small, like she was trying to hide it from me. She didn't even realize that the smallest smile could light up the darkest room.

"You don't have to. You can go back out to the—" I cut her off and turned to face her.

"You're right, I don't have to. But I want to. Let me help you, angel." Her eyes softened, giving me the response I wanted. I rolled my sleeves up and caught Katherine staring at my arms from the side of my eye. I couldn't help but smirk at how obvious she was when she stared.

Her back hit the counter beside the dishwasher. She opened it and started to load the first plate. "Thanks for coming," she said, looking at the plate I handed her like it was the most interesting thing in the room.

"Thanks for inviting me," I added, looking at the side of her face. Her skin seemed soft. I wanted to run my fingers down her cheek. Get a feel for what I'd been missing.

"The girls were glad you could make it."

"Are you glad?" I asked, wanting to get the real meaning behind her statement. She finally met my gaze, her almond whiskey eyes boring into mine. There was so much unspoken tension between us. I yearned to know more. To hear more come from those luscious lips.

"Yes." I stepped closer to her, seeking her touch. Seeking the warmth she gave my body. It was like a shot of espresso, instantly waking me up. It made me feel alive, like I'd jumped off a cliff and managed to fly. I felt like I kept getting into debt, constantly paying for a drug, only to experience the high all over again.

Moving closer, her scent became stronger—vanilla and lavender. I could hear the small gasp escape from her mouth as I wrapped my arm around her waist and pulled her in. I placed a finger under her chin and lifted her face toward mine. I could see all the details of her face, from the small mark on the side of her eye to the tiny slit in her eyebrow.

"I am, too," I spoke.

Her eyes fluttered shut, and I admired her from a different angle. Having her in my arms felt right. I'd never felt this way over another person, never cared about another person like I care about her. I had no clue what all that meant, and I didn't know what to do with it. Whether to pursue it or hide it. Whether it was smart or utterly ridiculous.

I cleared my throat, letting go of her. Her eyes opened, giving me a look of confusion. I didn't know why I did any of that. My body had a mind of its own around her, and I needed to control it more. Things had been fine between us, even after the Halloween party. I couldn't risk that so soon, with the election right around the corner.

I knew most of it was my fault because I had initiated it. But not now. If I had met Katherine under any other circumstance, I'd go for it. I'd go for her.

"Right, I'm going to—I'll be right back," Katherine stuttered as she ran out of the kitchen. I deserved that. I was the asshole sending mixed signals to her. If only I could think without my dick and more with my brain.

Katherine left the kitchen, and she didn't come back. I finished cleaning up and left everything spotless, like it would make up for messing with her mind. I exited the kitchen to find everyone already leaving. Aaron was sitting on the couch, reading what I knew were emails.

"Ready?" he asked, straightening his tie as he rose. I gave him a firm nod, giving the ladies a goodnight. I still couldn't see Katherine, giving me the impression that she had hidden in her room.

"Tell Katherine I said goodnight. I'll reach out later," I told Elaina, as she accompanied us out.

"I'll be sure to tell her. Have a safe drive back home," she said to Aaron and me. The door slammed shut in my face, the sound like a slap to my face.

"Eventful night, no?" Aaron added, seeing the look on my face, like I'd fucked up bad. And I knew I had.

CHAPTER 26

ADAM

Today was the first of December. I hadn't seen Katherine since Thanksgiving, and I had only myself to blame. I'd only received emails in reference to her writing, and that was about it. I was positive that if I wasn't her boss, I'd be getting nothing. But an email would do, a clear sign that she was alright and out of trouble.

I'd thought of scheduling multiple meetings just to see her. But my mind always went back to how I had confused her that night, how I was about to kiss her, but left her waiting. She wanted time away from my complicated ass, and that I could understand. I wasn't hurrying her. She had work to finish, noting that her deadline was drawing close.

I hadn't seen her in days, and it was like a constant needle poking me. A need to see her face, to analyze all her facial features once again.

With that, a thought came to mind. Katherine worked at Avenue, but I wasn't sure when her shifts were. If I were to pay a little visit, my chances of seeing her tonight were slim. But any chance of seeing Katherine was worth taking. The time on the clock was 9:32 p.m. I'd been at the office all day, trying to pull together the important details of Katherine's book.

Perhaps she was working a shift right now. I sat in my chair, staring at the view behind my desk, contemplating if it'd be a good decision to go. I glanced over my shoulder at the clock on my wall—9:33 p.m.

Fuck it. I'm going.

I let Henry know that I needed a ride. I headed downstairs to the parking garage and drove toward a club I absolutely despised but had the woman that I felt the complete opposite about.

After what seemed to be a long ride, I arrived at the entrance of a building with the name Avenue in all big purple neon lights. For a club that had highly listed clients, the interior seemed tacky. Too tacky for my own taste, at least.

I didn't waste time getting out of the car and making my way inside. I passed the bodyguard with much confidence, walking in like I owned the place. I might as well once I gained my CEO position. Diego would have to bow to kiss my feet the moment he realized I owed him jack shit.

The bodyguard didn't seem to follow me or try to stop me. Lazy and useless. For a Ford, it was quite an embarrassment. Yet, it could be that Diego saw my entrance and somehow allowed it. Whichever it was, I didn't give a fuck. I was here for one thing only.

The dance floor was filled with drunk, sweaty people, as usual. I tried to make my way without someone touching me or pulling me to dance with them. With much determination and a few pulls away from drunk girls, I made it to the bar. I desperately wanted Katherine to be the one who greeted me, but it was her curly-headed friend, Celeste.

"Excuse me, I'd like a drink," I called out loudly, above the music.

"And I'd like to go home, bud. But we all got to wait," she

screamed, as she made a drink for the man who'd asked before me. Her back was to me, so she didn't realize it was me yet.

"Fair enough. It's not all I want, though," I added, hoping that it would catch her attention. I needed her to tell me where Katherine was. I was sure she worked a shift tonight; it was a feeling I had.

"I'm going to spray you down with beer, if it's what I think. Don't—" She finally turned around and paused when she saw it's me. Her eyes switched from annoyance to anger. I instantly became confused. Why was she giving *me* that look? "Might just spray you down, anyway." I was taken aback by her response.

"What—" she cut me off as she handed the man his drink.

"I don't know what you want from me." She crossed her arms and lifted her right eyebrow. She knew about Thanksgiving. Why else would she be treating me like I killed her beloved cat?

"Is Katherine here?" I asked, helplessly wanting her answer to be yes. She stared me down, like she was considering whether she should tell me.

"No. She's not," she said as she turned back around and took another person's order.

"Why?" She ignored me while speaking with the other customer. "Hey! I was here before him. Which means you must attend to me first. Is that not how your job works?" I knew it was low of me to call her out and tell her how to do her job. But I was running out of options. I needed answers.

"Sure, sir." She spit out the two words like they were bitter on her tongue. "What do you want?" She said it as if it were a burden instead of a question.

"A whiskey sour," I responded with a smug smile on my face. "Why is she not working?" I commanded of her. She scoffed at me.

"You sure are bossy. Thinking you can order people around whenever." She smirked, like she was trying to calm herself. To not explode. I knew I was poking a bear right now, but again, I didn't care.

"Sure. I need to know." She was making the drink right in front of me. Shaking cups and pouring liquids.

"If you must know, you airhead, she's working on her book. She has been stressed lately, trying to finish it up with the deadline *you* gave her. I'm taking her shift so she can focus." At that moment, I knew Celeste might hate me, but I didn't dislike her. I instantly respected her for protecting and looking out for Katherine. It was rare to find such loyalty.

"How come she didn't reach out to me? It's what I'm here for." A stupid question left my mouth.

"You think she's going to reach out to you?" She slammed the drink in front of me. "Please, tell me you aren't that stupid." My eyes widened at her boldness to call me out. I usually wouldn't let it slide and make them regret it. But she was right. What she said to me was all true. Not one lie came out of her mouth.

"Right." I looked down at my cup and played with the rim. Celeste studied me as she wiped her hands clean with a cloth.

"It's Christmas." She began speaking. It was the first of December and everyone was starting Christmas celebrations. Jesus, give me a break. "It's going to be Katherine's first Christmas alone. Valery heads back to Barcelona, Elaina heads to Washington to visit her family, and I head to Florida to visit mine." There was a hesitance in her voice. "If you're here, maybe you could reach out to her by then. I'm hoping that I won't regret telling you this information, yes?"

I nodded, knowing that I was going to change all my plans for a woman who didn't want to see me.

"Good. I better not," she said as she walked away from me and got back to work.

"Where are you going this time?" Aaron asked as he sat across from my desk. Every December, I left New York City and went somewhere tropical. Last year, I went to Hawaii for the entire month and worked online. It got way too fucking cold for me here, and I hated the cold. I might have been cold-blooded when it came to my emotions, but not my body. Fuck no.

"Nowhere. I'm staying here in New York." My brother stilled. He looked like he had missed something. I was staying for Katherine. Knowing that she was about to spend her first Christmas alone, I couldn't leave. I wasn't sure I could go, regardless.

"But you hate it here in December. You haven't stayed in *years,*" he explained, trying to figure this out.

"Yes, and now I'm staying," I confirmed, not wanting to give him much of a hint behind the reason for my stay. He leaned back in his seat and studied me, as if he could find the answer written on my face. I mirrored his movement and stared at his face in return.

There was a bit of hesitation on his side as he built up the courage to assume something. I saw him sit up straighter, rolling his shoulders back like he had figured it out. "Does this sudden stay have to do with a certain someone?" I tried not to react to his words, knowing he'd figured it out.

Shit. He sensed my motives, but I couldn't have him thinking it made me weak. Or worse, that it distracted me. "Not a some-one, Aaron. A *something.*" He hummed in response.

"And this something is..." he prompted, eagerly awaiting my response.

"The elections. It is far too close for me to fly out of state. I need to be around in case Edward decides to hit us with yet another splendid surprise." I scooted my seat closer to my desk, reaching for my filing cabinet. "Like this one."

I pulled out a file on my uncle, more specifically on his

current behavior toward his author. "Our uncle has an ally in the literary world. He's going against the will and getting help." Aaron's eyes widened as he grabbed ahold of the file, flipping frantically through the pages.

"It's cheating. With this proof, we could win the position." He was right about that. A fraud like this could have him thrown out of the elections faster than the speed of a bullet. Though it would feel good to step into the position of CEO, it unfortunately would not give me the satisfaction I would like.

I wanted to see his face when he realized he'd lost to me even with the help. Pathetic. My eyes met Aaron's gaze. "Yes, but that will not be necessary. I will bring out the files once I am CEO and use them to throw him out of the company. For good." I grinned at the vision of him getting physically thrown out of the building. It was tempting to do it now, but again, all good things come to those who wait.

The files were returned to my hidden file cabinet, locked. Aaron smiled. I imagined he was more than pleased with my plan. I most certainly was. I glanced at my clock, my mind quickly going back to a pair of amber eyes. I rose from my seat and headed toward the door.

Aaron looked at me, confused. "Where are you going?" he asked. I rolled up the sleeves of my black sweatshirt, fixing the Patek Philippe on my wrist. I usually wore a suit, but today called for a different type of wear. Comfortable, but presentable.

"I have a matter that I need to attend to." Aaron was quick to stand. He knew where I was headed, but he would not acknowledge it.

"Alright. I will see you later?" I nodded in response as I held the door open for him. He walked out, and I closed the door behind me. We both walked across the hallway side by side for a moment before turning in opposite ways.

I remembered Celeste telling me she was leaving this morning. Katherine would be left alone today, and I had an idea of where she might be. I felt quite confident in it. She had no idea that this Christmas would be different. It would be her first alone and it would be my first accompanied. I waited for a warning not to go, but nothing stopped me. I was determined to find her and see her. Even if she didn't want to.

CHAPTER 27

KATHERINE

I waved goodbye to the girls at their terminal gates from the doors. Celeste, Elaina, and Valery were all going back home for the holidays. They all happened to book the same day to fly back, which left me to say goodbye to all of them at once. I knew I would need to face this moment for some time now, but part of me didn't want to acknowledge it. I tried tricking my brain into thinking they would be right back home tonight as a coping mechanism.

Though I knew deep down that I would be alone. The holidays were a time to spend with loved ones, but I figured it would benefit me to be alone, to finish the book. At least that was what I kept telling myself. I hadn't forgotten my deadline. In fact, it was engraved in my mind. It was the one thing my mind constantly went back to, other than Adam.

I had not heard or spoken to him since Thanksgiving. It was partially my fault because, I would admit, I had been avoiding him. So much had happened between us in such little time. Or it felt that way.

After standing at the doors for thirty minutes, I turned to leave. I ordered a taxi to the place that helped me bleed on paper.

As the taxi started to drive, I looked out the window. Time passed until I arrived at the 'Happily Ever After' bookstore.

This tiny pink building brought me peace, inspiration, and hope. I paid the taxi driver before jumping out of the cab. I headed toward the entrance covered in roses, and I noticed the store seemed emptier. It was missing a fair number of books on the shelves.

The doorbell rang as I pushed it open. "Judy?" I called out, waiting for an answer. Nothing came; the place was silent. I felt uncertain about walking in, but I suspected Judy to be somewhere in the back. So, without much thought, I wandered to the table I usually sat at to write.

I got settled in the seat, placing my laptop in front of me. I inhaled a breath before I began to type. *Alright, Katherine... let's get to work.* Suddenly, I felt the hairs on my neck stand, like I'd been struck by lightning. The air in the room became heavier, making it feel smaller than it actually was.

"Katherine." A deep voice caressed the back of my ear. I turned to find Adam in casual wear, a style I didn't usually see him in, but one I found myself completely obsessing over. He had a muscle-fit wool sweater on, the sleeves rolled up, paired with black pants. His watch was the first thing that caught my eye, as it shone and stood out from the black. His hair was brushed back, with a strand falling on his forehead, making him look effortlessly hot.

I hadn't responded to him, and he noticed as his bright green eyes bore into mine. I cleared my throat, fighting to gain back every bit of my own consciousness. "Ahem, what are you doing here?" I quickly realized it was the rudest way to greet someone. I shyly shook my head as I tried to find the right words.

"It seems that I grew to like this spot. It's very..." He paused as he looked around the empty store. "Engrossing," he finished, looking pleased with himself. My cheeks turned pink as I took into consideration that he might have been talking about me.

"Right," I choked out. "Well, I was just leaving, so..." It was a lie. I was planning to stay here until closing time. But plans changed the moment I saw Adam. He looked intrigued as he watched me stumble out of my seat and tried to scramble my belongings together.

"Please, stay. I'll leave you. This is your spot, after all." I caught the hint of humor he tried to fit in, but I could tell he didn't want to leave. "It doesn't feel right to make someone leave when they were here first." That was why I stood and grabbed his wrist carefully.

"No, no. It's fine. I was just about to leave and grab something to eat," I said. He didn't look me in the eye; he's too busy having his eyes fixed where my skin made contact with his. My body flushed with heat, and I could feel my nipples push against my shirt. They could cut glass at this point. It was peculiar how my body reacted to his. And this touch was as innocent as they came.

"You're hungry?" he asked, grabbing my wrist with his free hand. He began to caress the side of my wrist with his thumb as he waited for my answer.

"Yes," I said, unable to look away from his hand.

"Let me take you to dinner?" he asked without warning.

"I don't know..."

"It's just dinner, Katherine." I looked up to find his eyes already on me. His eyes softened as I sighed, and I knew I should say no. But I wanted more time with Adam. He gave my body a rush of adrenaline by just looking at me.

"Okay," I whispered. He grabbed my bag from the chair and grabbed my hand, leading me out of the store. We stepped outside, and I found his driver, Henry, already out front. Adam opened the door for me, and I climbed in, feeling his eyes on me. He followed and shut the door behind him. "So, where are we going?"

"Somewhere nice," he said, his voice cool, but it warmed me up.

"Nice as in dressing up nice?" I asked, looking down at my clothes. I was wearing a pair of jeans with a pink crop top and sneakers. My hair was wavy. I had washed it this morning and let it air dry. I was in no position to go somewhere "nice." Adam followed as his gaze roamed up and down my body.

"Relax, angel. You look *nice*." A simple compliment had me blushing once again. Adam smirked as he saw the sudden change of color on my cheeks. "We're having sushi. The restaurant is decent, but not as 'nice' as you're thinking," he reassured me, not taking his eyes off me. Adam's eye contact was intimidating; he knew how to use it to his advantage.

We reached the destination, a sushi lounge with blue neon lights. Adam's idea of 'decent' was pretty vague. For someone like me, who was middle class her whole life, it was pretty damn nice. I instantly felt underdressed as I did minutes ago in the car. "This is decent to you?" I whisper-shouted as we walked into the restaurant.

"Is it not?" he responded. As we reached the host, he gave her his name, and she instantly grabbed two menus and showed us to our table. Every woman here was wearing heels. There were no sneakers in sight, except mine. We took a seat in a small booth in the corner. The lights were dimmed, but still bright enough for others to see what I was wearing.

I shifted in my seat as I looked around the room. My head was down the entire time, trying to hide from everyone. "Everything alright?" he asked me cautiously.

"I'm the only one wearing sneakers," I said, feeling insecure. He looked down at my sneakers and glanced around the room. He sighed as he shook his head slowly. I became wary that I'd done something to disappoint him.

"You look perfect. You are perfect. Better than anyone else in the room, if you ask me." I didn't expect him to say that. I was shocked as I sat trying to understand the words he'd said. He looked down at the menu before meeting my eyes. "How about we take this to go? I think sushi tastes better at home than it does here." His voice was soft, and yet I knew he was saying it to make me comfortable, and I appreciated it.

I bit my bottom lip and nodded, relieved that he didn't seem annoyed. Years ago, Martin hated it when I'd shown any sign of me feeling uncomfortable. He'd make me feel bad for it, but Adam only strived to make me feel better.

The waiter came to order our drinks and Adam told them about our change of plans. He ordered his choice of roll, and I ordered mine. Adam also asked for an order of dumplings he saw me looking at on the TV, like he read my mind and knew I'd be too self-conscious to ask for more than one meal. Another bad habit from when I was with Martin. It had been so long since I'd dated, but I noticed I still held on to the way Martin treated me.

Our order came in to-go bags, and Adam paid and left the table with my hand in his. This felt natural—us. I wasn't sure if this was even a real date. All I knew was that I wanted it to be, and that it was going to hurt me in the long run.

I stood behind Adam as he reached for his keys in his pocket. He pulled them out and inserted the key, unlocking the door. He swung it open, holding it for me to walk in. I shuffled in with the bag of food in my arms.

As I stepped into Adam's penthouse for the first time, I was speechless. It was absolutely stunning where he lived. It was bachelor pad style, with a breathtaking view of the city. Most of the furniture was dark colors, mostly black. Black seemed to be his favorite color, from what I could see. I saw a staircase on my right. Not only was his penthouse spacious, it also had two floors.

I was guessing the second floor was where the rooms were and his office, but I didn't ask. The door shut behind him and I was brought back to reality. Adam walked up behind me and placed a hand on my back, guiding me in the direction of the kitchen.

His kitchen was spacious, the cabinets all black, the entire kitchen was blacked out. There was an island with stools and two or three lights casting down on the counters. The view of the city was behind us, the city lights brighter than the lights in the kitchen. It was like a fever dream. I noticed the windows wrapped around the entire penthouse.

I placed the bag of food on the counter as Adam bent down to open a cabinet and pulled out two plates. "You must really like black," I spit out without a second thought. He chuckled with his back to me. He turned around with two cups in his hands now, settling them on the counter.

"I wouldn't say I like it. I'd say I cope with it." It was ironic. Everything was dark, but he looked like the only bright thing in the room. His sunny blonde hair and bright green eyes stood out against the colors surrounding us.

"You don't have a favorite color?" I asked, trying to grasp an understanding of his answer. He looked into my eyes, making me feel like I couldn't hide from him. He nodded without breaking eye contact.

"Amber, honey brown," he said, his voice husky. This would be the first time I heard someone say the color *amber.* So random. But he seemed so sure of his answer, almost as if the answer was so obvious. "Let's eat. Sushi tastes better when it's still fresh." He grabbed the bag and took out the food, setting it on the plates.

"Go on and sit anywhere you'd like. Make yourself at home," he added. I strolled out of the kitchen and went back to the living area. I circled around the gray couch that seemed comfortable to sleep on and sat on the carpet in front. There was a small coffee table in the middle. I had completely ignored the table with seats not so far away from me and sat on the floor.

It felt like home to me, and I didn't usually sit at a table to eat. Adam walked into the living room, expecting me to be at the table, only to find me on the floor. I smiled up at him shyly, unsure how he would deal with this. He only grinned and brought the plates to me. He placed them on the coffee table in front of us and took a seat on the floor next to me.

"I don't usually use this spot to eat, but it'll do," he said with a grin on his face. I was desperate to see his smile again. To see the dimples hidden in that beautiful face of his. Instead, I scooted closer to him and reached for my plate. He handed me a set of metal chopsticks, not knowing that I had no idea how to use them. I always used my hands to eat sushi. I didn't think of that when he said that's what we would be eating.

I quickly became embarrassed and tried to grab the first piece of sushi with the chopsticks. It sucked terribly as it kept slipping out of my hand. Adam watched me through the corner of his eyes, eating his sushi roll so effortlessly. Of course, he had metal chopsticks and of course he looked hot using them. What couldn't this man do?

But I didn't give up. I kept trying until the piece of sushi I so desperately tried to put in my mouth completely ripped apart. I sighed heavily as I glanced at the destroyed piece. Adam scooted closer until his knee graced mine and grabbed the second piece of my roll with his chopsticks. He lifted it up and motioned it toward my mouth. "Open," he ordered, and I obeyed without hesitation. I opened my mouth, and he slipped the piece in. I closed my mouth around the chopsticks, and he pulled them out.

I covered my mouth with my hand as I tried to swallow the food. "You grab the chopsticks like this," he instructed, showing me. "Let the back end of it rest in the crevice between your thumb and index finger, and the front-end rest on the bottom of your ring finger. Then lay your thumb over the chopstick." I mirrored his actions, grabbing my set of chopsticks. I felt silly, but I was determined to learn.

"Like this?" I asked. He leaned closer and nodded.

"That's it," he assured me. "Now keep the bottom chopstick fixed while moving the top chopstick. Place pressure around the piece and pick it up. Slowly." I followed his instructions as I lifted it. "Good, now eat it while you can," he said as he saw my grip on the piece loosen. I quickly shoved it into my mouth and chewed. Realizing I had done it, I put two hands up in the air as a victory sign. He laughed, showing all his white teeth and the dimples I hadn't seen in a while.

Jesus, those dimples would be the end of me. Adam was gorgeous, but smiling Adam with dimples was as sexy as it got. I felt a flush of warmth pool at my lower belly. As I swallowed the food, I couldn't seem to look away. Even after he was done laughing, he was still smiling.

"You should do that more often," I spoke. He looked down at my lips and licked his own.

"Do what?" He seemed completely unaware of the effect his smile had on me. I reached and touched the side of his jaw with my fingertips. His smile dropped lazily as he leaned into my touch.

"Smile more. It looks good on you, Mr. Pearson." His smile returned, small but sure. His hand covered mine.

"I only smile around you, angel," he admitted. My entire body felt warm, a sense of arousal hitting me like a bomb. I wanted to climb on top of this man and praise his body, his smile, him. No one had been able to make me feel this way before.

But instead, I looked down and said, "It's getting late. I should get back to my apartment." Even though I dreaded being alone. Adam seemed to catch on as he saw the change in my face.

"You're staying alone?" I was confused about how he would know.

"How—"

"Celeste told me at the bar," he explained. Of course, Celeste would definitely tell the man I'd been trying to avoid that I'd be alone. The man I was insanely attracted to.

"Right, well, yeah." My voice shook at the vision of me being in my dark apartment alone, with locks that could be easily broken. I didn't worry about these things when I was with someone else. Especially with Elaina, who kept a base-ball bat underneath her bed in case of break-ins. She knew how to use it, but I didn't. They'd probably take it from my hand and hit me with it. I wasn't Harley Quinn, not even close.

"Hmm, and you don't like the idea of being alone," he said, reading my mind exactly right.

"Well—" I started, but I was cut off.

"Does your apartment have security?" he asked.

"If the skinny lobby boy and his pet rat count, sure." I tried to bring humor into the conversation, but I failed miserably. "I'm sure I'll be fine. I—"

"Stay here," he said, certain. Except the idea was absurd. Me, stay here with him? Same room? "I have a guest room on this floor, ready for you to take. You'd have your own space. I'm upstairs if you need anything. The security here is good," he explained, and suddenly I was disappointed that I wouldn't be sharing a room with him. Jesus, Katherine.

"No, I couldn't—" He raised his hand, shaking his head.

"Please, you'd be my guest. I'm offering. You know it's safer here." He was right. I'd feel a whole lot better here and sleep better at night. Maybe. But I was doubtful, unsure if I should take his offer.

"I—" I looked around the living room. This place was like a fortress, impossible to get into. It was safe and comfortable. I'd avoid Adam during the day and hide in my room at night. It could work. "Okay, I'll stay," I answered.

He gave me a relieved smile as he rose from the floor, holding a hand out for me to grab. I lent him my hand, and he helped me up. "I'll show you to your room," he said as I walked behind him. I followed him into a hallway; his penthouse had no business being this big, and we were only on the first floor. He turned a corner into a guest room. The walls were painted—yes, you guessed it—black. The bed frame was velvet forest green, and the covers were bright yellow.

There were two nightstands on each side, with lights dangling from the ceiling. I would never think these colors would go so well with each other, but they did. It was a mix of modern and retro. Whoever designed his house truly had talent. "This is your room. Make yourself comfortable. We can retrieve your belongings tomorrow for the time of your stay."

Somehow, Adam made this sound like business, but it was something he was doing to help me. It didn't help him whatsoever. "Thanks for letting me stay here. You don't have—" He walked closer to me, stopping me.

"Don't worry about it. Think of it as a boss looking after his clients." Way to make it seem like a business proposition. But again, it was what we were. Nothing more, nothing less. Right?

"Okay, well, thanks," I said as I sat on the bed. The mattress felt like the type of fluffy cloud I dreamt of as a little girl. I could fall into a deep slumber here and never wake up. Unless someone woke me. Adam stared at me like he was studying me. I looked down at his pants and found a bulge of his arousal. He was hard by just looking at me spread on a bed.

"No problem. Goodnight, Katherine," he said as quickly as he could, running out of the room. I opened my mouth to say goodnight, but he was gone. Long gone. I turned my head on the pillow and curled into a ball, wrapping myself with the fluffy gray blanket that was placed on top of the mattress.

Heaven was what it felt like. My eyes flapped closed as I fell into a deep sleep. The memory of Adam and where I was still burning in my mind.

I woke up in a sunny room. The curtains on the windows were completely open, casting in the light of the bright sun. The building Adam lived in had its penthouse next to the stairway to heaven. So unbelievably high up in the sky, all I could see were clouds and the sun.

I rose from the bed and looked around the room. With the light, I could take in all the details in the room better than I could last night. Every lining, every painting, every object. But I was quickly distracted by the smell coming from outside my door.

Possibly coming from the kitchen. The smell of bacon and pancakes captured my nose. I felt as if I was a cartoon floating to where the smell was taking me. I was still in the same clothes as yesterday, since I had nothing to change into.

I tiptoed to the kitchen to find a woman in an apron with a tight, small bun on the top of her head. When she saw me, she greeted me with a smile. "Buenos dias!" *Good morning,* she says, flipping a pancake on the pan. Her wrinkles showed as she smiled, and I noticed some streaks of white hair in her brunette color.

"Buenos dias," I responded with the same smile she gave me. Soft and welcoming. She pointed to the stool on the other side of the island. "I'm Katherine," I said as I placed a hand over my chest.

"Hola, Katherine. Yo soy Petra," she added as she turned back around to the stove. The sound of sizzling bacon rang in my ears. My mouth watered in response. She handed me a plate, and I began to eat the delicious food. Adam wasn't here. He must have still been sleeping. It was still pretty early—seven o'clock.

Once I finished my plate, I was left satisfied. I thanked Petra and made my way toward the living room and waited for Adam to wake up so I could go back home and get my things. When I reached the living room, I found my bags packed with clothes on the couch. I was confused how my things got here.

I stalked toward the bags and looked through them. Yup, these clothes were definitely mine. My laptop and charger were also here. "Good morning, Katherine." I turned to see Adam in a tight black shirt and sweats, drenched in sweat. He had earphones in his ears, looking like he just came back from a run. While I, on the other hand, had just woken up and ate pancakes and bacon, thinking he was still asleep.

"How did you get this?" I asked, pointing at my belongings that magically showed up.

"I had Henry get your things from your apartment. Thought I'd save you the trip," he told me while plucking the earphones out of his ears. His breath was heavy, and his perfectly sculpted body was beyond distracting. He took his shoes off and then grabbed the hem of his shirt and peeled it off of him. His abs were rock hard and defined, covered in sweat. His sweatpants were dragging down, showing his adonis belt, but covering the spot I was compelled to see.

My eyes were glued to him, and I was hypnotized by him. "Everything good?" he asked with a smirk on his face. Of course, that bastard did it on purpose, just to see me sweat. Well, it worked, obviously.

"Oh yeah. Better than g-good." I stuttered the last word.

"Have any plans today?" he asked. I looked away as he walked around the couch.

"Going to write," I answered, trying to end the conversation. It was too hard to focus while he was standing in front of me without a shirt.

"Okay, I have a meeting to attend to. But afterward, I'd love to sit and go over what you have so far. That's what I'm here for, anyway," he reminded me. I nodded, only understanding the first sentence and the last coming out of his mouth. He shook his head while chuckling to himself on his way up the stairs.

He stopped halfway up and looked back, only to find my eyes glued to his ass. "I could also lend a hand. If you need it." He winked at me before continuing up the stairs. This was just *great.*

He was messing with me, and I didn't blame him. I was easy to mess with. I ignored what happened and opened my laptop and got to work. I moved all around the penthouse, testing which area I was able to write the most in. I knew it sounded stupid, but it was a real thing.

Throughout half the afternoon, I wrote three chapters, and I felt proud of it. Feeling closer to the end.

CHAPTER 28

ADAM

I LEFT THE OFFICE EARLIER THAN I DID ON REGULAR DAYS because I wanted to go back home to Katherine. I didn't think she'd take my offer. I'd hoped she would, and she did. For the first time in years, I had a strong need to leave the office.

I stopped by the bookstore to check if Katherine left to come here. I hadn't checked the penthouse yet, but I didn't want to arrive and not find her there. It was on my way, and stopping didn't hurt. I strolled in and the doorbell rang, notifying my entrance.

"Hello!" a heavy accent greets me—Judy. The woman who owned the store and a friend of Katherine's. She had her hair up and was wearing a pink sundress that matched her store. She looked stressed, exhausted even, but didn't show it in her voice.

"Hello, Judy," I greeted her, and she squinted her eyes at me. She recognized my voice but didn't realize who I was. She reached for her glasses on the counter and put them on.

"Adam! Hello, dear. I apologize. A woman my age starts to lose her vision little by little," she joked, pointing to her glasses. "What can I do for you, dear?" I glanced around the store and noticed it seemed to be emptier, missing books on the book-shelves.

"Books selling out quickly, I see," I said to congratulate her, but her face only seemed to lose the small amount of light it had. She appeared to be sad, tired of keeping up this act. "Are you okay, Judy?" I asked, worried she'd break down right in front of me.

"I'm sorry," she wheezed, covering her eyes.

"No, please, it's alright. Is there something wrong?" I would try to get more information about what was happening.

"It's the store. With the sudden change of rent, I'm unable to keep it up." She gasps in between words, unable to speak. "I'm closing the store. I don't want to, but I have no choice," she said while she shrugged in an attempt to brush it off.

My mind only went to Katherine, and how devastated she'd be if she knew her favorite place on earth would close for good. This store wasn't something I'd pick to come to regularly, but I could agree with Katherine when she said it was unique.

I decided to step in and take matters into my own hands. "Judy, how about we make a proposition," I said, as I pulled out a chair from the coffee table for her to sit in. She only looked at me with confusion in her eyes, but she followed my lead and took a seat. I settled across from her and began to speak.

I left the store after speaking with Judy for about two hours. I'd spoken to lawyers and business colleagues and came to an agree-ment that seemed good enough. I wasn't planning to spend much time there, but it worked out perfectly.

Unlocking the door, I walked into the penthouse to find Katherine propped up against the couch with her laptop on her lap. She had her headphones on as she typed loudly on the computer, not noticing my presence. She was facing the view of

Manhattan, the night allowing the lights to shine on her face. A masterpiece casually sitting in my living room.

I took advantage to stare at her in action, when she was in that hole that writers go into when they write. A whole different world I'd always felt jealous I couldn't experience for myself.

I decided not to interrupt her and let her continue to write. I slowly stepped around her, not wanting to distract her, but she stopped me by saying, "Hey, you're back." I turned to see her taking her headphones off and closing her laptop.

"Yeah. How's the writing?" I asked, pointing at the laptop she was gripping.

"How come you don't have a Christmas tree yet?" She ignored my question completely, but had a mischievous glint in her eyes. Where was this girl going with this question? I stepped back and shrugged out of my jacket, rolling up my sleeves.

"I don't do decorations." I cut it short and simple, getting straight to the point. "They take too much work, and I don't care whether or not I see lights in my house. I already see enough outside." Her mouth propped open in complete shock. "What?" I asked—she hadn't closed her mouth yet.

She sat up, crossing her legs and rolling her shoulders back, like she was getting ready to give me a lecture. "There is no way you just said that," she proclaimed. "You need Christmas decorations. How else are you supposed to get into the holiday spirit?" I chuckled at her seriousness.

"I don't think I have the ability to get in the holiday spirit, angel," I explained as I reclined on the couch next to her.

"That's the most ridiculous thing I've ever heard." She spoke with her hands, waving them in the air. "I think you've never given yourself the chance to get in the mood."

"Oh yeah? You got the cure, Dr. Know it all?"

"I'm serious, Adam," she added, annoyed at my sarcasm. I was messing with her because she was hitting a spot that I didn't want her to reach. I didn't want her to know the dark side of me.

The memories that haunted me late at night. "Why don't we go get a Christmas tree? I have decorations at my apartment."

I took a second to process this; it was going to be a fucking pain to accomplish. But then I took a second to study the look on Katherine's face. She was slightly biting her lip, anxious to see what my answer would be and how—or if—I'd go along with it. Should I?

Fuck it.

I grabbed Katherine's chin by my fingertips and tilted it toward my face and gave her an answer. "Okay, we'll get the damn Christmas tree." She shrieked excitedly, like I'd just agreed to give her a million dollars. She jumped up from the couch and ran to the door, putting her shoes on and grabbing her jacket.

"Come on, let's go before all the good ones are gone," she explained as she waved to me to come toward the door.

"What? Now?" I asked, confused and unsure of where we would even find a Christmas tree at this time, but I was not slow to match her pace.

She was making me feel excited, like a child, and I was just along for the ride.

"Yes, now! Are you kidding? We've already wasted so much time!"

It made me smile how she was treating this as a live or die situation. It was only the first few weeks of December. I was sure there were enough trees to pick from. And if she didn't like any of them, I'd find one she did want. Price wasn't a problem.

After aggressively fitting my feet into my shoes, I raced behind her. She was holding the door for me to walk out. I grabbed the door from her and closed it behind us, locking it. "Alright, where is this secret tree place?" I teased her as we approached the elevator.

"I'll tell Henry; he's the one driving," she teased back. It was playful, but it triggered the tiniest bit of jealousy toward Henry.

"Not today. It's his day off. I'm driving us," I lied. He drove me throughout the entire day, but Katherine didn't need to know that. "Looks like you're going to have to tell me, after all." I grinned at her, quickly satisfied with my decision.

"*You're* driving *us?*" She seemed surprised, as if she expected me to not know how to drive. It wasn't that I didn't know, I did, but I'd rather not. The elevator doors opened, and we walked in. I pressed the button to the garage.

"Yes," I clarified. "I'm quite the driver." She snorted under her breath, causing me to turn my full attention to her. "I'm sorry, did you have something you want to add?" She covered her mouth, not realizing she snorted so loudly.

"No, I didn't think you knew how to drive," she admitted, looking at the numbers decreasing on the pad. The elevator slid open as we reached the garage, showcasing a number of luxurious cars. I walked out as Katherine stood still with her mouth slowly opening wider and wider.

"Something wrong?" I asked, smirking to myself. She quickly closed her mouth and followed me. There were multiple floors underground for parking space, which gave me the opportunity to buy an entire floor. There were five cars parked and spread throughout the floor, giving each car a greedy amount of space.

"Which one's yours?" She looked around the lot.

"All of them," I said with a bored tone. Not many took me as a car guy, but I had a secret love for them. Something Micheal and I shared.

The five cars parked were a Pagani Huayra Codalunga in a pearl color, a Bugatti La Voiture Noire in matte black, a Rolls Royce in black—my day-to-day car Henry drove—a McLaren Speedtail in white with black stripes, and a Lamborghini Veneno in a metallic silver color.

I headed toward the wall that held the keys to each car and reached for the Lamborghini fob. "How are we going to fit a tree in that car?" Katherine said as she followed behind me. The thought of having to deal with a tree had completely flown out of my mind the moment I saw my cars.

"I'll have my men bring it," I said, not wanting the tree to scratch the car. I always had a bodyguard present with me everywhere I went. They kept their distance from me, so I wouldn't have to deal with their presence.

"Your men?" she asked, not having noticed them. Which was good; meant they were decent at their job. I nodded as I opened the door for Katherine on the passenger side. She looked up at me with a glint in her eye. "Can I drive it?" she asked with a huge smile on her face.

"You have experience with driving cars like these?" I asked, already knowing the answer. She shook her head, knowing I'd won.

"No... but you could teach me..." She moved closer to me, brushing her thighs against my legs. I looked down at the interaction, trying to keep a clear mind. "Please..." She tilted her head as she looked up at me. I was quickly lost, staring at her lips. The thoughts of wanting to take ownership over them came rushing back. She was good.

The word 'please' coming from that mouth, in that pleading tone, did devious things to my mind. Deep down, I had a horrible feeling that whenever this girl said please, I would go to any length to do what she wanted. "You want to learn?" My voice was huskier than before. She nodded without breaking eye contact. "Very well." I wrapped my hands around her waist, moving her into the seat. "Sit and watch me drive. You can try on our way back."

She sat, and I grabbed the seat belt and buckled her in place. My movements were slow and soft, not wanting to hurt her. She grabbed my arm, making me turn my face to hers. Our faces were only inches apart. I brushed my nose against hers and she let out a soft gasp. She smelled as delicious as she always did, and I was lost in yet another lavender haze.

She was leaning in, surely wanting the same thing as me. I wanted nothing more than to feel those lips on mine again, but the thought of having an uncomfortable Katherine in my house didn't allow me to. So, I moved back with every ounce of willpower I had. I closed her door and headed toward the driver's side.

Once I was all settled in, I started the engine. Katherine had her body and head facing the window, away from me. "Where are we going?" I asked in a soft voice. She handed me her phone with the address put into a maps app, and I grabbed a hold of it and turned the radio on.

The song 'On My Mind' by Ellie Goulding started to play, and I was about to switch the radio until I noticed Katherine quietly singing to it, so I left it. The song talked about not understanding why a certain person was constantly on your mind, and I couldn't help but find it ironic how I could relate to it. A little too much.

The drive to the market was quick—twelve minutes tops. We arrived, and I found Katherine to be in a much better mood once she saw the trees. It was an outdoor market with different types of trees displayed with price tags on them. Tall, short, thick, slim trees lined up in rows.

Katherine got out of the car and made her way to the trees. I turned off the car and followed her, annoyed that I needed to run after this girl. I turned into a row, and I didn't see Katherine. As I continued to walk down, the smell of the trees hit my nostrils, and I was reminded of the moments I had as a child. Decorating my own Christmas tree.

From the side of my eye, I caught a glimpse of brown hair all the way down the aisle. I moved closer and found Katherine smelling the side of a tree with a smile on her face. "Found the one we're taking?" I asked, and she opened her eyes in shock. She hadn't realized my presence.

"How long have you been standing there?" She avoided my eyes and ran her hands over the branch.

"Long enough to know you want this one." I stepped closer to her, wanting more clarity about why she seemed upset with me. "What is it?" I demanded as I pushed her against the black fence behind the tree. I propped both hands against the fence, caging her in.

"What are you talking about?" she asked angrily, struggling to get away.

"What is it that you want, Katherine?"

She was quiet, playing a game that was pissing me off. And truly, I had built up too much sexual tension to participate. "I—" She struggled to get the words out. I placed a hand on the side of her neck, rubbing in slow circular motions. I moved closer to her, our lips only a breath apart once again.

"What. Do. You. Want?" I said, my voice low as it had ever been. I sounded like a hungry wolf, ready to devour his untouched lamb, and I got the feeling this lamb wouldn't run away.

She did the same movement of brushing her nose against mine as I had done in the car. "I want you to kiss me," she said softly, almost as a whisper. My heart began to race, my palms sweaty. I had never reacted this way to a woman who wanted to be kissed. Much less a woman who asked to be kissed. This wasn't just any woman, though. It's Katherine. My Katherine.

She just didn't know it yet.

But I was quick to give her what she wanted. I brushed my lips with hers and kissed her. Our kiss was soft but hungry, the type of kiss that made you want to burn each other's clothes off and praise one another. Her hands ran up to my neck and mine down to her waist and ass. I gripped and squeezed her ass cheek and she moaned into my mouth. I was lost in her scent, her touch—in her.

I forgot where we were until I heard a couple of voices getting closer to the tree.

"This one's nice," a female voice said.

"Perfect, let's get it," a low voice responds.

If it weren't for those voices, I would have kept going. But I wasn't about to have a couple of strangers take this tree from Katherine. She wanted it, and she'd get it.

I let go of Katherine and fixed her hair for her before turning. "Wonderful tree, isn't it?" I said to them.

"Yes, it is," the woman said, surprised to see me climb out from behind it.

"Unfortunately, it's recently been purchased by this wonderful woman." I pointed toward Katherine, who was climbing out from the back with flushed cheeks.

"Oh," the man next to the woman added.

"Terribly sorry, folks. I'm sure you can find another great tree." They looked at each other, seemingly suspicious, but nodded and went on their way. I held Katherine's hand and ran to the front to purchase the tree.

"I can't believe you did that." She giggled, looking as beautiful as ever.

"You said you wanted it. I was going to make sure you got it," I said to her, holding her hand in mine. It felt good, it felt right. I let Katherine drive us back, and to be honest, she couldn't have driven it better for her first time.

Afterward, we went back home and began to decorate the tree. Christmas music played in the background—Katherine's choice—and it was the first time in a long time that a holiday didn't seem like the burden I thought it was.

CHAPTER 29
KATHERINE

Spending the Christmas season with Adam was going better than I thought. From the invite to stay at his house to the kiss at the tree market. I was now here decorating a Christmas tree with Adam; he was mostly standing next to me, handing me the ornaments. But that kiss. The kiss was better than I remembered it to be. Maybe it was the fact that things were slowly changing between us.

I received a piece from Adam and tiptoed to hang it on the upper left side of the tree. I tripped by mistake and dropped the ornament. It shattered on the ground and sliced a cut on my right foot. "Ah," I said to myself as I noticed the blood from the cut.

"What?" Adam asked as he hurried to my side. He spotted the minor injury on my foot and his eyes widened. He instantly climbed over the shattered glass and carried me out, even though I was perfectly able to walk myself. He held me in his arms in a bridal pose and took me to the couch to lay me down. "Stay put."

"Wasn't going anywhere," I joked as I saw him walking toward the kitchen. He returned with a first aid kit in his hand and set it on the coffee table across from me. He opened the red box that had all types of bandages—triangular, crepe rolled, etc.

Adam pulled out disposable sterile gloves and a clean cloth that had already been dampened with water. "It's a small cut, not a vein cut." He shook his head slightly while smiling.

Seriously, though, he was doing a bit much with the gloves. It already smelled like a hospital with all the tools he was pulling out. "Relax, angel. I'll clean you up good," he said as he grabbed the crepe rolled bandages.

"This isn't how I'd imagine you'd 'clean me up' with a warm damp cloth," I joked, but suddenly realized what I had just said. My eyes widened and my cheeks flushed red as he met my gaze.

"Sorry to disappoint. I wasn't aware that was even an option," he teased while quirking a brow. He knew that I felt utterly embarrassed. Why would I even say that out loud?

"That—That is not what I meant." I tried to fix it, but desperately failed as I noticed his grin grow wider.

"I'm unaware of what you mean... How did you mean it, then?" He seemed so happy with this, like he enjoyed seeing me nervous and tripping around him. I wanted to take the next flight to Canada at this point. After that kiss and this outburst, he definitely knew I was having thoughts about him. *Very* inappropriate thoughts.

"Not important," I spoke.

Adam had already cleaned up all the blood and managed to put some healing ointment on my cut while I was distracted by our current conversation. He began to wrap the bandage around my foot, then around my ankle to secure it.

"Everything you say is important, Katherine," he said in such a low voice, I almost missed it. "There, all fixed." Fixed, it was. I didn't even feel like I had a bandage wrapped around my foot. Not an ounce of pain was felt while he cleaned it.

"Thanks," I told him as I bit my bottom lip, unsure of what else to say. I tried to push myself up from the couch, but briskly felt a pair of hands wrapped around my waist, pushing me back down.

"What do you think you're doing?" He grabbed the pillow behind him and placed it under my foot.

"Finishing the Christmas tree." It was almost done; all that was left were the lights and the star. Everything else was done. I had chosen to do a red and white pattern, and it reminded me of a candy cane. Perfect for the occasion, if you asked me.

"The hell you are," he spurted out. "You just injured yourself, so you need to lie down for a bit. You can't put weight on it just yet." God, he was acting like I had broken a bone.

"My 'injury' is the same as a paper cut."

"Yeah, a fucking deep one." He crossed his arms, showcasing his muscles. Yeah, I for sure wouldn't ever get tired of that view. "Just stay off your feet for now." Looking into Adam's eyes, I knew it'd be hard to fight him. He was too damn stubborn.

"Fine, but I'm going to need some type of entertainment," I argued, annoyed that I was giving in to him so quickly. He sighed and brushed his hair back with his hand, again flexing his muscles. I couldn't tell if it was on purpose or if his body naturally looked good from all angles.

He took a seat next to me, leaning back. "Alright, then, what would you like?" He asked, like any answer would be valid to him. *Your pants off would be nice, sir.* Yeah... I was definitely feeling horny. I shook my head, focusing back on what Adam was saying.

"Talk to me," I answered, pleased with my choice. This could be a good time to get to know Adam more as a person. To know who he really was.

"Katherine, I am talking to you." He was acting sarcastic with me, but I also had a feeling it was his barrier talking.

"I mean, tell me more about yourself. Like your childhood," I explained. He shifted in his seat uncomfortably. It was probably hard for him to open up, but I was just asking, hoping he'd agree. "Please?" I whispered. He met my eyes with his lips pressed together. He simply nodded, but didn't say anything. "I can go first. Ask me a question."

He sat up and looked at me as if he knew exactly what to ask, but hesitated to ask it. "Has it always been just you and your mom?" And there it was—Adam being curious. It wasn't the first time I'd gotten that question, though, but this was the first time that I'd answer it honestly.

Adam didn't make me feel uncomfortable. I actually felt that sitting here, on this couch, next to him, was my safe space. "Well." I tried to figure out the right words to use. "No... not always, at least." He tilted his head ever so slightly.

"My dad, he, uh... He wasn't the best dad. He wasn't much of a family man, either," I started.

"His best friend was alcohol. I don't think I've ever seen him sober, if I'm thinking about it. He began cheating on my mother, and I knew because I could hear her cries at night, talking about it with her friend. I was little, but I could still understand everything. Things were good between him and my mom until, well... me." I nibbled on my bottom lip, trying not to cry. "One day, he came home, packed his bags, and walked out the door. He, uh— He never came back. He didn't even bother looking back at me, and it made me feel as if I had never existed to him. That I was only a burden to him, something he was stuck dealing with. The reason he left," I explained, and I felt Adam's hands rubbing my back in support.

"I don't understand how anyone would willingly leave after knowing you." I felt a teardrop fall down my cheek. "Hey, hey. It's okay," he said in a soothing tone. I nodded and wiped away my tears as Adam tucked my hair behind my ear. "You got questions for me?" He tried to change the topic.

I looked at him, trying to decide what to ask him. Something that wouldn't make him shut down. As I scanned him, I looked down at his chest. His shirt was pulled to the side, showing the edge of a scar on his collarbone. The same scar I had seen that night at the hotel. I'd been curious about it ever since.

"What's this scar? How'd you get it?" I asked, pointing at it. He looked down to where my finger was and sighed. I didn't push him; I let him come to me. He lifted his hand to swipe the last tear from my face before speaking, sending butterflies to my stomach.

"It happened a long time ago, when I was a child. Most people carry scars that they get from their childhood as a memory, like riding a bike and falling. But I didn't have a regular childhood. I had to grow up rather fast." I was looking so intensely at him, craving more of his story. I noticed he took a break to sigh between lines. "My mother was a phenomenal woman—sweet, kind, loving, and quite beautiful. She had these slender hands that always brushed my hair back when she had the chance. I used to hate it back then, but now, I'd give anything to feel that again."

"She sounds exceptional. What happened to her?" Adam's breath became shaky as he regained the courage to continue.

"It was summer, and my mother had decided to take my brother and me to the beach house for summer break. I was eleven at the time. I remember sleeping in my room next to my brother, who was fast asleep, and heard silent screams from the kitchen. I got out of bed to go see what was happening, but as I reached the kitchen, I saw two men attacking my mother. They had her held down on the counter, beating her. She saw me and screamed for me to go back to my room and stay there. As her son, I wanted to save her from the bad guys. I tried to fight them off, but unfortunately, being small and skinny didn't help. One of them had a knife and cut me. I think they were trying to reach for my throat, but I was way too fast for them." Adam was focused on the story as I imagined him as a child going through this. I couldn't help but tear up at the image.

"The police were on their way, and they made a run for it.

Leaving my mother thrown on the floor, incapable of moving on her own. I dragged my way through the floor toward her. They had stabbed her. She was slowly losing blood, and I saw her die in my arms. She had tears in her eyes and whispered how much she loved us. The paramedics came and rushed her to the hospital and my father came for my brother and me. Not a day later, they pronounced her dead. It was too late, and she had been more injured than I thought. If only I could have fought them off, if only—" Adam's cheeks were now wet with his own tears as he remembered everything, finally letting everything out.

I reached across the couch to hold his face in my hands. I kissed him softly, tasting the salt on his lips.

"It's not your fault," I told him and kissed him again. "None of that was your fault, Adam."

I knew that opening up was hard for him, and sharing this story meant the world to me. I was hoping that after everything I had shared with him tonight, with honesty, he'd know I was telling him nothing but the truth.

He stayed frozen in place, unable to move.

Suddenly, he kissed me back. Deeply and intensely, like he couldn't get enough. It was not as sweet and slow as the kiss back at the tree market. No, this was a desperate kiss. Like we were the only thing that was holding one another. We both just shared the deepest, darkest parts of ourselves, and in a way, we now understood one another. His tongue tangled with mine, his hand in my hair.

Our kiss happened to last a while until Adam pulled me on top of him by my hips. He pulled my shirt over my head, leaving me with only my bra on. His lips dragged all the way down my neck and stayed there as he nibbled and licked a spot that had me going crazy. He pulled down the straps of my bra, revealing my bare chest to him, and held me tight to him. Then he ran his hands over my breasts, unable to look away.

"Fucking hell, Katherine," he groaned. "Your body is perfect."

I leaned further into his touch, seeking and wanting more. I became more aroused as he praised my body, and I felt the bulge in his pants become thicker. He took my breast in his mouth, flicking the nipples with his tongue until they hardened. He sucked on them in turns, back and forth, building the sensational waves of pleasure into tsunamis.

The air in the room became thicker, and the space in the room appeared smaller. It was as if Adam had taken over my world, turning every bit of attention, breath, and movement toward him. For him. I wanted him to suck on my breast forever. It was so achingly good that all I could do was moan and grind against him. He flipped me on to the couch, my back lying against the cushions as he hovered over me.

I was gripping his shirt in my hands, pulling him closer to me. His face was still buried in my chest, having me withering against him. When he finally got low enough, I pulled the end of his shirt over his shoulder, wanting to get rid of it. He smiled in response and pulled the shirt over his head, his chest now bared to me. I ran my hands over his arms, his chest, his abs, feeling each muscle in his body tense. He returned his attention to my lips, kissing me and pressing his chest against mine. I held him close to me, gently scratching his back.

It was far too late. I didn't know how much time had passed since I'd been on this couch with Adam. Time didn't seem to exist with him. He unbuttoned my jeans and peeled them down my legs. He moved slowly and carefully pulled my injured foot out of the hole and landed a kiss on the bandage.

He refocused his energy between my legs, pulling them apart, grabbing me by the hips and burying his face in my pussy. He was using his fingers, lips, and tongue in ways I never would have imagined. I'd never experienced this type of pleasure, never experienced so much care in my life.

I tried to move away, only for him to pin me in place, seeking out my most sensitive spots. He slid two fingers inside me, pumping them in and out while focusing his mouth on my clit, sucking and licking. I began to feel the pressure of my orgasm building as I continued to grind against his face. I was so wildly stimulated; I didn't have the voice to moan anymore.

I looked up at the ceiling as my orgasm finally exploded inside me, my vision reaching the stars. It was a vision of bright brilliance, so intense, so dazzling, I could almost cry. My legs were shaking, and my heart rate was nowhere near normal.

"Oh my god," I said softly, trying to regain strength in my voice. He climbed back up to me, placing a delicate kiss on my lips. He tried to move away, but I held him back, kissing him deeply. He kissed me back, groaning in my mouth.

"You're going to be the death of me," he spoke and continued to kiss me. I wrapped my legs around his hips, pulling him down and close to my entrance. I felt his dick straining against his pants and shamelessly ground against the friction. "Fuck, Katherine." He was looking down at the movement, at the sight of us pressed together with only the material of his pants between us.

I reached for his pants and began to unbuckle them. Adam looked me straight in my eyes and grabbed my hand, stopping me. "Katherine," he said, like he was trying to talk some sense into me.

"What? Don't you want to?" I asked, confused.

"Fuck, of course I want to," he growled. "I don't want to rush you."

"You're not." Even when I was withering against him, completely baring myself to him, he still thought whether it would affect me or not. Whether I'd want to or not.

He spared me a quick smirk before placing both his hands on my ass and picking me up. He was carrying me like I weighed nothing, heading straight toward the stairs. Adam was way taller than me—six-foot-two, almost six-foot-three. And I was small, around five-foot-four. I wrapped my hand around the back of his head, kissing and sucking on his neck. It seemed to trigger him as he gripped my ass harder in his hands, groaning in my ear. As we reached his room, he dropped me on his bed, ripping his pants off in the process, leaving only his boxers on.

I sat on the edge of the bed and could visibly see how big he was. It had my mouth watering in ways I didn't know it could. He stood in front of me, his chest rising and falling aggressively as I looked up at him. I reached toward his boxers and pulled them down, watching as his dick sprung out, large and thick, with pre-cum leaking from his tip. I gripped it and gave it a soft tug.

"Fuck, baby. You're killing me," he said through gritted teeth, and I was feeling a bit more confident about taking charge.

I took him in my mouth, closing my lips around his tip, and sucked. He let out a soft growl, which encouraged me to keep going. I took more of him in my mouth, careful not to choke on it. He was big and I couldn't fit the whole thing in my mouth. "You're doing so good, baby. You look so pretty with my cock in your mouth." I moaned around his cock, continuing to suck and twirl my tongue around his shaft. I used my free hand to cup his balls, delicately kneading. I closed my eyes to try to take more of him, but suddenly felt him pull out of my mouth and throw me in the center of the bed.

I opened my eyes to see him hovering over me, his scar, his blonde hair messed up, his green eyes piercing into mine. He looked perfect, like a dream. I opened my thighs so he could position himself closer to my core. I wiggled against him, which had him fluttering his eyes shut. He was so close. He was right at my entrance, and it was driving me crazy. I grabbed his dick and slid it up and down against my folds. "Fuck," he groaned.

"Tell me to stop," he said. I slowly shook my head. "Katherine, tell me to stop before it's too late."

"I can't," I told him, speaking the truth.

"If we do this, there's no going back. You'll be mine, Katherine, and I don't think you'll like what that means. So, tell me. To stop." He searched for any signs of discomfort in my eyes. I couldn't say no now. I wanted this. I wanted him. I'd be lying to myself if I said I hadn't thought about this moment multiple times.

I opened up to him, told him what I couldn't tell anyone else, and I knew he could say the same. I wasn't worried about messing up. I was worried I was going to fall harder than I already had.

"I don't want you to stop. I want you, I want this. Please." I didn't bother lying. He smiled and positioned his tip at my entrance. I was wiggling again, desperate to feel him.

"I know you want this, baby. I do, too. I'll go slow." He sunk into me, only stretching me by an inch. I moaned at the feeling. He was bigger than I thought. "Are you okay?" he asked as he saw the small look of pain on my face. I nodded in response, wrapping my hand around his arm, encouraging him to keep going. "Inch by inch, baby," he reassured me.

He sunk deeper inside me, and only halfway inside me, I felt completely full. I was worried I wouldn't be able to fit all of him inside me. I looked down at where we were connected and saw a good amount still needing to enter me. "I don't think it's going to fit," I admitted. He simply shook his head and kissed my neck.

"Of course it'll fit. You were made for me, angel." He kissed my chin and continued to move. Every inch he slipped in, he pulled out, then added another inch. He was moving slowly, not wanting to hurt me. It had been such a long time since I'd had sex. It felt a bit tight, especially with his large size.

Once he was fully seated inside me, I felt so full. I moaned as he moved in and out of me. "You feel so fucking good. Fucking perfect," he groaned in my ear. I could tell he'd been holding himself back, so I placed my hand on the side of his cheek and directed him to my face.

"Faster," I told him.

"You sure?"

"Yes." And with that, he unleashed himself and went hardcore, pounding into me. I screamed his name at the top of my lungs as he lifted a leg over his shoulder. "Oh my god, yes!" I screamed again as I felt another wave about to hit me. He pressed his thumb on my clit with just the right amount of pressure that had me exploding once again.

"Yeah, just like that, baby. You're doing so good for me," he growled, and I moaned in response, his comments only keeping me going. I felt my third orgasm ripping through me as he took my breast in his mouth and sucked while he used his hand to play with the other one.

"Fuckkk," I yelled, feeling sweat beading on my forehead. His breaths and strokes became unsteady as he exploded inside me and collapsed on top of me. He buried his face in my neck, his body shaking from his orgasm.

My legs were locked around his waist. We stayed there in that same position, regaining our strengths. I could feel his heart beating against my chest, his heart just a couple of inches from mine. Separated by flesh and nothing else.

He finally lifted up and pulled out with a popping sound. He left to the bathroom and came back into the room with a damp cloth. He cleaned my thighs and my pussy. It was aching with pleasurable pain, but he was careful as he wiped along my skin.

"Is this how you wanted me to clean you up?" he joked as he cleaned up the last of his cum. I didn't realize a small comment about a wet cloth would lead up to this moment hours later. I smiled at the thought.

"Exactly like this." He smiled and grabbed a blanket folded from the edge of his bed and climbed back up next to me. He held me in his arms and pulled the cover over us. I placed my head on his chest, right where his heart was, and fell asleep to the rhythm of his heartbeat.

Nothing would beat this moment between him and me.

CHAPTER 30

ADAM

I woke up the next morning with Katherine's body draped over mine. Last time I had woken up next to her, I had left with my tail between my legs. Instead, today, I lie here and soak up the warmth of her body. Her soft breasts pushed up against my chest, her arms wrapped around my waist. I looked down and saw her face fully at rest.

Her hair was tangled and free, her lashes shadowed over her cheeks as she continued to sleep. Watching her sleep brought me the most peace I'd ever experienced. This wasn't the first time I'd seen it, but it was different. We were different.

Being in her presence felt like being bathed by the purest kind of sunlight. A light that shone through the grayest clouds, it felt liberating and vibrant… hopeful even. I didn't usually use the word hope. I saw no true meaning to it until now. In this moment, I realized that she was my salvation, even though I wasn't worth saving.

It was incredible how a person could walk into your life and turn it upside down. Showing you the beauty that this world held, how it looked through her eyes. How a single Christmas tree made her happy, how she expressed her love through stories, how she seemed joyful in spite of all the evil surrounding her. I knew after last night that I was not capable of letting her go. I was not capable of feeling this way for any other human being.

As I continued to breathe in Katherine's presence, she moved against me, slowly coming back to life. She fluttered her eyes open and met my gaze. She was the most beautiful woman I'd ever seen. She had never looked better than she did in this exact moment.

"Hi." She yawned while doing the smallest, cutest stretch. She had no idea what she did to me.

"Hi," I said back, admiring the way her nose crinkled as she woke up. "How did you sleep?"

"I slept surprisingly really well. Probably the best in a long time."

"You're welcome." I smirked. She rolled her eyes at me as she pulled the cover over her head. I went underneath with her, shying away from the light shining in through the window. She smiled as my eyes met hers. Her hand landed on my chin, rubbing small circles with her finger.

"I like this," I admitted, looking at her almost golden eyes.

"Like what?" she asked, biting her lip.

"This. You, here with me."

"Me too," she said, holding back a smile. I was already smiling, my dimple penetrating my face. She moved her fingers to my dimples and blushed. I moved closer to her and kissed her softly, soaking in the way she made me feel.

Happy.

We stayed there in our own little world for a few minutes before getting up and heading to the kitchen to have some breakfast. Katherine sat on a stool behind the island, staring at me as I whipped her up some pancakes. I wasn't a chef, but pancakes couldn't be that hard to cook.

Though, I still managed to slightly burn them. If Katherine didn't like them, she didn't show it. She was eating them like it was the best batch ever made. I knew she was lying, but I found it cute that she tried.

"So, what do you want to do today?" she asked as I took a seat at the stool next to hers. I was about to answer her, but was interrupted by my phone ringing and vibrating on the counter.

I reached for it to see who was calling—the Pearson Book Group main office.

I picked up and heard Richard's voice over the phone. Having my family lawyer calling me from my office at this time set me on edge. I imagined the worst possible scenario. *I lost my right to the will,* went through my head.

"Adam. Good morning, I hope I'm not calling at a bad time." I looked over to Katherine, who was staring at me, confused. I laid a hand on her thigh and gave it a small squeeze before I left the kitchen.

"Good morning, Richard. No, this is a perfect time. What can I do for you?" I asked, wanting him to spit it out. I managed to walk into my home office to take the call.

"Well, I've been up to record with your and Mr. Edward's reports so far... I'm very impressed with the work you both have done for your authors. The reason I'm calling is to check in on you. I've noticed you've taken a little break from promoting your author's book, and I'm a little concerned whether it's finished or not. That is very important." Crap, I'd been so caught up in Katherine that I'd slowed down on the marketing side of her book. I was sure Katherine had also slowed down on the writing, hinting at the fact she hadn't finished her book.

We'd both gotten so caught up in each other that we'd put those things aside. If Richard hadn't called this morning, I would've gone the entire day without paying any type of attention to this project. Christmas was only a few days away, and February first would be right around the corner. Time was going by too fast. I swear, I felt like it was working against me.

"Of course, I appreciate your concern, Richard. I can assure you, the book is almost finished. I'll manage the rest. I've been working and sorting out events for this coming month. Thank you for your call," I told him. He called because deep down he knew it would be a waste to hand over the entire franchise to my uncle.

Having my uncle in charge was like handing over a billion-dollar company to a teenager who didn't know two fucks about it. Equaling pure disaster for all involved.

"Alright, I'm glad to hear it. I'm truly rooting for you, Adam." I could tell he meant it sincerely. My uncle always despised having Richard as our family lawyer, but my father insisted. With that, he ended the call.

Walking back out to the kitchen where Katherine was, I knew I'd have to bring up business. I didn't want to, but I had to. I had a responsibility that must be fulfilled, and as much as I'd hate to admit, we were still working together. She worked for me.

I came close to Katherine, who was finished eating, and turned to face me. "What was that about?" she asked with curiosity in her eyes. She looked breathtaking, with no makeup and her hair tied up in a bun. *Focus.*

"Work, nothing important," I said. She nodded and didn't question me. She trusted everything I said. "Speaking about work. How is the book coming along? Are you close to finishing it?" Katherine hummed under her breath.

"I'm kind of close. I really only have about six or seven chapters to write, and I think I could wrap it up then. I'm just... I'm stuck on which way I should go." Hearing this didn't exactly ease my nerves. I didn't usually feel nervous when I was in competition with anyone, but this was so damn important, especially considering that Victoria had her book done.

"I see. How about we spend the day brainstorming? We could write a layout for the last few chapters, so it'd be easier to finish it." I tried to suggest a work day in the nicest way, trying to make it seem like it was her idea. I knew it was an asshole move of me, and if there wasn't so much on the line, I'd say to hell with all of it. But that wasn't the case. I didn't know how many times I had to remind myself of it.

Clearly a vast amount.

Katherine took a moment to think about it and answered me. "Yeah, I guess that would help. I'd have to leave the house for brainstorming. My creativity seems limited when I'm in a plain space." I knew what she meant by that; it was also the same reason she adored going to her little pink bookstore. Today, I had the perfect spot to take her to.

It used to be a multimillionaire's personal library. It wasn't exactly filled with modern day literature, but it was a place inspiration spilled out of one. I personally thought it was the cultural space, but I'd leave it up for Katherine to decide.

"Perfect. I know just the place."

The Morgan Library and Museum on Madison Avenue was where I took Katherine. Like I said, this wasn't a spot that people could use as a workspace—it was a museum.

I had my assistant rent out the entire library for us, so no one would interrupt us. Since I had such a high position in the literature world, I was able to do it. It would be just me and her in this big library. I couldn't help but have a good feeling about this. The Morgan Library housed one of the world's foremost collections of manuscripts, music, drawings, and ancient works of art. It was filled with history—home to the finest artists, thinkers, and writers.

The entire building itself was big, with different types of rooms that held the works of a specific category. I led Katherine to the one room I knew she'd appreciate. I hadn't forgotten what she told me the first time she brought me to the bookstore—her motivations, goals, and even favorite novel.

We walked into the library filled with only the best works of literature. Examples of some of the earliest printed books on display, along with classics. Most of the books were locked behind gates, but the bookshelves were close enough to stick your hand in to touch and feel the covers. Katherine wandered around the room, exploring the different types of novels, poems, and letters from history.

She matched the room perfectly. She was wearing a ruffle-sleeved maxi dress with a front slit in a solid khaki color, and her hair was loose with natural waves. The khaki and the color of her hair matched the vintage colors surrounding us. In my eyes, she was the most priceless work of art.

"This is beautiful. It takes my breath away," she said as she stuck her hand through a gate to touch a red book cover with golden edges.

"I know," I admitted, completely gawking at her. She finally looked at me and smiled. That smile… I'd pay any amount to see it on display at all times. I took her hand and led her to where they had Charles Dickens 'A Christmas Carol' along with 'The Little Prince' on display in a glass compartment.

Katherine placed her hand against the glass, as if she was trying to get as close as possible to them. "Pretty amazing, isn't it?" I said to her while she continued to stare in awe. I grinned to myself, knowing that the next thing I was going to show her would be her favorite. "Come," I told her as I stepped away, heading to the next thing.

I stood beside a table where the pages were laid out. There was no glass compartment, there was no gate. It was completely within her reach. She could touch it, feel it in her hands, and turn the pages to analyze the work.

Finally, she came to stand next to me. "What's this?" she asked. She seemed as excited as a child would be in a store filled with candy, though she stayed still, not reaching for anything until I said it was okay.

"Why don't you go ahead and take a look?" She gave me these unbelieving eyes and moved toward the table. "You can look through it, but be very gentle with the pages," I explained as she reached for the first page. I gave her a few seconds to discover what it was.

Her face lit up like never before, and I knew that she had figured it out. "No. Is this?" She checked again and re-read the first line. "This is—"

"It's the first manuscript of Pride and Prejudice," I clarified.

She continued to flip through the pages with glassy eyes, completely astonished by the gesture. I remembered the day she told me that it was her favorite novel, one of the novels that encouraged her to begin writing. I specifically asked for them to leave this out for us. I had paid a grand amount for it, and clearly, it was worth every damn penny.

"I figured since this was the one novel that helped you begin writing, it could also be the one to help you finish yours." I couldn't see Katherine's face with her hair in the way; she was hiding from me. Her sight was still glued to the manuscript laid in front of her.

"You did all of this for me? To help me finish my book?"

I stood there without an answer. Yes, I did it all for her, and if only she knew that I would do *anything* and *everything* for her.

Katherine turned to face me with tears in her eyes. She ran into my arms and slammed her lips against mine. Her lips were soft and tender as a blossom; they felt heavenly.

"Thank you," she whispered against my lips.

"You're welcome, angel."

We spent hours sitting in this library, brainstorming and writing. Katherine seemed to be on a whole different level; she knew exactly what she was going to write about. She had this face she put on when she was fully in the zone where her brows scrunched together, her eyes narrowed, and her lips became plump from the number of times she bit down on them.

I adored this version of her; she was free in her own mind, expanding her creativity with no one to tell her otherwise. As she wrote, I worked on planning future events, marketing ideas, and artwork.

Victoria, my uncle's author, had gained a generous number of readers this past month. Which meant we'd need to really make a good impression with our marketing plans, with ads, book influencers, and collaboration events with best-selling authors in the romance genre. Victoria might have gotten a head start, but we'd pass her the second Katherine released her book.

That, I was positive about.

"Okay, I officially have only four chapters left to write before completely finishing." Katherine yawned, stretching her arms above the chair. She hadn't moved from her position in hours.

"Excellent," I said as I stood and made my way to her. I stopped only inches behind her, my hands shoved in my pockets as I tried to control myself from grabbing her. "Are you sore?" She rotated her head to face me, giving me a shy smile.

"Just a bit. Nothing a good stretch couldn't fix," she answered, her voice extremely low.

"A good stretch, huh?"

She nodded, turning back to her computer with stiff shoulders. I reached to place my hands on her shoulder and began rubbing in circular motions. I did it with a certain amount of pressure, careful to make it pleasurable for her. She groaned beneath my touch, tilting her head to the side as I moved toward her neck.

Her heartbeat was fast, rapidly beating against her skin. She was becoming warmer, her shoulders beginning to loosen up a bit. "Is this helping?" I whispered in her ear, and she let out a small gasp and nodded. She didn't answer me with words, but her body was doing the talking.

I moved my fingers along the edge of her dress. Only three

buttons held her breasts from spilling out of it. I got the sight and the feel of them yesterday, but today, I was just as desperate to experience it all over again. It was addicting. She was addicting.

I'd never truly understood the meaning of being addicted to someone. To only crave the feel, the taste, the smell, even the sound, of a certain person. Being this close to Katherine, to hear her small gasps and whimpers, nearly undid me. I could say that I'd never had that.

Not with anyone.

Right as I was about to keep going, she stood from her seat and dragged me around the chair. She pushed me to sit and climbed on top of me, the rest of her dress covering our legs. Her hands landed on my chest as she looked into my eyes.

"What am I going to do with you?" I spoke without thinking, words spilling out of my mouth. But Katherine only smiled and drew close to me. This girl kept me on my toes, and I'd willingly go along with anything she wanted.

"You're different from what I thought you'd be," she admitted.

"Oh yeah? How's that?"

"You seemed really intimidating at first, but now I see that you're a softie at heart." She giggled, and I couldn't help but chuckle along with her. "People just need to get to know you."

"No, angel, I'm only a softie when it comes to you," I clarified as I brushed her hair out of her face.

I caressed her cheek and her chin before pulling her in for a kiss. The kiss quickly developed into a desperate need to have each other. She unbuckled my pants and pulled them down enough for my cock to let loose, and it hit her inner thigh. I tugged her panties to the side and moved a finger along her folds.

I groaned at finding her wet for me. My lips attacked hers. I bit her lips,and shoved my tongue into her mouth, sucking the breath out of her lungs like I was in survival mode, needing her air to live.

She ground against me, hungry for more. I lined myself up at her entrance and pushed the head between her lips. It felt impossibly wet and extremely warm. Katherine threw her head back as she sighed with pleasure. I grabbed her hips in my hands and pulled her all the way down.

We both gasped at the exact same time it went in. This wasn't just sex, it was a connection. She cried out into my mouth, biting down hard on my lip, drawing blood.

Still, I kept going with shallow thrusts, continuing to push myself inside her, until our bodies were tight together. No space between us. It was too much. I couldn't stand it for much longer. It was taking everything within me to not blow inside her. It felt too good.

She was getting wetter and wetter, helping me slide inside her easier. Our mouths were locked together, and she was clinging to me. We were entwined with one another in every possible way.

As her body bounced on mine, I had a full view of her breasts. I'd never seen skin so creamy and flawless before. Her nipples were a light pink, barely darker than her flesh. She was simply the most angelic woman I'd ever seen.

"More, Adam. I need more!" she screamed against my ear.

I gave her what she wanted and lost all sense of control, rapidly and aggressively thrusting into her. She squirmed above me as she clenched around me, causing me to lose my cool and come with her.

We both came down from our highs a few seconds later, covered in sweat and out of breath. Katherine caressed my face as I admired her. Her hair uncontrollably messy, her cheeks flushed with my favorite color of pink, and her gleam of sweat making her look like she was glowing. Looking like a goddess on top of me.

Caving in, I let my guard down, resting my head on her chest where I could feel her heart beating. Most would say I was showing weakness, and hey, maybe they were right.

"Adam," Katherine whispered in my hair, interrupting my thoughts.

"Yes, angel?"

"I love you."

Shock entered my system as I realized what she said. My skin paled and my muscles tensed. I wasn't expecting it.

CHAPTER 31

KATHERINE

'I love you.' Three words, eight letters. The one thing I thought I'd never have the balls to say to someone again. I wasn't going to say it, but it slipped. I felt extremely vulnerable in that moment, connected with Adam.

I was sitting on his lap, face-to-face, and pouring my feelings out to him. His face lost a bit of its color as his shoulder tensed underneath my hands. I had no idea what was going through his mind right now, if he even felt the same for me.

"Adam?" I said in a low, hurtful voice.

I was calling after him because I was desperate. I was calling out for him, even though he was right in front of me. I didn't want to be the girl who fell for the guy and willingly gave him my heart when he never intended on keeping it. Who never intended to give it back.

Adam remained unresponsive. I was swiftly losing my patience, knowing I should keep the last bit of dignity I had and leave.

"Right, of course. I get it, no worries," I managed to spit out, feeling the most embarrassed I'd felt in my entire life.

I pushed myself off his lap and fixed my dress. Without

sparing him one look, I grabbed my bags off the table and made my way toward the door. It all seemed to kick in for Adam once I was inches away from the nearest exit.

"Wait, wait Katherine." He raced behind me. "Hold on!" he desperately said as he gripped my right arm, pulling me back to him. "What... what just happened?" he asked. He was out of breath, but he only ran a few inches to reach me.

"I don't know, Adam. I told you I loved you and you ignored me. You didn't say one thing," I yelled back at him, but then I realized it wasn't his fault if he didn't feel the same way. So, I looked him in the eye and took a deep breath. "Listen, I get it if you don't feel the same. You're not obligated to. But at least say *something,* so I'm not sitting there like an *idiot* waiting for your response."

"Katherine, that's not—" He spoke, but I held my hand up to stop him.

"Let's just go, yeah? I really don't want to talk about this right now."

"But..." He tried to explain, but I honestly didn't think I had the strength emotionally to hear the next few words that would come out of his mouth. I was afraid they were not going to be what I wanted them to be.

"Please, not now," I said to him before turning around and walking out the door. He followed behind me the entire time, keeping a distance of five feet. I could hear his steps behind me, matching mine. He was giving me my space, but he was close enough to watch me.

I walked out and found the car already parked outside, waiting. Henry, Adam's driver, got out of the car to open my door. I hesitated at the door, thinking about how difficult it would be to ride in the back alone with Adam.

"Henry, can I ride with you in the front?" I asked hurriedly.

"Oh, I don't know, miss. Mr. Pearson regularly likes his guests to ride in the back with him," he explained. I knew I was asking something he wasn't used to. I wouldn't want him to get in trouble. Adam came up behind me, only inches away.

"Is there a problem?" he asked with a dominant voice that sent a shiver down my spine.

"No, Mr. Pearson, but Miss Katherine would like to ride in the front," Henry said. Adam didn't look at Henry while he was speaking. He was looking directly at me. My back was facing him, but I could see him piercing his eyes into the back of my head through the car window.

"I see... well, whatever she wants," Adam said as if it were poison coming out of his mouth. He didn't like it, but he was obliged to do anything I asked for right now.

I hadn't taken a glance at Adam yet. I felt like it would kill me to see him. Instead, I settled for the reflection of him; his jaw was locked and his whole body expression was tense.

Henry opened the front passenger door for me, and without a second thought, I got in. The privacy wall in the back was closed, and I instantly felt relieved. Henry came back to the driver's seat and drove.

Not even five minutes passed before Adam rolled down the privacy wall from the back. Now he could see and hear everything that was happening in the front. I didn't look back at him; I refused to give him the satisfaction. But I wasn't as strong as I'd like to think. I pulled down the sun visor and flipped open the mirror. I waited a few seconds before taking a small peek at him through the mirror.

It was ridiculous that I had to settle for the reflection of his face. As if he were my own personal medusa, eyes far too beautiful, like they would turn my soul to stone...

When I looked in the mirror, I found Adam's eyes meeting mine. He was already staring at me, and he didn't flinch or look away. I saw deep desire and regret in his emerald green eyes, and my heart began to beat out of my ribcage. My chest was heaving like I'd suddenly lost all the air from my lungs.

There weren't many words to describe the way those eyes hypnotized me. It was like magic—there was no true explanation for it. All I continued to think about was how doomed I was. How doomed my poor heart was.

The car made a harsh turn, which seemed to break me from the spell. I closed the mirror and pushed the sun visor back up, upset with myself for giving in for so long. I turned my body to face out the window, glancing at the buildings we were passing and the people on the streets.

After what seemed to be the longest car ride of my life, we arrived at his building. Christmas Eve was tomorrow, and the girls would be back from their trips not long after that. I'd be able to leave his penthouse then.

Guilt hit me as I realized that I wasn't completely happy with the thought. I was quick to push the feeling back down where it came from and got out of the car. Adam and I made our way back to the penthouse in silence. I didn't speak, and he didn't dare to upset me anymore.

I was going crazy because I didn't want to hear from him or look at him, but I was so desperate to hear the words I wanted from his mouth. I was mad that he wasn't saying anything.

We made it to the door, and Adam unlocked it and held it open for me. I waited a few seconds right out the door as I felt Adam's eyes on me. My sight was on the ground, pretending that my shoes were the most interesting thing to me at the moment.

Finally, I couldn't stand to be under his gaze, so I ran through the door when I felt the tears building up in my eyes.

"Fuck," Adam said under his breath as he shut the door and ran after me. My sight became cloudy as the tears filled my eyes more and more. If I blinked, a tear would surely fall. I was running as fast as I could, trying to reach my room to lock myself in.

I was inches away from my room. I stretched my hand out to

reach the door when I felt a pair of hands pull me back by my waist.

"Let me go!" I half sobbed, not wanting him to see me like this. So upset over him. Over what he didn't feel for me.

"Katherine..." Adam began to reason with me, but I wouldn't hear it.

"NO!" I yelled at his face.

"JESUS CHRIST, WOMAN. LET ME SPEAK!" he yelled back, which startled me. My mouth shut closed as I looked at him. His chest was rapidly rising and falling from the chase. The look on his face wasn't one that I recognized. It was pure desperation. "Katherine, let me talk. *Please.*"

I was in full shock because Adam wasn't a man that begged for anything or anyone. Biting my lip, I gave in and gave him a nod. He released a breath he'd been holding in this entire time.

"My father only loved one person in his life: my mother. She was the light of his life, his purpose to live is what he used to say. When she died, my father was a disaster. I lost my mother, but I also felt like I lost my father," he said, holding a good grip on my hands, like he's afraid I'll run away from him.

"I had to take care of my brother. I practically raised Aaron. I had to learn how to run a business to soon take over our empire. Within all that time, I believed that love was a sign of weakness and without a weakness, you're invincible. Impossible to reckon. I always told myself I was never going to be one of those people who set themselves up for failure.

"But then I met you. You walked into my office without realizing you'd be the change in my life. Within time, I learned how much I enjoyed being in your presence and how much I've come to crave it. You slowly began to bring me back to life. I was in total darkness, and you were the light that guided me out. I know I should have said something when you told me you loved me. I'm a fucking dumbass because you *are* my once in a lifetime,

Katherine. I didn't understand what it meant when my father used to say it to my mother, but now, I do."

I was beginning to cry and smile at the same time as he continued to speak.

"I love you, Katherine. I'm only going to love one person in my entire lifetime and it's you. I saved it all for *you*. I fell in love with your soul before I could even touch your skin. I fell in love with your words before I even knew they came from your lips. You changed my world, angel. I'm so fucking sorry if I made you think I felt otherwise." His hands are running through my hair, moving it out of my face.

It felt as if I was on cloud nine right now.

"We're really going to need to work on your timing," I said as he grinned. He pulled me against his chest and stole a kiss.

We stood there for I don't know how long, lost in our lips, and our spoken words roaming around us. Out of all the declarations of love I'd read in books, I could say that Adam's was by far my favorite of all time.

Christmas Eve came around, and Adam was needed at the office. He had some errands to do, and I offered to stop by later. Not knowing how long he'd be away, I didn't want to risk him spending Christmas alone. First, I wanted to stop by the bookstore to finish up my last chapter. I planned on surprising him after it was done.

I thought it'd be the perfect present. It only meant that we go forward with everything else. I could tell it meant a lot to him to see me succeed, and it was sweet how a man like him would want that without it benefitting him. It showed how selfless he was, and I wanted to show him how much I appreciated that.

Henry gave me a ride to the bookstore. I told Adam I could walk and take the subway, but he detested the thought. I didn't fight him. It wasn't horrible to be driven to places for free. It was actually pretty great.

The doorbell rang as I entered my favorite place on earth, ready to breathe in the space and suck up the energy that I needed to finish this last chapter. But as I walked in, I noticed the shop itself seemed incredibly slow. It hadn't been that long since my last visit, and yet, it had seemed to change drastically.

Judy came into the room with an empty cardboard box in her hands. "Oh, Katherine. Hi, I didn't hear you come in," she said as she set the box on the counter. Looking at Judy's face, I could tell she was exhausted. The bags under her eyes were darker and the wrinkles on her forehead looked more ingrained.

"How have you been, Judy?" I asked. She sighed in response, gazing at her shoes for too long. I thought she wasn't going to answer.

"Well, not great, if I'm being honest." I gave her a questioning look, encouraging her to explain further. "I'm losing the place... I've been packing books in boxes for the past week."

The news hit me like a train. I wasn't expecting Judy to close the store. I always thought it'd stick around forever. I knew it was naive to think that, but how could I not when I had been given the opportunity to find a place such as this? It was impossible not to.

It pained me to find out the truth behind Judy's stress, but now I understood her. "You're closing? Why?" I asked, trying to hold in my tears. I didn't want to upset Judy more than she already was.

"The landlord raised the rent, and it's too much for me to cover all by myself. I wish I could, but the bookstore isn't doing as well as I'd like it to." Judy walked over to the shelf in front of us and stacked books in her arms to put into the boxes.

"Oh, Judy..." I couldn't imagine how this made her feel. For me, it was mind wrecking.

"It's alright, hon. I actually might have a plan. I don't want to get your hopes up, either, but I think someone can help us," Judy explained with more peace on her face than she had seconds ago.

"Then why pack if you're not sure?"

"I don't want to jinx it. We'll see how it all plays out. Either way, I'll be okay." She closed the box and secured it with tape on the folds. She reached for my hand and held it for comfort. "Don't worry about it, just continue to write at that table as you always do. It'll make things feel a little normal."

I nodded and headed toward the same coffee table positioned in front of the window without saying another word. I settled in my seat and took out my laptop from my bag. One more chapter and it'd be done. It was exciting to be this close to the finish line when you've been running the race for years.

Hours passed. Judy packed half the books away, and I finally came to the closing sentence.

'At last, I can say our forbidden love was the greatest love there was. It's the love that was worth fighting for and useless to fight against.'

The End.

There it was... the last page and the two words that made a writer feel accomplished. I stared at the words typed on the screen with the biggest smile on my face.

I did it. I actually did it.

I checked the time and realized I'd been sitting in this chair for the past four hours, figuring out the end. It'd be Christmas in three hours, and the streets of New York were hectic this time of year. If I wanted to make it to Adam's before twelve, I needed to leave now. I jumped out of my seat and prepared myself to face the craziness outside these doors.

"Judy! I'm leaving. Merry Christmas!" I yelled from the door. A few seconds later, I heard Judy scream back as I walked out.

"Merry Christmas, Kat!"

I ran across the streets of New York, hopping on and off the

C train to see the one face I'd come to admire the most. The closer I got to Pearson Book Group, the faster my heart beat.

I entered the building and headed to the elevator, up to the eighteenth floor.

When the elevator doors opened, I found a crowd of people gathered on the floor. It looked like a Christmas party. The ceiling was stuck with paper snowflakes cut-outs, covered in silver glitter, and a medium-sized Christmas tree fully decorated at the center. There was a jazz holiday playlist playing in the background, people dancing and talking, with plastic cups in their hands.

If I knew there was a work party, I would have put more effort into my outfit choice. I was wearing a regular red cotton sweater with black jeans. My hair was straight and put in a low, messy ponytail. I quickly ripped out the scrunchie and let my hair loose.

I tried to make my way through the crowd, squeezing between people and saying constant "excuse me's" until I got to Adam's office. It was right along this corner, and as I came close to it, I was stopped by a woman dressed in a red tight dress. Her blond hair fell effortlessly down at her sides, and her crisp blue eyes bore into mine.

"Katherine, didn't think *you* were coming," she said in distress.

"Hi, Victoria. Yes, I came," I answered, wanting to end the conversation before it started.

"I've heard it's been a slow past month for you... that must suck for you, honey. *So sorry.*" Her apology was as phony as a three-dollar bill. She was hinting toward the fact that I was the other author who hadn't finished her draft, and she enjoys that. Today, I wasn't her anymore, but she didn't know that yet.

"Hm, I'm sure you are, Victoria. Can you excuse me? I have to speak with Adam," I told her.

"Oh, sure. He's in the restroom. He's fixing himself up. You know how it is when you come across a sudden... special encounter." This bitch. I know she's not trying to imply what I think. "He did look rather handsome in that suit..." Red clouded my mind. I needed to leave the conversation as fast as possible.

"Excuse me," I spit out and bumped past her shoulder as I walked away. How dare she? She couldn't be serious. There was no way Adam would do that to me. It was obvious she was trying to mess with me. She'd found a way to really irk me.

I entered Adam's office to find it empty. I dropped my bag on his office couch and took a seat. *Okay, Katherine... just because he's in the bathroom doesn't mean the rest of what Victoria said was true.* He wouldn't do that to me. He wouldn't hurt me like Martin did. He's different.

My mind began to play tricks on me, betraying me by over-thinking. Not a few beats passed before Adam returned. He entered the office, shutting the door behind him. As soon as he saw me, he broke into a smile that showed his dimples. "There you are," he said in a tone that melted my heart.

"Hi," I said back, not knowing what else to say.

"Thirty minutes more, and I was going to hunt you down myself," he joked as he made his way to the couch, taking a seat next to me. He stared at me, my head down. "What's wrong?" he asked.

"Nothing. I just—" I looked up at his face, and he was patiently waiting for me to speak. Worried to know what it was that was bothering me. Sometimes, I wished he wasn't so perfect; it physically pained me to see him and not feel a thing. "Was Victoria in here?"

He appeared to be taken aback by my question. "No. Wait, she stopped by to ask a question. She was in and out quickly." I shut my eyes at his words. I wanted to believe him, to trust him. "What did she say to you?" he said to me. It wasn't a question. He knew she said something.

"She implied that... you know." His expression changed like a flick of a switch.

"Absolutely not," he blurted out. "Never in a million years would I even look at another woman the way I look at you. I couldn't even if I wanted to. You've made that impossible for me to achieve, angel." He spoke the words with such certainty, like he could live and die by this.

"I mean it, Katherine. No one," he reassured me. Deep down, I wanted to believe him, and I chose to believe him. Every good relationship was built on trust, and I trusted Adam. He hadn't given me a reason to think otherwise, so why would I start now?

"I know, I know," I began, wanting to forget Victoria altogether. "I didn't realize you guys were throwing a party."

"Honestly, I wasn't aware until a while ago. I never stick around for these things. I usually take my work home, but I agreed to see you here." His hands grazed along my thigh, and I was slowly forgetting the reason for my being here.

"Hmm, why do I find that hard to believe?" I quirked a brow, pretending to be suspicious of him. I knew he wouldn't stay. He was too much of a grump for this.

"Believe it." He leaned in and kissed me. His lips traveled from my lips to the nape of my neck, licking spots that heightened my senses. My eyes rolled back as I sighed.

"Wait," I breathed, wanting to tell him the good news. Adam leaned back, facing me again. "I actually have a surprise for you." He looked me up and down, not expecting me to waltz in here with a surprise.

"Okay... what is it?" he asked, dubious.

I reached for my laptop, resting it on my lap. I uploaded the last document saved in my drive and turned the screen toward him. "Read that last page and let me know what you think?" I told him.

"You want me to edit a chapter for you now?" he responded,

like that was the surprise. Had he ever been surprised before? To think that was what it was.

"No silly, just read it," I encouraged him. "Go on."

He glanced at the screen, scrolling through the last page. I became excited when I saw he reached the end of the page, with those two magical words typed. I waited for him to catch up and realize what his surprise was. I thought he noticed when his body went stiff.

"You're finished?" he asked in disbelief. It had been a week since he took me to the museum and helped me with possible outcomes. I still had about four chapters due, but I'd written them while Adam spent time at the office. I hadn't presented him the chapters this past week, so he was completely stunned.

"Yes, I finished." I couldn't hide my smile even if I wanted to. But Adam didn't seem as happy as me, and I was a little confused. "What? Is there something wrong?" I asked him.

"No, it's just… No, it's great, Katherine, I'm glad," he stuttered. I wasn't sure if he meant it.

"Alright…" I was skeptical about his reaction, but I didn't want to further ruin the moment. However, it was not exactly what I had in mind for when I told him.

"Let's move on with this," he said before rising from his seat and walking toward his desk.

CHAPTER 32
ADAM / KATHERINE

ADAM

I tried my best to look as if I was overfilled with joy by Katherine's completion of the book. I really was happy for her, but the only thought that passed through my mind was the fact that I wouldn't have her around me as much as I'd like. I wouldn't be working with her one on one anymore. I was disgruntled with the thought, but it was bound to happen.

Katherine was seated in front of me as I typed away on my computer. This was where it all ended, where we did a release and marketed the hell out of her book. The next goal was to reach a specific label for Katherine in the literature industry and gain my authority as the new CEO.

I figured if I focused on the next steps, the last wouldn't sting as much. The truth was, I'd fallen for Katherine. I told her I loved her, and I meant it. I didn't realize I would become the fool who fell in love, but now it was my weakness. The only part of me that was capable of bringing me pain.

I brought it on myself. I had signed Katherine with the intention of *using* her to get what I wanted. I was forced to work with her individually, and I dreaded it in the beginning. The truth was something Katherine could never know.

She'd never forgive me... I wouldn't forgive me if I were her.

As I worked on editing the last five chapters, I noticed the time on the clock. Twelve. It was officially Christmas, and I was working with Katherine in front of me. I should be enjoying her.

"Merry Christmas, Katherine," I told her as I focused on fixing my cufflinks, unsure of what else I should say.

"Merry Christmas, Adam." I smiled at her saying my name. I never got tired of hearing her say it. She spoke it with such grace, such delicacy, it felt as if she were caressing me with her voice. I was instantly reminded of the first time I heard that voice at the coffee shop.

I was not somebody who reminisced memories, but the feeling of being close to losing her was the reason for it. I gazed into her eyes and saw a pinch of sadness.

"How was your day?" I asked her, curious about where she'd been, what she'd been doing, and with whom she was doing it with.

"It was fine. I spent most of my day at the bookstore." She didn't name the exact bookstore, but I knew which one she was speaking of. It was the only one that brought her joy and inspiration.

"And how was that?"

Katherine hesitated before answering. She was questioning if she should tell me what she was truly thinking. In my mind, I was desperate for her to elaborate.

"Judy told me she's closing. Most of the shop was empty when I went... It felt different, a bad different," Katherine explained. Of course, I already knew this. Judy was quick to tell me the issue when I last visited.

I knew Katherine would be devastated with the news, which was why I had jumped into action and taken care of it myself. Judy continued to pack the store, even though I told her I would manage, but since there wasn't much news on it, she believed it wasn't worth holding on the process of packing.

The landlord had been a real piece of work. He was an ass who wouldn't answer his emails as quickly as I'd like him to. He answered my last email about a week ago, and I had sent him a response with a deal he wouldn't be able to resist.

The number on the screen was beyond what he was asking for. He immediately answered me, selling me the property. I was now the owner, which left me to decide the rightful price for rent. Knowing Judy's situation, I'd lower it to half the last price she dealt with before the sudden increase.

The bookstore was saved and would be around until Katherine's last breath; I'd make sure of it. I was never going to let her favorite place in the entire world be taken from her. But I decided to stay anonymous as the new owner. I didn't want Judy or Katherine to know I was the one responsible.

Hearing Katherine's distress over the possibility of losing the place informed me that I had made the right choice by saving it. I didn't like seeing her like this, but I'd deal with it knowing it wouldn't last long.

"I was sorry to hear that," I said.

"It's fine. It's not your fault." She played with the ends of her hair before saying the next thing. "Elaina and Celeste fly in tomorrow," she said, and I knew exactly what that meant.

"Oh," I responded.

"Yeah, so I can finally get out of your hair," she said in a humorous tone. She was trying to hide her pain behind it.

"You don't have to."

She paused for a second, taking in what I said. I couldn't tell if she understood what I was implying. Katherine staying in my place had been the best thing I'd experienced in a long time. I couldn't imagine how it would feel to come back from the office to nothing but quiet in the penthouse. I used to hate it, and that was before I had Katherine there.

"What are you..." Katherine asked, but I interrupted her.

"Meaning you can stay, if you'd like. You don't have to move in, but you know..." *Shit,* why was I nervous? It wasn't like I was asking her to marry me. "...keep a spare key and keep some of your things there. Maybe even stay over more than you would at your own apartment."

"So, basically, move in with you?" she summarized, because it was clearly too difficult for me to do so. I'd never asked someone to move into my personal space. I'd never wanted someone to.

"Yes," I confessed.

Katherine tried to read me from across the room, her head tilted slightly to the right, studying me for any sign of unsureness. But she'd never find it. I'd never been so sure about anything in my entire life. I wanted Katherine with me. I wanted her to be the last sight I saw at night and the first sight I saw in the morning.

"Okay," she said.

"Okay?" I asked as I rose from my chair and made my way around the desk toward her.

"Yes, okay," she assured me with a small smile.

Who knew two simple words would have such an impact on me? I reached for her, my hands running through her hair as I brought her lips to mine. Excitement had my blood rushing through my veins and my heart beating wildly. This was it. All of it. She made me feel alive.

She was mine. Mine to find, mine to keep, mine to praise.

~

KATHERINE

The last two days had been a dream. I never thought that I'd be where I am with Adam today, from expressing our feelings to moving in with him. I was currently at my old apartment that I shared with Elaina, and I was packing the things I'd like to bring to Adam's. I had Henry waiting downstairs; Adam sent him to pick up the boxes to take the penthouse.

After this, I had to pick up the girls from the airport. Part of the reason I was choosing to pack right now was because I didn't know how I was going to tell them I was moving in with Adam. I didn't know how I was going to tell them about the drastic changes that had happened since they'd been gone.

I hadn't been telling them things in the past phone calls we'd had. I guess I was a bit scared of what they'd think; their opinions meant more to me than they should. It felt wrong to have kept something this big from them, so I planned on taking them to lunch and telling them there.

How were they going to react to all of this? I had no idea. But I hoped they took it well because I loved Adam, and whether or not I'd want to admit it, he'd become a big part of my life. He had played such an important part in making my dreams become reality.

"Miss Trujillo? Are you all set?" I jumped at the voice; I turned to find Henry at the door. I hadn't realized I left the door open. "Are you alright, Miss Trujillo?" he asked.

"Yes, I'm fine. You scared me." I tried to laugh off the shakiness of my body.

"My apologies, miss, it's been quite some time that I've waited downstairs. I came to check on you," he explained as he walked in.

"How long have I been here?" I asked, unaware of the time. I'd been stuck in my own head as I packed and packed.

"Three hours, miss." Three hours?? I should have been at the airport an hour ago to pick up the girls. I was late, and I didn't even notice.

"Oh, my gosh! We have to leave now, Henry!" I yelled as I ran out the door. Poor Henry ran behind me, not asking any questions. We went downstairs to the car and got in.

"Where to?" Henry asked. He wasn't supposed to take me to the airport. But I guess he was our ride for today.

"The airport. I have to pick up some friends, and I am terribly late. I didn't even realize it while packing," I explained to Henry as he drove down the street.

"Alright, miss, no worries. I'll have you at the airport in twenty minutes," he said as he focused on the road, leaving me to think in the back of the car. Showing up at the airport in a black Rolls Royce would certainly raise questions.

Surely, after twenty minutes Henry pulled into the terminal the girls told me they'd be at. Henry parked, and I got out of the car, looking for a sight of blonde hair, curly black hair, and black, almost violet, straight hair. Not long after, I found them standing outside the doors with their luggage.

I walked toward them, waiting for them to notice me. Celeste turned to see me and broke into a grin. She yelled and sprinted toward me, her arms wide open as she tackled me with a hug. Her body weight almost knocked me off my feet but didn't because of the pole that happened to be behind me.

"Kat! Hey, girl. I missed you!" Celeste said, with her arms locked around me. This girl had a crazy amount of strength in those small arms. Elaina and Valery walked toward us with luggage in their hands.

"I missed you, too. How was the trip?" I asked as Elaina and Valery came up to us. Elaina gave me a side hug and Valery gave me a big, soft one, much more delicate than Celeste's.

"Well, the trip was interesting," Elaina said.

"It went well, though I have to go back to Barcelona tomorrow," Valery said. I frowned at her words; I didn't know why I thought she'd be back in New York for good.

"What? Why?" I asked, disappointed to not have more time with her.

"I know. I wish I could stay, but I still have three months before I finish culinary school. Then I can come back here and open my own restaurant," Valery explained. I tried not to be sad and focus on the fact that she planned to come back for good in a while. Though, her leaving tomorrow sparked a thought in my mind that I'd need to tell them today.

"Okay. Well, I was hoping I could take you guys out to lunch. I have some news I want to share with you," I told them as we walked back to the car.

"Jesus, it must be nice," Celeste said as she noticed the black Rolls Royce. She had no idea that it was our car.

"Yeah, it is," I replied as I came to a stop in front of the car.

"What? Do you want a picture with it?" Celeste asked as she took out her phone. She really had no idea...

"No, I don't. Actually..." I walked around toward the trunk to open it. Henry got out of the car and came to the back.

"Miss Trujillo, please allow me to help," Henry said as he reached for the bags in Elaina's hands. Celeste's jaw dropped to the floor as Elaina and Valery stood there in shock.

"Shut up. Did you win the lottery and not tell us?" Celeste spit out.

"When did this happen?" Elaina asked after Celeste.

"That's what I wanted to speak to you guys about." I opened the door for all of us to climb in. After Henry finished loading the luggage into the trunk, he drove us to a small diner nearby.

We got seated at a round table and ordered drinks. I wasted no time and began explaining everything that had happened this past month. As I explained all the details, I'd gotten a bunch of surprised expressions and open jaws. When I finished, I sat there anxiously, waiting for them to voice their thoughts.

The table was quiet for a minute, and I swirled a straw in my drink as I only got more anxious by the second. I was itching for their approval.

"Okay, let me get this straight. You and your current rich, attractive publisher are, like, together?" Celeste questioned as she took a sip of her strawberry lemonade. I nodded in response.

"Score girl!" she exclaimed.

Celeste's words brought a shred of peace to my mind as I waited to hear what my other two friends thought. My attention flew to Elaina, who hadn't said a word since we sat at the table. She'd been quietly listening, and I knew she was the one with the most questions. Elaina was the friend that worried about the rest of us.

"Are you happy?" Valery asked when she realized Elaina wasn't speaking.

"Yes, very," I answered, while looking at Elaina. She released a deep sigh, reaching across the table to hold my hand.

"Are you sure about all of this?" she finally asked. I knew Elaina felt a certain way about my decisions with Adam. I lived with Elaina, and I'd be moving. It was going to feel different for her. Also, I knew she didn't want to see me get hurt; she had already seen me at my worst.

"I've never been so sure," I told her. Elaina only nodded and gave me a small smile. "And I'll keep paying my part of rent until you find a new roommate," I assured her. I was moving out without letting her know in advance, so it was the best thing I could do.

"I knew you would, thank you." She gave my hand a gentle squeeze before letting go. "I trust your judgment on this. If you believe this is the best option for you, then I am fully on board. *We're* fully on board," she said as she looked around the table.

Everyone surrounding me at this table loved me; they only wanted the best for me. I didn't understand why I felt so worried. I should have known that they were going to be supportive, no matter what. As long as it made me truly happy.

"I have one last thing to tell you guys," I said as I remembered to tell them the news of my book finally being completed.

"There's more? Remind me to not leave for a month again," Celeste joked. She was right, though. The one month that I thought was going to be lonely for me, difficult even, turned out to be everything and more.

"I finished the book. It's finally getting published."

"What?!" Elaina yelled at the top of her lungs. Celeste jumped up from her seat to squeal along with Valery.

"I know! It all happened so fast; *I* can't even believe it," I confessed.

"When are you going to release it?" Elaina asked.

"Next week, actually," I answered. Valery frowned, registering the thought of not being there.

"I'm sorry I won't be here to support you. I really would have loved to," she said as she looked down at the table. I walked around to her chair and leaned down to give her a back hug.

"It's alright. I know if you could, you would. No worries, though. I'll ship you a signed copy," I persuaded her, which worked because she lightened up a bit.

"Please do."

"I am so happy for you, Kat. December ended up being your month. Who knew?" Celeste voiced. The server came by to check on us, and Celeste whispered something in his ear.

"Sorry, ma'am, we don't have tequila here," the server said out loud.

"You asked for tequila at a breakfast diner?" Valery asked Celeste in a humorous tone.

"Spare me, will you? This calls for a celebration drink," Celeste responded. She looked back at the server with glinting eyes. "Are you sure you can't do anything?" She fluttered her lashes at him. Yup, it was great to have her back.

"I can whip up some mimosas, if that works," he said, caving to Celeste in a matter of seconds. I had yet to see a man not give in to Celeste, but that'd be the day.

"Perfect!" She winked at him, and when he left, we all burst into laughter. "What? You try to do the same," Celeste said, irritated with all of us.

"Nope, only you can manage to do that, C," Elaina said.

It felt great to have my girls back. Now I felt a sense of harmony with the decisions I'd made. I had a good feeling about everything; I hoped it stayed this perfect. I couldn't help but feel that it'd be taken away from me because nothing had ever been so perfect for me.

Nothing was as good as it seemed. But then, maybe, just maybe, this time, it really was.

CHAPTER 33

KATHERINE

TODAY WAS RELEASE DAY FOR MY BOOK. ADAM HAD ORGANIZED an event at the Union Square Barnes and Noble. To my surprise, it was overflowing with readers—readers who had been interested in my work since we presented it at the book convention. The store was massive; the biggest bookstore in America, with a record of four floors.

The event was being held on the fourth floor. The space was decorated with red, gold, and white balloons for the theme and had multiple posters of the book cover plastered around the building. Adam also had catering done with some cookies and cupcakes shaped in swords and crowns. We had multiple chairs set up in front of the stage, where I'll be taken up for Q&A.

However, we didn't start asking questions until later. Until then, I stood at a table with numerous copies of my book stacked and a book launch backdrop. I was to sign these copies for the people that walked in. I must say that this day felt bizarre, dreamlike, if you will. I was holding my book in my hands. It was surreal.

It was an exciting day. Seeing multiple faces made me

anxious... I doubted the feeling would go away. That was until I saw a familiar face in the crowd. He cleared the way through the swarm of people with the intention of getting to me and me only. His face was written with determination and his green eyes held me in place. It was as if he had me tied up in his lasso, and instead of reeling me in, he was coming to me.

I should focus on giving these readers my full attention as I signed their copy, but it was just so damn hard. The past three days had been heaven since I moved into Adam's penthouse. I'd gotten to know him on a deeper level, having late night talks until the sun rose, then hiding away from the light to avoid the reality of time. And the sex... Don't get me started on the sex. No man had ever made me love sex as much as I did with Adam.

Everyone went through their 'honeymoon phase' in a relationship and they said that it faded away at some point, but I was convinced that it would never happen for us.

"I was so excited to read your book. I've been waiting two months for it!" A woman admitted to me, bringing me back down to earth. She had bright blue eyes and brown curls framing her face. She kind of reminded me of Celeste, but her eyes made her distinct.

I smiled from ear to ear, satisfied with the comment. "Thank you so much! You have no idea how much that means to me. I hope you end up liking it," I answered. She smiled as she grabbed her signed copy and put it in her tote bag that seemed to be filled with books from shopping around the store.

As she walked away, the next person in line approached. Right as the next person approached me, I felt two rough hands sink into my hips, pulling me toward a big, tall frame. "Hi, angel, how's your hand doing with all those signatures?" I jerked my head back to meet Adam's gravitating eyes.

Heat clouded my judgment, and suddenly I was feeling aroused. I was quick to forget there was a question asked. I could feel my cheeks flush in response instead. Adam noticed and leaned down to my ear.

"I asked a question. Are you going to answer me?" he whispered, and I could feel his hot breath against my ear. It instantly spread goosebumps over my arms.

"Yes, my hand is doing fine."

I forced myself to turn and face the reader in front of me to sign their copy. Adam hadn't moved from his current position; I could still very well feel his body heat radiating from his navy suit. I loved it when he wore his suit, which was almost every day, but every time I saw him in it, it was like experiencing it for the first time.

I knew my mind should be in this event, but again, my brain woke up with its favorite thought. *Adam.*

"We're doing the Q&A in twenty," Adam confirmed. "I'll see you behind the stage, angel."

The time had passed me by. I hadn't even realized I'd been standing in the same position this long. My hands felt it, my legs definitely felt it, but my mind was oblivious to it. I checked the time on my phone. I was eager to go backstage with Adam alone.

I signed about ten other copies before making my way to the stage. My nerves were building slowly as I passed the black metal folding chairs set up on the right and left side of the room. The stage was a wooden platform with a blue couch placed at the center, with yellow cushions. It looked comfortable, but the idea of sitting there in front of an audience made it less so.

Before walking on, I walked to the back, to the curtains behind the platform. Once the curtains closed, I was surprised by everyone I was close to. Elaina and Celeste were here, Auther and Judy were here, and my mother, who I didn't think would make it. I bounced back with shock.

"Surprise!" they all screamed. I was overwhelmed with joy and relief. I was beyond nervous having to present my book in front of so many different faces. I hugged everyone and thanked them for coming.

"Adam gave us a call," my mother said as she wrapped her arm around my shoulder. "We wouldn't have missed it for the world."

Adam had the idea of bringing everyone out here today for me. He knew that I would be feeling anxious, and he brought my family to me when I didn't think of it. In that moment, I knew that Adam knew me better than I thought; he thought of all the details. This wasn't part of his job, almost everything wasn't part of his position. He didn't *need* to work individually with me on my book. He didn't *need* to edit all the chapters himself. He didn't *need* to be the only one reaching out to me about my book. He didn't *need* to do this event himself, and he most definitely didn't need to bring my family for me to feel more at ease.

He went above and beyond when he didn't have to. And I loved that about him.

"I am so proud of you, girl," Celeste said, with Elaina holding both of their own copies. I smiled at the thought of them running to get a copy before they sold out.

"Congratulations, Kat!" Auther exclaimed, with Judy giving me two thumbs up behind him. They left for their front row seats while my mother stayed behind to talk to me.

"It's your big day, and I am beyond proud of you. You finally put yourself out there," she told me.

"Thanks, Mami, but I couldn't have done it without Adam."

"Adam was a big help, yes. But you did it all. You wrote every paragraph, every sentence, every word, and every letter. Up to the very period at the end of each sentence. Without your story and your creativity, he would have had nothing to work with. So, really, Adam couldn't have done it without *you*. Therefore, I am proud of *you*," she explained as her hands landed on my cheeks, holding my face.

My mother's words hit me more than I'd like. I never looked

at it that way. I always gave myself less credit than I deserved, and she helped me realize it. My mother's words were the confidence boost I needed to get on that stage and speak, knowing that no answer could possibly be wrong. Because I made up the answer. I basically made up the questions that come along with it.

"You're right, Ma. Simpre tienes la razon." *You're always right.*

"Ay, Mija, mother knows best." She gave me a wink and let me go, leaving me behind the curtain alone. A few seconds later, I poked through the blue curtains and saw that almost every chair in the room was taken.

I no longer felt nervous. I felt ready. Seeing people interested in my work made me realize that I was good at what I did. I was a writer, and I should have faith and trust in it.

In myself.

"Ready?" Adam spoke behind me, also poking through the curtains with me. I jumped at the sound of his voice. I never heard him come in.

I took this time to turn and face him. His handsome face was suddenly confused.

"What's wrong?" he asked. I chuckled at the fact that he thought something was wrong when he did everything in his power to make sure everything was just right. He was ridiculously selfless; it wasn't real. It couldn't be.

"Nothing," I answered. "Absolutely nothing," I tiptoed and pulled him down by his neck and kissed him. He reacted fast and wrapped a hand around my waist, pulling me closer to him. His other hand cupped the back of my head as he nudged his tongue on my lips, seeking an entrance. I granted it to him and fell quickly into a rhythm that would be hard to break.

That was until he broke it. He pulled away, panting just as much as I was.

"What's this for?" he asked with hooded eyes. Already

caught up in the haze that seemed to always be there between us. Something we produced, me and him.

"Everything that you've done. All of it," I confessed. "You didn't need to do all of this for me. Especially not alone. Thank you for seeing something in me when not a lot of people saw it." Adam looked into my eyes, and I saw a shift in his face. His smile dropped a bit, but he was quick to pick it back up. "Are you okay?" I asked as I tilted my head.

"You shouldn't be thanking me, Katherine, really. It's not necessary," he said.

"Don't be ridiculous. You probably deserve more than a thank you."

"No, I don't." I looked at him, not understanding where this was coming from. He didn't say anything else, but held me tight. It was as if he was scared that I'd slip from his grip, that I'd run away from him. His hands were wrapped around me, his eyes set on my chin.

I reached for his jaw and pulled his gaze to my eyes. Right as I opened my mouth to speak, he said something before I had the chance.

"Good luck out there. You're going to do amazing. I'll be right here when you're done," he told me as he released me. He distanced himself from me, but still held my arm, then slipped down to my hand, then my fingers, until he completely let go.

I watched him disappear as I heard a woman on the stage speak through a microphone. I heard her introduce herself and start my introduction. The woman called my name, and I didn't hear it until the second time. My mind seemed to have walked out of the room with Adam. I shook my head and forced my mind to get back to my task at hand.

Walking through the curtains, my friends and family were seated in the front row. I scanned through the crowd to find Adam, but I didn't see him. I continued to walk up the stage and shook the woman's hand, taking a seat beside her on the couch.

"It's so nice to finally speak to you, Katherine. Your book has been released today, and by the looks of it, it's already doing incredibly well," she said. "The novel seems amazing. I mean a princess and a bodyguard, a forbidden love... I just have to ask. Where did you get this idea?"

I stared off at the crowd and hesitated to answer. I considered running offstage and out of the room, but then realized how unfair it'd be to those who gave up their time to be here. I must respect it and put my feelings aside. The reality was, I didn't know what to think of my feelings. I didn't even know how to deal with them.

Everything was great until I thanked Adam. It triggered something inside him. I long to know more about it. I yearned to get to him and demand answers. But now was not the time.

"I've actually been working on this novel for a while. I started when I was eighteen and stopped for years until I found my publisher, who thought the draft had potential. I can't tell you how I came up with the ideas because I don't even know. I got lost in my mind and entered a world that my brain created," I answered.

"Amazing. I actually have several questions written here in my notes." She chuckled as she pulled out her phone. The crowd chuckled alongside her. I sat up straight, preparing to answer them.

"Alright, let's hear them," I told her.

Twenty questions later, the Q&A was coming to an end. We allowed some readers in the crowd to ask questions to close with; a total of six people asked a question. With that, we ended it. I shook hands with the woman and walked off the stage. The first person in my mind to speak to was Adam.

I didn't see him throughout the entire time I was up there. I worried that he left for whatever reason, but then remembered that he was my publisher. This event was as much his as it was mine.

Auther and Judy were the first to walk up to me. They were holding hands while walking. Did I miss something? I thought to myself.

"You did so good," Judy said.

"Good job, Kat," Auther added.

"Thank you. I am so glad you guys came. And..." I looked down at where their hands were joined together. They followed my eyes and chuckled.

"We've been going out recently. I decided to go down for a coffee at his cafe and we actually bonded over you. I told him the news about the shop and how much it affected one of my top readers, you. And he said he knew you," Judy explained.

"Yes, and we sat down, had a coffee, and it turns out..." Auther said, lifting their hands. Judy blushed at the gesture. I never thought of them together. I was almost mad that I hadn't thought of it sooner.

"Wow," I said as I processed everything. "That's amazing. I am happy for you both."

"Thanks, Kat. We just wanted to come and say our goodbyes before leaving," Auther said.

"Okay. Well, thanks again for coming." I waved them off while smiling. They waved back while walking out. They actually looked great together. Auther and Judy deserved to find one another, and I was glad they found each other; and all it took was a coffee.

I couldn't help but think about how it was also a coffee that brought me to Adam the very first time we met. Well, a double espresso, if I was being specific. And a run in at my old job at Avenue. The last thing I had done for them was decorate for the Halloween party. But I didn't get any more calls for shifts; it was never a permanent job. I didn't need it since signing with Adam.

I had to find him; I knew he was here. I took a look around the fourth floor, searching through each aisle stocked with books. Right as I was about to give up, I found him in the romance aisle on a phone call. He turned and saw me, then turned back around to speak on the phone.

"We'll be there after we're done here," he said before he hung up.

"What was that about?" I asked him, disappointed that he missed the interview for a phone call.

"It was Aaron. He said we need to stop by the office for a meeting. We need to present our numbers along with my uncle's," he explained. "How was it?"

I paused before responding. I thought about bringing up our last conversation, but I didn't want to stir up complications. Not yet.

"Yeah, it was good," I answered him.

"Good," he responded.

We walked back out to the event and wrapped things up. Signing the last copies left, speaking and taking pictures with readers. I said my goodbyes to Celeste, Elaina, and my mother. She'd leave with the girls to go back to the apartment, where she'd be using my old room. With that in my mind, I felt at ease to leave.

Adam and I arrived at Pearson Book Group not long after. Adam didn't speak a word to me during the entire car ride. I couldn't figure out what was bothering him, why he was suddenly distant. Earlier this morning, he was fine, normal, his usual self with me.

We entered the building and headed straight to the elevator. He pressed a button and waited about three seconds until the doors dinged open. He gestured for me to go in first with his hand and walked in behind me. Once the doors shut, the vibe between us darkened. I looked over to Adam. He was biting down so hard that his jawline popped. His hands were in the pocket of his pants as he stared at the elevator numbers slowly increasing. The conference room was on the twenty-fifth floor, which took longer to reach than our usual ride.

I could feel the air tighten as I leaned against the wall. Adam turned his gaze to me; he looked me up and down with desire in his eyes. I bit down on my lip, attempting to keep my cool. He pressed the stop button in a smooth movement as his jaw ticked. I wanted to look away from him, but I couldn't. I wanted him and I knew he wanted me. I was about to speak when Adam slammed his body against mine, pinning my hands above my head. His chest was heaving along with mine.

"Adam—" He slammed his lips against mine, desperate to taste me. At first, I was stiff and unyielding, not knowing how to respond to him. But then my eyes fell shut as I allowed him to run his hands over my skin. His lips tasted sweet and bitter, a mix of chocolate and whiskey. He spread my thighs with his leg and ground his thigh at my center. I gasped and my lips parted, allowing him to slide his tongue into my mouth.

Every thought left my mind, any anger I felt toward him went into our kiss. He dropped my hands and grabbed my left breast. I wrapped my hand around the back of his neck and yanked him down, closer to me. I suddenly felt desperate to feel him on a closer level, to feel us become one.

Adam placed his hand on the wall, closing me in and gaining balance. He let out a low and heavy growl at my ear as I unbuckled his belt. With his other hand, his fingers slid under my flowy dress.

Once I freed him, his cock sprung out, hard and heavy. He shoved his fingers inside me as I wrapped my hand around his base. His eyes were more lustful than ever. Hungry as a lion.

"Someone might see us when the elevator opens," I breathed as I saw the elevator still moving up floors. He immediately pushed the stop button on the elevator. "What if they hear us between floors?" I asked, overthinking.

"I don't care. Let everyone in this damn building hear those beautiful sounds that come out of that pretty little mouth." His voice came out rough and husky. I moaned at his words and his tone.

"Katherine," he moaned into my mouth. "You're so fucking stunning." I smiled against his lips and continued. I needed this. We needed this.

He lifted my leg over his arm, positioning himself at my entrance, and slipped inside me. Adam leaned his head back, letting out a deep, growly moan. His hands wrapped tightly against my waist, pulling me down on him.

Oh my god, this felt so good.

He grabbed a handful of my hair and pulled down, biting the side of my neck. It sent waves of heat through my body. I clung to his neck even harder and squeezed around his cock. I shook against him as I let my first orgasm ride over.

He continued to pound into me, searching for his release. I started to ride his cock again, rolling my hips against his. Adam groaned, squeezing his hands on my waist so tight, so rough and so starved, I knew I'd be left with bruises. It weirdly turned me on even more, making me desperate to reach climax once again.

"You're mine, Katherine," Adam growled in my ear as his movements became sloppy. "No one can take you away from me. No one." I squeezed around him once more. With that, he erupted inside me. The second orgasm was even stronger than the first. The strongest I'd felt.

If he wasn't holding me up with both his arms now, I would have hit the floor. My legs were trembling; they were completely giving out on me. Adam pulled my underwear back in place and put my dress down with a boyish smirk that had his dimples showing. He held my face between both his hands and planted a soft kiss on my forehead.

He pressed the stop button again and fixed his pants. The elevator continued to move up floors. I managed to fix my hair in place and control the strength in my legs. Once the doors opened, he gave me a quick wink and walked out.

I followed Adam to the conference room where the meeting was being held. As we entered the room, we were greeted by half the faculty, along with Aaron and Mr. Edwards, Victoria sitting next to him silently. We were the only two standing in the room. Everyone else was seated around the table. If I didn't know any better, I'd say they were waiting on us.

"Mr. Pearson, I'm glad you could finally join us," a man in a sky-blue suit said. He was probably the chairman. I felt like I should have known these people, but I didn't. Matter of fact, I hadn't seen half of these people outside this conference room. They were mostly new faces for me.

"Apologies for being late. We came from an event. But please, continue," Adam told the man as he looked back at me with a smile and motioned me to a seat. He pulled out the chair and pushed it in once I was seated, and took the seat next to mine. Across from me was Victoria, and she didn't look happy with me. Well, to be fair, she never liked me, but today she hated me.

"Alright, since we're all present now, we can start with the presentations. Edward, please start us off," the chairman said.

"Very well." Edward stood and made his way to the front of the room. "Ms. Stonefield's book has been out for two months as of today, and our numbers have been heading in the right direction. We've been able to land her a position on the best-sellers' list at number ten."

Victoria was sitting quietly, watching the presentation with much pride. She was grinning as she took a few looks at me. *In your face,* was probably what was going through her brain. I couldn't say or do anything while Edward continued with his presentation.

I couldn't lie; their numbers were impressive. Victoria and Edward had managed to sell about ten thousand copies in two months. I began to slowly lower myself in my chair, wanting to hide myself under the table so no one could see how intimidated

I was feeling. It wasn't the numbers, it wasn't the publisher, it wasn't everyone else in the room. It was Victoria's way of belittling me with just her looks. She was staring directly at me the entire time.

"Ignore her. Trust me, our numbers are better," Adam whispered in my ear. He was the only one who recognized my discomfort.

"They are? But we just released it today. How could that be?"

"Because I've been working on it every day. Why do you think today was such a success? The numbers of pre-orders we have are just as impressive, even more so."

Adam finished his sentence as Edward closed the presentation. He looked very pleased with himself as he took his seat.

"Adam, you're up," the chairman said.

Adam rose from his chair, fixing his tie as he pushed his seat in and gave me a wink before walking to the front.

"Ms. Trujillo has released her book today, but our numbers have been quite good. Mr. Edward, I was sure your numbers were accurate, but I must ask, when was the last time you checked the best-sellers list?"

Edward tensed in his chair. I could see the low shade of red that rose on his cheekbones. Everyone in the room looked back at him, confused.

"Last week, why?" He said the last word bitterly. He didn't like to be questioned or provoked. That was the one thing he and his nephew had in common.

"Well, if you had checked this past week... you would have noticed that Ms. Stonefield isn't number ten on the list anymore. Ms. Trujillo is."

Edward's face was now the darkest shade of red, next to Victoria's, who looked like she'd been robbed blindly. Aaron, who was sitting two seats away from me, chuckled. I, on the other hand, was shocked. I wasn't aware of this sudden change.

"That's absurd. I would have noticed," Edward argued.

"Yes, well, you didn't. Ms. Trujillo has sold around fifteen thousand pre-orders. Therefore, bumping you off the list," Adam explained.

"You won't be there for long," Edward yelled, slowly losing his temper.

"You're absolutely right. You can get back to ten. When Katherine's at first." Adam looked over to me and smirked, giving me another wink, which made me blush. I caught Edward staring at me out of the corner of my eye.

"I beg your pardon? When who is first?" Edward questioned.

"Ms. Trujillo," Adam corrected.

"Hm. Very well... congratulations," Edward said as his whole demeanor changed, like a light bulb had gone off in his mind.

The entire room clapped alongside Edward. Adam also saw Edward's switch, and he became suspicious of it. But he didn't question it as he took a seat. He slipped his hand under the table, reaching for me. He moved his hand to my inner thigh and squeezed.

Victoria glared at me like I had killed her cat... I would return the gesture, but my grin was hard to hide. I refocused my attention on Adam, who looked just as proud. I wondered how long he knew...

"When did this happen?" I asked, whispering in his ear.

"Yesterday. I wasn't going to bring it up until you made the top five, but..." I knew exactly why he said it. However, I wanted to know, regardless. It was a great achievement; not everyone could say they'd made the list.

"Very well... It seems that the both of you are headed in the right direction. We'll have another meeting at the end of the month. May I remind you, it will be the last," the chairman said before leaving. Everyone followed behind him, leaving Edward, Victoria, Adam, and me alone.

"Nice little stunt you pulled," Edward said.

"Stunt? It was pure facts. If you're upset with it, I suggest you work harder to change it," Adam told him.

"Adam," Aaron called.

"Yeah."

"They're asking for you in your office," he said.

"Alright, I'll be right there." Aaron nodded and walked back to his office. Adam leaned down to my ear and placed his hand on the small of my back.

"I'll be back. I just need a minute," he whispered. He didn't acknowledge Edward or Victoria as he left the conference room. Edward stared at Adam as he walked away,almost like he was imagining throwing daggers at his back.

Right as I was about to leave behind Adam, Edward stopped me.

"Victoria, do you mind giving Ms. Trujillo and me a minute?"

"Of course," Victoria smiled at him. As she passed me, her smile dropped, and she gave me a death stare.

"How can I help you, Mr. Edward?" I asked him, unaware of what to say, what to expect. I was uncomfortable with the fact that I was having a conversation with Adam's uncle, whom he hated, alone.

"I have to say, it's very impressive that you've managed to sell so many copies in such little time. Adam must really be devoted..."

"Yes, he's been great." I tried to avoid eye contact while speaking to him. Instead of catching a hint, he studied my face, searching for anything that would give me away.

"I'm sure he has been. Though Adam isn't one to do things without it benefitting him in some way." He spoke the words like he had a hidden meaning behind them. And I thought I knew what he was hinting at. As if Adam had been using me for personal reasons...

"You're wrong," I told him.

"Am I?" he prompted.

"Yes. He's helped me with my book without expecting anything in return. He's been kind and sweet, dedicated. He chose my book because he saw potential; that's why he volunteered to work on it individually with me. He's a Pearson. He didn't need to be all in."

While explaining how selfless Adam had been, Edward's eyes gleamed. He chuckled as he realized that it wasn't what he was thinking, but better.

"Oh, he didn't tell you, did he?" He smiled wide, thrilled to see my reaction when he told me whatever secret he was hiding.

"What are you talking about?" I crossed my arms and pierced my fingernails in my skin. I had a feeling I shouldn't stay to hear what he was about to say, but my feet were glued to the floor.

"Did you really think he'd be willing to help someone like you? No offense, Ms. Trujillo, but you were a nobody in this industry. The Pearsons don't publish just anybody, we only work with authors whose names are already known." I rapidly blinked as I continued to listen to Edward.

"Adam isn't CEO. There's an election between him and I. Part of winning the position is bringing an unknown author to the top of the best-seller list within six months. This entire time, Adam hasn't been helping you because he wants to. It's because he *has* to. Can't you see it? He's been using you to get to the top. Once he gets there, he'll forget all about you. Throw you to someone else and out of his hands."

Edward's words sliced through me like a knife. My heart dropped along with my arms. I could feel my legs giving up on me, and I reached for a chair and sat down.

"No, that can't be. That'd mean—"

"That you're nothing but a pawn in his game."

A tear dropped down my cheek as I stared at the floor. He *used* me. Everything he'd said to me, everything he'd done, it was to get what he wanted.

"Seeing your reaction, I can tell this wasn't a professional relationship." He chuckled as he rubbed his chin. "Well, I'll give you some privacy. I believe we now understand one another concerning Adam. Have a good rest of your day, Ms. Trujillo," he said before walking out the door and closing it behind me.

Once I heard the door shut, I broke into a hysterical cry, letting everything out. I wanted to scream at the top of my lungs, how could I be so stupid? Maybe if I hadn't come to fall in love with him, it wouldn't have hurt so much.

But I did. God! How could I be so naïve?!

He'd been keeping this a secret from me, and it wasn't that he was dedicated to me, he was dedicated to an act for his job. Was all of this just a lie? I was this idiot who always hoped for better and never worse. And look at where it had gotten me.

I was a mess. I wiped the last of my tears off my face and got up. *Take the last bit of dignity you have left and leave.* I was going to take a deep breath and leave the room. Before I did, I reached for my phone and called the one person I thought of.

It rang as I waited for the person to answer. After a few rings, they finally picked up. "Katherine?"

"Hi, Ma."

"What's wrong?" my mother asked, hearing the tremble in my voice.

"I'm coming to the apartment; I need to get a few things from Adam's penthouse now," I explained.

"Did something happen, mija?" I tried to hold back tears when she asked, pushing them down, stubborn to let more out.

"I'll tell you later." I hung up the phone and walked out of the room. I ran down to the lobby. I found Henry sitting in a chair, reading a magazine, waiting for Adam and me.

"Henry?" I called out to him.

"Yes, ma'am?" he answered.

"I need you to take me home now."

"Of course, Ms. Trujillo. Is everything alright?" I didn't

blame him for asking. I was sure my face looked red and puffy from crying.

"Yes, Henry, I'm alright. Please, let's leave."

Henry nodded as he walked to the car. I followed behind him, wanting to leave as fast as I could before Adam realized and tried to stop me.

CHAPTER 34

ADAM

I left Katherine in the conference room and headed to my office. I was enjoying my little victory against my uncle. The look on his face was priceless, pure shock. I wanted to enjoy the moment much longer, but I was called to my office for a chat. When I walked in, I was greeted by HR.

There was only one reason HR would come unannounced, and it was never good. This was the first time I'd had them in my office. Aaron closed the door as I approached the man and woman standing at my desk. New faces I hadn't seen before. Last time I checked, our HR was Yolanda.

But that was a long time ago. To be fair, I had been incredibly busy these past six months. Seeing as I was not the 'boss' yet, Yolanda's release was out of my control. Which was unfortunate, because she never gave me problems. She was smart enough to avoid me. It was clear these two didn't get the same memo.

"Good evening. What can I do for you?" I started by asking. I was keeping my face as still as water, not once losing my composure. I kept my hands in my pockets and held a high posture. One thing about me was if something troubled me, I'd never show it.

They clearly tried to intimidate me. Standing instead of sitting, positioned near my desk and my work. Not saying one word, so I'd be compelled to start talking before they'd even addressed the reason for their appearance. I knew this because I had used this technique more than I'd like to admit. It worked like magic on the weak-minded. I should have been offended that they thought it would work on me, but honestly, it almost made me laugh.

"I apologize for coming unannounced, but we've received a tip on a matter that is considered a violation of our code," the woman said. She didn't show much emotion while speaking. I didn't think she could with her tight-ass ponytail snatching her face back.

"Of course. Please take a seat." I gestured toward the two chairs placed in front of my desk. "Before we begin, what are your names?" I asked them both as I briefly glanced at my watch, keeping the time on my mind. I didn't want to keep Katherine waiting for too long.

"I'm Carla, and this is Antuan. He's just starting with us." She was older than me and Antuan looked around my age. Perhaps even younger.

"Great. Now, could you explain what exactly this 'tip' was, and most importantly, who it was from?" I rested my forearms on my desk, leaning forward, yearning to get the information out of them faster.

"Unfortunately, I am unable to tell you who gave us the information." I noticed that Carla was the only one speaking. Antuan was silent, with a straight face. In fact, he hadn't said a word since I entered my office. I looked behind Antuan to lock eyes with Aaron, making sure he was also aware of this.

It could mean nothing, or it could mean something. Either way, I knew I had a witness if anything decided to slip out of their mouths. While Carla continued to speak, I turned my gaze to Antuan. If anyone was good at being intimidating, it was me, and I was going to get this fucker to talk.

"So, it's been brought to our attention that you've been having a personal relationship with Ms. Trujillo. May I remind you that this company does have a no-dating policy." Hmm, shocker. I wonder who gave them this information.

Alas, I couldn't go after the bastard unless I had proof. I knew it was my uncle; he was turning toward his last options. I was remarkably close to winning the CEO title, and it was finally getting to him. I needed to play my cards right.

"I am well aware of this policy, *Carla.* This is considered *my* company. I'm a Pearson," I confronted her. Rising from my seat, I arranged my cufflinks correctly, so they were pointing in the same direction, all while fixing my gaze on Antuan once again. "It seems you have forgotten that as you waltzed into my office, accusing me of breaking *my* code with no evidence. So, tell me. Why should I not fire you on the spot?" I managed to speak these words coldly, with no sympathy for the two doing their jobs.

"I—" Carla tried to get out a sentence, but Antuan was too desperate to regain points. He spilled it all out for me.

"Edward Pearson gave us the information; I have the email he sent. I'm sorry, Mr. Pearson. I love my job; it's the only one I've been able to get, and I can't afford to lose it." And there it was. The little bird sang out every detail I needed. It was almost pathetic he gave in so quickly. I knew there was a purpose for his presence.

I glanced back at Aaron, who shot me back a "told you" look while crossing his arms.

"Good choice," I told Antuan.

"So, I get to keep my job?" he asked as he got up from his chair, Carla looking down at the floor as she made her way to the door.

"For now. And I'd appreciate it if you could forward me the email Edward sent you."

"Done," he spit out as he walked out behind Carla. Carla looked immensely annoyed with Antuan; she didn't even spare him a look as she left the room. After I obtained the position, I knew to add Carla right under Edward on my list of people to fire. As for Antuan, he was temporarily on it under Carla until he proved his loyalty to me again.

"That was something," Aaron said once he shut the door.

"He's desperate. He'll try everything. It's only a few days until the election comes to an end." My uncle would be deranged enough to hold on to a grudge over some decision my father made years ago. He was competing against me for a reason. If he really had what it took to be CEO, he would be in charge right now.

"Can't blame Edward for going this route."

"What do you mean?"

"I mean, it's so damn obvious that you and Katherine have something going on. It's the way you look at her. You've never looked at someone like you admired them. Shit, you've never looked at me like you admire me, and I'm your brother."

"*Younger* brother," I argued, as if it would dial down his main point.

"Right, whatever makes you feel better about it. All I'm saying is, be smart and not so goddamn obvious. Last thing we need is HR on our asses." Aaron never bullshit when it came to winning. It was us or Edward.

"Don't you think I know that? I got them off our backs."

"For now. I'd find Katherine and inform her that people are sniffing around the both of you. Let's hope Katherine's a better actor than you are." Aaron had a point; Katherine wasn't aware of the stakes. It was our asses on the line.

"Alright," I spit out.

"Yeah, I am right," Aaron said. I rolled my eyes, annoyed

that I had to agree with my younger brother's advice. It didn't bother me to take it, it bothered me that he was prideful about it. It puffed up his ego, as if it couldn't get any bigger.

"Shut up and help me find Katherine." Aaron brought his arms up in surrender with a smug face, agreeing to help me.

With that, Aaron and I ditched my office to find Katherine. I left her last in the conference room, so that's where I went first. We entered the office and found it empty. It was unlike Katherine to leave without at least notifying me. I told her to wait, and she left.

I tried not to take it to extreme lengths; it could mean nothing. I reached for my phone in my pocket to check if she left any texts or calls. As my phone lit up, there was nothing from Katherine, only a text from Henry.

> Henry: Ms. Trujillo asked to be taken back to
> the penthouse. I will return for you in thirty
> minutes, sir.

Relief hit me as I realized that Katherine was back at home, safe. That text was sent about an hour ago, which meant Henry was downstairs waiting for me. I turned to Aaron and let him know I was leaving the office early today.

Once I arrived at the penthouse, I walked in to find it quiet. I could hear my own footsteps as I stepped into the living room.

"Katherine?" I called out. My voice echoed around the big space. I heard nothing but silence. I shrugged out of my coat and set it down on a chair. I rolled up my sleeves and took myself up the stairs to check the rooms.

"Angel?" I called out to her again. I entered the main bedroom and found the bed made and untouched. I entered the bathroom and noticed that none of her things were on the counter. Objects that were regularly there, like her toothbrush, hairbrush, creams, and the cute pink headband she puts on when she's getting ready and unready, were all gone.

Desperation took over me as I swiftly checked the cabinets, praying that it was Petra who put her things away and not what I was thinking. She wouldn't leave me. *Unless she knew...* the thought creeped into my mind.

I'd opened all the cabinets except one... I looked at the wooden furniture like it was holding my entire life in it. I reached for the handle and pulled it open to find... nothing.

Nothing that was pink, nothing that was insanely small for a full-grown human, and nothing that belonged to Katherine.

I rushed back into the bedroom to check the drawers she used for her clothes. Empty. I checked the nightstand on her side where her charger was usually plugged in. Gone. I rushed back down to the shoe closet to check if her slippers or heels were there. I didn't know why the thought of checking made sense, but I'd search everywhere if it meant I'd find something. Anything to hold on to. I searched, but the only pair of shoes that were here belonged to me.

She was *gone.* Her things were *gone.*

She knew.

No, she couldn't know. How would she know? No one knew except Aaron, Micheal, and...

"Edward," I said to myself as the pieces clicked together like a puzzle. His name was distasteful on my tongue, pure hatred as I clenched my teeth down.

I left her in the conference room alone with Edward like a fucking dumbass. I basically handed him the opportunity to fuck everything up. How could I be so stupid? How could I let this happen on my watch? I was always attentive to my surroundings, and I left her alone with him.

The urge to kill Edward was big, but the urge to find Katherine and beg her to come back to me was bigger. I had to find her. Explain everything to her. Maybe she'd understand.

I paused at the door with my hand on the doorknob. Who was I kidding? She wouldn't forgive me. She hated me. It was why she left in a hurry with all her things. I just asked her to move in; I wanted her home with me. And now she was gone because of me.

I turned around, facing the living room, looking at the couch I'd always find her on, writing. I remembered the peace that I felt when I saw her. She was my calm in a storm. She was my anchor that held me down in an unforgiving sea, never letting me stray. She was the light that shined over my darkest days.

The penthouse was never quiet with her in it. It was never lonely with her here. She made this place feel like home when I was never capable of doing it myself. The reality was, I needed her. With that, I left in search of Katherine.

I ran across the city to get to her; I had never run so much in my life. It felt like hours until I got to her apartment. I stood outside her door and knocked three times with the last amount of strength I could gather. I was exhausted, but it didn't stop me from getting here. My chest heaved as I desperately gasped for air. My hair was a mess, my clothes were damp with my sweat, and I had no doubt that the look of worry was written all over my face.

A few seconds later, the door opened to reveal Elaina. She had her blonde hair wrapped up in a messy bun, and she had a pair of blue sweatpants on with a matching blue sweater. She looked anything but pleased to see me. If anything, she looked like I had ripped her favorite shirt to shreds.

"What do you want?" she asked bitterly.

"Is Katherine here?" I asked desperately. I tried to look over Elaina's shoulder to see if Katherine was around, listening. But she quickly blocked my view, pushing me back with a hand on my chest.

"Why do you want to know?" She crossed her hands, looking at me in disgust.

"I need to talk to her." Elaina didn't say anything. She was guarding the door with her tall frame; I had never met a woman as tall as her before. The thought of Aaron being the only one who could pass her by a few inches passed through my mind. I quickly shook off the thought and asked her once again.

"Is. She. Here?"

"No. She's. Not." She gave me the same tone I was giving her. Damn, this girl was hardheaded.

"Katherine!" I yelled past her.

"What are you doing, you lunatic?! Leave!"

"Katherine!" I ignored her and continued to call out for Katherine. I needed to speak with her, and it needed to be today. I'd sleep outside this door all night until she spoke to me. Elaina tried to shut the door in my face, but I placed my foot in the door to stop it from closing. Elaina didn't like that.

"Are you insane?! I'll call the cops!" she yelled back. I was about to call out for Katherine again until I heard her soft voice in the back.

"It's okay, El," she said behind her. We both turned to look at her. She was wearing pink pajamas and her hair was down. She had no makeup on, but she looked more beautiful than ever. I let out a sigh of relief as she came up to Elaina and me.

"Are you sure?" Elaina asked.

"Yes. I'll be back inside in a minute," she told her. Elaina nodded and turned to give me a dirty look before leaving us. I hadn't looked away from Katherine since she came into my view. As soon as the door shut, Katherine began talking.

"What is it?" she started. She has her arms crossed and her posture straight. She wasn't beating around the bush or trying to be nice. I didn't blame her.

"I looked for you in the penthouse, but all your things are gone. Angel, I—" I motioned toward her, trying to hold her in my arms, but she backed away.

"Don't. God, what are you doing to me? What do you want from me? Well, I know what you want from me. You basically used me."

"Katherine, I'm sorry. I didn't—"

"Was any of it real?" she asked me with cloudy eyes. I could see the sadness written on her face, the feeling of defeat as she released her shoulders.

"Of course it was real. How could any of it be fake?" I leaned down so that I could be at the same level as her while speaking.

"All of it was fake, Adam. You used me from the very beginning. You're *still* using me to get your precious CEO position. God, I was such an idiot to actually believe that you picked me and decided to work with me because I was so special. Now I find out I was a project to you. An ally to get what you wanted." I could see the tears rolling down her face, and it felt like someone repeatedly stabbed me in the heart. No, worse. Like someone ripped my heart out of my chest.

She was crying because of me, because of my bullshit. The only woman I'd come to love was hurting, and it was my fault. Her light was dimming right in front of me, and I was desperate to fire it up again.

"Katherine, it wasn't like that. Okay, in the beginning it was, but I didn't think we would turn out the way we did. I'm sorry, baby. I never meant to hurt you."

More tears rolled down her face as she bit her lip and shook her head. This was the worst feeling of my entire life. I never thought heartbreak could cause physical pain. My chest physically hurt.

"I need time. I need to be alone and away from you. You lied to me and that's something I can't get past. I put all my trust in you, poured all my love into you, and gave you all of me. I'm sorry, Adam." I feel a streak of wetness roll down my cheek and neck. I reached to wipe away the tear that had come out of me. *Shit.* I was crying and I never cry. It had been years since I'd cried.

"Katherine, please. Don't leave me." I knelt down on the

floor in front of the woman who was breaking my heart, begging for her to stay with me. To not let my fuck up ruin us.

"I'm sorry," she sobbed as she walked back inside and shut the door, turning the locks.

I stayed kneeling on the floor, looking straight at the door. Feeling numb to my own body, my mind relived the moment over and over. 'I'm sorry,' her voice rang in my head. I lost her. I had everything I wanted, and I had to go and fuck it up.

You still have one thing left, my inner voice reminded me. At the end of this week, I was going to get my position. At least I had that. Maybe it would make me feel something.

I got up from the floor and stood outside the door for hours, until the time on my watch forced me to leave the building and get ready for work. The walk back was shameful. The only thing on my mind was Katherine and the look on her face. It would haunt me at night when I slept, it would haunt me while I was working, it would haunt me every second of the day.

CHAPTER 35

ADAM

ONE MONTH LATER...

It had been a month since I last saw Katherine. I'd been numb; my body, mind, and heart, all numb. I considered myself heartless before, but now it was different. I didn't exactly feel like I had a heart most of the time, but it was there. It was broken and incapable of working or even caring. I'd been working like a robot for the past few days, finishing the last bit of marketing for Katherine's book.

I hadn't moved from my chair in over a day. I stayed overnight, drinking from my liquor cabinet. I wouldn't have noticed the time passing if it wasn't for my brother finding me here.

"Jesus, you look like shit. Possibly worse," Aaron said with a grimace as he came into my office unannounced again. I was wearing the same suit as yesterday, and I was sure the bags under my eyes were severe.

"Thank you, brother. Anything else?" I said, as I bent over my desk.

He stayed quiet, and I thought, just for a second, that he left me to die alone in peace. That was, until I heard Micheal's aggravating voice coming in my office.

"Jeez, bro, you look like SpongeBob in that one episode where he's begging for water," he said as Aaron chuckled beside him.

"That's a beautiful description," Aaron said.

"Oh, I know."

I forced myself up on my chair and looked at them both with murder on my mind. These two were always together in the worst possible timing. Micheal was wearing his motorcycle gear, telling me he rode his bike here today, and Aaron was wearing one of his best suits.

"Why are you here?" I asked both of them. They glanced at each other with confusion written on their faces.

"What do you mean? It's the big day," Aaron said, and I looked at him, becoming just as confused as they were.

"Election day, bro," Micheal clarified. No, election day was on the third. There was no way that today was the third. That would mean I'd been locked in my office for more than twenty-four hours. I reached for my phone to check the date, and what do you know, it was the third of January.

I had a few drinks on the first, that was pretty much all I did for New Year's. To be honest, all I could think about was how I was starting this year without Katherine and what a mess I'd been without her. I drank to the misery of wanting her back.

"So, what the fuck happened to you?" Micheal asked as he shrugged out of his motorcycle gear and put it on my furniture. "It looks like you've been here for days."

"Katherine left me," I admitted. It felt horrible to say it, like I was accepting the truth and the reality of losing her. "I lied to her about using her to get CEO."

"Ahhh, so she found out and left your ass in a minute." I stared at Micheal, careful not to lose control and squeeze his throat until I saw the light in his eyes go out. "Alright, well, lucky for you, I have great experience with women."

"How's that going to help, Mike?" Aaron said while rolling his eyes.

"It means you get killer advice," he answered with confidence.

"Great, just what I need," I said sarcastically.

"Before I tell you what you're going to do, I have to know this one thing," Micheal said as Aaron left the room.

"Go on," I told him. I was definitely at rock bottom if I was actually considering Micheal's advice.

"Do you love her?" The room fell silent as I took in what he said. Did I love her? I couldn't breathe without her; I couldn't function right without her. I couldn't even go home knowing that, when I did, I'd feel her absence. That was why I'd been locked in my office and sleeping on my couch like a loser.

"Yes, I love her," I answered Micheal with confidence. Not one doubt ran through my mind about what I truly felt.

"Alright then. Show her." Micheal crossed his arms. That was it? That was the advice? Show her? "Listen man, I've never been in love, but if I was, I'd show her I loved her, that I'd put anything before her. If she felt like she was used, show her she's wrong and the moment you realized you loved her, you dropped everything for her." Huh, that was not the worst advice I'd ever heard.

"You know, that's not the dumbest thing that's come out of your mouth," I complimented Micheal.

"Thank you?"

"It's time," Aaron said as he walked back into my office. Micheal and I rose from our seats. I fixed my suit the best I could to make it seem like a fresh fit, then made my way across the hall to the room where my future was held. I got a 'good luck' from Aaron and a 'break a leg, actually that'd be funny' from Micheal and went inside.

"Adam Pearson, glad to have you join us," Richard, our family lawyer, greeted me. I looked around the room and saw my uncle and some people from the board present.

"I'm glad to be here. I apologize for my tardiness; I was completing the last of my work." I took my seat and listened to them talk, presenting my uncles and my work for a few minutes.

"Edward, please rise." Dread filled my stomach as my uncle was called to the stage and not me. I saw everything I'd risked, even Katherine, for nothing. "I'm very sorry to say this, but you did not win the election, therefore you do not get the CEO position." I looked up from my lap in shock. The look on my uncle's face was the one I'd been working so hard to see. And now, looking at it, I felt nothing. I didn't feel pride or joy or relief.

"Adam, I'd like to congratulate you on winning the position. I know you will do great things for The Pearson Book Group." The words coming out of Richard's mouth didn't give me the pleasure I was hoping for. It certainly didn't make me feel better. I still felt... empty.

I stood up and marched over to the front of the room, beside my uncle. "Thank you. I feel honored to have been given this position. You have no idea how hard I've worked toward this. My first decision as CEO is finally giving my uncle the retirement he desires." I looked straight at my uncle, who couldn't look worse.

"You son of a bitch," he stated under his breath and stormed out of the room without looking back. That, however, made me feel good. He had it coming for what he did to Katherine.

"My second decision is to pass on this position to my brother, Aaron Pearson. I unfortunately cannot accept the offer, and I must hand it over to someone who I know will do good with it. No one better comes to mind," I announced as I called my brother in. I'd gone through painstaking lengths to ensure my position, but I now realized I didn't want it. I'd taken risks that involved the pain of someone who I'd come to love, and who made me happier than this position could ever make me.

Aaron seemed stunned by my request, but walked up to me.

"What are you doing?" he asked.

"What I need to do." I winked at him and waved everyone in the room goodbye. I passed by Micheal, who was leaning on the door frame with a knowing smirk on his face.

"Go on and show her," he said, and I patted him on the back and made my way to Katherine. I needed to show her just how much she meant to me, that I'd do anything for her.

CHAPTER 36
ADAM

I had Henry drive me to her apartment. I was sitting in the back of the car, staring out the window and thinking of ways I could show her how much she meant to me. How much I couldn't live without her. She'd been the only thing on my mind every day. I'd hallucinated multiple times, seeing her in my kitchen cooking, my bed sleeping or laughing, my shower washing her hair, and even my office when I went to work. That was how hopeless I'd been.

Looking out my window, I saw a figure the same as Katherine's walking along the sidewalk, wearing a long brown coat with a brown beanie on. I was suddenly convinced I was hallucinating again, that was, until I saw her face. I jumped from my seat and leaned against the window to get a better look. I smiled at the sight; she looked stunning.

"Henry, slow down, please," I said as I put my window down and called out to her.

"Katherine." She looked at me immediately and it felt like my heart stopped beating. The last bit of air left my lungs as her eyes met mine. I missed looking at her face. I had settled for looking at a picture of her for the past few days, but man, nothing compared to the real deal. She quickly looked back down at the ground and continued walking.

"Let me give you a ride. It's cold." It wasn't that cold outside, but I didn't know what else to say. I was stating the first things that came to mind.

"I'm fine!" she yelled back. That was the first time in days I'd heard her voice. God, I was acting like a creep right now, obsessing over any little thing she did.

"It'll be faster," I tried to convince her, but she wouldn't budge. She was stubborn, and I have got to admit, it was one of the things I loved about her.

"I want to walk," she responded firmly.

An idea popped into my head as I opened my door and got out of the car. "Henry, you can have the rest of the day off," I told him at the window.

"Are you sure, sir? How will you get home?" he asked, obviously concerned with the sudden change.

"I'll manage," I said, certain of my decision. Henry drove off, leaving me exactly where I wanted to be—with Katherine.

I walked toward her until I came up beside her. She said she wanted to walk, she never said she wanted me to leave. At least, that was what I was telling myself.

"I'll walk with you, then." She stared at me with squinting eyes. I was hoping she'd say yes, or at least allow it.

"Why?"

"Because I want to. We don't have to talk. Just walk." She looked at me suspiciously, and it made me want to laugh. I held it in and waited for her answer.

"No," she said as she continued to walk, leaving me behind. I let her walk a couple steps ahead of me, and I walked behind her with a decent amount of distance between us. I wasn't going to let her walk outside alone. I'd rather be here than anywhere else. It wasn't safe.

At least this way, I knew she was safe.

She didn't spare me a look, and that was okay. She didn't need to look at me right now. I only wanted to look at her. Be in her presence without a word being spoken. As she reached her building, I felt my heart physically squeeze. She was about to walk inside without saying anything. I didn't know when I'd be able to see her again, so out of desperation, I spoke.

"Angel," I said softly, scared to be rejected again. Even if I deserved it. I was expecting her to ignore me, but to my surprise, she stopped and turned.

"Don't call me angel." She was quick to correct me, and it hurt me more than I'd like to admit.

"I'm sorry, Katherine." I tried to switch to her name, so she wouldn't run away from me.

"What do you want, Adam? Don't you have things to do now that you're CEO?" She said it as a reminder to leave, or as a hint to get out of her hair. As much as she didn't want me here, I just couldn't leave. I refused for her to walk away with my heart and leave a void in the middle of my chest. I could hear my heart in her hands, beating desperately, never wanting to leave her hold.

"I've made arrangements for my absence from the company. I..." I paused to look in her eyes and swallowed hard. "I gave it up, Katherine."

"You gave it up," she repeated, not getting what I was saying. "Gave what up?"

"The position, the job, I gave it all up," I confirmed. She stared at me, not blinking. It was almost as if she'd gone into shock. "It all means nothing without you." She was quiet as she looked into my eyes.

"You still used me, Adam, lied to me since the beginning," she suddenly said. I could tell she wasn't telling me that, she was reminding herself to stay away.

"I know I fucked up. Trust me, I know. But believe me when I say this, I'll try every day until you give me another chance." She let out a half chuckle, half sob.

"Listen..." she started.

"I lost hope," I talked over her, demanding that she listen. "I lost any tiny bit of hope I had when my mother died. I was consumed by darkness until I became darkness. It's always been like that—until you. I always assumed that light was so frightened by darkness that I'd never get a taste of what it could feel like. But you taught me that darkness craves light, Katherine, and your light is so damn bright, I wanted to get just a piece of it. I was okay with not getting it at all. Until I had it all.

"You gave me hope, Katherine. You gave me every ounce of hope. Hope to become a better man for you, hope to make you as happy as you make me, hope that you'll forgive me, hope to give me a second chance, and hope that you'd love me half as much as I love you." My face softened as I realized Katherine's tear rolling down her face.

"A spark is all you need to ignite hope. And you, angel, are my spark," I whispered as I wiped her tears with my finger. "I don't expect you to forgive me now. But I promise to show up every day to show you how much I mean every word that just came out of my mouth. I need you; I'll need you always."

Katherine bit her bottom lip and gave me a simple nod. It was a small interaction, but it felt bigger than that. It felt like the tiniest bit of progress, and that was better than nothing. She didn't say any words, and she didn't have to right now.

She walked inside her building, and I stood outside until I saw her lights turn on through her window. That was when I walked all the way back home. I was going to show up every day to walk with her. I'd walk miles for hours, if it meant I had a second with Katherine.

I was going to earn her love, her trust, and her heart.

CHAPTER 37

KATHERINE

A MONTH AND A HALF LATER...

ADAM HAD BEEN WALKING ME TO MY BUILDING EVERY DAY FOR the past month. Sometimes, he'd come with coffee or flowers. I thought that eventually he'd get tired and stop showing up, but I was wrong. He kept coming and walking with me without expecting me to say a word to him. Adam had also made a habit of dropping gifts at my apartment. Today, I entered my apartment to find a gift wrapped on the counter with a note.

> *After all the words*
> *And all the ink*
> *And all the blank pages painted black*
> *With the adjectives of you,*
> *One thing is abundantly clear;*
> *Nothing I write*
> *Will ever be enough*
> *To sum You up.*
> *-Poem by Tyler Knott Gregson*

P.S. No amount of words will ever be able to sum up the amount of love I have for you. -Adam P

I must have reread the note a thousand times. I held on to the piece of paper like it would fly away at any moment. He might not be a writer, and the words might not be his, but the intention of dedicating it to me was just as romantic.

I sighed as I stared at the pink-wrapped square object. Was it weird that I wanted to avoid opening it? It'd been difficult to stay away from him and put boundaries in place; harder than I thought. He poured out his heart to me outside my building a month ago, and the words still repeated in my mind.

"A spark is all you need to ignite hope. And you, Katherine Trujillo, are my spark."

"I promise to show up every day to show you how much I mean every word that just came out of my mouth."

"I need you; I'll need you always."

It took everything in me to not give in to him. I honestly had no idea how I managed to walk inside my building without saying a word to him. He didn't seem to mind as he continued to come every day. I was not mad at him, per se. I was scared to open up my heart again. I was afraid of handing over my heart and getting the stitches I put in myself ripped out. I shook off the thought and placed the note on top of the box.

This week, I'd been announced as New York's number one best-seller. I was now thinking of ideas for book two. It was true what Adam told me; he had given up his position to Aaron. He was who I'd been emailing for the past week. It was weird having to write Aaron instead of Adam; something about it just didn't feel right.

"Are you going to open it?" Elaina said behind me, bringing me out of my thoughts. I hadn't noticed her standing behind me. Celeste also came out of Elaina's room, wearing her paint-covered overalls and a confused look on her face.

"It's a free gift. FREE. Hell, I'd open it," Celeste said.

"I don't know," I told them, looking at the box indecisively.

"Que lo abras, que lo abra, que lo abra!" Celeste began to chant. Elaina tried to chant it as well, but her Spanish wasn't fluent. I bit down on the inside of my cheek, contemplating if I should or shouldn't.

After a few seconds, I gave in and ripped open the gift. I gasped loudly once I realized what it was. It was a typewriter. Not just any typewriter—Mark Twain's vintage typewriter that I'd been wanting since I was a teenager. Back then, many girls my age wanted a cellphone or a laptop, but I wanted a typewriter. I always thought it was so beautiful and thought it held the grandest amount of inspiration.

I never was able to get it myself due to how expensive it was. I brought my finger along the engraved letters at the center. 'Williams 39327.'

"It's real," I said softly to myself.

"An old typewriter?" Elaina questioned.

"It's not just an 'old typewriter'. It's Mark Twain's typewriter, a great poet. I've been dreaming of getting my hands on one. I never thought I'd have it in my possession, but..." I smiled at the breathtaking antique, and slowly, my smile started to fade.

"What's wrong?" Celeste asked as she saw my face.

"I can't accept this."

"Why not?"

"It's too much. I can't. I must return it. I'll tell him to take it back when I see him," I told the girls. "Until then, I am just going to leave it here. I'm going to the bookstore." I grabbed my bag and keys and left out the front door without another thought. I didn't want to look at it any longer. It was a big gift. I couldn't have him expecting something from me if I agreed to receive it.

I walked out of the front lobby and found myself waiting for Adam. He was usually always out front, early in the morning, standing with coffee. Today, he was nowhere to be found. I couldn't help but feel disappointment sitting at the pit of my stomach. I forgot the thought and continued making my way toward the bookstore.

Did something happen to him? Is he alright? I began to think of a very possible scenario that could explain why Adam hadn't shown. But then I realized that he probably stopped for good. Maybe he didn't want to deal with me anymore. He'd gotten nothing out of me, and he finally gave up.

As I came up to Judy's bookshop, I noticed more books placed on the bookshelves from the window. I instantly got a rush of excitement. Maybe this meant she was keeping the store. But again, I could be wrong. I opened the door and entered. The doorbell rang above me.

Judy was barely standing over a ladder, stocking the shelves with books. "Kat!" she greeted me as she put the last copies up on display.

"Hey, Judy. What's going on? Why are you reshelving?" I dropped my bag on the counter and made my way over to Judy. I held the ladder on each side so she could climb down without it tipping over.

"The rent went back down once the old landlord left! Oh, it's been such a week, but it's been a blessing," she explained to me. I smiled big, all teeth, and my cheeks started to hurt. This was the best news I'd had all day.

"That's fantastic, Judy. I'm so happy you're staying."

"Yes, me, too. I have Mr. Pearson to thank for this." I was taken aback by her bringing up Adam. Why would she be thanking him now? She retrieved more books from the counter and tried to climb up the ladder again.

"Hey, Judy. I hope you don't mind me asking, but why is it that you'd be thanking Adam?" I asked her as I held on to the ladder once again.

"Oh, well, the day I found out I could be losing this place, he came in looking for you and found the store closing down. I told him what was happening, and he willingly jumped in to help. No questions asked. He talked with his lawyer in front of me, and now, he's the new landlord. I saw his name printed in the new rental agreement." My jaw popped open as I registered the words coming out of her mouth.

"Why? I mean, why would he do that?" I asked. Judy looked down at me from the top of the ladder with a soft, knowing smile.

"Why? He did it for you. The only person as devastated as I was was you. And he certainly didn't do it for me, because I was a stranger to him. He did it for you. A very romantic gesture, if you ask me." She put up the last book in her hands and climbed back down. She closed the ladder and put it away in the closet. I was standing in the middle of the store, shocked.

"I—"

"I thought he had told you. I didn't think he would go through all this trouble for you not to know it was him," Judy said as she came up to me.

"I have to go find him," I told Judy. She gave me a nod and motioned me to go. I ran out of the door faster than I had entered it. I stopped midway on the street. I was running, but I had no idea where I was headed.

Tonight, I had a book signing and a celebration for my achievement of getting number one on the best-sellers list. I was sure I'd hear from Adam sooner or later today.

CHAPTER 38

ADAM

Aaron called, asking me to come by the office to help him with certain things. I agreed only because I placed all of this responsibility on him at the last minute. I was preparing for CEO my entire life, and he'd been preparing for it for a month now. I understood where his concerns were coming from. I never thought I'd be giving it away so quickly.

But then again, I thought of many things differently before meeting Katherine. She so quickly managed to change my perspective on everything. All that I once thought was right turned out to be completely wrong. I once thought love and hope were for poor suckers, a clear sign of weakness, until I became the poor sucker.

I had intended on meeting Katherine outside her building this morning, like I did every other. Our walks had become a solid part of my daily morning routine. I hadn't missed a day for two months, nothing would have stopped me. When it was cold, I stood outside with a coffee. When it was warm, I stood outside with flowers. When it was raining, I stood outside with an umbrella and my jacket in my hand, ready to give it to her.

Katherine had become my top priority; my entire world lay at her feet. I'd always had a void in my soul, and I had accepted the fact that I would feel that way for the rest of my existence. Nothing made me feel as complete as Katherine did. She was my person.

I stepped foot in Pearson Book Group headquarters for the first time in two months. I took the elevator to the eighteenth floor to my old office, where Aaron was now staying. So, perhaps I should start calling it his office.

Passing floors, my mind raced through my last memory in this very spot. The last time I felt Katherine's touch, how her skin felt against mine, the way her hips rocked with mine, how she managed to utterly consume me. She was as eager, as desperate, and as hopeless as me. Everyone else to hell, for that matter.

Katherine was mine, and she knew it. There was absolutely no denying it. Once mine, *always* mine. Even so, I had a feeling that this moment would be the last time I'd touch her like she was mine. I couldn't figure out how to bring the words out of my mouth and tell her how I was feeling. Tell her the truth before it drowned her along with me.

Stupidly, I hadn't, and now I dreamt of sacred moments with her. However, I was okay with settling for the ghost of her, *only* if I was promised to have the reality of her again. I could only hope the promise would be granted.

The elevator doors slid open, and I stepped out. I made my way to the office with the initials A.P. on the door. I stood outside the door with the intention of knocking until the idea of barging in, as Aaron always did, arose in my mind. I grabbed the doorknob, tilted it, and kicked the door open.

The door swung open with a loud banging noise as it hit the wall. Aaron jumped from his seat with a look on his face that reminded me of when we were kids. Pure shock. Still, it didn't pull out a smile, not even a chuckle, like I thought it would.

"Hello, brother, did I scare you? Apologies, it wasn't my intention," I said sarcastically as I walked in more calmly.

"Apologies my ass, forgot your manners so quickly? You've only been gone for two months. Did you lose your touch?" He paused with his hand on his chin. "Don't answer that. I already know you did."

"And yet you called for help," I responded.

"I was never supposed to be CEO, Adam. That wasn't the plan," Aaron said on a serious note.

"I know, but plans changed."

"When will you be ready to take the position? You and I both know I can't do this for long. I have other companies to run." Aaron owned three other companies, since he was never set to deal with the responsibility of being in charge of Pearson Book Group.

"When I handle my things." When Katherine took me back. "You called, I showed. What is it you need my help with?"

"Things?" He raised his brow, then sighed. "I'll give you two weeks to deal with your 'things'. That's it."

"Two weeks? I'll see if that works for me. I don't plan on rushing it." I stood before his desk. "I'll ask one last time. Why did you call me?"

"As you know, Katherine has reached number one on the New York Best-Sellers List." I knew that. I checked every day until she reached it. I sent her a gift this morning to congratulate her. "And you scheduled an event for her before you left. I need you to take over and prepare everything for tonight. You've worked with her every step of the way, so only you can plan this." Aaron looked at me with pleading eyes.

"You want me to take over," I repeated.

"Yes. I have to attend meetings for the other companies in hand. I'm unable to do it. I do believe it's mandatory we go through with this. All week, I've been receiving calls and emails from Anthony Kennedy, the owner of Hearts of Words. He believes, as our contract ends with Katherine next month, it'd be best for her to pass over to his company. I haven't spoken to Katherine about renewing the contracts due to..." He gripped his tie and fixed it. "Complications." He coughed while looking at me. He meant me, and that was fair.

"Anthony Kennedy? The bastard who's been trying to get a job here?" I laughed with anger. "That's ridiculous."

"Yeah, well, not when you read his proposal. He wants me to send it over to Katherine. Of course, I haven't. But I won't be able to keep it to myself when our contract ends," Aaron added.

"Right," I said, upset with myself, but even more upset at this Anthony Kennedy. Who does he think he is? Trying to take Katherine away? I didn't give a shit if it was business. She belonged here. Of course, she didn't fully trust me yet. I couldn't bring this up without knowing she forgave me.

Micheal's words rang in my mind as I thought about what I should do about Katherine. *If you love her, you have to show her.* This could be my chance; to plan tonight's event and earn time with her. Katherine wouldn't expect this from me, which was exactly what I wanted.

"I'll take care of it. You can leave my office now," I answered. Aaron looked taken aback, as if he wasn't expecting me to agree so quickly.

"Yeah, it's not your office yet. Not officially."

"You haven't moved into it yet. Therefore, it's still mine. Move." I kicked him out of my chair and settled in. My desk was exactly how I had left it. My files were organized in my bottom cabinet, my office supplies were still intact and set correctly, and the same number of pens were on my desk. Aaron clearly didn't touch my office. I wouldn't doubt it if today was his only time coming in.

"This office always did suit you," Aaron said as he looked at me at my desk with a slight smile on his face. "You belong here."

"I belong wherever Katherine is."

"Katherine also belongs here. At Pearson Book Group, as a

writer, and you as a publisher. You never thought that you and her were meant to work together? After all, Pearson Book Group is what brought her to you, brother." Aaron was right, but I knew that without her here, I would no longer fit. Neither would I want to.

"When did you become the wise one?"

"Don't fool yourself. I've always been the wiser one. I run three other businesses. How do you think I manage all by myself? I was that guy. Don't fuck with me," he answered.

"Alright, it's time for you to get the fuck out," I said, annoyed. Aaron might be younger, but that didn't stop him from being overly confident and assertive. He had accomplished more than the average twenty-five-year-old, and a proud ego came along with that. Unfortunately...

"Seriously, Adam, it's time for you to take over as CEO. I can't do it." I took in Aaron's words and thought. I gave up the CEO position because all I felt was guilt about the things I had to do to get it. But my brother was struggling and needed me. If the future of the Pearson Book Group depended on me, then I had no choice but to take it.

"Okay," I told him. "I'll do it under one condition."

"What?" he asked.

"I'll do it with Katherine by my side. I need to fix things between us first." I wasn't going to touch the position until I had her forgiveness. I needed her to be okay with the idea. "I'll have her back here with me. I don't care how long it takes."

Aaron nodded and exited my office, shutting the door and leaving me to work. I only had a few hours to pull this off the way I wanted to. Unfortunately, every location was unavailable. But luckily, I was a co-owner of a very charming small bookstore. I gave Judy, the bookstore owner, a brisk call.

"Hello?" Judy greeted over the phone with a heavy accent. I could never tell what it was, if it was Russian or Swedish.

"Judy, it's Adam Pearson. I was calling to ask for a favor." There was a sudden pause from across the line.

"Oh, of course, anything," she responded.

I explained my plans for using the bookstore for the event tonight. Judy instantly agreed when she found out the favor was for Katherine. There was a lot of work to be done in the store. We'd have to clear a space, move bookshelves and tables. But, in my mind, I had a clear vision of what Katherine deserved.

Once I tied down the location, I left to begin getting everything ready. Banners, flowers, catering, setups. Everything was going to be flawless.

I'd collected the flower arrangements and was now on my way to pick up catering. As I passed my building, I decided to stop by the penthouse. I have to admit, without working for two months, I had to occupy myself in some other way. Walking with Katherine was only for a few minutes a day, and afterward, I was left with nothing.

So, I'd dedicated myself to completely redesigning my study. The study was by far the biggest, most spacious room in the entire penthouse. It was the one room that screamed lonesome. After a month, it was finally done. I had no idea how this night was going to go, but I hoped Katherine would agree to come home with me to see it. Because I did it for her.

I dropped off a personal vase of red and pink roses with a note. The two colors that reminded me of her most—red, for the bold color she painted her lips with, and pink, for the color of her cheeks when she got flustered. They were the two colors that made her look like a goddess. Everyone had their colors, and these were Katherine's.

Afterward, I headed over to the bookstore and got to work. The entire time setting up, I was praying Katherine would like it.

CHAPTER 39

KATHERINE

Adam hadn't reached out to me the entire day. Not a phone call, not a voicemail, not even a text. A part of me worried that something happened to him, that he was injured or in trouble. Or maybe that was the first thing that came to mind because it was easier to think he was hurt than to think he had given up. If he finally came to the conclusion of abandoning me or moving on. I wouldn't blame him... I hadn't made any of it easy for him.

Yet, a part of me desperately wanted him to fight till the very end. To prove to me that he was worth taking another chance on, to convince me that what my heart wanted wouldn't hurt me. Because I deeply wished to be with him. I wished to spend every night lying beside him. I wished to be spending more hours of the day with him. My heart betrayed my mind every time I thought about the possibility of forgiving Adam.

Were the outcomes worth it? Would my heart heal with him or burn? Adam said I was his spark that ignited hope inside him. What he didn't know was that he was my spark that rekindled my ability to love on a higher level. He was the glue that pieced my broken heart together, but unfortunately, the glue had been temporary. I wondered if he were to glue me together again, would it be a stronger kind of glue? Would it be the glue that's impossible to un-stick?

There was only one way to find out, and the path had nothing but thorns. It was a path that required time and building trust. Roses were beautiful, they signified love and passion, but roses had thorns and prickles. The thorns, for me, signified that even the most passionate love could hurt. It could cut you and cause you to bleed. But the pain was temporary, and the cut would stop bleeding and heal with time. Many would cut the thorns off, but then you'd only be willing to take the beauty of it and not the pain that came with it. They'd be willing to modify it the way they wanted and not the way it had been created. It all came down to the commitment one was willing to take. Was I willing to take it?

The truth was, I didn't really have an answer. All I knew was that I missed Adam. But I wondered if that was enough. I constantly checked my phone, hoping to see a notification from him pop up. Instead, I only received a text from Aaron confirming the event for tonight.

He didn't bother to tell me the plans; he only sent over the location with the time I was supposed to make an appearance. Which was in about an hour. I clicked on the address and noticed it was being held at the bookstore. My mind swiftly went to Adam once again, remembering that he was the one who saved the one place he knew I felt most at home. The place I mentioned was my favorite spot in the entire world.

I still needed to talk to him about that. I needed to know the real reason he felt the need to take matters into his own hands. I wondered if he'd make an appearance tonight as well.

"What time do we need to be there?" Elaina asked as she walked out of her room in a towel. I stood in the kitchen with a cup of chamomile tea in my hands. It always made me feel calm in situations such as these.

"Uh, eight," I answered in a half cough. Elaina looked at me with a concerned face.

"It's seven. You should take a shower and wash your hair now. So you have time to dry it out and get ready."

"Yeah, you're probably right." My voice sounded more unsteady than usual.

"Celeste is coming a little later, eight-thirty. She said she had limited time to finish the piece she's working on before her deadline. Something like that. I don't understand the process of being an artist." She chuckled.

"That's fine." Her grin dropped as she studied me. I wished she didn't pay so much attention to me. I could fight my feelings by myself, but they always seemed to overtake me when someone who knew me was in the room.

"Are you okay, Kat?" Elaina walked across the living room to the kitchen where I was still standing, drinking tea between sentences. "You look uneasy. What is it?"

"Nothing. Really, I'm fine. I think I'll take that shower right about now." I smiled small, placing my now empty cup of tea in the sink, and made my way to the bathroom. I didn't bother looking back at Elaina because I knew if I did, she'd figure it out.

An hour passed, and we were in the back of a taxi, on our way to the event. I felt jittery. I didn't know what to expect from tonight. I kept my eyes on my lap, playing with the material of my red dress. Elaina had dressed me; she chose a glistening, off-the-shoulder, short-sleeved velvet sequin dress.

Elaina swore that red was my color. She said any other choice would have been a sin. Since she was the fashion expert, I didn't question her. I trusted her judgment. She paired the dress with white shimmery heels. The only jewelry I had on was diamond earrings. My hair was done in an up-do, showcasing my slim neck and collarbone.

At first glance, I thought it was way over the top, but again, Elaina insisted that it was perfect for the occasion. She wore a satin turtleneck dress in a metallic silver color that made her golden locks pop.

"This is your stop." The taxi driver spoke as he pulled up to the curb, parking right in front of the pink bookstore. The entrance was always decorated with red and pink roses, but they added lights to the floral circular decor. In the dark night, it looked beautiful, almost magical. A banner with my book was placed right next to the door, assuring its location and the event going on. Through the window, I could see the crowd of people inside with an open space.

"Hey, lady, you going to pay?" the taxi driver interrupted. Elaina seemed to be as consumed with the decorations as I was, since neither of us realized we were still in the cab.

"Here." Elaina scrambled through her small white purse and gave the taxi driver a crumbled up twenty-dollar bill. The taxi driver un-crumbled the money with an annoyed expression on his face. We got out of the cab and headed to the entrance. "This is really nice."

"I know." I stared at the building in awe.

We opened the door and walked in to find most of the book-shelves were gone, leaving a generous opening. There were about fifty people walking around without feeling crowded. There were breathtaking flower arrangements in vintage vases at each corner, and a stage set up right at the center of the room. My books were stacked on a table in the left corner with goodies beside it. Macaroons, cupcakes, and a tower of champagne glasses.

"Katherine, you're here! What do you think?" Judy emerged from the crowd with a big smile on her face. She was dressed beautifully in a satin green, long-sleeved dress. She had her silver-gray hair up in a bun; she looked like a pixie fairy.

"What do I think?" I repeated, looking around the room and taking in the scenery. "I have no words. Everything is stunning. You outdid yourself, Judy."

"Oh, darling, it wasn't me. I helped with the location, but it was all done by Mr. Pearson." My heart dropped at the mention of his last name. Only then do I remember that she was talking about Aaron Pearson, who was now taking care of everything. I just thought since everything was done in the way I dreamt, that it came from somebody who truly knew my deepest desires. It was silly of me to think that all of this was done by Adam.

"Oh, well, Mr. Pearson did an outstanding job." Judy smiled, pleased with my response, and headed to the tower of champagne to grab a glass.

I took a moment to walk around, noticing the small details that were placed in the room. I walked by the only bookshelf against the wall and noticed copies of Pride and Prejudice. I smirked at the memory of Adam taking me to see the manuscript, and how I had held it in my own hands.

The memory washed away as a man stepped on stage and began to speak at the microphone, saying how wonderful it was to help plan the event, a couple of 'thank you's' for coming, blah blah. I didn't pay any attention to it. I tuned him out as I made my way back to Elaina, who had a glass of champagne along with Celeste.

"Hey, C, you made it!" I greeted her. She looked up and down at me and whistled.

"Hey, you! You look hot, girl," Celeste complimented, as Elaina nodded proudly.

"Oh, I know. I did that." Elaina smiled as she took a sip from her glass.

"You really did. Can you dress me for the art gallery next month?" Celeste asked as she took the glass of champagne from

Elaina and took a sip. "Oh, wow, this is really good. It, for sure, is expensive." She hummed as she took another sip.

"There's a literal tower of glasses. Go get your own." Elaina rolled her eyes with a smile.

"But I'd rather have yours." Celeste fake pouted as Elaina left to grab herself a new glass. "So, this event is great. It's a shame Valery can't be here."

"Yeah, I would have loved to have all three of you here with me. But she'll be back soon to stay." Celeste nodded. "How's the art piece coming? Elaina told me you came a little later because you needed to work on it." She lit up with my question and started to explain her process. I was giving my full attention to Celeste until I heard the unexpected.

"Please welcome our event coordinator, Adam Pearson, who would like to share a few words before tonight comes to an end."

I abruptly turned toward the stage, cutting Celeste off as I saw Adam walking onto the stage. My heart thumped out of my chest. I felt like I could faint seeing him here, yet I felt relieved at the fact that he was *here*. He was wearing a black Zegna suit that made his dirty blonde hair look almost gold. There was a fair distance between us, but I could still so clearly see those emerald green eyes. The same ones that made me freeze in my place; the ones that made me feel like I was running through a maze and might never find a way out. And I'd be more than okay with being trapped.

His tall frame captured everyone's attention as he stood on the stage. He looked at no one but me. I didn't shy away from his gaze; I craved it. He looked at me intensely, like he was trying to take in as much as he could. He gripped the microphone in his hand and cleared his throat before speaking.

"Good evening, everyone. I expect everyone to be having a good time, yes?" Everyone cheered, lifting champagne glasses in the air. "I'm glad. I'd like to thank everyone who made an appearance tonight. It's very much appreciated. As you know, tonight, we are celebrating the success of a talented, amazing author in Pearson Book Group." Adam paused for others to applause. "She is, without a doubt, the best author I have worked with. It was an incredible honor to have someone who truly sees literature as a key to a whole other world. During my time spent with her, I came to understand the way she thought, and it really made reading her novel astonishing. I actually have a few things I'd like to say to her if that's alright with you." Adam shared his charming smile, which made everyone chuckle and women swoon over him.

He looked at me as he raised the microphone to his lips, a sense of longing in his eyes as he shut everyone else out. "Not everyone will understand what I am about to say, but I know you will..." Adam began his speech, and a sob got stuck in my throat as I realized what he's doing. He was quoting specific passages from an old English masterpiece, written by one of the best novelists of the eighteenth century—Jane Austen.

"What is he saying?" Celeste asked as she stared at him, confused. Without tearing my eyes from Adam, I whispered to her.

"He's quoting all the things Darcy said to Elizabeth Bennet in Pride and Prejudice by Jane Austen." It was incredible that he could quote Darcy word for word without having the book to read from.

"And why would he do that?" she asked, dazed by my response.

"Because he knows it's the book that made me want to start writing," I told her.

But what I found so romantic was that Darcy was so consumed by an unquenchable, limitless passion for Elizabeth's beauty and her mind that he felt compelled to propose to her. Despite himself, he loved her. He was completely and irrevocably in love with her. I wondered if Adam's reasoning behind quoting Darcy was to show me that he, too, had that boundless passion for me.

The thought of that being the reason scared me. I was afraid of experiencing a once in a lifetime love, a love I never knew I could feel for someone. I remembered the way my heartbreak over some high school relationship felt like my heart was physically tearing apart in my body. I could only imagine how this would feel. It would be unrecoverable.

Adam finished his last sentence and took a deep breath before sighing. "Thank you," was the last thing he said before stepping off stage.

The crowd began to talk and circulate through the room, filling the room with conversations and blocking my view of Adam. I saw him stepping off, but I couldn't see where he was going. I needed to speak with him. I didn't want him to leave. Not now, not ever.

"That was..." Elaina began, as she handed me a glass.

"So romantic! He started quoting from your favorite novel that related to your situation. God, that sounded beautiful. No wonder you like Jane Austen so much," Celeste said.

"Unexpected," Elaina finished her sentence.

"What are you going to do now?" Celeste asked.

"All I know is that I need to talk to him. I need this night to end quicker than I thought," I said to them.

"What are you going to say?" Celeste asked. I was about to answer her when a man in a blue suit walked up to me with my book in his hands. He had a Sharpie in his other hand and wore a charming smile on his face.

"Katherine Trujillo?" he asked.

"Yes?" I answered him. Elaina and Celeste grew silent behind me.

"Would you mind signing this? I read it the other day and thought very highly of it," he commented. He stood confidently next to me, handing over the book and the Sharpie. As he leaned in closer, I could smell his cologne perfectly. He had brown, almost black hair and green eyes, but not as bright as Adam's. He smelled good, but not as intoxicating as Adam. He was handsome, but he didn't compare to Adam and the way he made me feel when he was near.

"Of course. I'm glad you enjoyed it. It was one hell of a process getting it done, though." I opened the book to the first page and signed.

"Really? I didn't notice. It seemed like it flowed along perfectly for you." I smiled at his compliment. "I'm Anthony. I have a publishing company of my own, Hearts of Words. If you're interested, I'd like to speak to you about the contracts I could offer you. Work like this would be very much appreciated and not looked over."

"Oh," I didn't know how to respond. I wanted to decline the offer in the nicest way possible, since it'd be wrong of me to even consider the offer after all Pearson Book Group had done for me. "That's a kind offer. Unfortunately, I can't accept. I am currently signed with Pearson Book Group."

"Not for long, I heard. But I understand, and the offer still stands. However, I'd like to invite you to dinner. Possibly tonight, since we're dressed for the occasion," he added. I blushed, not because I liked him, but because it was so sudden. He went directly for it.

"Um, I'll have to see. I have to speak to a couple of people. Thank you for the invitation, though," I said, hoping I wouldn't have to answer him again. I couldn't go out with him while having Adam in the back of my mind. I couldn't do anything tonight without seeing him.

"Well, I'll stick around, then," he said as I returned his book and Sharpie. He walked away as another person approached me for the same reason: to sign their book.

CHAPTER 40

KATHERINE

After signing a few books, my hand became sore. The event was finally coming to an end, and it was a huge success. As I signed the last book, I said goodbye to Elaina and Celeste. I said goodbye to the many guests who came as the bookstore cleared, leaving just Judy and me.

I sighed heavily as I looked around, giggling to myself.

"Something funny?" My heart beat wildly as I turned to expect the one guy I'd been crazy to see. I came to face Anthony instead and instantly felt disappointed.

"Nothing, I was thinking to myself," I answered. I didn't have to speak to him any longer, did I? I just wanted this night to end. I only had one person on my mind.

"Are you going to take me up on my offer?" he asked.

"Oh, I—"

"I'm afraid I'm going to have to decline for her. Seeing as she'll be busy," a low voice said, and I felt trembles throughout my entire body. That voice... It brought warmth and made my hairs stand on end. I slowly rotated my body toward Adam, and there he was, standing tall and firm. His nose flared with anger as he stared at Anthony. The way he spoke was calm and cool; it could make one feel timid.

"You're Adam Pearson. Pleasure to finally meet you," Anthony greeted as he stepped closer toward him, offering his hand. I could sense he was wary about getting close to him, almost scared, but too prideful to show it.

"Yes, I am. Who the fuck are you?" Adam responded, looking down at his hand and completely ignoring him. Anthony chuckled as he moved back.

"Anthony Kennedy. I own Heart—"

"Hearts Of Words. I am aware of your company. Though, I'm confused as to why you're speaking with my client." I looked at Adam, baffled. I was technically now his brother's client. But I didn't want to correct him.

"I was about to take your *client* to dinner. I don't see how that concerns you." That seemed to make Adam upset, and he stepped closer toward me, wrapping his hand around my waist, pulling me into him.

"She's not just *my client.* Like I said, she declines, and she's busy *with me.*"

"I think I can decline for *myself,* Adam," I said, looking at Adam and then, turning my eyes back to Anthony, "Thank you for the offer again, Anthony, but I can't tonight. It was really nice to have you here. Thanks for coming and for the offer."

"Of course. Have a good night," he said, winking at me before leaving. Adam's grip on my waist tightened as he watched him walking away.

"It was really nice having him here, was it?" Adam said once Anthony was at a fair distance.

"What? No, what was all that about?" I confronted Adam as I loosened from his grip.

"I could ask you the same question," he argued, his brow furrowed.

"I asked first." I crossed my arms. The tension was so thick, you could cut it with a knife. He took a moment to stare at me and lifted the corner of his lips into a small smirk. Then he chuckled. *Chuckled*, right in my face. "What?!" I asked, irritated.

"You have no idea how beautiful you look when you're mad," he admitted. My cheeks instantly turned pink, my mind entirely bewitched.

"What are you doing here, Adam?" I asked, but I knew the answer. I wanted to hear it from him. I wanted him to admit and explain the reasons why he had done all that he'd done.

"Isn't the answer clear?" I stared at him, not saying a word. He sighed before answering. "I'm here for you, Katherine. I spent the last few hours preparing this perfect night for you." I closed my eyes as I listened to his voice. It was much harder looking at him while he spoke. I knew I'd give in too quickly.

"And that speech. I—"

"They might have been Jane Austen's words, but I meant every single one of them. I am not an emotional person, but with you..." He chuckled to himself. "You seem to bring everything out of me. I quoted Darcy because, in a way... you are my Elizabeth Bennet." He smiles shyly, dimples on full display.

"Oh."

"Yes, oh," he repeated, stepping closer. "I'm sorry, Katherine. I don't know how many times I need to say it. I don't know what I have to do to get you back."

"Adam..." I tried to turn down the conversation that was clearly about to happen.

"I love you," he said. "Katherine, all I can think about is you. At all hours of the day, it's you. I've never felt this way for any other woman." His breaths became quicker each second, his shoulders tensing as he got closer. I could feel his desperation to have me forgive him. "Please, angel, forgive me."

"I'm afraid you'll hurt me again," I whispered, embarrassed to share my fears. He held my face in his hands, caressing my skin as he stared into my soul.

"I'll never hurt you again. I'll never let anyone hurt you."

Adam's voice was serious, and in his eyes, I could see promise. I'd been a disaster without him. I pretended to be fine and to forget it, but the truth was... I wanted to forgive him as much as he wanted me to. So why was I fighting it? I could have it all with him; all I needed to do was put my heart at risk.

Though, it wasn't really a risk when my heart was already considered his, was it? It was only a matter of time before I understood that. Before I accepted it.

"Okay," I said, so soft and small, he could have missed it. But he was already so close, he could hear my own thoughts. His face transformed from worry to relief, his eyes softened, and his lips curved into a small grin.

"Okay?" he repeated, worried that he had heard wrong. I nodded, grabbing his wrists. Within seconds, his lips found mine once again. I leaned into his touch, his warmth, tasting his lips and his breath. The kiss was soft at first, time slowing. His arms wrapped around my waist and my hands wrapped around his neck. The embrace was strong, holding each other, scared that one might get away.

He gripped my hips toward his, squeezing me so tightly it hurt, but I didn't care. Our kiss turned into a hot, passionate act. His arms were strong and clutching me, but at the same time, his touch was soft and reassuring. He broke our kiss to look at me once again, and he smiled. He smiled so big, his dimples showed.

My favorite.

"What?" I asked, smiling back.

"I wanted to make sure this was happening. That I wasn't imagining it again," he admitted, shaking his head.

"Again?"

"I dreamt of kissing you like this multiple times. Honestly, if you knew how many times, you'd think it was a problem." I giggled at how serious he was. I never imagined Adam to be so open with me, telling me everything that was going through his mind. "I like it when you smile," he said, brushing his thumb against my bottom lip.

His fingers traveled down to my neck and rested there, drawing small circles at my nape. "You look beautiful," he whispered in my ear, bringing his lips down to the side of my neck. He leaves small kisses at my collarbone, tingles everywhere his lips make contact. "And your neck... it drives me insane," he said as he brought his lips back up to my neck. "I want to inhale you completely, be consumed by you entirely." He gently bit my skin, and I gasped in response.

"Do you have any idea how much I missed you?" he breathed. At a loss for words, I shake my head. "No?" he asked as his hands traveled up to my chest. "Should I show you?" I nodded, still unable to form words. "Yes? No?"

"Yes," I said in a half moan. His right hand gripped my right breast as he sucked gently on my neck. "Oh." I groaned, unable to control myself. I was lost in him. Time was irrelevant, thinking was useless, and the world surrounding us just didn't exist.

"I missed those sweet sounds," he admitted. He found my lips again, kissing them harshly. He pushed his tongue into my mouth, his hips pushing up against mine. We walked backward until my back hit the cool wall.

"What if someone catches us?" I asked, completely out of breath. My common sense hit me when I felt the cold against my skin. We were still in the bookstore, and anyone could still be here.

"No one's here. I had everyone leave at a certain time. I was waiting to get you alone," he said between kisses.

"You were?"

"Mhm," he murmured. "I needed to get your attention some way. And now that I have it," he reached for my hair and let it down, "I can show you how crazy you make me." He gripped the back of my neck as his free hand traveled under my dress and rested on my inner thigh. "How addicted you've made me." His fingers slowly moved closer to my center. I became desperate for any type of friction. I bucked my hips toward his hand and arched my back to get closer to him. His fingers played with the lace of my panties, making my knees weak in the process.

"Please," I begged. He wore a smug smirk on his face, shaking his head ever so slightly.

"Not so fast," he whispered. "I want to take my time." His thumb rested on my clit, the fabric of my underwear in the way. "To savor this moment." He added pressure, earning a moan from me. He suddenly turned my body around and pressed my chest against the wall.

He unzipped the back of my dress and let it fall to the floor. The material pooled at my legs. "Climb out," he ordered. I stepped out of my dress and kicked it to a corner. My chest was bare to him, my underwear the only kind of cover I have left. He abruptly turned me back around to face him. He stood before me, taking me in completely. "You are perfect," he told me, and I blushed in response.

His hands traveled from my legs to my thighs to my waist and to my chest. "Just perfect." He slammed his lips against mine, devouring me. He slammed his left hand on the wall, holding me with his right. He brought his hand back down to my stomach, inches from my underwear. He roughly tugged it to the side and slipped his fingers between my wet folds.

"Oh god." My eyes rolled to the back of my head. Every touch was so delicate, so precise. I didn't know how long I'd last. I needed to feel him. His fingers slipped inside me.

"Fuck," Adam cursed under his breath. "You're so wet. God, I missed this." I moaned against his mouth. He pulled his fingers out and ripped the material off me. I was completely bared to him, nothing in the way. I felt exposed, only wearing heels. My hair was down, and my red lipstick was smeared. There was even lipstick smeared on his lips and chin.

"Get on your knees." He spoke through his teeth. His jaw was clenched tightly. His jawline looked like it could cut paper. His green eyes were filled with desire, and his face was written with determination. I didn't question him as I got on my knees, feeling the hard, cold floor on my skin. He unbuckled his pants and pulled them down. His cock jumped out, hard and angry. "Open your mouth," he spoke. I was stunned, but followed his directions.

Before I could wrap my lips around his head, he shoved his entire cock in my mouth, making me gag in the process. "That's it. Take it like a good girl." He groaned as I get used to his size. I bobbed my head up and down his length in an even rhyme. "You're doing so good," he praised, gripping the back of my hair. I sped up, wanting to hear more from him.

Suddenly, he pulled out with a heavy groan. "Get up. Both hands on the wall," he demanded. Without wasting a second, I got up from the ground and placed both of my hands against the wall. "Bend over," he said so harshly that I shamelessly felt more aroused.

I waited with my head down, legs spread, and bent over. It wasn't until I felt his breath against my skin that I realized what he was doing. Adam kneeled behind me and licked my pussy. The feel of his tongue, warm and wet, was sensational. Almost too much for me to bear. "Oh my god! Adam!" I yelled as he flicked his tongue faster. He pushed two fingers inside me, helping my orgasm build. I was so close, I could taste it.

My legs began to shake. I felt as if I was on a roller-coaster, about to reach my climax. Just as I was about to release, Adam pulled away and stood up. I groaned in disappointment. "No, no, don't stop."

He chuckled behind me. Out of desperation, I pushed up against him. He moaned in response. "You were made to be my personal torture. You know that?" His hands wrap around my waist, helping me up. My face was pressed up against the cold wall.

"I need… please—" I tried to form words again, but it was useless. I felt like a fish out of water, desperate for oxygen. I needed him to breathe.

"Tell me how badly you want it. How many times have you thought about this?" he asked as he ground behind me.

"I—"

"Did you miss me, baby?" he asked, kissing the back of my ear.

"Y-yes," I answered, using all my strength to concentrate.

"Only I can make you feel like this, Katherine. You're mine. No one else's." He positioned himself at my entrance. I could feel his tip. I was desperate to feel him inside me. "Mine," he murmured as he kissed my back. "Say it. Say you're mine," he said as he gripped my hair in one hand.

"I-I'm yours, Adam." That seemed to flip a switch inside him. He rammed inside me with one push. My entire body pushed against the wall as a high-pitched moan escaped my lips. He was fully seated inside me.

"Fuck, you feel out of this world," he groaned as he kissed my shoulders. He slowly pulled out and pushed back in with the same force.

"Yes. Faster. Please go faster," I begged him. I wanted him to ruin me. I didn't care about my legs or my ability to walk. It had been too long, and I needed him.

"Hold on to the wall," was the only warning he gave me before he thrusted in and out of me with all his force. It was the type of rough that felt delicious, that many craved and couldn't have. The sound of our skin slapping against each other filled the room.

"A-Adam," I moaned, feeling myself getting close. "Adam," I whined. He gripped one of my breasts with his left hand and held me up with his right.

"I know, baby, I know," he groaned as he continued to slam inside me.

"Oh—Oh..." I yelled Adam's name from the top of my lungs as I finally reached my climax. Time froze, my vision became clouded. I swore I saw stars. Adam's thrusts became sloppier by the second as he, too, reached his climax.

He groaned roughly behind me as he pushed into me one last time. Sweat, beaming all over his forehead, fell onto my back. We could hardly catch our breath. He rested his head on my shoulder as he held me up. I eased up as I enjoyed the last flickers of pleasure.

"I love you," he said. "I loved you the moment you walked into my office. I loved you the moment I read your words."

I smiled as I touched his face, caressing his cheek. "I loved you from the moment I poured champagne on you." I chuckled to myself as I remembered the look on his face when I began to dry his pants with napkins.

I could feel him smile against my skin as he said, "You didn't pour it, you sprayed it at me." I giggled. "And that day, I knew I was a goner for you."

CHAPTER 41

ADAM

I FINALLY HAD KATHERINE BACK, AND IT FELT LIKE I HAD JUST conquered planet Earth. She was mine again, and no one was going to take her away from me. What I thought I'd feel once I was with her again was nothing compared to the real thing. Katherine was unique; there was only one of her. She stood before me, putting her red dress back on. She couldn't put her underwear back on because I had ripped them to shreds trying to get them off her.

I had been desperate to have her. I needed her like I needed oxygen. I stared at her as she fixed herself. I never thought I could grow even more fond of her. Yet here I was.

"Why are you smiling?" she asked, giggling. Her laugh—it was the only sound that could make me feel alive. That sound confirmed that what was happening was real. It wasn't a dream.

"I can answer that with one word," I told her, leaning against the wall. Unable to take my eyes off her.

"Oh, yeah? What's that?" She gave me a playful look. It was almost childlike. It made me feel as if I were a teenager again. Falling for the most beautiful girl in school, and constantly having to question why she had chosen me.

"You," I answered with much confidence. There was no better word to use. She looked at my darkness and saw only light. What I thought was doomed, she found hope. This woman was the bane of my existence and the very reason I woke up every day. I didn't think there was such a thing as going back. I couldn't remember life without her and could only see my future with her.

"Adam, as amazing as this is, I really need to talk to you," she said.

"Whatever you need. But can we take this conversation home?" I asked her without realizing that I called my penthouse our home. She seemed to notice as she stood still.

"I don't think it's smart to jump right back into things." She was probably right. It was the logical thing to do. But looking at her, all common sense got thrown out the window. Fuck being logical.

"I really want to show you something. Afterwards, we can talk, and I'll answer any questions you have. I promise." Katherine looked down at her shoes and began to walk toward the door, leaving me behind to watch her. I was confused if that meant she'd come or she'd go. I hoped it was the first option. Just as I was about to make an assumption, she turned her head back to me.

"Are you coming?" I smiled and hurried behind her. "This better be something amazing," she said playfully.

Oh, believe me, I'll make it worth your while.

"It is."

Katherine didn't ask a single question the entire journey to my penthouse; she waited patiently to reveal the surprise herself. I could see she was hesitant to come home with me, but her curiosity got the best of her, and I was glad it did. We entered the lobby and took the elevator to the top floor.

She stood near the doors, waiting for them to open. It was

quite funny seeing her get excited, like a child would. She was on the tip of her toes, counting the floors we were passing.

"Almost there," I whispered in her ear, and she leaned close to my chest.

"Hmm, don't tempt me," she whispered back. Staring into each other's eyes, I could feel the tension piling up by the second. If we didn't get out of this elevator, we'd be hitting round two soon. It wasn't until I heard Petra's voice that I was broken from the spell.

"Hola, Mr. Pearson. Acabo de terminar de limpiar el estudio. Salió muy bonito." *I just finished cleaning the study. It came out looking very nice.* I slightly twitched at her words, almost giving the surprise away. I tried my best to regard it and continue.

"Gracias, Petra. Que pases una buena noche." *Thank you, Petra. Have a good night,* I told her as Katherine and I got off the elevator, switching spots with Petra. The elevator doors closed, sending Petra on her way down and leaving an amused Katherine in front of me.

"I always forget you speak Spanish," she admitted, looking satisfied with the quick conversation.

"Yeah, one could say I have a bit of spice to me." I winked at her as I walked to my door, taking out my keys.

"I don't think spice is the right word... but it'll do for now. Until I find the right one."

"Take as much time as you need." I unlocked the door and pushed it open for Katherine. "After you," I said with a gesturing hand.

"And a gentleman when you want to be," she added, chuckling.

"I have always been and always will be a gentleman, angel. Don't get it mixed up." She walked into the penthouse, straight away slipping out of her heels and dropping them on the floor one after the other.

"What did she mean the study came out nice? You redid it or something?" she asked, as I closed the door behind me and removed my cufflinks, taking off my jacket in the process, leaving only my black dress shirt, and I roughly rolled up the sleeves.

"Or something," I answered. Her eyebrows creased, showing a visible V between her brows. It was easily one of the cutest expressions I'd seen on her.

"Can I see?" I chuckled as I realized I wasn't going to be able to downplay showing her the surprise.

"You want to see now?"

"Yes..." She giggled as she made her way to the study. Nerves began to take over my body as she got closer to the door. Behind that door was something she'd either hate or love. Find romantic or... too much.

"We can save that for later. I really don't recommend entering now..." I tried to talk her out of it, but in reality, I was trying to get out of showing her tonight. "It's probably dusty and needs a few more things." I asked one last question out of desperation. She put her hand on the doorknob and my heart began to race. "How about that talk?" Before I could continue the question, she'd shoved the door open.

At the entrance of the door stood Katherine, unmoved. She stood so still, observing the room I had made just for her. I had painted the walls pink and stuck pages that proclaimed love declarations all over. Bookshelves filled with romance novels, old and new. Flowers placed in every corner, filling the room with a floral scent. A desk at the center with a brand-new Macbook, waiting to be typed on. I left a special space for her future books and an area to put her vintage typewriter that I had gifted her.

I had remodeled it like the bookstore because she said it was her favorite place on earth. I went in with the thought of her *maybe* considering this place as her favorite spot, too. I could only dream that she would call my home her favorite spot in the entire world.

"This is the surprise?" she asked, looking breathless as she stared at the study. "You did all of this for me?" I walked up behind her, moved her hair to the side, and planted soft kisses on her shoulder.

"I want you to consider this space your spot, as inspiration. A place where you can allow your creativity to flow without limits." I rested my hand on her shoulder. "I want this to be home for you. With me." She turned to look at me.

"Did you buy the bookstore and rent it to Judy at a lower price?" Her question came out quickly, as if she couldn't hold it anymore. I didn't expect Katherine to ever find out about that, but I guess she did. I never wanted credit for what I did. I only wanted her to be happy. But now that she was asking, I couldn't lie.

"Yes, I did," I admitted.

"I can't believe it," she said as she walked into the room to take a closer look at the details. "I can't believe you," she added. "I can't believe you'd do any of this, much less for me. No one had ever done anything like this. *Ever.*"

"Anyone who has eyes can see the woman you are. You are a woman worth pleasing, worth loving, and much more. I never believed I was worthy of you. I mean, how could I be?" I shook my head, disbelieving this entire day. "When you left, the penthouse went back to the way it was before. Lonely. I didn't realize the void was so major until you left. I worked on this room every day since you left, hoping that one day you'd come back to me."

"I—"

"I don't think you understand the measures I am willing to take for you. I'll give you everything and anything you want. If it were to make you happy, the price wouldn't matter. Even if that price happened to be my soul, I would gladly hand it over." My voice came out huskier than I'd like. It was my personal oath.

"All I ever really wanted was you." She spoke over me. "I only wanted you." I stepped into the room and stood across from her. The air in the room felt tight, and my heart squeezed in my chest as I heard the words come out of her mouth.

"I've always been yours." I stared into her honey golden eyes that had a certain glint. Her long wavy brown hair fell over her shoulders, and her chest rose and fell. "My mind? It's yours. My heart? It's yours. My overall existence? It's yours, take it. I don't own it anymore." I stepped even closer to her, now only standing a couple of inches away from her.

Her scent intoxicated me, the familiar scent of lavender and vanilla clouded my thoughts as I leaned in toward her.

"I've always been yours. I've waited for what I believed would be endless to find you. But throughout that time, my heart knew I belonged to you." She smiled shyly as she stood next to the bookshelf.

"Smart heart of yours," I said, tugging her into my arms and taking her lips captive. The affection filled my heart with a satisfied warmth that I was never capable of feeling myself.

"Hmm." She broke the kiss and scanned the books by the spines, reading each title. She came across a vintage copy of Pride and Prejudice. She took the book out and flipped it open to a random page in the middle. It wasn't until she noticed the notes I'd left for her in the margins that she looked at me with a shocked expression. "You made notes?"

I simply nodded as she continued to read and flip through pages to see the other notes. I had annotated the entire book for her. I knew she'd be reading it again, and when she did, I wanted her to think of me for hours. Reading it from my point of view. It had also helped me pick out quotes I wanted to use in my speech. It was a win-win situation.

"Since when do you take notes?" she asked, putting the book back on the bookshelf. "I'll be reading all of them later."

"I'm a publisher. I write notes for a living." I brushed my hair back with my hand. "Now I'm not, but you understand what I mean."

"Adam, giving up your life's work for me was a great gesture. But not one that I liked. You've been working toward this your entire life and gave it up once you got it." I stared at her, bewildered by her words.

"I couldn't take the position of CEO knowing that I had lost you because of it," I explained to her. But she simply shook her head in the most delicate way. She looked elegant as she stood tall.

"And I forgave you. But if I'm being honest, it hasn't felt right since you left. Aaron is great to work with, but he isn't you. I don't feel the connection you and I had. We're a team." She couldn't have said it better. It was like a wave of relief washing over me.

"I'm glad you said that... I need you to come with me tomorrow."

CHAPTER 42
KATHERINE

I SPENT THE NIGHT AT ADAM'S AND WOKE UP, MAKING MY WAY into the study. *My study.* I entered the space in awe all over again; I didn't think I'd ever get used to walking in here. I'd always be left breathless every time I saw it.

Memories from the past six months came flowing back into my mind. The things Adam and I had been through had brought us to this very moment, bringing us together. I had successfully published my first book and managed to get it on the New York best-sellers list. I remembered warning Adam that his expectations were unrealistic for the time period. Now look at us.

I took a seat at my new desk, in front of the keyboard. My fingers were itching to type. I hadn't had that feeling in a long time. Where the first thing I thought of when I woke up was to write. It only happened when I had inspiration flowing around me. That was when I realized this office was filled with it, exactly how Adam had planned.

I spent a good two hours in my office, writing a draft for a new book. I looked at the screen, proud, feeling accomplished and unstoppable. As if nothing could get in my way.

"Morning, angel." Adam's voice pulled me out of the zone. I looked up and saw him leaning against the door frame.

"Morning," I said back. "I woke up wanting to write this morning," I admitted.

"I see that." He chuckled, making his way toward me. "I am glad you feel inspired here." He was standing beside me, looking at the screen. "Is this new?" he asked as he leaned down to read.

"Yeah." I smiled at him, moving the computer slightly to the right so he could read it easier. "It's book two."

"Book two?" He smiled. "What's the trope?" I chuckled at his book terminology. I loved that he understood everything about it. I think it's why we fit so well together.

"Well, it's an enemies to lovers' romance." His eyes lit up.

"Is it? Huh, one of my favorites," he said, resting his hand gently on my shoulder.

"I thought you didn't read romance like that." I squinted my brow at him.

"Katherine, why do you think I picked your manuscript out of several?" My eyes widened as I realized that he was right. He picked up my book, which happened to be a romance.

"But it's a fantasy romance."

"Yeah, that was my first fantasy novel that included romance. I usually stick with the regular. But that's why it stood out to me so much. It's one of the reasons I picked it. I listened to my gut and, turns out, I made the best decision." He tilted my chin up and planted a soft kiss on my lips. I felt a quick electric zap and completely lost my train of thought. This man made me feel like I was on cloud nine and there was nothing that could beat that. "When you're done, we need to make a quick appearance at the office," he added.

"It's fine. We can go now," I told him, logging off.

"Are you sure? It can wait." I got up from my seat and held his hand.

"I'm sure. I lost my train of thought when you walked

through the door." He flashed a wicked smile and grabbed me by my waist.

"Well, if that's the case, we still have some time," he said playfully.

"What—" Adam picked me up and draped me over his shoulder. "What are you doing?!" I quilled while hitting his back. "Put me down!" I laughed, almost out of breath.

He walked out of the office and up the stairs. As we passed a mirror, I could see a big smile planted on his face, dimples showing. "Almost there," he said as he reached the bedroom, throwing me onto the bed.

"We have to go!" I giggled as he climbed on top of me, placing kisses on my neck.

"Like I said, we got time."

We met Aaron in the lobby before running up to the office. I didn't know what we were here for, but I was guessing it was important since Aaron brought their family lawyer. Adam entered the building with his hand on my waist.

"Richard," Adam greeted once he stood in front of him and gave a curt nod to Aaron. "I am glad you could meet with us today."

"The occasion was impossible to decline. I'm very glad to be doing this," Richard said as he picked up his suitcase from the floor. "Shall we?" he asked, fixing his eyes on the elevator.

"Yes, let's make this quick. I have places to be," Aaron said, walking forward, leaving everyone to follow behind him. I was still confused about what exactly was going on. But regardless, I went along with it.

Once we reached the eighteenth floor, Aaron led us to the conference room. The same conference room where Edward told me everything. Adam burned a hole in my cheek as he stared, searching for any signs if I was uncomfortable. He squeezed my waist before he let go and pulled out a chair for me. Once I was seated, he took the seat beside me.

Richard sat across from us, setting his suitcase on the oval table, opening it, and taking out files. Aaron sat at the head of the table, leaning back in the same position as his brother. The Pearsons seemed to love leaning back in their seats; it almost made me laugh how identical they looked. Except, instead of blonde hair, Aaron's was brown, and instead of green eyes, his were sky blue.

"Alright, now, I understand that Aaron will be transferring the CEO position back to Adam, correct?"

"Yes," Adam and Aaron responded. I looked at Adam, surprised. He locked eyes with me and gave me a quick wink, reaching under the table to grab my hand. I was shocked that he was making the decision to come back the day after I told him it'd be the right thing to do. He took action immediately. I noticed how much my words meant to him, and I couldn't help but feel my heart ache.

"Great. Now, I know you both understand the position. But I have to go over it, due to it being part of the process of transferring." He pulled up a document and began to read it. "As CEO, you will be the main person responsible for managing Pearson Book Group, taking charge of expanding the company, driving profitability, and, in the case of public companies, improving share prices. Are there any questions for me regarding what I just read?" Adam gave Richard a blank stare as Aaron yawned in his chair. "I didn't think so." He chuckled as he pulled out the contract.

They might have understood it, but if it were me signing, I'd want a play-by-play about everything. Even if I did understand, I'd still want it.

"In this contract, Aaron will sign here, and Adam, you'll sign there," he explained before he handed Aaron the document first, along with a fancy gold and silver pen. Aaron scribbled on the paper and passed it down to Adam. I glanced down at where he was signing. Adam picked up the pen and signed with an ARP. He then handed the paper back to Richard.

"ARP?" I whispered to him.

"My initials, including my middle name, because me and Aaron have the same initials without our middle," he whispered back, while the room stayed quiet and Richard signed some papers himself.

"You have to tell me what R stands for," I told him.

"No can do." He shook his head stubbornly.

"Oh, come on. I'll beg. I'll beg to the point where you'll scream it." He rolled his eyes as he positioned his chair to face me.

"It's Rumble." He spoke so quietly that if I hadn't been so close to him, I would have missed it.

"Adam *Rumble* Pearson?!" I teased him.

"Don't say it like that. Better yet, don't say it at all," he said as my smile grew bigger than before. I knew it! Adam Pearson had something that made him human. A person with an awful or, at least, the most random middle name. It may sound weird, but I actually liked it. And I liked that I knew it even more.

"Alright, papers are signed, and it's official. Congratulations," Richard said, standing from his seat, reaching over the table to shake Aaron's hand and then Adam's hand.

"Thank you, Richard. Pleasure doing business with you," Aaron said, standing from his chair.

"Pleasure is all mine. If you need anything at all, please don't hesitate to give me a call." Richard secured the documents in his case and headed out the door.

"Thank you, Richard," Adam said.

"Congratulations! I am so happy for you," I voiced loudly as I threw my arms around Adam's neck. As he chuckled, I felt my heart melting with happiness. The sound vibrated from his chest into mine.

"Thank you, angel. But there's something missing." I pulled away from him and gave him a confused look.

"What?" Adam looked over my shoulder at Aaron, who gave him a quick nod and left the conference room.

"Remember when you said we were a team? And it didn't feel right to work with anyone besides me," he started.

"Yes..." I answered warily.

"Well..." Aaron came into the room again with a contract in his hands. It was the same packet I signed when I first came into Adam's office, only thicker.

"Katherine, I've only worked with you for two months. But even I noticed the potential you have as a writer. It's some good stuff. We'd be idiots to let you go," Aaron said as he placed the stack of papers on the desk.

"I can't imagine working as CEO without my best writer. I'd love to represent you. I want you to be a part of Pearson Book Group," Adam said, reaching for a pen in his suit. The pen was gorgeous, entirely silver with diamonds engraved. "I've only used this pen twice—the two biggest decisions I've made for this company. It was my mother's, and it's like she's here to witness it."

"Oh, Adam. I—" I reached for the contract and stared at him.

"I'll be in my office. Katherine, I hope you make the decision to stay with us," Aaron said, rubbing Adam's shoulder before leaving. The door shut behind him and left Adam and me alone.

"How long do you want to renew it for?" I asked him, reading through the pages.

"However long you'd like," he answered.

"I don't think they can renew it for as long as I want." I saw a hint of a smile on his lips as he leaned on the desk.

"Hm, perhaps you're right," he playfully responded. "They can't, but I can. Name it and it's done. Also, I'd like to add that

I'll be working on the next projects with you personally." Before I could speak, he continued. "I want to be a part of every idea, every note, every sentence, and every chapter you create. I want to be by your side when you get writer's block. I want to be a part of your inspiration." I could feel a tear running down my cheek as I listened to his beautiful words. He meant them, and I wanted everything he was offering. I never thought I'd be writing, much less finished with this book.

I was always in so much fear of failing. But like I did for him, he gave me hope, and hope is stronger than fear. As long as there was hope, there was no room for worry or doubt. I was lucky to have found him. I'd grown as a writer, and I was proud of the author I'd become. I couldn't have done it without him.

"Oh, yeah? What's in it for you?" I challenged him, walking closer to him, our chests only inches away from each other. He looked at me with admiration in his eyes. He turned the paper toward me and handed me his special pen.

I signed as he spoke. I put the pen down and handed him the paper.

"You've managed to do the impossible. You have taken my pain and turned it into hope. If you're asking me what's in it for me…" He tucked a strand of hair behind my ear as he moved his face closer to mine, our lips a breath of an inch away.

"Absolutely everything."

He slammed his lips to mine, hard and passionately. I melted into his touch with no resistance, letting myself become completely consumed by him. Allowing myself to see that contract as a promise. Allowing him to become a part of my heart, my soul, and my life.

Life had a funny way of working, but because of it, Adam and I had found each other. And you know what? I couldn't have had it any better. I guess you could say it was luck... but I called it hope.

EPILOGUE
KATHERINE / ADAM

SIX MONTHS LATER...

KATHERINE

"I think blue will pair nicely with gold." Jessica, our new cover designer, gave her opinion. It had been over six months that I'd been working under Pearson Book Group, another six months that I'd been with Adam. I was already finished with book two and was getting prepared to release it. To my surprise, multiple readers loved book one and begged for a second, and hell, I was going to give it to them.

"I think so, too. It's coming along great, Jess," I said, analyzing and absolutely adoring the art chosen for this cover. The first had a golden crown showered in red blood, and this illustration was a silver sword dipped in royal blue blood. It was different, yet it matched perfectly.

The writing process for this current book was as smooth as silk, thanks to Adam. The man who became my inspiration for my male character, for every word printed on paper. He swore it was the study he built for me, but it was him. He had helped in every area, just like he said he would. Signing that contract was the best decision I had ever made for myself.

Jessica and I continued brainstorming possible ideas that could outdo the current pick. I was completely fixated on creating the finishing touches, nothing could break my focus. That was, until I heard a familiar dark, raspy voice at the door.

"How's the design coming along?" Adam asked. I broke into a smile, feeling the same butterflies in the pit of my stomach. I could never grow bored with Adam, or his tailored suits. God, he was breathtaking. It seemed that no matter how much time passed us by, it would always be the same between us.

"It's coming along," I responded, avoiding his gaze. I turned around and looked down at the designs. I knew I couldn't finish doing what I needed to do with him here. But at last, it was too late. I could feel him staring at me so intensely, it felt as if we were already making eye contact. I could hear his footsteps marching over to me.

Throughout this entire time, I pretended as if his presence hadn't affected me. That I was perfectly capable of working with him in the same room as me. As I turned around, I came to face Adam. He was keeping a generous distance between us, but it felt like he was taking the entire space up for himself. He sucked out all the air in my lungs, making me breathless.

Yup... never getting bored.

"It's good. Better than the first design if you ask me," he said as he looked at the art spread out on the table.

"Well, I don't recall asking you. But, thanks," I responded, crossing my arms to hide the fact that my hands were shaking with excitement. I always felt like I had some type of adrenaline rush when it came to Adam Pearson. It was exhilarating, thrilling, and even stimulating. I thought it was the fact that I knew I was constantly playing with fire.

"You don't recall asking?" he repeated, with the certain tone in his voice that sent shivers down my spine. "Jessica," he called behind him. "Do you mind giving Mrs. Trujillo and me a moment?"

"Of course not, Mr. Pearson. I'll leave this here," she said, putting my cup of coffee on the desk, then left the room, closing the door behind her.

"You were saying?" Adam prompted, walking closer toward me, approaching me like a predator would his prey. He stopped right in front of me, gently playing with a piece of my hair. His eyes dilated and filled with challenge.

"I wasn't really saying anything. I just don't remember asking you which of the two covers you thought was better," I explained, quickly regretting poking the bear with a stick.

"Are you being smart with me?" The question came out so harsh, my legs were on the verge of giving out on me, and he hadn't laid a finger on me yet. If it weren't for the desk I was currently leaning on, I would probably be having this conversation from the floor.

I shook my head no, my chest rapidly rising and falling. "I wouldn't call it being smart. I think the right word would be honest." I turned my body around so I could face the table and the work laid out.

Adam didn't miss a beat to lean over me, his chest resting on my back, his arousal pressed up against my inner thigh. My throat went bone dry as I began to feel my own arousal.

"Must I remind you who I am?" he growled, biting my ear.

"Why? When you constantly scream it off the tallest building in New York." He chuckled softly behind me. I could feel the vibration coming off his chest.

"Oh, angel, you just love to push my buttons, don't you? You like it when I get angry." He said the last sentence like it was a fact.

"Mr. Pearson?" Jessica's voice spoke through the door as she knocked three times. My breath hiked as Adam pulled away from me. "Aaron Pearson wishes to speak to you," she added.

"Gives us a minute, Jess!" I yelled as nicely as possible.

"Are you ready to go to Europe?" Adam asked as he caressed my shoulder, completely ignoring Jessica, who was waiting on the other side of the door. Adam and I were leaving for Rome for a book signing event later today. My book had been translated into thirty different languages, and we were doing a book tour around Europe. I was more than excited.

"Mhm, but first I have to finish this before I leave. So..." I looked at the door, hinting for him to leave. He looked at me, amused, chuckling.

"Once we get to our hotel room, there's nothing that can save you from me. I am going to *ruin* you, and you're going to love it," he whispered in my ear, sending a shiver of anticipation down my spine. He then walked away from me, taking all the heat with him.

He opened the door to reveal Jessica, holding multiple packets of white sugar. She smiled shyly as she fixed her glasses. Her brown hair was tied up in a ponytail, and she was dressed business casual. She was a timid girl, younger than me probably, but the girl's got talent when it came to designing. I'd never worked with someone as staggering as her.

"Thank you, Jessica. I'll see him now," Adam said. He turned back to look at me and winked, with a smug look plastered on his face. With that, he left. Jessica walked in, taking his spot that I so much wished was still filled by him.

"Sugar for your coffee! I know you can't drink it without it." Jessica smiled as she showed me the packet of sugar she brought.

"Thank you, Jessica. That's kind of you," I thanked her, taking a packet from her batch.

"You and Mr.Pearson are really something. I can see the admiration you both have for each other," she commented as she worked her way around the table, taking a seat.

"Oh, you have no idea." I smiled to myself, forcing myself to focus on the art piece that once had my full attention. I ripped open a packet of sugar and poured it into my coffee. With a quick stir, I took a sip and continued working with Jessica with the thought of finishing what I started with Adam at the back of my mind. But I had all the time in the world with him. There was no rush. We would soon be on a plane, flying to Europe to meet many more of my readers.

Adam's promise kept ringing in my head. I had become more excited to be trapped in a room with him than to go out sight-seeing and meeting other people. I was going to visit a place I'd never seen before, and he was at the top of my to-do list. Because that was just what Adam Pearson did to me.

I couldn't wait for the time to get on the plane.

I shook with excitement; goosebumps ran up my arms as I felt a rush of heat take over my body.

ADAM

I'd visited Europe far too many times, more than the average person should. Each time was strictly for business. We have a very vast clientele in Europe and the UK, more than America. Our company held a very high standard for everything that had to do with audio, print, foreign, film, and television.

This time, it was for Katherine, more specifically, her book tour. Even though it was for work, I saw it as a vacation. Truthfully, I'd seen every moment with Katherine as a vacation. She allowed me to feel at peace, at full comfort. We'd fly privately in four hours exactly, which meant I needed to leave everything in order beforehand.

First, I headed to Aaron's office to see what the problem was. Aaron never called for me unless it involved something that needed an extra pair of hands. My brother was far too stubborn to admit it, but success always happened to be at the top of his list. It came before his stubbornness.

As I arrived at the entrance of his office, I saw him gripping his phone extra hard in his hand. His knuckles were white from the pressure. I lightly knocked on the door, which was already open for him to notice me. His eyes shot up from his paper and motioned me to come in with his hand.

"I understand. Yes, I assure you we will get to the bottom of this." He abruptly ended the call in a harsh tone. He threw his phone across the room, and it landed on the carpet near the door. Aaron sighed heavily as he dug his face into his hands.

"What's going on?" I asked, choosing not to beat around the bush to get an answer out of him. Aaron rarely got stressed, much less frustrated. This wasn't something minor; it was something major.

"We have a problem. One that's going to be a stick in our asses. Undeniably the biggest stick we've ever dealt with." He spoke with fury, his face reddened as he processed the call.

"What the fuck are you talking about? Spit it out!" I yelled, quickly losing my patience. What the hell could be happening that's so bad?

"It's Micheal Zhang," Aaron uttered with hatred. My mind went blank, and I was hit with bafflement.

"Micheal," I repeated, making sure I had heard him right. He nodded as he closed his hands in tight fists. "What did he do?" I needed more information. I couldn't just accept the answer to be 'Micheal' without an explanation. I considered Micheal to be my good friend; my only friend, to be frank.

I didn't know how vague this problem was. All I knew was that this better not interfere with our trip to Europe.

"It's not what he did that matters. It's more about who he did it with," Aaron answered, my brows knotting. "Dylan Cruz. Ring a bell?"

I stood quietly before Aaron, thinking about the time Micheal brought Dylan along to Avenue for his birthday. Brunette, with glasses, tall as an NBA player, extremely hard to miss. I remembered him. I nodded, waiting for Aaron to explain the rest.

"Well, Dylan Cruz owns Cruz Fine Art. A family business. They own the finest collections of art, holding exclusive work and vintage pieces that are worth enough to buy a country. The Cruzs are important people. No one messes with them," he explained.

"I'm aware," I told him, still trying to understand what this had to do with Micheal.

"Yes, well, what you're not aware of is Dylan's little side business. It seems that the young billionaire is a greedy bastard. He hires people to investigate certain art galleries, to learn the security systems and the history behind each art piece before he decides whether robbing them is worth his time."

"Micheal is stealing art with him for money." I spoke, finally putting the pieces together.

"Bingo, brother. I thought I lost you there for a second." Aaron stood from his desk and walked toward the liquor tray.

"Fuck. I knew Dylan had something going on. I was going to do a background check on him, but with everything that's happened lately…"

"You found a girl and fell for her. Yes, I know your sappy love story. But while you were busy stuck in Lala land with Katherine, I took it upon myself to check." I rolled my eyes at my brother saying the phrase "Lala land."

"You didn't find it sappy when you helped me get her back," I laughed. He shook his head as if I was far from that being the right answer.

"Oh no, brother, I always found it sappy. But I'll always help you with anything, even if it happens to be for a girl." I smiled as I stood beside him.

"Who was on the phone?" I asked, changing the subject as he poured himself a generous glass of whiskey.

"That was Diego Ford. As you know, he has a side business himself. We both know he doen't give a fuck about Micheal, but what he does give a fuck about is his money. Dylan has interfered with one of his clients' desired art pieces, and he's unhappy about it." Aaron handed me the glass and poured himself another one. I stared at the glass and held it instead of drinking it. "About one point five million dollars unhappy," he clarified. I instantly shot back the drink in my hand.

"And he asked for your help?" It couldn't be. Diego would rather die than to ask for someone's help. If anything, it was the other way around. I always knew to steer the other way. I didn't do business with criminals. It always ended badly. I expected Micheal to know that.

"No, he was the one who informed me that Micheal was in the middle of this situation. You know I consider him a friend as well," he said.

"Therefore, trying to get Micheal out of Dylan's 'art robbery' scandal, which would interfere with Dylan's plan instead of Diego's," I suggested, placing the empty glass cup on Aaron's desk.

"Correct, again."

"How do you expect we do this?" I asked, unable to come up with any solutions. Micheal knew what he was getting into, I didn't think he was aware that getting out was going to be the difficult part. What worried me most was the thought of him not wanting out in the first place.

"I don't know. But we need to figure it out sooner than later," he answered before he shot back his drink.

"It'll have to be when I get back from my trip." Aaron stared at me like I misunderstood the entire conversation.

"That's two weeks from now," he argued.

"Yes, it is, and this problem will still be here when I return.

You're more than free to begin contemplating possible solutions. Until then, I will be on vacation," I said firmly.

"It's not a vacation," he corrected me in a bored tone.

"To me it is," I admitted. "I'll be back, brother. Try not to run Pearson Book Group to the ground," I messed with him.

"I own more businesses than you, remember? When you get back, this place will surely be in its best shape," he responded.

I smiled before giving him a slight pat on his right shoulder. He mirrored my smile as he got back to work. I left him to it and exited out of his office, making my way to mine.

I made a mental note to myself to figure out a way to pull Micheal out of this. I made sure to place all the information Aaron has informed me of in a file and shove it in my immediate attention cabinet. *Once I get back from Europe with Katherine.* I was going to get to the bottom of this and make Dylan pay in the process.

I guaranteed it.

AFTERWORD

Thank you for reading Call It Hope! If you enjoyed this book, I would greatly appreciate it if you could leave a review on the platform(s) of your choice.

Reviews are like tips for authors, and every one is welcome!

With Love,
Amber

I am excited to note that book two is coming out 2026! Keep an eye out for it!

ACKNOWLEDGMENTS

I never thought I'd be writing a book, much less writing the acknowledgments.

This has been such a journey discovering my true passion for writing. Adam and Katherine mean everything to me, the first two characters that I somehow managed to bring to life. I want to thank everyone who helped my vision come to life.

To my editors, Sarah Wentworth at Indie Editorial and Sarah Daniels at Tormented Author Series, I simply can not begin to express how thankful I am for your help. The entire process of editing was flawless. There couldn't have been a better match or a better team, you both truly had hope in my book and that was more than I could ask for.

To Julie at Books and Moods, you played a huge part in bringing my book to life. It all began with a silly thought from my mind, and you managed to create something even better. Thank you.

To my mother, who constantly expressed admiration for my story and praised my writing. For always making me feel like I was the best, even though you had to because you're my mom. I don't think I could have finished this without you. You were the one who saw my vision and loved it as your own. Thank you for always being there.

To my father, who always supported my every decision. You never hesitated in investing in my dreams. For that, I thank you. I hope I made you proud.

To Max, my special little brother who taught me patience, it played a huge part in the process of writing this book. If I didn't have the patience, I probably would have never finished it. Thank you, and always remember, you can't blend in when you were born to stand out. I love you.

To Jazmin, my first reader, thank you for showing such enthusiasm and love towards this book. I couldn't have done it without it without your suggestions and feedback. Every author needs a hype reader, and I'm glad you were mine.

To Genesis, thank you for teaching me how to market this book. Your dedication and love towards it made it an experience I'll cherish forever.

To the rest of the family, there are a lot of you who supported me in this, but I want to thank each and every one of you for being the definition of what a family is.

And last but definitely not least, thank you to the readers who had the courage to pick up my book and give it a real chance. My dream in letters, paper, and ink.

ABOUT THE AUTHOR

Amber Lee developed a strong passion for reading and writing from a young age. She loves to write contemporary romances with plenty of steam, angst, and swoon. When Amber Lee isn't writing, she can most likely be found reading, binge-watching drama paired with sushi, or trying to learn a new language. An introvert by heart and an extrovert by mind, she dreams of traveling the world to learn about various cultures she can add to her stories.

You can find her online at amberleewriter.com and on social media @ambeleewriter

www.ingramcontent.com/pod-product-compliance
Lightning Source LLC
Chambersburg PA
CBHW020347010826
48973CB00005B/1306